"You don't have to."

"But I should." Wyatt reached for his hat and put it on. Then he walked toward Leah, and her breathing hitched. Coming very close, he walked by. That masculine scent she'd detected on him earlier was still there. Still appealing to her senses. . . .

Leah escorted him to the door. Once there, Wyatt turned to face her.

"Thanks for the invite," he said, leaning into the jamb.

"You're welcome."

Wyatt gazed into her eyes, and she had the strangest desire for him to kiss her. So when he moved a few short steps closer to her, she took one closer to him. His face was inches from hers, and she tilted her chin upward. Waiting. . . .

"Sweet as a kiss." Wyatt spoke in a low tone that rippled across her skin. "I wonder if it is."

Rather than kiss her on the mouth, he took her hand in his and kissed her wrist. Right at that point where her pulse zipped at a frantic pace. . . .

Acclaim for Stef Ann Holm

"A refreshingly original voice in romance fiction, with characters who leap off the page."
—Joan Johnston

HEARTS

"A marvelous historical romance . . . a stupendously smashing story."

— *Affaire de Coeur*

"*Hearts* is a superb historical romance . . . tidbits of history are cleverly woven into the plot. Truvy and Jake are a dynamic duo and the support cast adds to the authenticity of the fabulous fourth and final book of . . . [the] series."

— *Midwest Book Review*

"A very charming read."

— *The Philadelphia Inquirer*

HONEY

"Stef Ann Holm's *Honey* is a wonderfully rich, heartwarming, deeply romantic novel destined to go straight to the heart. Holm's many fans will be enthralled, and her legions of new readers will feel they have just unwrapped a very special gift. This is romance at its best."

— Amanda Quick

"Few authors paint as warm and wonderful a portrait of small-town America as Stef Ann Holm. The multi-textured plot and three-dimensional characters combined with that Americana feel create a bit of homespun perfection."

— Kathe Robin, *Romantic Times*

"With plenty of emotion and laughter, Ms. Holm effortlessly draws her audience into the vibrant realm of the early twentieth century."

— *Rendezvous*

HOOKED

"Stef Ann Holm dishes up a slice of Americana that is not only love and laughter at its best, but a darned good emotional read."

—Calico Trails

"Guaranteed to bring you hours of enjoyment, laughter, and love. Few writers bring small-town America to life the way Stef Ann Holm does. . . . She breathes life into engaging characters and creates a town where people seem like your neighbors: you'd move in, if you could."

—Romantic Times

"This is one book with a title that lives up to its name, as readers will be *Hooked!*"

—BookBrowser Reviews

HARMONY

"Stef Ann Holm has no equal when it comes to wit, style, and authenticity. For warmth, charm, story, and unforgettable characters, *Harmony* is a perfect run."

—Maggie Osborne, author of Band of Gold

"The most warmhearted, heart-stirring romance of the season."

—Romantic Times

"Ms. Holm is one of the best at writing emotionally intense historical romance that leaves nary a dry reader's eye anywhere."

—Amazon.com

Books by Stef Ann Holm

The Runaway Heiress
Hearts
Honey
Hooked
Harmony
Forget Me Not
Portraits
Crossings
Weeping Angel
Snowbird
King of the Pirates
Liberty Rose
Seasons of Gold

Published by POCKET BOOKS

STEF ANN HOLM

Portraits

POCKET BOOKS
New York   London   Toronto   Sydney   Singapore

An *Original* Publication of POCKET BOOKS

POCKET BOOKS, a division of Simon & Schuster, Inc.
1230 Avenue of the Americas, New York, NY 10020

Copyright © 1996 by Stef Ann Holm

ISBN: 0-671-51044-4

First Pocket Books printing September 1996

10 9 8 7 6 5 4 3 2

POCKET and colophon are registered trademarks
of Simon & Schuster, Inc.

For information regarding special discounts for bulk purchases,
please contact Simon & Schuster Special Sales at 1-800-456-6798
or business@simonandschuster.com

Cover art by Tom Hallman

Printed in the U.S.A.

Dedication

"In order to fully understand one's immediate existence, and to have the wisdom and capability of fully appreciating and finding contentment in the future . . . look back and be the better for it."

—Frank Wysocki

To Anthony and Anne
To John, Edward, Stella, Stephanie, Frank, and Joseph
To Victor and Agnes
To Dallas, Margaret, and Gloria

Remembered in portraits; remembered in life.

❧ Prologue ❧

> Prepare for calamity not yet in bud.
> —Chinese proverb

September 14, 1887
Telluride, Colorado

Some said the name Telluride was derived from the phrase "to hell you ride." This could have been true, because the streets were full of swaggering men, loud laughter, and half-clad women beckoning from saloon doorways. Harlen Shepard Riley had already seen other such wild and woolly towns that could select their names from that very same meaning. But in this case, he should have taken the phrase to heart. For it was in Telluride, on a crisp fall day when the leaves were turning and the world was golden, that the journey to hell began.

After a night of drinking and socializing at the Lookout Saloon, the five members of a gang known as the Loco Boys for their drunken and wild exploits got duded up on Colvin's suggestion to get their portrait taken. Manny Vasquez, Nate Bender, Thomas Jefferson Ellis, Colvin Henkels, and Harlen Riley hadn't had a likeness snapped of themselves in ages. They'd been too busy relieving vaults of their wealth and trains of their gold while wearing the vagabond disguises that were the trademark of Harlen's gang.

For the past five years, they'd been holding up banking institutions, robbing the railroads, rustling cattle, and stealing horses in nine states and territories. No other outlaws were bolder or more marauding. The spark of danger fueled their raids and gave them the thirst for more. Their total take to date was close to a quarter of a million dollars, though not a one of them had a whole lot to show for this obscene amount—except prime horseflesh and the best saddles money could buy. Dollars were squandered on aged liquor, expensive women, and foolish gambling.

But to Harlen, who was twenty-one, he was living as good a life as he could. Any hope for a decent future had been buried in his past mistakes.

Wearing brand new Stetsons, decked out in stylish city slicker duds, and armed with silver-engraved revolvers, the group went into Darling's Photography Gallery to immortally capture their impressive appearances on camera paper.

An iron horse weight held the door open to air the strong smell of acids and solutions that greeted customers. The fumes were so intense, Harlen's eyes watered. A cross breeze coming from lifted windows in the rear only marginally helped to vent the place. He idly wondered how they managed to breathe in the winter when the room had to be closed up against the elements.

The reception room was big and decorated with sofas, chairs, and tables that on a first glance seemed to be elegant. On closer inspection, the furnishings were in poor shape. The weave on the damask upholstery was worn thin, and the scrollwork carved into the cherrywood chairs and tables had numerous nicks. There had been some attempt at repair by way of a sloppily applied wood stain, but the chips were no less noticeable.

Harlen strolled to the middle of the room just as a man entered from a doorway off to the left.

"Good afternoon, gentlemen," he said enthusiastically. Attired in a suit soiled with tiny white spots apparently caused by a bleach of some sort, the proprietor was of middle age and appeared to be fit despite having to contend with the poisons of chemicals on a daily basis.

Colvin spoke up. "We want our portrait taken. All five of us. Together." Ever conscientious over his appearance, Colvin smoothed an invisible wrinkle out of his tie. He was forever trimming his mustache or combing pomade into his blond hair. Harlen had to admit, Colvin was the best looking out of the five of them. And the son of a bitch knew it.

"That would be fine. A sitting for five. My name is Edwin Darling, and I'm happy you've come to me." He gestured toward the doorway. "Will you step this way, please?"

"I'll go first and check things out," Manny remarked, his hand falling over the butt of the revolver he kept beneath his long coat. With his eyes halfway closed, as if he were trying to trim the world down so he didn't have so much to take in, he went after Darling. The rest of them followed.

The room they entered was brightly lit and had a pair of Grecian columns on either side of a backdrop painted with unusual trees and a fountain. There was a pedestal and a vase of dried flowers.

"Now then." Edwin arranged some chairs, not showing any intimidation over their being armed. Portraits taken of men wearing guns and spurs to show their bravado weren't uncommon. "Three will sit and two will stand. Proportioning is important."

Harlen hung back, watching as the man fidgeted and worked with the furniture. Thomas Jefferson sniffed around the bottles on the counter as Nate took out his tobacco bag to roll a smoke.

"You better not do that."

A child's voice caught them all off guard, but none more than Harlen. The admonition came from right at his side. He gazed down and saw a girl with two brown braids and wide, large eyes the color of honey, wearing a striped pinafore with a hole in one of the pockets. She was tall for an age Harlen guessed to be around nine or ten.

"If you light that, mister," she frowned at Nate, "you'll blow us all to smithereens. No smoking in here."

"Yeah," Thomas Jefferson clipped, while nudging Nate. "What kind of dumb ass are you?"

Nate stuffed the bag into his trouser pocket, his hand following as he shrugged and said quietly, "Just nervous is all. Thought I saw someone we knew outside."

"Who?" Harlen asked. With the kid standing there, Harlen didn't expect Nate to go into detail.

"An old friend of ours. Mr. Strawn."

Harlen nodded, hoping Nate was wrong. Thayne Strawn was a Merchants and General detective who had a lot of guts and was always itching to let off some steam. He apprehended his wanteds in whatever manner—legal or not—he could get them. So far, the Loco Boys had eluded him, but Strawn was no idiot. If he was out there, they'd better watch their backs.

"Little Darlin'," Edwin called over his shoulder while putting one of the wicker chairs into position, "could you get one of the Eastman dry plates for me?"

"Yes, Daddy."

"Now, you go here." Edwin gestured for Thomas Jefferson to sit in one of the chairs. "Then you and you." Nate and Colvin followed and were adjusted in their respective poses.

Harlen was glad the man didn't ask them their names. Some people were natural born talkers and questioners. Edwin seemed focused only on his work, which suited Harlen fine. He wanted the photograph completed as soon as possible so they could get out of Telluride.

"You, sir." He pointed to Manny and positioned him to stand between Thomas Jefferson and Nate. Then gesturing to Harlen, "And you. If you please, right here." Harlen stood behind Thomas Jefferson and Colvin.

Edwin went to his tripod, took the plate from the girl, and set it on top of the wooden camera box. Affectionately smiling at her, he said, "Thank you, assistant."

Little Darlin' beamed, and her sweet face caused a heaviness to settle in Harlen's chest. Right in the middle of his heart. Back home, he had three younger brothers and two younger sisters. The littlest, Mary, had been a baby when Harlen had left Moab. He wouldn't be able to recognize her if he passed her on the street. This greatly saddened him and brought to mind the homestead in Utah where he'd grown up. Most every day, he thought about his parents and their struggle to make ends meet. About the unfairness they had had to endure from the bank. If Harlen hadn't seen too few roses and too many thorns, he'd probably still be back there with a plow strap around his shoulder behind Old Dutch the mule, digging into land that could very well be taken from them again.

Scratching out such an uncertain existence wasn't Harlen's way anymore. He'd grown too cynical and too bitter against big-moneyed thieves saying they had his family's best interests in mind, when all along the greed of the bankers feasted on the homesteaders. So to Harlen, his crimes against banks were justifiable.

"You gentlemen look as stiff as dead dogs," Edwin said while peeking from the edge of the black cloth over his head. "If you'll forgive my asking, are you good friends?"

The boys were the only friends Harlen had. These men were as close to being his brothers without blood as anyone he knew. "We've been through just about anything a man can and still come out trusting each other with our lives," Harlen supplied.

Manny nodded his agreement.

"Then let the portrait show your loyalty to one another." Edwin came forward and placed Manny's hands on Nate and Thomas Jefferson's shoulders. Without being prompted, Harlen moved his hands to Thomas Jefferson and Colvin's shoulders.

Standing back, Edwin studiously gazed at them. "There's something else . . . something that isn't quite right . . ."

"I know, Daddy," the girl said. "It's the hands of the three in the front. They need to be turned just a little."

Edwin squinted. "Little Darlin', I believe you are right." He kissed the top of her head, and she giggled.

Just then, a woman appeared in the doorway. "Excuse me, Edwin."

She was so stunningly beautiful that she brought out a

gasp from Colvin, who claimed he'd laid eyes on, and laid, every fine miss this side of the Rockies. Well, he hadn't had this one. She was high quality all the way. The color of her dress brought to mind summer peaches, with the lace at her collar being the sugary cream. Her figure was perfect, the nip in her waist so tiny it was hard to believe the child in the room could belong to her. But the resemblance was there. The lady's hair was burnished brown and swept up high on her head with a feathered hat anchored in the back.

For some reason, the woman didn't quite fit in with the scene of the man in a stained suit and a girl with a torn pocket. With her refined manner and smooth voice, she looked and sounded as if she belonged on a stage in a big city.

"It's quite all right, Evaline."

"Forgive my intrusion, gentlemen," she said, her tone so low and husky, Harlen noticed Colvin had to shift in his chair. "I'm going to the post office now, Edwin. I'll return shortly."

"Yes, Evaline, dear." Edwin resumed his station beneath the cloth, having put some of the boys' hands on their thighs and some resting casually on the armrests of the chair. "That was a good suggestion you had, Little Darlin'."

The child smiled, but her smile was for the woman exiting the gallery. She trailed after her. "Good-bye, Momma."

Evaline stopped and allowed the girl to clasp her arms around the fullness of her skirt. "Behave yourself."

"I will, Momma."

The woman hurried along, not really cold toward her daughter but not really all that warm either. Harlen's own mother, despite having six children underfoot, had had a loving touch and kiss for each of them at any hour of the day. Maybe that should have been enough to make Harlen feel contented and secure enough to stay in Moab, but he'd been a part of the land as much as he'd been a part of his parents' love. Above all things, Harlen had valued his freedom too much not to fight back.

"Your gold watch is causing a glare," Edwin was saying,

motioning to Harlen. "Please tuck the chain in farther. Thank you, sir. I'm about ready."

He disappeared inside that tunnel of dark cloth and bounced back a number of times, then came the muffled command, "Smile, gentlemen."

Harlen tried, but he wasn't much good at it.

Edwin didn't take the picture. He popped out from the cloth with a frown.

The girl laughed. "You all look as if you've just been laid out on an undertaker's table and are waiting to be embalmed."

Her attempt at trying to make them crack smiles fell short. Edwin slipped a brass cap over the lens, then inserted that plate into the back of the camera. He'd already poured a granular compound on a platform that was head-height, and at his shoulder. After a final scrutiny of the group, he removed the brass cap and counted to the tap of his foot. Then he ignited that compound and a flash lit the room brighter than the sun. The explosion had them all blind and groping for their guns.

Edwin capped the lens and put the plate into a case, then started upon seeing five guns trained on him. Shoving Little Darlin' behind his back, he stammered, "Eh . . . gentlemen . . . is there a problem?"

"What kind of picture is that you took?" Manny asked suspiciously.

"An artificially lit photograph." Confusion and a thread of fear were mirrored in Edwin's eyes. "I assure you, I did nothing out of the ordinary." The little girl's tiny hand fit around her father's waist as she peeked out from the side of his coat. "You may relax, gentlemen."

Harlen eased the tension from his shoulders, not realizing how tight his muscles had been. They reholstered their revolvers and shuffled out of the positions Edwin had had them in. The studio now smelled like a barrel of rotten eggs. Colvin held his nose.

"The photograph will be ready shortly. You can wait in the receiving room." Then he gazed at his daughter and commented lightly, "Little Darlin', why don't you come and help Daddy?"

Clearly he wanted the child safely by his side after what had happened with the loose guns.

"Didn't mean to alarm you," Harlen stated before Little Darlin' could reply. "We won't be taking our guns out again."

"It's quite all right." But Harlen could tell it wasn't. The man was still unnerved.

Little Darlin's eyes fell on Harlen and she stared at him. "I'll get you freshwater for the bucket, Daddy."

Edwin vacillated, then said, "All right. Go through the house and use the pump out in the yard." Then he went into a small room that appeared to be lit by a singular yellow flame.

The girl held back, watching as the boys filed out. Harlen was last, so she kept her gaze on him the longest. Before he exited, he paused. Reaching into his breast pocket, he withdrew a fancy snowdrop caramel. He was partial to candy and always had a few pieces on him.

Harlen offered the caramel to her while saying, "You're a credit to your daddy, sweet pea."

She gazed at him with hesitation, her little fingers quivering as to whether to accept the confection from him.

"Don't have to take it if you don't want to," he said, moving to put the candy back in his pocket.

Her hand darted out and she snatched the caramel lickety-split. "Thanks, mister."

Harlen smiled, then walked through the doorway and met up with Nate. The two of them stepped onto the boardwalk for a smoke while Colvin, Thomas Jefferson, and Manny stayed inside to look at the *carte de visite* collection and pictures in the stereoscope.

"I swear, Shepp," Nate said, calling him the last name of Harlen's most used alias—Harvey Shepp. "I saw Thayne Strawn around that store over there. And you know he never travels alone."

Harlen nodded, exhaling. He stood back a ways to stay in the shade of the awning. No sense in tempting fate and standing out in the glaring sun if in face Nate had seen Strawn. "I reckon it could have been him."

"It was you, T. J., and Colvin who held up the bank here in eighty-three."

Back then, Telluride had been called Columbia and Harlen hadn't yet met Nate and Manny. Just he, Thomas Jefferson, and Colvin had been into horse racing until no one would race Colvin's mare anymore because she never lost.

A childhood recollection hit Harlen, and he smiled to himself. Betting on mustangs was a far cry from betting on the grasshoppers leaping across his mother's garden. He and Daniel and Robert would tie strings to the legs of the hoppers then let them go, betting an unpleasant chore as their ante.

Harlen sighed heavily, the picture of his innocent youth clouding as a wagon rambled in front of the photography gallery. After abandoning the horse racing, T. J. and Colvin suggested they rob the Columbia Security Bank. Harlen had gotten too used to easy money to earn it honestly, and frankly, he liked the idea of stealing from a bank, since they were all operated by a bunch of crooks anyway.

He, Thomas Jefferson, and Colvin had made off with thirty-one thousand dollars—just over ten thousand apiece.

Harlen glanced at the corner where the Columbia Security Bank used to be. A hardware store now occupied the spot. He wondered if their robbery had busted the depository, and wasn't sorry if it had.

"If Strawn is in town, we'd better get the hell out of here soon as that photograph is ready," Harlen suggested.

Nate crushed his smoke beneath his boot. "I'm for that. 'Bout time we paid a visit to the Silverton Miners Bank and make a withdrawal."

Harlen pulled smoke into his lungs and thought on that a moment. They'd already sized the bank up and had decided to relieve the vault of its assets. If Strawn and his boys were in the neighborhood, better that they go south for a while. And after the job, even farther south. Maybe down to Mexico.

After a time, Colvin stuck his head out the door. "Photograph's ready."

Harlen and Nate put out their smokes and went inside. Having not seen Strawn or any detectives, Harlen allowed himself a little breathing room in the studio.

Pride beamed on Edwin's face as he showed them their formal portrait. Harlen stood over Thomas Jefferson to get a better look. Not a one of them had a hint of a smile in his expression. They looked like a bunch of somber preachers. But despite that, the image was a good one. And with Edwin's coaching, the five of them did resemble a group of men who'd known both good and bad times together. There was a certain comradery in the soul of that photograph that came shining through.

Reaching for his wallet, Harlen paid Edwin his fee. "We're obliged, Darling."

"You're welcome, gentlemen," he replied.

They all filed onto the boardwalk, Colvin inspecting his reproduction with a critical eye. "I shouldn't have put my hand down there. Looks like I've got it on my crotch." Colvin bumped Manny with his elbow. "Does that look like I've got my hand on my crotch?"

"No. Looks like you've got your hand on your fly," Manny replied. "You must have been thinking about that lady who came into the room."

"Damn . . ." Colvin let out his breath in a soft whistle. "She was something."

Nate's hand came down on Harlen's shoulder and he cautioned Harlen quietly, "Over there by that hitching post. The man with the derby . . . three others with him."

Harlen's stomach knotted. Thayne Strawn of the Merchants and General Agency conversed with some other detectives, by the look of their suits.

"Boys," Harlen said in a low voice. "I don't want any sudden moves or raised voices. We've got us a problem here."

Manny moved in, his hand on his gun.

Thomas Jefferson reached for his revolver, and Colvin tucked the portrait into the inside pocket of his coat.

Nate kept his head down, his hat tipped at an angle so his face couldn't easily be seen. "Across the street. Four of them. M and G's. Thayne Strawn in the middle."

Colvin swore.

"We'll walk on over to the livery, get the horses, and take the east road out," Harlen said, his fingers instinctively curling around the wooden butt of his Remington-Rider .44. "I think we should split up. Colvin and T. J., you go first. Me, Manny, and Nate will follow a short distance behind."

Colvin and Thomas Jefferson started walking. Harlen kept his gaze trained on the men across the street who were talking with folded arms, as if they were discussing something as unimportant as the weather. None of the detectives had even glanced his way. Harlen took up the slack and began trailing T. J. and Colvin. He kept to the inside of the boardwalk, making pedestrians go around him.

They reached the livery, saddled their horses, and mounted. Harlen took the lead, heading down one of the alleys, but having no choice other than to cross over at Main Street to connect with the southeastern route out of Telluride toward Silverton. He kept his gray roan, Blue, loping at an even gait through the obstacles of rigs and other riders filling up the road.

He and the boys were about in the clear when Thayne came out of nowhere from behind the dry goods building. He ran to the corner, pistol raised, cheeks red, and meaning business. Harlen had to rein Blue in, the horse digging his heels into the dirt.

"Harlen Shepard Riley, throw down your weapon in the name of the Merchants and General Agency."

From various points in a small circle at the intersection, Thayne's men had them surrounded. The same call to drop weapons was issued to each member in the gang.

None of them complied.

Harlen was the first to damn the consequences and spur his horse forward. A hot bullet whizzed by his ear, so close he could hear the sizzle of his hair being singed. The rest of the boys followed him, revolvers drawn and returning fire.

Harlen didn't want to kill any of the detectives. He aimed only to disarm and put a man out of commission. Blue's speed gave him the advantage to do so, as a moving target was harder to hit than a stationary one.

Chaos erupted on the streets, hindering a fast getaway for the boys, because they had to dodge frantic citizens. Harlen sharply veered Blue to the left as a group of men sprinted out in front of him to duck behind a watering trough. Women scattered up boardwalks, leaving their parcels in the street to be crushed by Blue's pounding hooves.

Though Blue had been trained not to spook at the sound of gunfire, the roan acted skittish as Harlen directed him away from the armed men giving him pursuit on foot.

Edwin Darling ran alongside of Harlen, then swerved. Harlen gave Blue a hard right spur to avoid knocking the photographer down. With only a moment to view what was going on, Harlen watched Edwin fall to his knees in the street beside a pool of peach fabric. His mournful scream cut through the pandemonium as he lifted his face heavenward.

"Evaaaaaaaaa!" The sound that came from Edwin's throat went through Harlen like a dull blade.

Foreboding prickled his skin. Without being told, he knew what had happened. Evaline Darling had been caught in the cross fire and killed.

Harlen kept on riding because he had to. Thoughts of whose bullet had taken the life of that beautiful woman ate at his gut. That the fatal shot could have been caused by him brought rose bile to his throat.

As he whisked past the photography studio, Little Darlin's small face seemed to fill the window. Their eyes met for a second that felt like forever. In that flash of time, Harlen saw devastation and hate registered on the girl's face.

That look would haunt him for as long as he lived.

❧ 1 ❧

A lost inch of gold may be found,
a lost inch of time, never.
                              —Chinese proverb

August 20, 1904
Eternity, Colorado

Some inebriated fool was shooting the bottles off Marshal
Scudder's liquor tree. Rooted in the corner lot of Eighth
Avenue and Main Street, the tree nearly took up the entire
yard of the marshal's office. Leah Kirkland could see the
stunted scrub oak—long dead after a lightning strike—
from the upstairs window of her house two blocks away.
Midmorning sunlight glittered off the variegated colors of
glass stuck on gnarled branches through the bottle mouths.
Amber, green, caramel, blue, and crystalline were being
picked off with wanton bullets.

As soon as the first gunshot had been fired and she heard
glass breaking, Leah knew there'd be an arrest. U.S. Marshal Benard "Bean" Scudder had been sticking his empty
beer bottles on that tree for as long as anyone in Eternity
could remember, and those bottles being blown to pieces
would set the lawman off faster than the shutter on her No.
2 Bulls-Eye Kodak.

Ka-Boom!

Leah winced at the sound that spelled doom. This time
the weaving culprit hit the top rung of the straight ladder

Marshal Scudder kept propped against the tree. Taking aim, the gunman tried again and hit his mark. Blue shards fell. As far as Leah could tell, he'd hit one of the Pabst Blue Ribbon bottles. On wobbly legs, the drunk stopped to reload his revolver. She didn't recognize him and took him for a passing drover who'd gotten drunk at one of the saloons. Most likely the Temple of Music or the Gold Belt, where neither bartender was known to cut a man off after he'd consumed his limit.

Casswell Tinhorn, with his blacksmith pliers in his rear pocket, ran down Seventh Avenue toward the Aspenglow River where Marshal Scudder spent his Saturday afternoons fishing. There would be aces to pay as soon as Casswell came back with the marshal.

Leah let the Nottingham lace curtain fall into place. Without question, she'd be taking the lawbreaker's photograph for a charge of drunk and disorderly. She'd been snapping mug shots for the arrest records almost two years now. Ever since she'd established a gallery in her home after her husband's death. Her photography studio was the only one in Eternity. Her specialty was shooting feminine scenes: mothers, children, pets, domestic activities, gardens, homes, and portraits. She also snapped criminal suspects' faces when the need arose, and photographs for the *Eternity Tribune* when something newsworthy needed a picture with the article.

Turning away from the window, Leah strode across the converted bedroom. The colors of her studio were old blue and ivory. Turkish rugs, silk draperies, upholstery chairs, and pottery made up her work area. The pungent smell of chemicals was apparent even though the four windows were thrown open. Easels on casters and painted canvasses took up an entire corner of the room. The space was light and airy with its skylight, low-raftered ceilings, and innovative decorative touches. She used the water closet as her darkroom, printing her negatives in the window.

Leah went to a narrow mahogany table that butted against the far wall. Its finish had long since been ruined by thoughtless placements of silver nitrate and potassium iodide bottles. A stack of photographs she'd taken for use in the stereoscope tipped over and she shoved them upright, searching through the clutter for a single negative film plate. The Bulls-Eye Kodak, the Buckeye 1899 model, and the Kombi, covered in black-grain morocco, were all good for a sufficient mug shot. But she selected the Buckeye, because she didn't have to use a tripod and it could be loaded in daylight. It was practical, compact, portable, and with developing costs at a minimum to produce the three and a half by three and a half-inch pictures. She packed the necessary equipment in a case with a shoulder strap.

Florencio Constantino sang Verdi's "La donna è mobile" on the Edison, but Leah didn't take a minute to shut the phonograph off. The shooting hadn't subsided, because Bean Scudder didn't run too swiftly. He worked hard at his short, choppy steps to get anywhere quickly. Unless he picked up the pace at mealtime to get to Mrs. Scudder's table. But Leah didn't know that for sure. She was going by pure speculation and the girth of Bean's paunch.

Heading out the door with her straw hat indifferently pinned over her topknot, Leah briefly glanced at her reflection in the hall mirror. Her hair was never quite smooth and in place, because she spent so much time beneath a black focusing cloth. The chronic state of her coiffure was disheveled.

The sun was high and warm as Leah walked the pebbled path to the road. She had a large front yard with a walkway lined by rosebushes and leading to a whitewashed, split-rail fence that went right up to the street. Leah hoped her mother-in-law made Rosalure and Tug stay inside her house and continue making candy, instead of letting the children out to investigate the noise. She didn't want them getting underfoot with a lunatic in the road.

Opening the gate, she saw Casswell Tinhorn return to the Anvil and Forge blacksmith shop, and Bean Scudder lumber up Seventh Avenue wearing an india rubber pneumatic boat. The tube resembled a big black doughnut with foot holes in it so the great outdoorsman could float like a cork on the water to catch all those unsuspecting trout. With a canvas creel slung over his shoulder, a fishing rod in his left hand, and a gun raised in his right fist, Marshal Scudder bore down on the offender with the fury of a black bear who'd been disturbed in his den. If the town hadn't appropriated funds from the city treasury to buy Bean a Smith & Wesson hammerless safety revolver that couldn't be fired unintentionally, Leah might have been more fearful. Scudder had a problem with going off half-cocked when he was mad . . . or tipsy. But the marshal's current revolver required direct pressure simultaneously exerted on the stock and trigger to discharge it. Accidents were impossible. According to the ad, the hammerless safety revolver was the only absolutely safe arm for pocket or home protection. This greatly relieved the citizens of Eternity, who used to run in hiding when Bean Scudder was holding a gun.

Leah kept to the sidewalk, but in the event of an emergency, she planned on hiding behind a tree. Her Queen Anne–styled home was a singular dwelling on the block. The rest of the lots were overgrown with box elder, sage, and the lingering July colors of columbine and verbena. Depending on which way a person was traveling through Eternity, her residence was the first or last they encountered. She liked being set apart from the central commotion of Main Street. From her porch swing, she had an unobstructed view of the Eternal Mountains and the enormous cross the First Presbyterian Church had mounted back in the mid-1880's.

"What in the hell?" Scudder hollered as he neared the gunman. "I say, what in the Sam *hell* is going on here?"

The drover gunman, wearing downtrodden spurs and shaggy chaps, swiveled on his boot heels with the firearm still in his grasp. "Huh?"

"Drop it!" the marshal ordered, fumbling with the stock and trigger of his hammerless.

Leah immediately ran across the street to the opposite corner. She took cover behind one of two wooden Buddhas stationed in the entryway of the Happy City Chinese Restaurant. From there, she peeked around the Buddha's broad, weathered shoulder to see if it was safe to come out.

Marshal Scudder, rather than resorting to using his Smith

& Wesson, was able to apprehend the suspect without altercation. The reason was because the suspect had dropped his gun—and himself—in the dirt. He'd passed out cold on the ground in front of the liquor tree.

The marshal attempted to reholster his gun, but the rubber tube got in his way, so he held it along with his fishing rod. He wore hip boots that squeaked and sloshed from the water inside them when he took mincing steps. Huffing, he bent his knees enough to reach down and pick up the man's gun. With an awkward grunt and a totter, Bean straightened, then turned toward his office.

Leah dashed from her hiding spot and approached the prone suspect. Standing over him, she studied his pale face with its week's growth of whiskers, thinking a likeness exposed in his passed-out, drunken state might be more interesting than one taken of him awake with bloodshot eyes. She always tried to come up with new ways to improve her picture taking, whether she altered the lighting or used different lenses or poses.

"Mrs. Kirkland." The marshal's voice lifted her chin. "Guess you heard the shots."

"I did."

"Don't know why Moon couldn't hear them and handle this matter himself. Instead, I was dragged from a brown trout a nibble away from being on my supper plate." He glanced at the Buckeye in her grasp. "You brought your camera, I see. I'll have to have Moon help me get the prisoner in the cell and revive him so you can take his picture proper."

Scudder opened the office door and stood back so Leah could enter first. The marshal, wedged in the door's opening by the wide circumference of his pneumatic boat, had to shove himself inside. The line of his pole got hung up around the nose of his revolver as he struggled on stubby legs to get somewhere. With a scrambling of his squishy feet, he stumbled into the room, his boots leaving muddy tracks on the floor. Scudder flung his bamboo fishing pole, hammerless safety revolver, and the drunk's gun on his desk in a tangle of fine silk line.

Deputy Ferris Moon, with a half-smile on his thin mouth, was fast asleep on a cot next to a sunny window with one of those shady magazines draped over his skinny middle. Scudder kicked in the legs of the cot at Moon's feet, collapsing his bed and sending Moon hard on his backside. He came up sputtering, a shock of straw-blond hair falling into his surprise-widened eyes.

"Hang it all, Moon!" Scudder railed. "Didn't you hear that gunfire?"

Seeing Leah, Deputy Ferris quickly bunched the offensive magazine in his fingers and shoved the wad of paper beneath his right thigh. "I, uh, thought some kids were setting off leftover fireworks."

"Some kids," Scudder mimicked sourly. "You blame fool. A drunken cowboy was shooting up my beer bottles! And he got six of them." The marshal shimmied out of the rubber around his middle until the doughnut lay at his wet feet. He stepped out of it and rolled the tube next to his desk, where water ran off the plump sides and spread into a puddle. "On account of you sleeping on the job, Deputy Moon, you'll be filling out all the necessary paperwork."

Ferris's face fell.

"Mrs. Kirkland, you may set up your camera. We'll bring in the perpetrator now."

Leah was left alone. She rested her case on the corner of Marshal Scudder's desk and loaded her camera. She was figuring out the best angle of light in which to shoot the mug shot, when Deputy Moon and Marshal Scudder came through the doorway. Bean had the cowboy's shoulders, and Ferris had his legs—visibly mindful of those can-opener spurs at the heels of his boots. When they got the prisoner to the cell, they put him on the bed none too gently. The rough handling didn't rouse the man at all.

Scudder, who was panting from the exertion and had worked up a sweat, plopped into the chair behind his desk and switched on his five-inch Little Hustler fan to high. The appliance ran eight hours on one charge and was rearing to go when Scudder needed to dry his perspiration. Unfortunately, Leah had seen him engage the fan on several occasions, and on each of those occasions the marshal hadn't had the foresight to move the papers on his desk out of the way. As in past times, they flew across the room like a flock of pigeons. A Pinkerton warrant stuck to the dusty windowpane, and Bean peeled it off.

"Hang it all!" Scudder swore, then turned the fan in the other direction, where the only damage it could do was ruffle the Mister Brew beer calendar hanging on the wall by a thumbnail tack.

Leah politely said nothing about the papers sailing to the floor. She picked up the few that landed at the tips of her shoes and set the documents on the marshal's desk. "If you would be so kind as to sit the man up for me," she said.

"Certainly," Bean replied. "Deputy Moon, frisk the prisoner for contraband, then sit him up. After that, throw a bucket of water in his face."

"That won't be necessary," Leah volunteered. "I believe I can still capture a perfect likeness with his eyes closed."

"But he won't look the same," the deputy commented as Leah entered the open cell with sunlight streaming in through a high northern window.

"Well, Deputy Moon, this man is probably arrested more times with his eyes closed than when they're open. An accurate picture for future reference would be one of him in his present condition, I think."

Ferris Moon scratched his head, alternating his gaze on the prisoner's face and the sorry state of his appearance. "I reckon you could be right, Mrs. Kirkland."

The deputy left and she set her camera on the bedside. The smell of liquor was strong on the man, and she held her breath as she made a few minor adjustments to his posture. She placed his right hand across his middle, and his left hand on his left thigh. Picking up the camera, she stood back and looked through the lens. Not quite right. Several more fine-tuning positions of his body, and she was satisfied he looked like a drunken cowboy with a slightly Napoleonic pose. She'd put his hat on his lap to cover the one button she'd noticed had been left undone. A blush stole into her cheeks, along with a quick glance at the deputy to see if he'd witnessed her embarrassment. But he wasn't paying her any attention. With a puzzled frown, he sorted through the papers that had danced around the office with its four cells.

Leah took the picture and stowed her things in the case as Marshal Scudder came inside, his hands cradling pieces of colored glass from his beer bottles. They made a crunching sound as he dropped them in the rubbish bin. With a combined grievous sigh and snort, he looked at Leah. "It galls me to see this sort of defacing of property. What is this world coming to?" Scudder's gaze fell on the hardwood ice chest, and he licked his lips. "I'll have to drink a few extra beers today to make up for the broken bottles."

Leah raised her brows. She didn't condone telling a person he should have a drink—especially if the person was known to overindulge. But neither did she think an occasional drink was a sin. The Italians drank wine. *Vino,* she corrected in the language she'd been diligently trying to learn.

"Get out of my chair, Moon," the marshal grumbled with a wave of his hand.

The deputy stood and stuffed his hands into his pockets with a bewildered gleam in his eyes. "I can't figure out all those papers."

"Lock up that cell, then go outside and clean up the rest of that glass." Scudder slumped into his swivel chair, which had a wide seat for wide seats. "This has put me in such a state of aggravation, the next stranger who comes through my town, I'm liable to lock up if he so much as looks at me the wrong way."

Leah wouldn't want to be that unsuspecting soul, for once Scudder made a threat he always went through with it.

Wyatt Holloway stood in the shadow of a towering cross, not feeling the least bit spiritual. Instead, he gave the mountainside some of his best blasphemous words.

Encountering the landslide some hundred feet down from the cross's base was a hell of a note to end the trip on, but what had he expected? That the area would have remained exactly as it had been seventeen years ago? That he'd retrieve the buried sixty-thousand dollars in twenty-dollar gold pieces, with five- and ten-dollar coins and a balance in currency. Be able to buy a ranch right off, settle down, and get married so he could have some kids? Nothing in life fell into place that easy. He should have learned that by now.

Lowering to a crouch, Wyatt ran the palm of his hand over the loose stone. There were small rocks and big chunks of light yellowish pink sandstone. As if he hadn't had enough of sandstone.

Wyatt shaded his eyes and looked up, gauging the distance to the cross, hoping that he'd miscalculated. No. He was in the right spot. But the crevice and its markings were gone. Years of nature had taken its toll. Heavy snows had probably done the most damage. The spring thaws hadn't helped any either. From the looks of the terrain, the landslide wasn't recent.

Standing, Wyatt removed his hat and rubbed the sweat off his brow with the back of his duster sleeve. At least the cross was still here. Without it, finding the money would be like searching for a calf lost on a thousand acres of mesquite—if indeed the money was still here. Could be that some lucky miner unearthed the extra gallon-sized Yellow Crawford apricot cans years ago. Then where would he be without the money bags that had been hidden inside? He didn't want to accept the sixty-thousand dollars not being here as a possibility. Because without it, his fresh start was no start.

Wyatt grew thoughtful, pondering his next move. Buying his horse, the saddle, gear, and tack had set him back. All he had to his name was twenty-two dollars and eighty-seven cents. He'd been planning on using the cash to buy himself a fine woman and a few nights of unbridled pleasure. To really live it up for a couple of weeks, then claim some prime acreage in either Montana or Wyoming and settle down. Now he couldn't even spare a quarter for a kiss. He'd have to purchase a pick, ax, shovel, chisel, and hammer, to name a few items. Tools that fit into his hands like second nature.

Wyatt took in his surroundings, thinking that if he had to be stuck somewhere, this place rivaled Eden. Walking to a slope of silky meadow grass, Wyatt sank down into the inviting cushion and reached into his shirt pocket. He unwrapped a piece of strawberry taffy, popped the confection into his mouth, and slowly chewed, savoring each sweet burst of the treat against his tongue. For a long while he sat there, taking in the palette of countryside colors that seemed brighter and more vibrant than he'd remembered.

The breeze was soft and warm and drowsy. Perennial streams as pure as crystal came dancing down from the high peaks. The foothills were thick with cottonwood, piñon, juniper, and aspens. Bluebirds and sparrows sang from the branches, a music Wyatt thought sweeter than the saltwater taffy. He could stay where he was indefinitely, marveling in the freedom of wide-open space around him. The sun, the same one that had held him prisoner as he'd toiled and sweated on Table Rock, was no longer an enemy he couldn't flee. Wyatt could move out of its simmering rays whenever he wanted. Right now, he preferred to bask in the hypnotic warmth while he ate his candy.

From his position on the mountain, Wyatt could see all four boundaries of the town below him.

Eternity.

Well, it hadn't stayed eternally the same. Back in '87, the town had been nothing but a tent city with not more than four hundred miners and nary a woman in sight. Wyatt's vantage point allowed him to see four streets running north and south, and seven running east and west. False fronts, what looked to be native stone, and wooden structures made up the town now. The streets were wide enough for two-way traffic. But at least there wasn't a single one of those skunk-smelling automobiles scaring the hell out of the horses and leaving a trail of smoke to choke a person. Though Ford's Boss of the Road and the Model B Cadillacs weren't present, the electrical wires were. Wyatt had seen them so thick in Boise City that there was hardly a visible speck of sky left.

Eternity was a regular civilized place, yet still looked like one of the sleepy little Western towns he was used to from the old days, except for the wires. Its bypass from the evils of present-day vices was most likely attributable to the fact the city was in a deep valley, fifty miles from anyplace, and surrounded by ranges—notably the San Juan.

Glancing up, Wyatt estimated the time. Several hours past noon. The sky was like a blue bowl of soup. Clear, with cloud dumplings to cast slow-moving shadows over him. When the clouds hit he was given a few minutes respite from the shimmering August sun, but when they moved on he was reminded of the heat.

He could use a cool drink. One of those Coca-Colas would have been just the ticket. The carbonated beverage was about the only thing the new century had to offer him that he could see was of monumental importance. All the rest was nothing but trappings and useless gadgets.

Finishing the taffy, Wyatt rose and went to his horse, July. The black was put together well and had a lot of bottom to him. Wyatt had been lucky to pick up the gelding for twelve dollars. After untying the lead rope, Wyatt mounted and nudged July down the winding trail of the mountain.

As he entered the town, he rode past a fancy house with music and diaphanous curtains flitting through the open window sashes. A man sang with orchestra instruments, but Wyatt couldn't understand a word. The singer wasn't from around these parts. He sounded like a foreigner. There must have been some kind of important concert going on, though there didn't seem to be an audience in attendance. The curb was empty of buggies. The white-and-blue stone residence itself was decorated with gables, dormer windows, and scalloped trim that looked like a gingerbread house. The placard planted in the grass read Leah Kirkland, Photography Gallery.

Wyatt had never heard of a female photographer before. He shied away from cameras and the people behind them.

While approaching the center of the town, Wyatt came upon an oddity that caught his attention. Different-colored beer bottles were strung out on a tree like Christmas ornaments. Next to the tree was an office.

Usually Wyatt could spot a lawman about as far as he could see one. They had a certain way of conducting themselves in an official manner that was like a red flag. But in this instance, the sign nailed to the building front tipped him off that the man in the shade was United States Marshal Benard Scudder. That, and the slice of sun—just enough to cut across the man's chest—flickering off the badge pinned to his fishing vest. He sat beneath the awning on an overturned apple crate drinking a High Hog beer. A cold one from the looks of the water droplets sliding down the bottle and dribbling on his pants leg.

A vague pang for a drink hit Wyatt but was gone before the old need came to fruition. He'd had his last taste on September 18, 1887. He'd gone too long without a whiskey to start up again. Liquor was nothing but trouble for him. It always had been.

Lifting his gaze to the marshal's face, Wyatt gave his craggy features a cursory look. Nothing stood out more than the handlebar mustache that appeared to have been given a good grooming with a heavy coat of pomatum wax. The russet twist of facial hair was a whopper, the biggest growth Wyatt had ever seen on an upper lip.

In Wyatt's experience, lawmen weren't always worth what they were paid. There were those who liked doing nothing at all, and those who liked to detain a person for doing nothing so they could throw their weight around. From the bulge of the marshal's stomach and the glint of purpose in Scudder's eyes, Wyatt sensed this man was a combination of both.

He was about to avert his gaze—because eye contact with the marshal would spell a challenge—but he was too late. Scudder saw him and pursed his lips. Standing, he hitched his pants with his left hand, though his suspenders were doing most of the work. Scudder's stomach started at his celluloid collar and didn't end until his belt. Or rather did, but his belly didn't know that. It flowed over his buckle like bread dough left to rise too long.

"You there!" he sternly called to Wyatt. "Get off of that horse and come on over here, boy."

Wyatt hadn't been a boy in over two decades, and he resented the degrading remark. But the last thing he wanted was trouble from the fat marshal, so he dismounted and led July to the sidewalk.

Stepping down the few steps of the porch, Marshal Scudder shuffled to the decorated tree and shoved the High Hog bottle on one of the empty branches. He took two steps toward Wyatt, then stopped as if to say, "You'll come to me, not me come to you."

Wyatt moved in as far as he could without putting his horse on the walkway. Even standing in the street, he had the lawman by a good head and a half.

"What's your name, boy?" Scudder asked, his hand slipping on his revolver butt to emphasize his authority.

"Wyatt Holloway."

"Wyatt Holloway." He tapped his temple with a pudgy finger as if to get things working. "Wyatt Holloway." The repetition of his name made Wyatt think the gears in the marshal's brain were spinning, arbitrarily trying to connect him with some unsolved criminal act and make the lawman look like a hero for apprehending the culprit right in front of the city jail. Well, it wasn't going to happen. Wyatt Holloway's record was so clean, it was invisible. "Doesn't sound familiar."

"It wouldn't."

"Where you from?"

Scudder was really pressing his appointed duty. There was no law saying Wyatt had to give up that information if he wasn't under arrest, so he figured a lie was in order.

"Billings."

"What in the hell are you doing so far away from Montana?"

"Checking out possibilities farther south."

The marshal gave him a stern going-over with a narrowed gaze. "Where'd you get that antique gun?"

Wyatt glanced at the '79 Remington-Rider .44 caliber double-action revolver at his hip. He didn't favor the newfangled automatic pistols. This was the gun he'd been trained to sharpshoot with. He knew how it operated, and he was used to compensating its kick for perfect accuracy. "Picked it up in a secondhand shop."

Scudder cracked a snide smile. "Does it still work?"

"Last I fired it."

The corners of the lawman's mouth went grim. "You won't be needing to fire it in my town. Just how long do you think you'll be checking out prospects in Eternity?"

Wyatt couldn't exactly say he was passing through, even though no one had the right to know his business. But if the digging was slow to bring results, he might be here for a week. He'd have to come to town if he ran out of food, and he couldn't sneak around. He wondered if there was a claim office to check whether someone might have already put a stake on that land not knowing that Wyatt had a stake in what was buried beneath the rocks.

"I can't rightly say how long I'll be."

"Then you need for me to set you straight. If you stay, you got twenty-four hours to get yourself a job. You don't have one by"—Scudder checked the time on his pocket watch—"four thirty-nine tomorrow, you'll be run out of my town, boy. I'll be considering you a vagrant at precisely four-forty." The marshal snapped closed the lid on his watch and shoved the timepiece into his tight pants. "Seeing as there's only one opening in town, I suggest you act on it. Quick. Before someone else snaps up the position."

Wyatt didn't have the opportunity to ask Marshal Scudder what job he was referring to. A woman approached them holding a small envelope. She was tall and slim, wearing one of those shirtwaists with a man's tie at the throat. He couldn't get used to a woman putting on an article of a man's attire. Her skirt was narrow, pronouncing the slender shape of her thighs, yet she wore one of those bustles that gave a man a false image of a lady's derriere. The rest of the skirt fabric flowed to a wider hem at the bottom where her lace-up shoes—which were only halfway laced up—peeked from beneath the cotton print. One of the laces was untied, though she apparently didn't care. She stepped on the black ribbon without putting a hitch in her purposeful stride.

"Excuse me, Marshal Scudder, but I have your documentation ready." She handed the lawman the flat envelope, then gazed in Wyatt's direction. "Pardon the interruption."

She had straight brunette hair that was messed up beneath her straw hat with a plum-colored ribbon on it. Wispy strands fell into her golden brown eyes. The way her hair tumbled in a flyaway manner around her face gave off the effect of a woman who'd just been in bed . . . and not alone.

Wyatt checked himself before he thought further on that. In broad daylight, a lady like this wouldn't have been doing something like that. His base need for a woman had him thinking along those lines. But still, she did have that look about her. That radiance . . . like she was content about something. He made a quick search of her left hand. No wedding ring. Could be she had herself a lover.

A dark smudge was at the hollow of her cheek, but he passed that by, gazing at her mouth, the lips full and pink. Her eyebrows arched with a slight pitch to them. He found that attractive in a woman. Especially when her complexion was pale and her brows darker.

"Benard!" a shrill female voice called from around the corner and had Wyatt cringing. "Benard Scudder!"

The marshal turned to the woman with a grumble. "What is it, LaRaine?"

"Your fried chicken is going to be on the table in fifteen minutes. You'll be home then if you want to eat it while it's hot."

Scudder's face brightened. "Why, yes, sugar puss. I'm on my way just as soon as I give Moon his orders." Then to the lady who'd brought the envelope, he said, "Thank you for the fast work. I'll have Deputy Moon log this while he's on his night-shift duty."

Then to Wyatt, Scudder said, "You better get on over to the Happy City Chinese Restaurant."

"What for?"

The marshal headed for his office and called over his

shoulder, "The dishwasher job. Like I said, you don't have lawful employment in twenty-four hours, I've got a cell with your name on it, boy." The marshal's parting comment was spoken through a snicker that Wyatt didn't appreciate.

The lady's clearing her throat startled Wyatt, and he turned toward her. "He's not kidding, you know." She stood pretty close, considering that he was a stranger, and she was not in the least bit giddy around him or afraid. The fragrance of carnations came to Wyatt, smelling so fine and erotic, he'd forgotten such a floral scent existed. Hard-pressed not to pull the lady into his arms and drag his nose across every inch of her skin, he forced himself to listen to what she was going on about. "I'd suggest you do as he says, or he will lock you up. He's had a bad day. A drunk shot six bottles off this tree."

Wyatt lifted his brows, his pulse so heated he could barely think. Her friendly advice invited him to flirt with her. He hadn't engaged a woman in conversation in such a long time, he decided to test the waters. He used to be able to send the ladies into bashful giggles. "You've got a cute smudge on your cheek, darlin'."

"Oh, do I?"

But that was it. She made no coy attempt to wipe it or ask him for a kerchief to do so.

He knew he'd changed physically, but had hoped that he still could charm a woman. Maybe it was because he was big now. Not the same lanky kid he used to be. His body had hardened like sandstone. His muscles had been cut and chiseled to well-defined slabs of flesh from years of back-breaking labor. He'd had his nose broken, so his face wasn't that of a pretty boy anymore. And his hands were too large, with the knuckle joints bulky from abuse. He didn't think too much of his appearance these days. He wasn't ugly, but he wasn't that willowy young man who could mount a horse by making a running leap into the air and landing squarely on the horse's back.

In short, he was thirty-eight and beginning to feel his age.

"Leo opens at five," she was saying, snapping Wyatt out

of his thoughts. "I doubt there'll be a line for the job, but you never know."

Then she scurried up Eighth Avenue, sometimes stepping on that shoe ribbon as she disappeared from his view.

Wyatt refused to accept that the only job to be had in Eternity was as a dishwasher. He'd had some blacksmithing experience, so he'd checked at the Anvil and Forge first and talked with a man named Casswell Tinhorn. But he didn't need any help and directed Wyatt to the Happy City Chinese Restaurant. Before he went on, Wyatt made arrangements to put July up in a stall for the night in the livery, then he set out on foot.

He spent all of ten minutes walking both sides of Main Street, making inquiries that were shot down within seconds. He'd had hard-luck jobs before. He'd done worse than dishwashing—and without pay—because he'd had no choice. Cannery work and washing and pressing laundry were low on the list. Breaking rock in the quarry had looked a lot better afterward.

As Wyatt ended his full circle, one of the last establishments on this side of the street was the Happy City. The place stuck out like a sore thumb with its twin carvings of two fat guys in underwear, in front. There was a short tower over the entry door that had an upward-curving roof over each story. Its red paint was peeling and in dire need of a fresh coat. From outward appearances, it looked like the owner didn't have a buck to his name.

Wyatt wandered over to have a better look, not because he was considering the job but because the sign in the window looked invitingly familiar to him. It was that same red sign he'd seen throughout the country at various eateries.

Refreshing and Delicious
Coca-Cola .05¢

That made Wyatt pause and deliberate. He was thirsty and could go in and have a glass to think over his other options. When he opened the door, the smells that met him were some of the strangest aromas he'd ever had the displeasure of smelling. He hadn't a clue as to what Chinese food was.

The place wasn't well lit, but he clearly saw the porcelain cat with fangs and a grin to put a laughing madam to shame. It sat in the vestibule, almost as if to distract customers from coming in. Chinese watercolors of tradesmen and an oil portrait of a guy in a black cap who looked as if he was important hung on the wall. There was a lot of colorful silk screens, and a red lacquered cabinet with brass hardware that appeared out of place with all the plain pine tables.

A man parted the curtain of reedlike beads that separated the kitchen from the dining area. He was a good-looking fellow. Not too short and with a pleasant face that disguised any attempt Wyatt would have made as to his age. His almond-shaped eyes were as black as his hair. He squinted against the smoke curling from the cigarette clamped in his mouth.

"We don't open till five for supper."

Wyatt wasn't sure how he'd expected the man to sound, but having an accent that reminded him of a fellow he'd once met from New York hadn't been on his mind.

"Wasn't looking to get a meal. I just wanted a cola."

The man gave him a tentative glance, then shrugged. "Sit down."

Wyatt did in the rawhide-bottomed chair he'd been pointed to. He took his hat off and ran his hand through his windblown hair. The table was situated at one of the front windows where wooden shutters had been pushed open to allow lingering sunlight in. A candleholder with a fat candle inside was on the table, causing Wyatt to glance at the ceiling. No electric lights.

The man had gone into the kitchen, the reeds stirring behind him. Wyatt saw a younger fellow at a square butcher's table. He held a cleaver and whacked a raw chicken into parts faster than a roper hog-tying a calf in a contest.

Returning with two cola bottles, the man gave one to

Wyatt, then sat down opposite him. Using an opener, he flipped the caps off each bottle.

"You aren't from around here," the man remarked as he took a sip of cola. He still had his cigarette. The stub dangled in his fingers.

"No," Wyatt replied.

"You look like you're out of place, mister."

Wyatt did feel sort of out of place, only he didn't want to admit it. "I could say the same about you. You're no westerner."

"No far-easterner either," he said as he lifted his chin a notch. "Born and raised in Brooklyn, New York."

Wyatt hadn't taken a drink yet, uncertain if he wanted to share a conversation and a Coca-Cola with a stranger. He'd grown distrustful of his fellow man, with circumstances being what they had been most of his adult life. But as soon as the man replied with blunt candor, Wyatt warmed up to him a little.

"Leo Wang," the restaurateur offered with an extended hand.

Wyatt took it. "Wyatt Holloway."

"Where you from, Mr. Holloway?"

"Wyatt," he amended. "Up north."

"Ah, a man who doesn't want people to know too much about him. I'll respect that." Leo drank again, noticed Wyatt hadn't, and frowned. "You don't want your Coca-Cola?"

Wyatt lifted the bottle and drank that first sugary sip that always slid down his throat better than fine bourbon. There was something about this cola stuff that really appealed to him. He couldn't exactly say what. He'd had sarsaparilla before, so he'd known the texture of carbonation in his mouth. But this was just like the sign said: delicious and refreshing.

Scudder's obnoxious face suddenly appeared in the window. He tapped on the glass with his gun tip. Leo gave him a big smile, and Wyatt had to at least acknowledge him with a nod. Then the marshal chuckled before walking off. It annoyed the hell out of Wyatt to think he was being followed, or encouraged to do something he didn't really want to do.

In the marshal's wake, Leo's smile fell, and he muttered, "What a pain in the tail butt."

Wyatt smiled. "You don't like the local law officer?"

"About as much as I like hot dogs."

Wyatt didn't know what a hot dog was, and took it to be some kind of Chinese food, but he didn't want to insult Leo by asking him if he really ate dogs. A good feeling had settled over him and he didn't want to ruin the moment.

The front door opened and two kids—a girl about the age of nine and a boy no older than five—wove their way around the tables, a woman not far behind them. She was the same one from in front of the marshal's office.

Leo stood and took his bottle with him. "The cola is on me since we both think Bean Scudder is a windbag." Then to the children who were scraping chairs back, "Hey, Rosalure and Tug. Have you been behaving yourselves today?"

The girl smiled. "We were at Nanna's house making candy. Tug ate too much. He says he's got a stomachache."

Not saying anything, the boy slid his chair out and slipped onto the seat, his face not much higher than the table. He made fists out of his dirty hands, stacked them, and plopped his chin on the top.

"I'll bring you a glass of milk, Tug," Leo offered, and went through the reed curtain into the kitchen.

Wyatt glanced at the woman.

"Hello, again," she greeted. Before sitting, she paused, indecision on her face and in her eyes, then she squared her shoulders and walked directly toward him. "I suppose on a chance meeting it isn't necessary to introduce ourselves, but I believe twice within the half hour would." She extended her hand, and he was late on taking her smooth fingers into his own. The shock of making contact with her soft feminine skin had him startled over the magnitude of his reaction. He'd never dreamed the mere touch of a woman's hand in his could awaken such a response as the fire spreading to his groin.

"Leah Kirkland," she said in that brisk voice of hers.

"Holloway," he countered, fervently trying to disguise the rasp of desire in his voice.

She lightly pumped his hand, then pulled away. A faint tint of a blush was on her cheeks, but she managed to tamp it down before it got the best of her and colored her face. He noticed the smudge was gone. "Well . . . enjoy your dinner. I recommend the yen ching chow mein." She took her seat without a backward glance and reprimanded the boy for poking his finger into the candle wax and making shavings out of it.

Leah Kirkland . . .

The name played over in his head until he could place it. Hell, she was that female photographer. One of those infernal picture-takers. It had been a photograph that caused many of the miserable things in his life. He never wanted one made of him again, so he was going to have to avoid her. Because a reprint of his likeness would be lethal. If the picture ever circulated, they'd know where to find him.

And Wyatt Holloway was a man who didn't want to be found.

❧ 2 ❧

**A maiden marries to please her parents,
a widow to please herself.**
                              —Chinese proverb

Men didn't intimidate Leah. After all, she'd been married
to one. Being in the photography profession necessitated
touching, bending, and molding a man's body to suit her
creativity when she worked. She'd learned how to disassoci-
ate herself from anything that could be construed as intimacy with strangers or town acquaintances that other women
would have found embarrassing. To Leah, it was her job and
responsibility to capture the sitter in his most flattering
angle. That meant adjustments and physical contact with
members of the opposite sex.

When her term of mourning had ended three years ago,
Fremont Quigley, the postmaster, and Leemon Winterowd,
the owner of Everlasting Monuments and Statuary, had set
up appointments within the same week. After that initial
sitting, both men had requested a new photograph of
himself once a month, until she'd come to the conclusion
that their only purpose in having their portraits taken was
to give them the opportunity of having her hands on their
shoulders and their chins. Put off by their tomfoolery, she'd
gently but firmly let them know she wasn't interested—

though neither had taken the hint to heart, for both continued to try and attract her attention.

Her career precluded courting, but that didn't mean she was adverse to remarrying if she met a free spirit like herself. In the spring of 1902, there had been someone she'd considered until he revealed his true opinion of women professionals. Frederick Warrick was an article writer for *National Geographic* magazine and had been sent to Colorado to do a piece on mining towns that had become cattle towns. In the beginning, she'd found him breathtakingly handsome and quite the charmer. Then he told her his ideal of the perfect wife was submissiveness and domesticity. He'd suggested she should dispose herself to the lesser "arts" such as needlework, embroidery, and china and miniature painting, and give up photography if she wanted to land a husband.

Until she met a man as passionate about something as she was about photography—and who accepted that not all widows were candidates to be teachers or seamstresses—she wasn't looking for a suitor.

In the interim, she'd made plans. Big plans that she had only confided to Leo. Her mother-in-law, Geneva Kirkland, would never condone her behavior, much less come close to understanding why Leah had to go to Italy to study.

Geneva was a sore subject with Leah. For her children's sake, she tried to be civil. But soon Leah wouldn't have to contend with Geneva anymore, because Leah would be on an adventure to Europe, stopping first in New York City to visit the infamous brownstone where Photo-Secessionists made their spiritual home in the Little Galleries at 291 Fifth Avenue. The mere thought of meeting the dynamic *Camera Works* editor, Alfred Stieglitz, brought on gooseflesh to Leah's arms.

She'd already sent Mr. Giuseppe Ciccolella in Lombardy, Italy, one thousand dollars to reserve her space in the Veneto Academy for Image Artists. She wanted to study photography in the quaint villa like the great Stieglitz had. To learn all his secrets from the masters and become so renowned, her name would be recognized with Austen,

Brigman, and even the former first lady, Mrs. Cleveland. Leah's dream was to win the coveted first prize in the New York Amateur Photographer contest. With the proper tutorage, she could have a chance.

The glass candleholder tumbled onto its side, pulling Leah from her thoughts.

"Tug, what did Momma say about putting your fingernail in that candle wax?"

Tug made no reply. From the exaggerated pout he gave her, he was still angry because she'd taken his hat from him for inappropriate conduct. Flushing Rosalure's musical bird figure down the toilet was not to be tolerated. Tug had had to forfeit his beloved Roughrider Roy cowboy hat for a week as punishment.

"Momma said not to put your fingernail in the candle." Leah answered her own question with a reprimanding tone that made Tug stop and pay attention to her, "Thank you, Tug. That was a good boy."

His nose wrinkled and he sighed with high drama. "Sure do miss the ol' Roughrider," he drawled. "A man just ain't a cowboy without his hat."

Leah folded her arms. "You'll have your hat in due time."

Rosalure stuck out her tongue at her brother. "Serves you right for flushing my Precious down the unmentionable."

Tug jutted his chin forward and returned Rosalure's gesture.

Intervening, Leah stretched her hands across the table and kept her children at arm's length. "There will be none of this at the supper table. You keep to yourself," she told Tug, then repeated the same admonition to Rosalure.

Leah pressed her fingertips to the bridge of her nose; not only the weight of her hair gave her a headache today, but also the bickering of her children. Though they had their disagreements, for the most part, Rosalure and Tug got along as well as could be expected between a boy and girl with a five-year spread in their ages.

Each day with Tug was a struggle for Leah. Raising a son without the direction of a husband was difficult. The habits of little boys perplexed her. Tug constantly brought home "treasures": snakeskins, fossils, beetles, and animal dung. Rosalure had never done such a thing, nor had Leah when she was a girl.

She sometimes grew resentful of her husband, Owen, passing away when Tug had been four months old. Her son had no father figure in his life to guide him, and Leah didn't know how to communicate with a boy who took pleasure in poking the eyes out of a live sucker fish. The only close male relative who could shed some light on the subject was her father-in-law, Hartzell. But he saw Tug as a commodity, a future successor as manager of the Eternity Security Bank—a position Hartzell now occupied as founder and owner.

Leah blamed herself for Tug's scampish ways. If she'd spent more time with him in his infancy instead of letting Geneva coddle him, Tug might not be so willful. During Rosalure's formative years, Leah had been a mother and wife, giving her daughter all her attention. With Tug, Leah was a widow raising two children on her own, which necessitated that she bring in an income to supplement the modest premium of her husband's Phoenix Mutual life insurance policy. Between the demands put on her by Marshal Scudder, the *Eternity Tribune,* and her own clients who came to her home studio, Leah fell short in the mothering department. The hardship of guilt for extending herself too far from her children weighed heavily on her. But she did the best she could given the set of circumstances she found herself in at the age of twenty-six.

Tug had made a tight ball out of the wax shavings, and before Leah could stop him, he flicked the ivory marble with his forefinger. His missile missed his intended victim, Rosalure, and sailed through the space separating her table and Mr. Holloway's, hitting the man on the shoulder of his duster.

"Tug!" Leah's voice was severe and laced with horror. "Apologize this instant!"

Mr. Holloway turned in their direction, catching Tug's eye. To Tug, anyone wearing a wide-brimmed hat, worn-out boots, noisy spurs, and a holstered gun was a cowboy. Mr.

Holloway met all the criteria, and therefore gained Tug's full attention.

"Sorry," Tug mumbled.

Glancing in Mr. Holloway's direction, Leah noticed he'd returned to staring out the window as if nothing had happened. Some people weren't fond of children, and she sensed Mr. Holloway was not, or else he would have written off Tug's prank with a smile. At the very least, an irritated smile. Instead, he'd glowered. At her.

She'd thought they'd had a favorable start when he'd teased her about the ink on her cheek. Flirtatious remarks from Mr. Quigley and Mr. Winterowd had never caused a tingling sense of excitement to spring to life in her. The experience had been an awakening one. Her reaction to Mr. Holloway had been purely physical. That had never happened to her before. Though Frederick hadn't lacked in looks, she'd been attracted to the writer before the man.

Mr. Holloway's lean fingers gripped the circumference of a cola bottle, and she recalled their introduction. Though the contact had been brief, she hadn't anticipated his hand feeling so warm and gentle. His knuckles were thick with calluses on the joints and roughening his palm. A hand like that had to have been beaten into such a condition by years of demanding physical use. She wondered what he'd been doing for a living. She'd never known cowboy work to add such bulk on a body. Wranglers around here were lanky and nimble. Mr. Holloway was a big man and a good head taller than her, which was rare. She was used to trading gazes with most men at eye level, with some exceptions, of which Marshal Scudder was one.

Mr. Holloway's upper body filled out his duster, his muscles rivaling those of the prizefighters that had once come through Eternity with a touring show. His powerful shoulders were wide enough to be a boxer's, wider than anyone's she knew. His neck was thick, and his face hard-featured. At present, she was granted a view of his profile, which was rugged and somber. He had an appearance that she couldn't exactly say was classically handsome, yet there was an appealing something about him.

Afternoon sunlight streamed in from the window behind him, giving an auburn tint to his dark brown hair. He took a drink of his cola, licking his lips and drawing her attention to the lower half of his face. His mouth was full, its shape pleasant and making her aware that a long time had passed since she'd been kissed. On that subject, she reflected a few seconds, then quickly shoved it out of her head. There was a slight bump on Mr. Holloway's nose, as if the bridge had been broken a time or two.

"What can I get for you, Mrs. Kirkland?" Leo had come to the table and stood by, ready to take their order. Hearing him call her Mrs. Kirkland, as opposed to Leah, sounded funny. But Leo had insisted that in mixed company they retain an air of formality. She supposed he was right. Having a man as her closest friend did leave open the door to gossip and rumors. Oh, she was friendly with women, but most didn't share her interests. Trude Barlow, the wife of the *Eternity Tribune*'s former editor, had moved to Iowa last year with her husband, leaving Leah with no one in particular to converse to about photography. Now Delmar Sheesley was the newspaper's editor in chief, and he didn't care one iota about the shading and lines in the photos she gave him, just that he could print the halftones clearly and they didn't cost him more than fifteen cents apiece. Leo was the only person who recognized her creativity and would listen politely about the pros and cons of certain developing fluids and the like.

After a hasty glance at the menu she knew by heart, Leah said, "I think I'd like the chicken foo-yung. Rosalure?"

Rosalure added, "I'll have the same."

Leo gazed at Tug. "The usual for you, pardner?"

Tug propped his chin on his fists again and nodded.

"Very good. Two chicken foo-yungs and one spreadable American Clubhouse cheese sandwich on white bread."

Then Leo went to Mr. Holloway's table and they conversed in low tones before Leo left for the kitchen. Tug's gaze went with Leo, then back to Mr. Holloway as he sized him up from his hat to his boots.

"Momma?"

"Yes, Rosalure?"

"I asked Nanna to make my birthday cake for me. I hope you aren't mad."

It was no secret Leah couldn't hold a candle to Geneva's cooking and baking—nor anyone else's. Her mother hadn't been handy in the kitchen and had never showed Leah how to manage one either. She could make passable meals, but for the most part they ate at the Happy City or at her in-law's home. "No, Rosalure, I'm not mad. What kind did you ask for?"

"French cream with white icing and pink flowers."

From prior years, Leah knew Geneva would outdo herself and make Leah very much aware of how simple it all was. And that anyone could do it. Well, Leah wasn't anyone, and she couldn't make a French cream cake with white icing and pink flowers. Even if she had the recipe, nothing ever turned out the way it was supposed to, so she'd given up trying years ago.

Tug squirmed in his chair, absently kicking one of the table legs.

"Oh, and Momma?" Rosalure said.

"Hmm?"

"I wanted to make the party favors I saw in Nanna's *Good Housekeeping* magazine. We'd need some lace and ribbon. And we could hand-cut the invitations, but we'll have to make sure they're delivered in time. The twenty-eighth is almost here."

The twenty-eighth was indeed approaching, and Leah should have had invitations already sent out. She wasn't at all ready to host a party. That meant she'd have to organize her home and really tidy it up. Geneva would be snooping in every cranny, just waiting for the opportunity to say something about lint or dust.

Mr. Holloway shifted his legs, the star-shaped rowels of his spurs making a metal clinking sound and attracting her attention to him. His posture was relaxed, but he tapped his blunt fingertips on the table. She wondered if he was bored or preoccupied by the prospect of having to find a job if he wanted to stay in town. A dishwasher certainly wasn't high on the pole of prestige, but Leo would be a fair boss.

Promptly at five-fifteen, Netha and Wilene Clinkingbeard, twin spinster sisters who were a year younger than Leah, arrived at the Happy City just like they did every Saturday night. They were as thin as broom handles, with pale complexions and hair that matched the orange of early carrots. Not strong on looks, they were, however, quite popular at the First Presbyterian Church for their perfect harmonizing while singing hymns.

After their obligatory hello at Leah's table, Leo showed them to their usual spot at one of the front windows. This evening, the two sisters nearly crashed into one another to get a better look at Mr. Holloway, whose larger than life presence filled the room. He sat one table behind them. Netha, who always took the southern side of the table, went for the northern chair so she'd have an unobstructed view of Mr. Holloway, only Wilene had already dropped her hand on the chair's back. There was an awkward moment when the sisters fought over that single chair before Netha conceded her loss and went to her regular place at the table.

Wilene blushed the color of geraniums as she dropped her napkin on her lap. Ruggedly handsome men didn't show up in the Happy City too often. Not that Leo's restaurant wasn't a fine dining establishment. But most of the cowboys in Eternity preferred a thick-cut chop or steak down at the Coffeepot Cafe or the Beaver's Corner Saloon.

Leah thought the spectacle the sisters were creating was rather offensive. Fawning over Mr. Holloway, and his not even noticing that they were talking loudly about their primrose garden, was in poor taste. Leah could grow flowers, too, but she wasn't broadcasting her talents in a voice for the entire restaurant to overhear.

"Yen ching beef for two." Leo repeated the sisters' orders to them, then paused at Leah's table to give Tug his glass of milk. "How's the stomach, pardner?"

"Okay."

"You don't look so green anymore."

"Reckon not," he muttered, his gaze fixed on Mr. Holloway's silver spurs.

A handbell rang from the kitchen, signaling to Leo that another order was finished. "Bet it's yours," Leo said, then parted the bamboo curtain to retrieve the hot plates from his nephew, Tu Yan.

Leah's gaze had followed Leo's departure, and she began speaking while facing forward. "Tug, I'd surely like it if you tried to eat all your cheese sandwich tonight. You need to eat something wholesome after all that candy . . ." Her words trailed as she eyed the empty seat across from her.

"He's over there, Momma," Rosalure whispered, pointing under Mr. Holloway's table.

Tug had crawled beneath the table—no minor feat considering the butts of his authentic Buffalo Bill Octagon-wood-and-rubber six-shooter defenders were protruding from holsters that sagged at his Wild West woolly chap-wearing hips. In tight spaces, some part of his outfit usually got hung up on something, and disaster struck.

Mortified, Leah held her breath, uncertain how to retrieve her son without Mr. Holloway noticing. Thankfully, his scrutiny remained on Main Street.

Dropping her napkin as if by accident, Leah bent to reach it and waved her hand at Tug. "Owen Edwin," she said in a low tone and purposefully addressed him with his given name. "You come out from there right now."

He ignored her, one pudgy finger inching forward to touch the shining spur at the back of Mr. Holloway's heel.

The Clinkingbeard sisters craned their necks to get an eyeful. Leah, still leaning over the floor, casually smiled as if nothing was wrong.

When Tug spun the rowel, Mr. Holloway brought his feet in and jerked his gaze from the window, then lifted the tablecloth.

"Mister, are these Eureka spurs?" Tug asked, as if it were a common occurrence for a boy to sit at the boots of a diner.

Mr. Holloway returned, "Where did you come from?"

Wordlessly, Tug pointed in Leah's general direction. She straightened and plastered a smile on her face. Mr.

Holloway's gaze moved to meet hers. The unfathomable depths of his blue eyes tore right through her, making her heart pound against her ribs. She hadn't noticed the intensity of the color before, nor the brooding line of his brows that suggested a stubborn streak.

"My son is curious about your spurs," she said, trying to cover her incredible embarrassment by making light of Tug's being beneath the table. "Are those Yippee spurs?"

"Eureka," he corrected.

Leah wanted to crawl beneath the table herself. "Of course."

"Gee, Momma, Yippee spurs are kid toys." He gave her an accusatory glare. "You won't let me have a pair because you said I'll hurt myself with them."

She knew the name had sounded familiar.

After jingling the rowel of Mr. Holloway's spur, Tug shimmied out from the floor to stand directly in front of him. "I'll bet you can really ride 'em, mister."

An irresistible grin dazzled against his tan skin. "I used to."

Aiming his finger at the enormous gun strapped to Mr. Holloway's thigh, Tug asked, "Is that loaded? Have you ever shot anybody with it?"

"Tug, really, Mr. Holloway doesn't want to be bothered with your questions." Leah rose quickly from her chair and went to Tug, laying her hands firmly on his shoulders in an effort to turn him around and march him back to the table.

For a little guy, Tug could really dig his heels in. She couldn't make him move. Quick on his feet, he ducked out from beneath her hands. "Is that a genuine Stetson, mister? Can I try it on?"

Before Mr. Holloway could reply, Tug had snatched the felt hat from the tabletop and plopped it on his unruly hair. The crown slipped down his face, and he pushed the sweat-stained brim back. He took on a rough-and-ready stance, chest laid back, hips thrust forward. "There he is," Tug declared. "Ol' Sidewinder in the middle of the street!" Then he fast-drew one of his rubber guns and proceeded to "shoot" up the window.

Mr. Holloway's laughter was a full-hearted sound. Hesitantly, Leah joined him, but as soon as he heard her, his voice went cold. She swallowed the lump in her throat.

"Tug, give Mr. Holloway back his hat," Leah said evenly, not letting Mr. Holloway's hooded eyes get the best of her.

Just then, Leo came up to them. "Your supper is on the table, Mrs. Kirkland."

Leah glanced at Rosalure, who was eating and pretending as if Tug wasn't causing trouble.

"Thank you, Mr. Wang," Leah replied properly. Then to Tug, "You quit this fooling around." She hoped her threat sounded as if she meant it. "Our supper is going to get cold."

"I want my Roughrider Roy hat," he complained. "I'm a sissy cowboy without it."

The Clinkingbeard sisters had gone from sly peeks to bold stares at the commotion Tug was causing. Leah was furious with herself for allowing the situation to get out of hand. She was a confident and a capable businesswoman, but when it came to Tug, she second-guessed her instincts and never was sure which way to turn.

"Seeing all the fuss he's making," Mr. Holloway said, "I don't care if he wears the hat while he eats. So long as I get it back when he's done. Which makes me somewhat skeptical, given the boy's name."

Leah blushed profusely. Tug's nickname suited him. Ever since he'd been a baby, once he got something he wanted, she'd had to tug it out of his grasp. "I really don't think that's necessary, Mr. Holloway. Tug should give you the hat right now."

"I'm not wearing it at the moment, so I don't need it."

The ears on the Clinkingbeard sisters suddenly appeared two sizes larger. If they hadn't been listening in, Leah would have insisted Tug return the hat. But the fact that there was an audience made her want to smooth things over as quietly and as quickly as possible.

"Very well. Tug, you may wear the hat while you are eating. What do you say to Mr. Holloway?"

"Thanks, mister."

Leah returned to her table with heat on her cheeks. She couldn't eat, and absently stirred her food around the plate with the tines of her fork. For long minutes, she didn't dare look in Mr. Holloway's direction. When she finally mustered the nerve, she observed him taking a sip of his cola. Bubbles rose to the upended bottom of the bottle. She grew fascinated by the way he swallowed with long gulps that made his Adam's apple softly bob.

He caught her staring, and she swiftly looked away. But not before she felt the full impact of the speculative appraisal he'd given her.

Toying with a sliver of chicken, Leah recanted her earlier thought about Mr. Holloway. It wasn't children he disliked. It was her.

Leah's eyes on Wyatt disturbed him, and mixed feelings surged through his thoughts. He found her undeniably attractive. The strength in her slender carriage and her self-assured walk didn't lessen her femininity. The aggressive yet soft touch of her hand ignited unbridled images in his head. He'd been without a woman for so long that his body's response would have been the same no matter what curvy thing had approached Scudder. His bad luck she was a photographer. Someone he hadn't wanted to encounter.

His initial reaction after realizing what she did for a living had been to refrain from noticing both her and her boy. But he'd been hard-pressed not to bust a gut when the kid hurled a pebble of candle wax at him. The antic reminded Wyatt of something he would have done as a kid.

Wyatt had missed being around children. He'd always liked them. Having five younger siblings, he'd grown up with a sister and two brothers tagging after him. They'd done their share of troublemaking. Their mother had given them what for when they'd turned muskmelon rinds inside out, strapped them onto their feet, and skated around the floor, smearing juice and pulp all over the place.

Gazing at Tug, Wyatt saw a bygone reflection of himself. Though he hadn't had a store-bought toy gun, he'd had a wooden one his father had carved. He'd been encouraged to find his amusement in the hills and fields with Robert and Daniel, and Todd, when he could toddle along. The boys learned the wilder world of men at a young age by capturing ground squirrels, while Ardythe had been encouraged to stay behind and take her domestic play outdoors by setting up imaginary households on the porch. With sad blue eyes, she'd watch the brothers run off, and Wyatt saw that she was yearning to come after them but minded her ma out of respect.

Wyatt had had a lot of time to think about the children he hoped to have. He'd come to the conclusion that whether he had girls or boys, he'd teach them lessons in life equally.

Every man wanted a son, and Wyatt was no different. If he was lucky enough to have one by next year, he'd show his boy all there was about wrangling. How to wear his hat, how to ride, how to rope, and a million other things around the ranch. If he had a daughter, if she was interested, he'd set her up with a dependable and well-trained gelding and teach her how to herd the cattle.

Wyatt's mouth pulled into a grim line. The vision was well and good, but by the time a child could be outfitted with a horse and snug little saddle, Wyatt would be halfway into his forties. He'd be getting a damn late start on fatherhood.

There was nothing more fleeting than years, and Wyatt had wasted too many of them. As soon as he got the money, he vowed, his life would change for the better.

Wyatt stared at the supper plate Leo had left in front of him minutes before. Leo had talked him into a dish called trout with black bean sauce. Wyatt hadn't had fish in nearly twenty years. He'd forgotten how it tasted. He knew too well the nothing-flavor of overboiled beef twice a day, with tough steak, hard potatoes, gravy, bread, and syrup for breakfast every morning. If he ever had another bad steak, he was going to puke.

A hollow emptiness punched Wyatt's gut as his stomach gnawed. He couldn't remember ever being so hungry. The endless fresh air and the arduous ride in the saddle getting his muscles used to the feel of a horse again had done him good.

The silver-skinned fish was presented whole and decorated with slivers of green-and-yellow things Wyatt couldn't identify. But the arrangement looked like something from a picture book, with a side bowl of fancy rice that had scrambled eggs in it. The food smelled appetizing enough, so he dug in.

The fish was moist and flavorful, though he was still a little doubtful about the green-and-yellow shreds, so he pushed them off. The black beans had an odd texture, but were a welcome sight from flat boiled greens. The meal, though foreign to him, was much better than the Van Camp's Boston baked pork and beans he'd grown weary of eating for the past month.

As Wyatt ate, he periodically glanced at Tug. The boy was good-looking. Just like his mother and sister, only his coloring was fairer than the girl's. His hair was a light brown and his eyes were hazel.

Wyatt pondered the whereabouts of the boy's father. It was very unlikely that it had been the embrace of a lover's arms Leah had been basking in when Wyatt had first seen her. Now he assumed she was married, only she didn't wear a wedding ring. But times had changed. A man couldn't tell very much about a person just by looking at her anymore. It could be she was a widow. That, or her husband ran off. The latter unexplainably aroused anger in Wyatt.

"How do you like the fish?" Leo drew up to Wyatt's table with another cola.

"It's pretty good," Wyatt replied after swallowing.

"Of course it's good."

Wyatt accepted the cola. "Thanks." He took a satisfying drink, then asked, "Does that marshal take an evening round after his supper?"

"The only thing Bean Scudder takes after his supper is a Bromo-Seltzer for his heartburn."

"So he stays home?"

"Until nine the following morning."

Wyatt nodded. He was planning on setting up a camp at the outskirts of town and didn't need a snoopy U.S. marshal tripping into his site in the middle of the night. "Does that deputy of his do anything?"

"Moon?" Leo snorted. "Moon's about as useful as Scudder. Neither one could shoot the center out of a quarter a foot away from them. It's a good thing Eternity isn't a wild, shoot 'em up town or we'd all be put to bed with a pick and shovel." Leo's eyes fell on Wyatt's long-nosed revolver. "'Cept you. You look like you could defend yourself."

The bell rang, but Leo ignored it.

Wyatt observed, "Your cook in there could defend himself with that cleaver."

A second peal sounded, followed by a series of *ding-dings.*

Leo yelled something in what Wyatt assumed was the Chinese language. Then facing Wyatt again, he said, "Tu Yan cooks faster than I can keep up with. Don't ever sneak up on him, he doesn't speak a word of English."

"Why would I sneak up on him?"

Grinning, Leo lifted his brows. "Because you're thinking on that dishwasher job I've got posted in the window."

"How do you know that?"

"I know how Scudder makes introductions and threats." Leo tapped the ash from a fresh cigarette. "The job pays twenty dollars a month, plus meals. And in your case, seeing how you enjoy that Coca-Cola so much, those are included."

Leo walked off before Wyatt could speak. He had been thinking about the opening, but not because Bean had put the thought into his head. The truth was, Wyatt needed the money the job would pay. He'd worked in Boise City as a trench digger to buy July and the supplies that had gotten him to Colorado. But now those supplies were about gone, and he didn't have the cash to buy replacements. Seeing as the only position available in Eternity was dishwasher, that meant employment at the Happy City Restaurant.

Wyatt savored the last bites of his supper, eating slowly and without anyone breathing over his neck. The habit of wolfing down his food had been a hard one to break. But he'd succeeded in the past month in enjoying his meals and tasting every last flavor in them, even if it was pork and beans.

As he wiped his mouth and set his napkin on his plate, Leah approached the table with her son. The boy still wore Wyatt's boss of the plains Stetson that had seen better days. Both of Tug's hands clamped the brim, keeping the crown anchored at the back of his head. Reluctance to give the hat up and even a faint shimmer of tears showed in Tug's eyes. "I like this hat. It's a man's hat. Who wants a Roughrider Roy when they can have a real hat that smells like horse poop?"

"Owen Edwin," Leah scolded. "That language is unacceptable. You take this hat off and return it to Mr. Holloway. Right now."

Tug pouted but didn't make a ready move. Wyatt's gaze rose to Leah's. Dismay lightened the brown of her eyes. It had been unfair of him to treat her with cool indifference. Who she was and what she did had no bearing, just as long as she didn't point a camera at him. Still, that didn't mean he wanted to socialize with her. He'd be polite, if and whenever they crossed paths. But he'd make sure he kept any subconscious thoughts of her intoxicating feel and the carnation fragrance on her skin from influencing the searing need that had been building within him.

"I need my hat now, Tug," Wyatt said, hoping that his subtle bid would influence Tug into giving up the Stetson without an argument with his mother.

Tug didn't say a word to him when he slid the hat off his head and handed it over. The brim was a little out of shape and rumpled, and the worn dent in the crown slightly crushed.

"I ain't got no hat and I ain't got no spurs," the boy said in a shaky voice to his ma. Tug swiped his rapidly blinking eyes with his scraped up knuckles as he battled with himself not to cry. "I'll never be a cowboy for real."

Then Tug ran out of the restaurant and Wyatt watched him race down Main Street.

"Excuse me." Leah left Wyatt's table, gathered her pocketbook and dashed off after her child. The daughter walked out slowly as if nothing amiss had happened, nibbling on a cookie Leo had given her.

Leaning back in his chair, Wyatt couldn't help feeling somewhat sorry for Leah Kirkland as she lifted her skirt and snowy petticoats to chase after her wayward boy. The two women sitting at the next table huddled their heads together and chattered like a pair of parakeets. He heard a few of the words: disgraceful, unruly, typical. They didn't sit well with him. He knew what it was like to feel helpless about a set of circumstances. A man had to do the best he could, and he supposed it was the same for a woman.

Wyatt laid out his bedroll at the timberline cutting across the mountain just before the trees gave way to the brush and wildflowers. This high, and with the break of pine boughs to help conceal him, he'd felt safe in coaxing a low-burning fire to life.

He'd lingered at the Happy City for a while, talking to Leo about the details of the job. Leo wasn't open on Sunday, so he didn't have to report for work tomorrow. Monday would be soon enough. First light, he was going over to the hardware store to buy the tools he needed. He hoped they'd save him from kitchen duty on Monday by digging up the money.

The snap of the campfire pulled Wyatt's thoughts in a different direction. Down the old path. He stared, mesmerized by the flames, thinking back . . . way back. To a time that was bygone and best forgotten. But he couldn't. No matter how much he wanted to forget it, the past was always there. The doubt. The shame. Tonight, he saw himself in the fire. The way he used to be . . .

❧ 3 ❧

You may change the clothes;
you cannot change the man.
          —Chinese proverb

September 15, 1887
Silverton, Colorado

The smell of breakfast sizzling in a frying pan on the campfire did nothing to entice Harlen's appetite. His stomach, sour from too much liquor the night before, made thinking about food impossible. He kept visualizing the young girl's face. Seeing the accusation and pain in her eyes.

Honest to God, Harlen had never killed another living soul in all his life. The double-barreled shotgun he carried in a saddle holster was mostly for show, because he avoided needless violence and never used that firearm in a shootout. When being pursued by peace officers while on horseback, he fired his Remington-Rider, a piece with an accuracy he knew, because hitting a rider was a last resort, and then he never aimed to kill.

Yesterday was the first instance when a woman had been hit. And Harlen's .44 could have been the cause of her death. Bullets had been flying every which way in the confusion. That had him spooked. He hadn't been able to control his shots as much as he wanted to.

"So it's Mexico," Thomas Jefferson said, dragging Harlen from his hellish thoughts.

51

"Too many authorities know us up north. Down south is the only way." Nate drew on a cigarette, the smoke mixing with his words.

Manny sat on his haunches. "We'll need traveling money."

"Silverton Miners Bank." Colvin stirred leftover beans into the salt pork. Setting the bent spoon on a sooty containment rock that rimmed the fire, he stood. "We know the layout. Know who the manager is and what kind of pistol he keeps. Pierpont Farnham couldn't hit a bull's ass with a banjo. So we know we're safe on that account."

Nate gazed at Harlen. "You've said two words at best this morning, Shepp. What's on your mind?"

Harlen popped off the top to his bottle of rye. Taking a slow drink that burned down to his navel, he licked the flavor from his lips. "We've got no choice but to rob that bank. We need the money."

"I heard tell two days ago their assets were up to sixty-thousand dollars," Thomas Jefferson remarked. "That'd be twelve a piece. Enough to get us where we need to go."

Harlen nodded. He didn't really want to talk about robbing the bank or forming a plan. He wanted to talk about the woman. Evaline. But in that regard, the Loco Boys weren't like him. They didn't see things the same way. The woman's death was an unfortunate accident to them. And that was it. When they rode on, what had happened in Telluride was no longer their concern.

Maybe they were right. Letting the incident eat away at him wasn't going to change anything. What was done was done. There was nothing he could do. Hell, it may not even have been his bullet. Rounds had been coming from everyone. Could even have been a detective's bullet that had hit Evaline Darling. Then Harlen wouldn't have the guilt so strong on his shoulder. There was still the matter that, had he and the boys not been in that photography studio, the shootout wouldn't have occurred. But he couldn't keep going around with what had happened. It was over. Finished.

Yet for all his coldhearted reasoning, Harlen couldn't forget.

Downing a long pull of the rye, Harlen's voice grew raspy when he said without emotion, "Since we're going to rob that bank, we'll need a plan, boys."

Silverton was framed to the south by the Sultan Mountains, had few trees lining the main street, and was built up with a moderate population of miners. Other businesses prospered, but the bank held the true wealth of the city. The brick institution was located next to the Grand Imperial Hotel.

The Loco Boys had split up near the North Star mill. Thomas Jefferson and Manny posed as trail-weary cowboys with their dusty scarfs over their noses and mouths, riding ahead and checking for the whereabouts of the sheriff. Nate and Harlen rode across Main Street made up like saddle tramps. Colvin walked alongside their horses dressed in ragged clothing, wearing hobnailed shoes and carrying a sloppy-looking roll of ragged blankets. Inside was a concealed, ready rifle. Colvin was the insurance man in case anything went wrong. He was supposed to enter the bank and sit down to cover any unexpected emergencies. The only trouble was, on the way into Silverton he'd run into a skunk.

Before Colvin could pick the weasel off with his Colt, he'd lost the fight but good. Old pretty boy Colvin Henkels smelled like month-old eggs left out in the scorching sun to rot.

Dismounting, Harlen slip-tied Blue's halter rope to the hitching post out front. He frowned over the stink brought on the breeze when the wind shifted. Colvin hovered near the bank entrance, his hat pulled down over his eyes. They all wore their hats low. Each man had altered his facial appearance, either by soot, scarves, clay mixed up to make their complexions darker, false scars, or temporary hair coloration from ashes. Whenever they pulled a job, they'd always worn disguises. There was only one time that came to Harlen's mind when they hadn't. That was in Montpelier, Idaho, some two years ago, when he and the boys had been drunk and feeling cocksure of themselves.

Nate nodded to Harlen, and the two of them entered the building. The interior was small and poorly lit through the yellowed curtains, with just one male customer who departed on their entrance. An empty bank was a better bank to hold up. There were two teller cages, but only one of them was in use at this midhour of the day. A clerk and cashier stood at the wooden counter going over accounts. They lifted their visored heads when Harlen and Nate came in, but went on writing when Harlen moved for the table at the center of the room, produced his wallet, and began filling out a depository note.

Glancing out of the corner of his eye, Harlen saw Pierpont Farnham at his desk in the enclosure. The man was preoccupied with stacks of ledgers, an ink pen and a tablet in which he scribbled figures. Snug in one of those desk drawers was a loaded pistol, though that thought didn't trouble Harlen, because he knew Pierpont couldn't hit a sitting target much less a moving one. And Harlen planned on moving out of the bank quickly.

As soon as Colvin slipped inside, the room was filled with a god-awful smell. Harlen strode to the counter, cursing the bad timing of that skunk. The teller took out a handkerchief and wiped his eyes behind the glass of his spectacles. The stench was so thick, they were all choking on the vapors coming off Colvin's hole-riddled coat.

"I'd like to make a deposit," Harlen said over the teller's cough. But as he began to slide his money across the polished surface, he paused. Then in a muted tone, he went on to say, "On second thought, I'd like all the money in the bank."

The teller and clerk looked at him as if he were joking.

Harlen pulled the side of his coat back, calmly removed his Remington from its holster, and pointed it at the clerk's head. "Make any sudden movements or noises, and we'll shoot you down."

The two men gazed over Harlen's shoulder. Harlen knew

that Nate and Colvin were backing him up and there was no question as to who was in charge of the situation.

"Be quick," Harlen advised, "and no one will get hurt. I want the cage unlocked. Get the key from Farnham."

The teller went on shaky legs toward the manager's desk and made the request without looking back.

Farnham leaned past the teller's middle and made eye contact with Harlen. Harlen's menacing expression didn't crack. The manager stood, taking from his desktop a ring full of keys that rattled when he walked.

Nate had positioned himself by the cage door, and when it was unlocked, waved his gun at the manager and teller, signaling them to move them toward the far wall. "The vault. Unlock it," he ordered, while Harlen dealt with the shaken clerk.

"Everything in the till. Put it in here." He took out two empty grain leather satchels that he'd tucked inside his coat. Opening the tops, he laid them on the counter.

The clerk stuffed money into the bags, with trembling hands.

Harlen yelled for Colvin to cover him while he entered the vault with Nate, who'd been carrying two satchels himself. They took piles of twenty-dollar gold pieces, five- and ten-dollar coins, and stacks of currency.

Pierpoint, with eyes watering, sputtered his offense at Colvin's rankness. "You smell like a polecat."

Colvin swore at Farnham, but it wasn't enough to keep the manager quiet. Either he was stronger on brains than he was on his aim, or he was just plain stupid.

"But a polecat is a sight better looking than you," Farnham added with a wheeze.

Harlen heard Colvin threaten to shoot Pierpont where he stood. That shut him up. Nate had taken almost all the legal tender there was in that vault. Harlen took up his two bulging satchels. Nate carted the other two to be given to Harlen for the ride out. It would have made more sense for Nate to keep his bags and not tax Harlen's horse with the extra load. But a code with the Loco Boys was that their leader was in charge of the booty until they could get to a place where they could split the money among them. Everyone trusted Harlen, and they'd always operated this way.

"In the vault, gentleman, and close the door." Harlen's directions were punctuated with the point of his gun.

The three bankers shuffled into the gated vault with its bar doors and closed themselves off behind the iron. Nate threw the keys. They slid across the floor and hit the floorboards far from reach of the captives. As Harlen made his way to the exit walking backward, he spotted Colvin at the counter scribbling on what looked like a piece of paper, and leaving it behind. There wasn't an opportunity to ask him about the note until the five of them were riding hard out of town.

"What was that you left back there, Colvin?" Harlen shouted over the earth-pounding hooves of the horses.

Colvin answered in a rush of defiant words. "No one calls Colvin Henkels a stinking, ugly polecat. I left those sons of bitches Darling's photograph of us so they could see just how good-looking I really am. I wrote my name on the back."

"You did what?" Harlen roared.

"Hell, we've never been caught before and it ain't no secret what we look like. That man insulted me. I'm no ugly, smelling bum, and I take offense to anyone who calls me one."

Harlen's nostrils flared with fury. "Colvin, you've just made a serious mistake in the name of arrogance."

But with a posse hot on their trail, Harlen couldn't right the wrong. The portrait would be discovered, and so would their identities. Even though Colvin was right, it was no secret that Harlen Riley alias Harvey Shepp ran the Loco Boys. And everyone knew their names besides. But leaving a picture as a calling card was opening the door for blame. Now there was no denying it had been them stealing from that bank. They might as well have gone in without their disguises.

Harlen prompted Blue toward the ridge and the fresh horses that Thomas Jefferson and Manny had saddled and hobbled next to a stand of cottonwoods on the other side.

But once Harlen hit the apex of that ridge, he lifted his hand to hold the others back. Reining to a sudden halt, Harlen saw the horses grazing. But he also saw at least a dozen waiting lawmen holding rifles with the barrels gleaming in the sun.

Jerking his finger, Harlen signaled an alternate direction, and the boys rode down the crest over the same trail they'd just come up. Without stopping to see if they'd been spotted by the lawmen, Harlen gave orders. "We're going to have to split up. Nate, T. J., and Colvin take Kendall Peak. Manny and I'll cross Bear Mountain. We'll all meet down on the other side of the Mexican border as soon as we can get there."

The men nodded and the group separated. Harlen steered Blue to the west, Manny keeping in stride with him. But they were unable to elude the lawmen. A cloud of dust to their right was a sign that horses were bearing down on them. They'd been spotted on the ridge and were being pursued. Blue had a lot of sand in him, and even though the distance was great enough for him to outrun the armed men, the tired horse couldn't do so with the heavy load he was carrying. Manny would have to break away and Harlen would have to try and trick the posse.

Harlen motioned for him and Manny to part. Manny kept to the west while Harlen veered north—straight for the lawmen, only he had Blue hug the high brush and thickets of trees for cover. Changing course, he followed South Mineral Creek, sticking to the water to cover his tracks.

Knowing about a mining encampment called Eternity quite a stretch north of Silverton, Harlen headed in that direction instead of south with his partners. He was going to need a fresh horse if he wanted to cover some distance without stopping. And he had to do something with the money.

For endless hours, Harlen rode Blue hard. As nightfall neared, Harlen grew more convinced that he hadn't been followed. He rode the steep trail on the mountainside that overlooked the camp. Eternity was nothing more than a newborn town with tents and hardly a real building. The

San Juan range rose above the muddy street. In the impending dusk, lantern lights glowed from within the tent walls as miners were preparing their suppers.

Dismounting and leading Blue across the unstable rocks, Harlen found numerous crevices and nooks in which to hide the money. But it wasn't until he came upon the lofty wooden cross, which seemed to be cast in gilt from a reflection of the sun's fiery descent, that Harlen was satisfied he had a marker he couldn't forget.

The impending cloudless night offered him enough light in which to see. A mound of trash littered the far edge of the clearing, and he searched the rubbish for something in which to enclose the satchels. Finding extra gallon Yellow Crawford apricot cans, he unstrapped the grain bags. They were too fat to fit into the cans, so he put all the coins into the oversized tins, which were still sticky from fruit syrup. With four remaining cans, he stuffed the satchels with the currency inside them to keep the paper protected against rain if it came in the next day or two. Then he selected a deep cache some hundred feet down from the cross's base. The pale rock was loose and rough as he buried what he had figured to be sixty thousand dollars. He didn't expect the cans to be there long. Two days at best. Then he'd come back when the lawmen tired of the chase, retrieve it, and ride down to Mexico.

When Harlen was finished, he stood and gave Blue an affectionate pat on the chest. The roan was too fatigued to go on. He bid the horse a silent farewell, knowing that he'd gotten too attached to this good animal, but also knowing that in his calling, nothing stayed the same for long. Since he couldn't go into town and make a trade, he'd have to leave Blue in someone's pasture and hope they'd take care of him.

As the burning sun went to bed for the night and darkness hid shady doings, Harlen snuck into Eternity unaware that the living grave of crime was closing in.

❈ 4 ❈

There is many a good man to be found under a shabby hat.

—Chinese proverb

There was an electrical storm brewing. One of those windy monsters that lay a hand on everything with enough of an annoying flutter to ruin a photographer's day. Especially since Leah had to take an outdoor shot.

The bothersome rustling put a northwestern spin in the weather vanes, caused the rosebush stems to make their flowers dance, and had the grasses in yards undulate to the wind's tempo. It had to be this Monday that Wert McWhorter had chosen to have his esteemed garden and orchard photographed. Leah had tried to convince him to postpone, but he'd insisted on having a photograph to mail in the midafternoon post. The sudden rush was due to an advertisement he'd read in *Illustrated American Gardener* about a green-thumb contest. The prizewinning photograph and essay, to be sent to Wahoo, Nebraska, had to be postmarked today at the latest.

Mr. McWhorter had been in a tizzy all morning, sweeping and preparing his garden. He had a small orchard of nectarine, peach, apple, and plum trees. No more than five trees apiece, but a respectable amount and in lovely color this time of year. Leah had to admit, Wert McWhorter could grow things. Better than the Clinkingbeard sisters.

Gazing at the hazy sun beneath the arch of her hand, Leah saw the natural light was fading fast. Large white clouds scudded across the sky, giving way to a blanket of gray to the east.

"Mr. McWhorter, I've got to take the photograph immediately. Have you secured the owls?" she called from her position in the street.

Mr. McWhorter lived on State Street, one block up from Leah. His yard was immaculate and in prime condition from April to September. This was due in part to his endless toil, but also because of the wooden owls he had perched on swiveling stands. They were authentic replicas of great horned owls. Mr. McWhorter had meticulously carved and painted them himself. He'd put the fake birds of prey up to discourage sparrows and the like from feasting on his orchard fruits and garden delights. Apparently they worked, for her own garden had been picked clean of strawberries, while Mr. McWhorter was still getting a harvest from his plants.

"All I have to do is secure Clarence," Mr. McWhorter said, putting a shim in the ball bearing beneath the circular platform on which the owl perched. He'd given all three of the owls names. Why anyone would want to personalize a fake owl, Leah couldn't guess. She attributed his attachment to them to the fact that he was an elderly bachelor and perhaps desirous of companionship in his later years. A tabby cat would have fit the bill, but he'd chosen wooden owls. He'd never married, but that hadn't stopped him from learning to do his own washing and cooking—an accomplishment Leah applauded, as her own left much to be desired.

Leah ducked beneath the cloth of her camera. In the ground-glass lens, Mr. McWhorter stood upside down next to his plum tree. The leaves were darker, lending a contrast to the snow-white summer suit he wore. It was too bad the deep red leaves were moving. They'd blur in places unless she chose the precise moment of vague stillness in the wind to snap her photo.

Coming out from the black fabric, Leah put her fingernail on her lip and studied the scene. The balance was off. The shapes and tones didn't complement one another. She spied a lawn chair on the veranda.

"I believe the portrait would be much improved if you were sitting in that wicker chair."

"Sitting?" Mr. McWhorter held onto a hoe. "But it won't look like I'm a gardener if I'm sitting."

"Of course it won't." She went to the picket fence covered with climbing morning glories. She stood on the street, and he on the inside of his fence. The orchard and garden stretched to the sidewalk, to the delight of many passersby. "You don't want to appear too eager when entering a contest." She knew. She'd entered the New York Amateur Photographer's competition twice. This year she just had to win, because she would have form. The Stieglitzian form of the great Alfred Stieglitz. Relatively simple. More of a composition and balance than of rhythmic order. She'd been trying too hard to have shapes outdo one another.

"You see," Leah said, while more firmly attaching her hat by its long pin, "in the world of art, one must make things relative. Since this is a contest for the best garden, you must impress upon the judges that it is because of their magazine that you have this lovely setting to enjoy. Thus, the chair. And while you are sunning yourself in that wicker chair, you shall be holding and faux-reading this month's issue of *Illustrated American Gardener* to show them what their time-saving tips have meant to you."

Mr. McWhorter's Scotch golf cap blew off, and he quickly ran after the hat as it tumbled up the steps to his veranda. "I think you have something there, Mrs. Kirkland." Grabbing the chair, he set the legs firmly beneath the shade of the plum tree as per her instructions. After a quick dash into his house with a slam of the screen door, he returned with the magazine and sat down.

Leah smiled as she looked through the camera. The scene was much improved. Just one last bit of direction. "Now

Mr. McWhorter, you must imagine you are President Roosevelt, and you are in command of this orchard. Nothing can defeat you. No bird or bug is too great a problem for you. You are the master gardener."

Mr. McWhorter's gray brows fell into a serious line. His expression was regal and confident. *Wonderful!* Now if only the wind would cease for one second, everything would be perfect.

Wyatt walked to work along a back road called State Street, hoping to avoid a run-in with that short-arm-of-the-law marshal. Yesterday, the hardware store—along with everything else except for the saloons—had been closed and locked up tighter than a chain gang, so he'd spent his Sunday excavating rock with a fat stick. The primitive method had produced more swear words than sandstone fragments. Poking around with a stick wasn't his idea of time spent in a worthwhile manner. After more than eight hours, he didn't have a thing to show for his effort.

Though he hadn't wanted to admit it, he'd pinned too many hopes on finding that money by sundown. It had taken him less than fifteen minutes to bury the bags. How come he couldn't exhume them in the same amount of time? By six o'clock, he'd called it a night and had saddled July for a ride. While loping over the hills as the sunset emerged, he'd accepted the fact that he was indeed a real dishwasher. It was a bitter pill to swallow and a humiliating one at that. He didn't care how nice a guy Leo seemed to be. Washing dishes was washing dishes, and he'd done that line of work before. There was nothing satisfying in it.

This morning, Wyatt had been the first inside Carlyle A. Corn's Hardware Emporium when he'd opened for business at seven o'clock. Carlyle was bald at the crown, wore denim coveralls, and had a wide gap between his front teeth that made Wyatt ponder the man's ability to tackle eating the cobbed vegetable that was his namesake. Corn had been a real gabber, the kind of man that Wyatt steered clear of. Carlyle had questioned him on the prudence of his mining equipment purchase. No one had struck anything around these parts for years. Wyatt had lied and said he was thinking about doing some placering as a hobby in the near future if he could rummage up enough money to buy the required three hundred by fifteen hundred-foot parcel. He'd convinced Corn he wanted to be prepared in the event of an opportunity.

After buying the necessary tools, Wyatt had had to sink some money into a can of coffee and a pot in which to brew the grounds. Of course, that meant spending another forty-eight cents on a coffee mill. He'd been sorely tempted to have Corn write him up some cigarettes, too. But he couldn't really afford them, and besides, a cigarette wasn't fully enjoyed unless he had a whiskey to go with it. Wyatt could never pick up another shot glass of rye, so the smokes were out. He bought an M. M. Royal chocolate bar instead. That and a canister of Quaker Oats, a half-dozen Libby Luncheons that came with keys on the bottoms of the rectangular tins to open them, and a pack of tutti-frutti gum.

Afterward, he'd gone over to check on July's treatment. It was hard for him to trust a modern smithy. Too many years had put a distance between his way of seeing things and theirs. Back in the good old days, he never had to question the service he was getting, because what was rendered was always reliable. Probably because he'd had a name for himself, and no one would dare cheat him. But now he was Wyatt Holloway and not known, which suited him fine. Only now he had the added worry of making sure July was properly taken care of. Stables tended to feed their animals too much grain and graze them on grass that was too hot, rather than give them a balance of straight hay and good exercise. Wyatt promised that no matter how tied up he got in his digging, he'd try and give July a workout for an hour each morning so he wouldn't go sour.

He hadn't been able to work the horse this morning, which he regretted but vowed to rectify tomorrow. Wyatt had spent the better part of the breakfast hour breaking in his new pick and ax, but with no luck. He had to be at the Happy City by eleven, so he'd headed out frustrated and agitated.

Wyatt tipped his head so the brim of his hat wouldn't catch on the breeze. He'd never been partial to wind. In fact, he hated it. Many times up on Table Rock, he'd had to cut stone with flying sand putting grit in his eyes. With this kind of wind, usually a thunderstorm wasn't far behind. That's all he needed. Wet rock and mud to paw through. Wasn't anything going to go right?

State Street cut through the foothills and dirt swirled in the road in tiny whorls. As Wyatt approached the city block where homes were built, he figured all the houses had to be owned by bankers and well-to-do merchants, because they were all two and three stories with wraparound verandas and chimneys for practically every room. He'd seen these types of homes in Boise City on Warm Springs Avenue, but few if any before that. Ranch houses were single-storied and plain, with simple accommodations that put a man at ease. These grandiose residences weren't his idea of comfort.

Too late, he saw Leah Kirkland standing smack in the middle of the street with her camera. The breeze fluttered her light-colored skirt, showing a good display of her ankles. He couldn't see her face. She was ensconced beneath the camera cloth. She popped out and spoke enthusiastically to a man sitting at the base of a tree.

"I believe I got a good shot," she said as the first plump drop of rain hit Wyatt on the jaw. "It won't take me too long to develop the photograph. You'll make the post."

As she turned to reach for a case, she spied him. An uneasiness pressed down on Wyatt. He couldn't exactly change directions and go back the way he'd come. The doodad trimmings on her hat seemed to wave at him, but she said nothing. He couldn't blame her. He hadn't been very congenial toward her at the restaurant.

"'Morning, Mrs. Kirkland," he offered in an amicable tone, trying to make amends.

She hesitantly smiled. "Hello, Mr. Holloway."

He had no opportunity to say anything further. A flash of

lightning went off brighter than the sun. The wind kicked up in a great flurry. An object sailed toward him on this sudden gust that shook all the leaves on the nearby trees.

"Look out!" she cried.

It was too late. An owl sailed from the yard and buffeted him in the side of the head. His hat was knocked from him, and he swore a clump of his hair had been ripped off with his Stetson. Raising his hand, he fingered the lump forming behind his temple, feeling as if he'd been given a blind punch.

"Damn," he mumbled, gazing at his feet where the great horned owl rocked on its back. The bird was dead. In fact, petrified. Wyatt toed the wooden owl with the tip of his boot, then bent down and grabbed his Stetson before it blew away.

"Damn," he repeated, thinking the only explanation for the bird's state was that it had been struck by a bolt of lightning.

"Clarence!" A man's hoarse cry came from the yard.

Leah spun on her heels and ran to Wyatt. "Mr. Holloway, are you all right?"

She instantly laid her palm on his forehead, her fingertips light on the rising bump beneath his hair. Her tender and caring ministration was totally unexpected. Before he got to thinking too much about her satiny hand against him, he reminded himself that she was a mother and prone to nursing. The gesture was more of an automatic thing for a woman.

Wyatt shifted his weight to get out from under Leah's touch. "I'll live," he assured her, but the relentless pounding of his head brought to mind a cattle drive being ridden across his skull.

Rain began falling in a splash of heavy droplets as the gentleman in the white suit came over, picked up the owl, and cradled it in his arms as if the bird was a sick child. "Clarence! You've got a chip on your shoulder." Glancing at Leah, the man spouted, "I've got to get Clarence inside and repair him. All this moisture could ruin his insides and he'll puff up like a dandelion." He sheltered the owl within his coat. "Thank you, Mrs. Kirkland. I'll call on you at twelve-thirty to pick up my photograph."

Leah nodded against the rain that was now making a stinging descent. "I think you'll be pleased, Mr. McWhorter."

McWhorter sprinted through the open gate and went quickly into his house as another flash of lightning lit the gloomy sky.

Wyatt had to ask, "Was that a fake owl?"

"Yes. The wind must have jimmied the shim right out of his base and picked him up. I'm sorry you got hit with it. Mr. McWhorter should have apologized, but I'm afraid he's not himself right now. Are you sure your head is all right?"

"I'll let you know as soon as my double vision clears."

"Truly?" she gasped. "Then you must go directly to Doctor Hochstrasser's." She took him lightly by the upper arm. "Can you walk?"

"There's nothing wrong with my legs," he replied. "And I was only kidding about the double vision."

Leah paused and gazed at him, blinking the rain off her thick lashes. The bobbles on her hat had gone limp, and the wisps of hair framing her face were stuck to her cheeks. Soon she'd be soaked through. So would he—a predicament he could think on no further without a provocative picture coming to mind. "You can't see two of me?" she questioned.

"Pretty as you are, the possibility would be welcome." Her lips parted a fraction at his compliment. "But, no, darlin'. I only see one of you."

She abruptly let go of his arm, her expression bewildered. "My equipment is getting wet."

Going to the camera, she removed it from its three-legged support and wrapped the top and sides with the black cloth. But with the water splattering the street, she had no place to set the wooden box while folding the tripod. She struggled with both, not asking Wyatt for his help.

That she didn't bruised his ego. Before he could think, he went to her and snatched the camera from her arm. "You're going to drop it."

She bit her lip but didn't argue with him. Loosening the screw on one of the tripod's legs, she folded the three sections.

With a lead feeling in his gut, Wyatt gazed at the Kodak in his grasp. He'd never held an image taker before. He hadn't anticipated the heaviness of the fine wood-grain box.

Gathering the tripod and a case, Leah juggled them in her arms. The wind threatened to snatch the full-brimmed hat from her head. Her lashes fluttered against the sparkles of water caught on them. He didn't want to notice her eyes, and lowered his gaze. A mistake. The thin white fabric of her blouse had become near-transparent and adhered to the generous shape of her breasts. He'd always been attracted to women with some depth to their curves. He could see the contoured outline of her corset cover and the delicate lace and ribbons at the shoulders of her chemise. An involuntary tremor of arousal began to heat him.

He shot his eyes to hers, meeting the purposeful gleam in the brown color that showed intelligence and the spirit of her independence. She reached for the camera, but he didn't relinquish it.

"You can't run holding all this," he said. "I'll see you home."

For a moment she seemed frozen in limbo, but then acquiesced. "We need to hurry. I can't redo the shot in this weather."

Nodding, he took off in a sprint after her. The hem of her skirt skimmed the street, the soft, swishing motion of her bustle catching his attention with its naturally alluring sway. She was quite adept at running in high heels, and more than once hopped over large puddles.

They reached the house at the end of Main. The soles of her shoes crunched across the tiny pebbles of the pathway. As she climbed the veranda steps, he noticed a lasso lying on the white planks of the porch. Without missing a step, she kicked the rope aside. Iron-cast soldiers and a baseball were strewn across the cushion of the summer settee, and miniature pewter dishes and a tea service were still set up on a wrought table.

With a snap of her wrist, Leah turned the front doorknob and gained entrance into the foyer. He drew up behind her but suddenly froze, his mind and body flinching. He retreated a step. The odor of photography chemicals, though not overly pungent, jumped out at him. There was enough of a sharpness in the air to choke and pull at Wyatt's memory. He squeezed his eyes closed, not wanting to bring forth the image of a little girl's face that had been so filled with hatred.

Wyatt felt Leah's presence close to him; he could pick up an elusive hint of her floral perfume and was able to breathe again. His eyes opened. She stood not a foot away from him, examining him with a concerned gaze. "You really did hurt your head," she said compassionately. "You'd better come into the kitchen and dry off so I can see if you're bleeding."

Walking around him, she shut the door, and he was caught in a house with smells that brought on the haunting fringes of a nightmare that hadn't gone away in seventeen years.

"You'll have to excuse the disorder," Leah said, depositing her tripod in the umbrella stand. "I was experimenting with lighting earlier this morning when Mr. McWhorter called." The ring of her shoes was buffered by the runner of oriental carpet that spread through the entry hall over an intricate parquet floor. Rosalure's lawn tennis racket was in the path, next to Leah's white duck tennis balmorals. She and Rosalure had played against Pinkie Sommercamp and her mother last week. Leah had never been organized, but at least she'd been tidy enough to encourage customers to keep coming back to her upstairs gallery for portraits. Today was just a hectic day.

Leah didn't look back to see Wyatt's reaction to the clutter as she shook the rain from her hands, then took the Kodak from him. She set the camera on the hall table, not bothering to check her appearance in the gilt-framed mirror above after she removed her bolero hat. She could bet she looked her worst. There was no sense in confirming it.

Besides, she wasn't altogether sure she wanted to catch Mr. Holloway's eye. His attitude toward her had been running hot, then cold, and now warm. She didn't know what to think of him.

"The kitchen's this way," she stated, and turned around.

The parlor was indeed a mess as she entered the room with glassware and painted arabesque pottery strewn on various plant stands and tables. She'd even been tearing up the kitchen. It had been a fluke, really, that had made her consider photographing the scrub bucket. She'd tripped over it on her way with the last pedestal jar and cracked glass vase. Emptying the cupboards hadn't been her intention, but once she started a project it took on a life of its own, and she wasn't satisfied until she knew she'd used and tried every means available to her to capture the perfect picture. So the bucket had been pure inspiration when a light prism had caught on the hoop iron. She would have dropped everything—if the pieces hadn't been breakable—to get her camera. As it was, she set the delicate objects on the worktable, hurriedly collected her Buckeye, and caught the bucket's image precisely when the cloud cover diminished the light that had streaked across the oilcloth floor. And just as Mr. McWhorter cranked her doorbell with enough energy to jam the winder and render the chime useless.

Deep into the parlor, she held back a groan. Every free space was littered with most every piece of decorative glass from her kitchen cupboards and the dining-room sideboard. She glanced at Mr. Holloway to make sure he was all right. A glint of wonder held his expression, but he said nothing as he watched his step around a bowl of waxed fruit at the foot of her ottoman.

"You see," she plunged in, feeling the necessity to explain, "I was going to test the qualities of special velox and regular velox against the exposure and development of soft negatives and contrasty negatives. I needed still subjects. Inanimate things with line definition. Vases, bowls, pedestals . . . each has to be on its own plane for light variance, thus the tables . . . and on the floor." She connected her palms with the swinging door that led into the kitchen. "It's not always like this in here."

Once in the spacious kitchen, Leah bent and picked up the bucket without missing a step. She went to the sink, stuffed the plug in the drain, then grasped the brass fixtures in both hands and ran the hot and cold water together. In the same efficient motion, she flipped on the electrical wall switch, then dabbed her face dry with the linen towel that hung next to the stove. "Come stand over here beneath the light," she directed.

Wyatt reluctantly came forward.

She removed his rain-pelted hat and set it on the counter, feeling suddenly nervous. Disassociating herself from anything other than Wyatt's injury, she brought her hands to either side of his neck, with thumbs at the base of his ears. A muscle jumped along his jaw, and she grew so conscious of his nearness she could hardly think. The slight scratch of dark stubble beneath her fingertips made her tinglingly aware of Wyatt's virility. Under his steady gaze, she couldn't move. The blue of his eyes was startling and as vivid as a summer sky. Tracing the generous shape of his mouth with her gaze, she caught herself wondering what it would be like to be kissed by him.

Letting out an uneven breath and taking in a steady one to retain an air of sensibility, Leah hoped her half-lidded expression hadn't betrayed her wayward thoughts. She tilted his head, lifting herself on her toes to see properly. Skimming her fingers through the silky coolness of his long hair, she felt for and found the lump at the side of his head. Then she made a part so she could determine the severity of the damage. A thin line of blood colored the white of his scalp.

"Am I a goner?" The rich timbre of Wyatt's voice was low.

Leah lowered herself to her heels and shut the water off. "In my estimation, you'll live. Tug's broken his skin open a lot worse than this before."

"How is the boy? He was pretty torn up about not having his hat."

Dipping the dishcloth into the warm water, Leah was touched that Wyatt would inquire. "I don't like to punish him, but he's got to learn the difference between right and wrong. At times, I can't make him understand that."

"Your husband can't set him straight?"

Leah delayed squeezing the cloth out. Her eyes stayed fastened to the faucet. "I'm a widow, Mr. Holloway."

"I'm sorry," he returned with consolation in his tone.

Backing away from the sink, she managed a soft smile. "It's been a few years since my husband died. I've come to terms with my grief and have gone on." She rose the warm cloth to his head. "And you, Mr. Holloway? Do you have a wife?"

"No." Wyatt stood stock-still.

As she lifted her arm to blot the blood on his cut, her breasts accidently brushed against the front of his damp duster. She quickly backed away from his tense, hard body, feeling the heat of a blush creep into her cheeks. Not daring to meet his eyes, she fought to stifle the racing cadence of her heart and pretended as if nothing had happened. Keeping her distance, she stretched to reach his head, using a light stroke to clean him.

The Cilicia clock on the shelf above her sink tolled the quarter hour at fifteen to eleven. Within seconds, the other clocks in the house sang their various chords. The last to engage its tune was the European cuckoo in her studio. The bird's call faintly drifted to the quiet kitchen.

After rinsing the dishcloth a third time, she'd barely moved toward him when Wyatt's strong fingers gently encircled her wrist, preventing her from lifting her arm toward him. "I have to go." His husky voice wrapped around her like a velvet-edged blanket. "I took that job at the Happy City, and Leo wants me there at eleven."

He released her, and a twinge of disappointment left Leah's mind reeling with confusion. "Oh." The dishcloth in her hand fell into the water. "I'm sure Mr. Wang will appreciate the help. He's been without a dishwasher for two weeks."

"It's only temporary."

"You're moving on?" An instant of regret fluttered in her breast, though she couldn't fathom why.

"As soon as I'm able."

"Leah," Geneva Kirkland announced from the doorway. "You have company."

She and Wyatt broke apart, Leah flushing to the roots of her hair. Her mother-in-law's untimely intrusion caused guilt to sweep over her. "Geneva. I didn't hear you come in."

Tug loved to tinker with anything mechanical, and he normally cranked the door chimes whenever he plodded up to the front door. Only now the bell was broken—no doubt her son's perpetual abuse foreshadowing its demise—and Leah could have used that signal to prepare herself to face Geneva.

The stamp of Tug's feet vibrated the floor as he marched toward the kitchen. On a lighter tread came Rosalure. Her children filled the door's opening, standing next to Geneva without commenting on the articles that were strewn through the house. Three sets of eyes were on Mr. Wyatt Holloway. To Leah's recollection, there had never been a man in her kitchen besides her husband. It hadn't dawned on her until now. Mr. Winterowd and Mr. Quigley never came for supper. Just refreshment, and that was served either on the veranda in the summer months or when the weather cooled, on the davenport in her parlor. By the look on Geneva's face, Leah had broken some cardinal rule that men shouldn't be admitted into the kitchen.

"Can I wear your hat again, mister?" Tug promptly asked.

"No, Tug, you may not," Leah replied.

A dead silence clung to the room. Only the steady tick of the clock split through the thick layer of awkwardness that had suddenly fallen. Tug's question insinuated not only that she and Mr. Holloway hadn't had a chance meeting, but that Mr. Holloway was open to sharing his personal belongings with her son. Geneva would surely misconstrue things.

Leah looked at her mother-in-law and struggled to find words of explanation. Geneva was not an easy woman to talk to. Her appearance had always daunted Leah. Mrs. Kirkland wasn't a tall woman, but she was broad in body and built with a sturdy frame. Her hair was frosted with gray, though she would never admit to such a disgraceful sign of aging. She dyed her hair with Old Reliable hair dye. Leah had spotted the bottle on the bathroom cabinet shelf when she'd had to use the upstairs necessary in the Kirkland home. But that hadn't surprised her.

Geneva was a hypochondriac. She feared getting old and decrepit, so she used every trumped-up product available to keep her youthful and peppy. The latest she swore by was Dr. J. Parker Pray's Plixine toilet preparations, though Leah was dubious about its effectiveness. Geneva's peach-fuzz mustache was still somewhat noticeable even after several applications of the good doctor's powder.

"This is Mr. Holloway. He had an accident and I was seeing to his cut."

"I see." The fullness of Geneva's bosom appeared even fuller by her exaggerated collar.

"Mr. Holloway," Leah said, "this is my mother-in-law, Mrs. Hartzell Kirkland. You know Tug, but you haven't met my daughter, Rosalure."

"Hello," Rosalure returned, though rather than repeat the greeting herself, Geneva bluntly asked, "You're no doctor, Leah. Why didn't he go to Doctor Hochstrasser's office?"

Leah wanted to die. She and Geneva had locked horns on many prior occasions, but nothing recently.

Rosalure recognized her mother's discomfort and interjected, "Look, Momma. Nanna and I cut the invitations for my party." She plucked one from the basket she was holding and held the card out for Leah's inspection. "Isn't it lovely?"

Leah took the card that had been carefully cut from a fine-grade linen paper and festooned with a pressed flower, lace papers, and a gold tassel much like a fancy valentine. "Why, Rosalure, it is very lovely."

"I made some and Nanna made some."

Geneva shrugged as if her craft talents were nothing. "A little patience and a lot of hard work pays off."

As if Leah didn't know this. She lived by that credo every day of her life when she was in her studio.

"It was nice to meet you, ma'am," Wyatt said congenially to Geneva, though Leah doubted that was his true thought. He grabbed his hat from the counter and fit it over his head. He tipped the brim politely at Rosalure, then to Tug, "You be good and you'll get your hat back."

"I got six more days left."

"They're liable to go by fast if you don't think about them."

Leah left the sink. "I'll walk you to the front door, Mr. Holloway."

Geneva asserted herself in a firm tone, "He found his way through the front door, dear, I'm sure he can find his way out of it." Stepping aside, she offered, "Good afternoon, Mr. Holloway."

Leah tried to catch his eye to communicate with him. When his gaze shifted to her, she sent him a silent message that said she was sorry he had to leave in such a way.

"Thanks for looking at the cut," Wyatt said, then he walked around Geneva and went through the parlor.

Once the front door clicked into place and the children scattered to the icebox for a drink of lemonade, Geneva strolled into the kitchen with her put-upon face. "You know, no one could replace my dear Owen, Leah."

"I know that, Geneva."

"Mr. Holloway isn't of your social caliber," Geneva clucked. "His clothing was in disrepair. That hat looked like it had been trampled by a horse."

Leah was aware of that. But she was also aware that good men wore shabby hats.

❧ 5 ❧

**If you wish to know the road ahead,
inquire of those who have traveled it.**
                              —Chinese proverb

Wyatt was uncertain what to make of Leo's nephew, Tu Yan. For hours, he and Tu had been sharing the steamy kitchen of the Happy City. Seeing as how Wyatt couldn't speak a word of Mandarin Chinese and Tu couldn't speak a word of English, one would have thought there would have been a communication problem. But that wasn't the case. Tu never stopped talking, and oddly, Wyatt picked up on a few of the young man's gestures and could actually decipher a little of what he was saying.

But mostly, when Wyatt listened hard enough above the clink of dishes in the deep pan of soapy water, the inflections out of Tu's mouth sounded like "women hen you cry." Now why exactly Tu would be saying "women hen you cry" had Wyatt puzzled, though rather than insult Tu by shrugging his misunderstanding, it was easier to nod and smile his agreement at whatever he was agreeing to.

The night was hotter than a laundry pot left on the fire until the water bubbled down to nothing. Wyatt had opened the back door to coax a breeze into the stifling room. All those little pieces of paper Tu had stuck up on nearly every available wall space and shelf just sat on their tacks, motionless. Wyatt had asked Leo what all the symbols were for, and he'd said they were Tu's proverbs. Philosophical sayings and sages that Tu swore were good luck. But they weren't lucky in keeping the heat out of the kitchen.

Those big six-burners that Tu Yan kept fired up lent a bake to the room like a summer parch on the plains. Sweat ran down Wyatt's temple. He'd all but stripped down to his underwear. The worn sleeves on his shirt were rolled up a notch above his elbows, and he didn't mind the occasional splash of watery suds down the partially buttoned front.

He should have chosen a cooler set of trousers to wear, but all Wyatt owned by way of clothing were two pairs of faded jeans, a couple of soft-laundered shirts, some underwear and socks, a broken-in Stetson, scrub-scarred boots, and his single-caped duster. Not a hell of a lot to fuss over by way of extra laundry, but he was thinking now that drawers hemmed to the knees would be a smart investment.

Tu's palm pounced on the bell stationed at the sideboard. Wyatt had come to realize this meant another order was ready. This also meant more dishes to be washed. Wyatt had hoped that the place wouldn't be too crowded on a Monday, and that he'd have some time to dry his hands off and enjoy the sunset framed through the back door's opening, seeing as he'd been too busy around lunch hour to do anything but wash silverware. But he hadn't had any luck so far to savor the evening, and that sun was all but a blur behind the San Juans.

Leo came into the kitchen to get the steaming plates of what Wyatt thought looked like noodles with a lot of green things and chicken pieces spread across the top. Tu was a fiend with that cleaver, and Wyatt swore he'd never do anything to aggravate the young man.

"Take a break, Wyatt," Leo said around the cigarette clamped in his lips. The spent smoke curled into Wyatt's lungs. It didn't help that Tu indulged in Nestors, also. Wyatt was having a hard time talking himself out of starting up again with all the temptation surrounding him. Mostly, he just breathed in, taking what he could from the air and telling himself that this was as satisfying. "Take a cola if you want," Leo added.

Wyatt was glad to pull the string from the apron around his middle, grab a Coca-Cola from the icebox, pop the cap, and step into the back alley for some fresh air. He sucked in the scent of vegetables, the odors of leaves, stalks, and stems of plants he couldn't name, and the leftover warm smells that the sun had left in the wood and brick that surrounded him. He took a cold drink of cola and thought that this really wasn't a bad place to be at this moment.

Leo was an okay man to work for. He gave Wyatt time to get out of the kitchen for a while and take a breather from the thick steam, hot water, splatter of oils, and all those odd smells. The heat had diminished his appetite, and he hadn't eaten his supper yet. When the dining room emptied, he'd take a plate and sit in the corner.

The crunch of boot heels came from the tall shadows between the buildings, and Wyatt tensed. He didn't wear his gun on the job, but he kept the .44 within close reach, wrapped in his duster on top of a cabinet in the kitchen.

When U.S. Marshal Bean Scudder ambled into Wyatt's view, Wyatt held back a curse. "Mr. Holloway," Bean said, then again, "Mr. Holloway."

Wyatt knew he was in for some kind of reprimand, though for what he couldn't guess. As far as he knew, he hadn't broken any laws by standing in the alleyway drinking a Coca-Cola.

"Scudder."

Bean drew in with about as much tact as a buffalo bull. "That's Marshal Scudder to you, boy."

Wyatt took a slow drink of his cola, the taste going flat in his mouth. He didn't want Bean to know he rubbed him the wrong way, so he put on his best indolent expression and gazed over Scudder's head—which wasn't hard—to steal the last vestige of the striking western sunset. It was all but gone. The only light in the confined space came from the four kerosene lamps that were suspended from the kitchen's ceiling.

The stream of soft yellow lit on Scudder's badge like a

moth drawn to a flame. "You did right by taking this job, boy."

"I needed a job," Wyatt concluded.

"You sure did. Because the choice was washing dishes or getting out of my town. I didn't force you to do either." The marshal belched. At least he had the couth to keep the noise beneath his breath. Hitching the straps of his suspenders higher on his shoulders, Scudder moved closer to Wyatt.

Wyatt could smell the odor of beer coming from the marshal's whopper mustache and skin. The man was half-drunk. "I was on a perimeter check of Eternity today," Scudder began with an authoritative ring to his tone, "and came upon what I'd bet my mother-in-law is your encampment. This being the case, you've violated city ordinance 4.023, which states, and I quote: 'Said parties affixing themselves and their property on parcels of city owned land, or the legally filed parcels recorded in the city clerk's office, is in effect, nesting on domains unlawfully theirs and will be considered as squatters and subject to incarceration by the city marshal if said situation isn't immediately rectified,' end quote."

This time, Wyatt did swear.

"No, boy, I don't believe the Good Lord will be damned in this instance. I'd consider one night camping. Two is squatting. And I know you've been up there for two. I can legitimately lock you up if you don't disband and relocate."

Resting the bottom of the bottle against his knee, Wyatt's opinion of the marshal went as low as it could.

"Eternity's got a wide city limit, boy. Just about any place you pick within a couple miles, I'm going to sniff out."

Wyatt couldn't afford to have Scudder looking for him. At least at the encampment Bean had already found, Wyatt had taken care to cover his tracks. He wasn't so stupid as to think that his camp couldn't be discovered. He really was in a clearing that wasn't hard to miss. So he'd thought ahead, kept his mining equipment hidden in a cache covered by brush, and rearranged the loose rocks this morning when he'd finished digging. Rather than leave a hole, Wyatt spread the sandstone out using his shovel to make the surface look a lot flatter than it was. This took some extra time, but seeing as Scudder had stumbled upon his diggings, it had been worth the effort. But that still didn't solve his current problem.

Where to go?

He didn't want to waste time riding several miles a day between his camp, the Happy City, and his excavation site. But he didn't have much money. Not enough to pay for a hotel for an extended stay, if that's what things turned into. There was something he had to do, and soon: ask about a discovery of money from that mountainside. Because if someone had dug up his satchels, he was as good as dead broke with not a single promise to his name. If that was the case, he'd have no reason to stick around Eternity and be squashed like a bug beneath Bean's thumbnail. But a question such as the one he needed to ask had to be offered in an offhanded manner, or else he'd cause suspicion to himself. Folks would want to know why he wanted to know.

"You ain't saying much," Scudder remarked.

"I'm thinking."

"You don't strike me as a thinking man, Holloway."

"That so?"

"No, so it's best I do your thinking for you. Get a room at the Starlight Hotel. It's clean and cheap. The widow Almorene East runs the place."

Wyatt wasn't all that keen on taking the marshal's tip but had seen the Starlight for himself, and the simple place looked to be about all he could afford. "How much time will you give me to pack up?"

"What time do you get off work?"

"Nine."

"You've got until ten."

"An hour in the dark to pack," Wyatt said with more than a thread of sarcasm.

"I could have said nine-thirty."

Wyatt held back a snort of ridicule. No good could come of embroiling the lawman into an argument. He didn't want to chance being thrown in jail; not after all he'd been through. "I'll be out of there by ten."

"Wise decision." Scudder made a move to mosey on, then paused and faced Wyatt, who was thinking the dishes were looking a lot better than Bean's face. "Just why did you pick that spot to camp? It's nearly into the timberline and not at all a convenient walk to town."

Wyatt had already thought of a pat answer, should he have to give one. "The view of the town was best from there. I'm a sunrise man, Scudder, and surely appreciate the colors of an eastern sky at dawn." Then an opening came, and Wyatt took it. "I may file a placer claim on that land if I can save enough money." That part was a lie, but it gave some legitimacy to his being there.

"Well, you'll have to be disappointed, boy. The land you're trespassing on is already deeded to Hartzell Kirkland, owner of the Eternity Security Bank."

A banker. Bitterness stirred inside him. It had to be a banker. And a banker with name connections to Leah Kirkland.

Suddenly all conversation left Wyatt, and he had nothing further he wanted to say to Scudder. He didn't like being made to look like an idiot with foolish dreams—not that he really was thinking about filing a claim. It was just that Bean thought him daft to do so, and that had Wyatt angered.

Without another word, he pushed off from the wall and went back into the hothouse kitchen. He set his Coca-Cola bottle on the counter and dunked his hands into the water that had grown a welcoming tepid temperature. His palms hit the glazed earthenware bottom of the sink, and he leaned his weight forward in thought.

Leah Kirkland's name had been drifting in and out of his mind during the evening. The blunt throb of his head served as a reminder that her hands had cradled his face. Her fingers in his hair were almost unbearable in their tenderness. He hadn't known such a kindness in so long, his eyes had surely showed the tortured dullness of his disbelief. He'd viewed himself as a pathetic man, a man so starved for love that he'd fed on, and made more out of, her exploring touch. When he'd felt her uneven breath on his cheek, when the soft curves of her breasts had grazed his chest, he'd wanted to bring his hands down the length of her back and fit her head perfectly in the hollow between his shoulder and neck, and hold her. To marvel in the small span of her waist, and feel her hips flattened against his. To kiss a supple mouth . . . and to rediscover the tickling sigh of pleasure on his lips.

It had been hard to remain coherent when she was so close to him. His thoughts had swum through a haze of feelings and desires aching for renewal. Those unforgettable minutes he'd spent in her kitchen had been the best he could recollect from a memory tarnished by years when nothing had been soft.

After he'd left Leah's home, he been able to think with fearful clarity. He could no longer ignore the mocking voice inside his head. Colorado was no place for him. He bore too many scars, both on his flesh and in his heart, from the little towns that dotted its perimeter. He'd been a different man then. Wyatt Holloway didn't belong in a place like Eternity. The wide-open ranges of Wyoming or Montana suited him better. That's where he was headed.

Wyatt tucked his thoughts away and tackled the fresh stack of dishes Leo brought in. Sometime later, when Wyatt was elbow-deep in dirty dishwater, he heard Leah's voice coming from the dining room. Glancing through an airy part in the reed curtains, he saw her sitting at the same table she'd been on Saturday night. The same table that had a direct view of him at the counter. Their eyes met, then Wyatt quickly averted his gaze. His blood pounded at his temples with a deflated thrum. Having her see him in his present low station in the workplace humiliated him. He didn't want her to watch him at the sink cleaning off the dishes that others had eaten on. Watching him wash hers, too, when she was finished and lingered over tea.

He kept his attention on the food he scraped off a plate into a loam bucket, but was unable to shut out Leah's voice.

"Good evening, Mr. Wang," she said.

"Mrs. Kirkland. A pleasure, as always," Leo replied. "How are you?"

"Very well."

"And the children?"

"They're dining at the Kirklands' this evening."

"I'll pack some of Tu's cookies for you to take home to them."

"They're spending the night at Geneva's, but I'll make sure they get them tomorrow."

Leo took her order and returned to the kitchen to repeat it to Tu. Wyatt wanted to rip his apron off and tell Leo he was through, but he couldn't. Instead, he made himself blind and deaf to his surroundings, something that he had learned to do over the years. He was glad to leave the kitchen for a while to empty the slop, but the next half hour passed slower than a funeral.

Leah leisurely ate her supper, alternately taking a bite of food and immersing herself in the magazine she was reading. At closing, Leo came into the kitchen with the last of the dishes. Everything but Leah's teacup and saucer.

"I'll be in my office totaling up the cash receipts," Leo said, holding onto a box and a device with a frame of parallel wires and beads. "When Mrs. Kirkland is finished with her tea and cookie, could you clear her table?"

Wyatt nodded. Leo was the boss, and Leo had to give him orders. Wyatt could take that. He just didn't want to be ordered to pick up after Leah. If he'd known how to ask Tu to do it, he would have.

After drying and putting away the clean dishes on the racks of the sideboard, Wyatt went to work on the heavy pans and gadgets Tu used for his cooking. With a plate in hand, Tu offered it to Wyatt with an explanation sounding like *"Chewing gee-want."*

Wyatt looked down at the four plump and crispy folded pancakes. "Thanks, Tu."

Tu merely smiled, then swept the floor and put his work space to bed. On a few glances to the empty dining room, Wyatt saw that Leah was making no effort to leave. It even seemed as if she was lingering, though the Closed sign had been posted on the door for a while. Wyatt drew up a chair in the corner and ate the vegetable-stuffed pancakes with his fingers, hoping that by the time he was done Leah would be gone.

She wasn't. So he took care of the pots and iron bowls, washing and storing them. When there was nothing left to do, Wyatt gave himself a few seconds to ease the tension in his muscles. Then he took off his apron and headed for Leah's table to clear it.

His wounded pride kept him silent.

She looked up from her magazine and gave him a soft smile. "How are you feeling, Mr. Holloway?" The twist of her burnished hair was lopsided at the top of her head, as if she'd been working and hadn't noticed her hairstyle was askew. He thought the casual disarray was seductive.

"I'm okay."

"I wish you would have let me do more for you. I feel somewhat responsible."

"I'm okay," he repeated in a voice that masked his disquiet.

Her fingers ruffled the magazine's edge, a thought apparently in the back of her mind that refused to be still, by the way she chewed on her lower lip.

Wyatt didn't wait for her to say her piece. He picked up her cup.

"Oh." She slid the saucer toward him. "Thank you. That's kind."

"It's my job."

"Yes . . ." Leah stopped fiddling with the magazine.

"I didn't think I'd see you tonight."

"I'm a regular customer."

Wyatt had no response. If he'd thought he could send Leah Kirkland from his mind, he now had to think twice. Because it didn't seem likely he'd be able to if she ate in the restaurant on a customary basis.

"I wanted to apologize for my mother-in-law," Leah said. "Geneva can be insufferable."

"She doesn't bother me." The two pieces of thin china rattled in Wyatt's big hand.

"I'm glad, because I didn't want you to think that you

aren't welcome in my home." She absently brushed the cookie crumbs on the cloth toward the center of the table. "Being new to Eternity, you don't know anyone and I wouldn't want you to feel like a stranger." Her eyes lifted to his with speculation. "You are going to be staying, for a little while?"

"Looks like it."

She closed her photography magazine and gathered it against her breasts. The motion pulled his gaze downward, but only for a fraction. "If you're in need of a good hotel, I can recommend one."

"The Starlight."

"Yes. You've already talked to someone."

"You could say someone already talked to me." Then Wyatt got to thinking about that mountainside and its being owned by Hartzell Kirkland. Leah might know something, if he brought up the subject in the right way. "I was camping up by that cross until Scudder told me I couldn't. There's a fine city view from there."

"That's my favorite spot. When the sunset hits the cross, it makes me think of church."

The cross made Wyatt think about bowing down on his knees, also. But with a pike in his hand instead of a Bible. "I heard someone in your family owns that land."

"Oh, did you?"

"Scudder told me."

"My father-in-law filed a claim on that property nearly ten years ago."

"That so. He have any plans for it?"

"None that he's ever told me about. Originally he was going to build a house there, but the architect told him the wash out from the snow would be detrimental to a foundation. And then there's been the landslides."

"Yeah, I noticed that." Wyatt spoke his next question in an offhanded manner. "He ever do any digging around up there?"

"Hartzell?" Leah's laugh was soft and light. "Good heavens, no. Hartzell wouldn't know what a shovel was.

Don't get me wrong, he's a dear, dear man. But my father-in-law is no outdoorsman. Why, he doesn't even hunt during hunting season with the rest of the men. He puts in long hours at the bank and wouldn't dream of leaving it for recreation, much less dig around in the rocks." Her smile remained as she stood up slowly, her body tall and trim. "Well . . . I'd better not keep you from your duties any further. If you do find that your head is troubling you, Doctor Hochstrasser's office is located on Fourth Avenue and State Street."

"I'll remember that."

The ruffles at her throat separated where a tiny pearl button had slipped free of its small hole. Available to his view beneath the flames of kerosene lamps, the hollow of her neck filled with soft shadows. Her skin was like peach-tinted cream, the mellow brown hair framing her face giving her a wild beauty. The pleasure he felt in looking at her was pure and explosive.

She gazed at him as if she were photographing him with her eyes. *"Arrivederci,* Mr. Holloway."

Blinking with bafflement, he asked, "Arriva-what?"

Firelight reflected the smile in her eyes. "That's Italian for 'I'll be seeing you.' " Then she said the word again with vigor and a dramatic lift of her hand, her fingers lithe as she went toward the door. *"Arrivederci, il signor* Holloway." There was an exotic and romantic flourish to the words in the way she spoke them, and after she'd left, the ambiance of the room seemed to dull.

Ahr-ree-vay-dayr-chee. *I'll be seeing you.*

Leah inserted her key into the lock and opened her front door. On an impulse, she cranked the bell. Nothing. She'd have to fix that. Perhaps it was time she got rid of the manual one altogether. With step-by-step instructions, she could probably install an electric ringer herself. One with a deep gong and five chimes that didn't play a melody. That would be modern.

She'd left the entry light burning low, and her shadowy

movements were cast on the stairwell. As she walked inside, she turned the wall knob by the door until the electricity clicked off and the vestibule grew bathed in meager moonlight. She knew her way around in the dark, and there was no threat of her stepping on anything. She'd tidied up the house before she left. Everything was back in order.

Entering the parlor, she laid the magazine on a tea table next to the Edison. Cranking the handle, she lowered the needle onto the record that was already on the turntable. There was a static-sounding hiss, then Signora Resky's soprano voice, accompanied by orchestra, went into an aria from the new Puccini recording *La Bohème*. Leah had read a review of the opera in the *Denver Post* that she'd purchased here in town. The reviewer said the opera drew hecklers at its Turin premiere, even with Arturo Toscanini conducting, and that the arias were nothing short of useless fodder for the soul. She didn't agree with the reviewer's taste. The music was lovely, the love story so tragic it made her weep.

Leah sat in the overstuffed armchair and propped her feet on the ottoman. Over the next couple of minutes, the clocks chimed ten o'clock. The last to toll was the pretty Ansonia clock on the mantel. The housing was bronze, with a fancy dial and two silver-cast croquet players, who rather than hitting a ball with their mallets took turns striking the bell on top of the time face.

Despite the music, there was an eerie quietness settling through the room. Tug wasn't here for her to read to, nor Rosalure for Leah to braid her hair before bed. She wondered how they would adjust to Italy. Was she being fair to them in making them come with her to pursue her dream?

Leah unlaced her shoes and let them fall on the carpet. She brought her knees to her chin and stared through the filmy curtains covering the windows. The oak tree branches outside were like giant arms rising to the heavens, to those family members she had loved and lost.

She had been devoted to her husband with a quiet camaraderie. She'd known him since the age of ten. He'd come into Telluride on business. Years later, she found out he'd given her father money to get their photography studio back on its feet after the murder of her mother. Each subsequent year, Owen Kirkland returned to Telluride. She grew up depending on him. They had a lot of common interests, and they were both only children.

When she was fourteen, Owen told her that he had a fiancée back in Eternity. This news devastated her, but she hadn't been able to arrest her feelings for him. During his short visits, he'd made her feel safe and secure about her and her father's future. The following year when he returned, he told her that he'd broken his engagement. Leah had been so relieved, she'd actually laughed and cried in her bedroom that night. At sixteen, Leah finally caught his eye romantically, and Owen began to treat her as his girl. Twenty-two days before her seventeenth birthday, Leah married Owen. It would have been the happiest time of her life if her father hadn't been taken ill with pneumonia late that summer and died.

She'd come to Eternity with Owen after her father's burial, and met Geneva and Hartzell. She was immediately warmed by Hartzell's welcoming friendliness. It was Geneva who rebelled against her baby boy marrying—and marrying Leah, a woman clearly not his better. Geneva barely spoke to her until she found out that Leah was pregnant with Rosalure. And after that, Geneva doted on her grandchild, though she didn't have as many kind words to say about Leah.

And then four years later, Owen went off to fight in the Spanish American War in Cuba and got sick. Only no one knew how serious, until after Tug was born . . . and then Owen was diagnosed with malaria.

Leah sighed. She didn't want to think about that right now. She leaned her head back and listened to the music. The lovely voice. The kind of voice she wished she had. The kind of quality she wished she could give to her pictures. That sadness and loveliness all in one.

At times, she wished Owen were still here for her to turn

to. But when she reflected on her marriage, she had to be honest about its stability. During the last years, it had been shaky. Owen had been married to his job at the bank, while she was left in charge of the house—a responsibility Geneva constantly pointed out she wasn't capable of—and the rearing of the children. But inasmuch as Leah resented Owen's long hours at the bank, she herself was guilty of the very same offense. She'd shortchanged Tug and even Rosalure by putting her studio first. Time gone by would never come back. A shared moment together was never to be had once the day was done. Leah needed to be with her children more, and vowed to rearrange her schedule to spend more time with them during the summer while they weren't in school.

Quiet tears streamed down Leah's cheeks as she sat in the dark. She should have recognized her fault before and done more to include Rosalure and Tug in her life. The opera music should have made her feel better, as it always did. But this evening it didn't. The sorrowful aria only served to remind her she was alone in this great big house with her multitude of clocks and nothing more than a passion to do great things to keep her going. If she failed, she would have to admit it had been an elusive portrait that she just couldn't capture. That would mean she'd be ordinary.

And Leah didn't want to be ordinary. In that respect, she was like her mother. Leah wanted to be somebody famous.

At first, Wyatt wasn't sure where he was. The bed beneath him was softer than anything he could remember, not the hard ground or a sagging cot. When he rolled onto his side, the wire springs inside the felt-covered mattress squeaked. As he opened his eyes, the window shade came into focus. Sunlight peeked through the cracks on the sides and lit the hotel room. Morning had come without a whistle to tell him he had to get up.

Outside came the ring of a hammer striking wood. Wyatt shifted onto his back, in no immediate hurry to get up and dress. It felt too good to lie in bed until he was fully awake. To languor in the crisp white sheets that smelled like clothesline air and a female's touch as she'd folded the starched linens with a precise hand.

Putting an arm beneath his head and bending his leg, Wyatt stared at the ceiling where a lightbulb on a cord hung above him. Last night, he'd triggered the light on and off at least a dozen times. Having never operated an electrical switch before, he couldn't figure out how that bulb of glass ignited an artificial flame.

City noises came to his ears, a populace of foreign sounds that he wasn't used to hearing. Voices calling out cheerful greetings. Bicycle bells. The grate of saws against lumber. When he had his ranch, he was going to revel in every birdsong, every horse's nicker, and every calf's bawl. He'd wake to the sound of his children's laughter as they rumpled their bedclothes and threw pillows at one another. He'd start each day with the warmth of his wife's body snuggled against his. They'd share a kiss and murmur their love for one another. And he'd finally know what bottomless peace and satisfaction felt like.

Wyatt exhaled a long sigh. Then he swung his legs over the bed's side, ran a hand through his tousled hair, and rose. The hardwood floor was a welcoming cool beneath his bare feet. A quick glance of the room in the daylight and he admired anew the tidy room Almorene East kept.

The walls were flocked with a crimson paper and didn't smell of dampness and sweat. Though the plain furnishings were sparse, he had everything he needed. The faint scent of lemon wax clung to the surface of the bureau, and inside the drawers was a printed paper lining. Down the hall, a bathroom with running cold *and* hot water was at his disposal. A pipe was anchored to the tub wall with a sprinkler called a shower bath. He wasn't quite sure how it worked, but figured it had something to do with the pull chain.

Picking up his watch on the dresser, Wyatt noted he'd slept later than he intended. He wouldn't have as much time digging as he wanted to before calling it quits to take July out. Rather than get dressed right away, he went to the window and nudged the edge of the shade aside so he could view Main Street. The Starlight was smack next to the Eternity Security Bank. He couldn't make out any of the building's front architecture, but he saw the sidewalk and men in suits going inside. In his mind's eye, Wyatt saw himself following them with deception on his mind. But that wasn't his way anymore.

Resting his forehead on the window frame, he watched a young boy on a two-wheeled bicycle dart between buggies. He had a bell on the handlebar that he engaged with a smirk whenever he got close to the horses. It spooked the animals and made Wyatt shake his head. Damn kid. On the corner of Main and Seventh was a popcorn-and-peanut wagon with a thick black cord strung out to its roof denoting that the equipment was functional because of the electricity. Its power source was the street lamp strung across the middle of the road.

The racket of construction continued, and Wyatt veered his gaze straight ahead on the other side of the street. A building was being erected, the framework nearly complete. On the outside in the lot's front expanse of dirt was a large sign.

Future Site of: Independent Telephone Co.

Then in smaller print:

Advantages of a residence telephone are friends can call you; does your shopping; calls the plumber; saves letter writing; saves time and steps; calls the doctor.
RESERVE YOUR TELEPHONE TODAY AND BE THE FIRST TO SAY "HELLO"

Wyatt dropped the shade into place. He was a stranger in an era he didn't recognize. The world had gone on and left him far behind. There was nothing here that he knew. From lights to showers, to telephones and automobiles. He was lost on a frontier of innovations.

Sinking onto the mattress, he cupped his head in his

hands. His mind swirled with doubts. Could he make it in this new place without reverting back to the old way of life with which he'd been so familiar?

He struggled with the uncertainty as the wood saw's grate penetrated his room, and the hammer kept on pounding. Like a gavel. Rapping. Over and over . . .

❈ 6 ❈

To one who waits,
a moment seems a year.
——Chinese proverb

October 4, 1887
Montpelier, Idaho Territory

Rap! Rap! Rap!

"Come to order!" The bailiff barked the demand above the authoritative slam of the judge's gavel. A late hush descended on the crowded courtroom as the Honorable Judge Erastus Peabody set down his mallet while the last of the spectators filed in behind the occupied seats. It was standing room only to hear the proceedings. This was the biggest criminal case that had ever been tried in Montpelier.

The leader of the Loco Boys had been apprehended and sent to Montpelier to face a jury on a grand larceny warrant that had been outstanding since November 3, 1885. Today was his arraignment and the whole town had flocked to the trial of the decade.

Harlen Shepherd Riley had been locked in a piss-poor territorial jail cell for nearly two weeks. Ever since he'd been extradited out of Colorado on the eighteenth of September, just a day after his capture in Montrose.

Twenty-four hours after splitting up with the boys, Harlen hadn't been able to collect the money and head south as he'd wanted. The area was swarming with members of a spread-out posse. On every trail to Mexico that Harlen had tried, some half-cocked deputy with a temporary badge on his chest was smack in the middle of the road on his horse. Waiting. Knowing that he'd be thinking to cross the border. So he had to stick to the high country for another two days, riding at night and catching some shut-eye during the day. The stocky bay he'd stolen in Eternity came up lame on Sunday morning, and he had had to divert to Montrose, a mining town farther north.

He held back until the street activity died down and everyone settled in the Glad Tidings Church for services. Despite keeping his face covered by a bandanna and the lowered brim of his hat, some smart Pinkerton detectives spied him. They immediately apprehended him and took him to the Montrose city jail. The sheriff was summoned from his pew to sign the necessary extradition papers.

Those damn detectives had had things all worked out. The capture was to be kept quiet, and they told Harlen their theory. Though they had no proof, they speculated that Harlen had stashed the sixty thousand dollars somewhere for safekeeping. They figured other members of the gang would begin asking around for him when he disappeared with the money, and in turn, give themselves away. There were enough law enforcers in the various counties and territories who knew of the plan and actually expected to contain Colvin, Thomas Jefferson, Manny, and Nate by the month's end. Harlen knew that none of his four comrades would fall for such a trick. They wouldn't think he'd absconded with the cash and left them high and dry. They'd go on to Mexico without him until he could meet up with them.

Since no positive identification could be made on the Silverton job, and since Harlen had had no evidence on him—namely, the money—it was going to be difficult to get a conviction in the Silverton Miners Bank robbery. Even though Colvin had left the portrait, the teller couldn't testify under oath that it was Harlen who'd stuck a gun in his face.

This hadn't come as any surprise to Harlen. Though he

had wanteds on him for numerous holdups, not a single witness could lay his hand on the Bible and swear to the court that Harlen had been the offending culprit.

The shootout in Telluride was a different matter. Even though they knew that it was Harlen, for none of the boys had worn disguises, there was no proof that it had been Harlen who killed Evaline Darling.

While Harlen sat in the Montrose jail, he'd heard a lathered-up lawyer acting on Strawn's behalf, arguing that Harlen should be tried as an accessory to murder. But a representative from the Merchants and General said that there wasn't a one hundred percent guarantee that Harlen would be found guilty. They finally had him behind bars and that's where they wanted him to stay. Only a clear-cut case of guilt could keep him in prison.

That's where Montpelier came in. And that's where that picture sealed Harlen's fate.

The cashier whose till he'd emptied in the Montpelier bank had a hobby: sketching. He'd been able to draw all five of the undisguised Loco Boys from memory, and had done an admirable job of it. There was no denying the like-for-like images of that drawing to the men in the photograph Edwin Darling had taken. Not only that, but there were two tellers and a manager, not to mention the half-dozen customers, who could identify Harlen in a court of law. It looked as if that portrait Colvin had left on a whim could wring Harlen's neck.

The Telluride and Silverton officials were willing to make a deal with the Montpelier officials. Lawmen in Telluride dropped the accessory to murder charges, and lawmen in Silverton dropped the larceny charges, with the promise Harlen would be severely prosecuted in Idaho and given a stiff sentencing.

This wasn't the first time Harlen had been arrested, so he was rather optimistic about his chances of getting off despite the big hoopla that he was going to be made to pay for his crimes. This arraignment was only a formality that his attorney, Richard Robison, had to come all the way down from Wyoming to handle.

"Order!" The sagging skin beneath Judge Peabody's chin shook against his tight collars as his voice bellowed through the courtroom. "This court is in session and I demand quiet. Those who cannot comply will be thrown out by the bailiff."

The room stilled to an ominous calm.

Handcuffed, Harlen sat at a table in the front next to Richard, while the prosecutors, Jason H. Edlin and Samuel Martin, the district attorney, were at the adjacent table. They wore expensive suits and had a lot of papers in their files. They looked prepared, and for a scant second Harlen felt a needle of worry prick his spine. But Richard had always gotten him off. This time would be no different.

"There being sufficient evidence to go to trial with, I order the defendant, Harlen Shepard Riley, to rise, hear his charges, and have his counsel enter his plea."

Harlen slid his chair back and stood. He refused to avert his gaze from the judge, who had an imposing look about him. That high and mighty look that said he wanted to make Harlen cower.

"On this fourth day of October, Harlen Shepard Riley is hereby charged with the grand larceny crime of armed robbery to the premises known as the Montpelier City Bank in Montpelier, Idaho, on November third, eighteen eighty-five. How does the defendant plead?"

Richard's tone was low and expert. "Not guilty."

"Having entered a plea of not guilty, and that plea duly recorded by the court clerk, the defendant will be remanded into the custody of the court, whereas he will be held at the Montpelier jail without bail until the twenty-fifth day of October, eighteen hundred and eighty-seven." The rap of the gavel cut through the room. "This court is adjourned."

Richard left his chair to stand next to Harlen as the bailiff came to take him away. Harlen had thought Robison could at least get him out on bail. But Judge Peabody was a hard-nosed officer and hadn't been persuaded by Richard's request earlier in chambers.

"I'll come to the jail straightaway, Harlen," Richard said

as he leaned to gather documents into his case. "First I need to speak with the district attorney."

The bailiff was leading Harlen toward the side door as Harlen replied in a restrained voice, "Don't you go making any deals for me, Richard. I'm not going to any prison. You got that? You've got to get me off."

But Richard's flat expression didn't hold the confidence Harlen wanted to see.

Later in the day, Harlen sat on the sagging cot in his cell, lounging against the wall while he smoked. At least the deputy on duty wasn't a tough guy out to prove he had the upper hand. He'd given Harlen a smoke when Harlen asked for one.

Richard Robison had come by earlier and tried to reassure Harlen that he was doing the best he could. Harlen didn't doubt his abilities. Richard and he went back to '84 when Harlen had saved Richard's life in a saloon brawl at Rock Springs. He hadn't known at the time that Robison was the foremost criminal lawyer in that area. From that time, Robison had become permanently indebted to Harlen, and the gang had used his services on more than one occasion.

Though Harlen was no stranger to the confines of a cell, he could never get used to the suffocating feeling of entrapment. At least his stays had always been less than a week. This was the longest he'd ever been incarcerated.

As the sun poured in through the tiny slice of window and the iron bars made linear shadows across his bed, Harlen took in his young life and tried to figure out just exactly why he'd ended up this way. He'd grown up in a home that had treated him fairly. He'd had two parents who'd taught him the straight and narrow, and had preached the Bible to him. But that hadn't been enough to keep Harlen out of trouble. He'd strayed, and it began that summer of 1881 when Whitt Trammel had come to his hometown of Moab in the Utah Territory.

Harlen's first arrest warrant had been issued when he was

fifteen. The charge: cattle rustling. His signature had been on a bill of sale for some hundred mavericks. A few of the hands who worked over at the Kittleman Ranch figured anyone with thousands of head of cattle wouldn't miss a few here and there. It took those tight-pursed, greenback-rich cattlemen with their fancy spreads a year to catch on to Whitt's scheme and start an investigation. When they did, the paper trail led to Harlen.

His one fault—if you could call it that—was a loyalty to friends and family that was never violated, even in the tightest spots. Those friends of Whitt's all had wives and children to feed on a poor wage. Even though Harlen hadn't rustled a single one of those cattle, he took the blame thinking that he could explain his way out of things. He was good with words and well liked in the community, but he found out that the only talking he could do to wealthy folks was from behind bars. Imprisonment seemed imminent, so he did about the only thing he could do to save his family from further shame.

He fled to Columbia, Colorado, to work in the silver mines.

At the age of sixteen, Harlen was arrested for horse stealing—the horse in question being his own. He'd left his colt, Samson, at a nearby ranch for eight months while he was working in the Revenue Mine. He paid to have the horse put up and fed, and planned to start breaking him in over the summer. But when Harlen turned down the rancher's offer to buy Samson, the rancher had a warrant drawn up. The charge was horse theft. Harlen's dad, Clement, was notified and he came to Columbia. It had humiliated Harlen to have his dad see him sitting in a jail. And though Clement didn't have to say it, he was humiliated for his son even though Harlen was innocent. Harlen swore that if ever such an incident occurred again, he'd never let his parents know.

Everyone in Columbia knew that Samson had been in that rancher's pasture for some time. So it did look as if Samson belonged to the rancher. Luckily, Harlen had had enough friends from the Revenue Mine to testify for him that the colt was his. And luckily, the jury believed him. He was acquitted.

There were other such incidents involving scrapes with the law. The time he was put in jail for rolling a drunk—which he hadn't. That was a dirty crime. He'd never stoop that low. And then there was the incident when he really had stolen a horse, though no one could prove it was he who'd stolen it, so he'd been released on insufficient evidence.

By this time, the west had three natural enemies encroaching on the wild land out of which Harlen's family was trying to carve a living: giant cattle companies, banks, and railroads. It was the end of an era when a man could roam the countryside with freedom on his back, and he was being driven out by herds of longhorns, cities springing up overnight, and rail crews cutting the prairie with lengths of steel and spikes.

Civilization was coming, and with it came corruption.

Harlen had known about corruption. The land his father had set aside for Harlen to start up his ranch had been repossessed by the bank on a trumped-up clerical error, and there hadn't been a damn thing his dad could do about the swindling. It was that unethical episode that stuck with Harlen most of his life. To his way of thinking, there was always somebody hanging around to cheat you out of something if he had a bigger bank account than you. The laws that were supposed to protect people and their rights only protected the man who already had more money than he knew what to do with.

By seventeen, Harlen had crossed the line and turned into a full-fledged outlaw with four other desperados: Manny Vasquez, Nate Bender, Thomas Jefferson Ellis, and Colvin Henkels. Their list of offenses included cattle rustling, horse thievery, bank robbery, and despoilers of the Union Pacific Railroad. Those U.P.R.R. fellows had sworn out more arrest warrants and hired more detectives from Pinkertons than any of the western barons put together.

Harlen robbed because he had every intention of buying

back the land bordering his parents' homestead with the bank's own money. But he always ended up sinking his cash into women and liquor, and anything else that gave him pleasure. So he'd have to rob again. High on whiskey, he began to lose focus of the land over the immediate luxuries he could afford to buy for the first time.

Over the years, Harlen had sent his folks honest money when he worked in the mines or wrangled cattle, but as soon as he started earning it dishonestly, he stopped sending them tainted support. He'd been raised to be a good Baptist and respected his parents too much to give them money that he hadn't rightfully earned on a paycheck. He realized his ambitions of buying back the land with stolen money would never happen. His parents would never accept it from him.

There had been many times that Harlen had tried to go straight. He'd even worked out a deal with the U.P.R.R. bigwigs with Richard's help. All charges were dropped against him. But things had gotten screwed up. People hadn't been where they were supposed to be when they'd said, and Harlen had thought the whole amnesty affair had been a trick. After that, he'd raided the railroad with a vengeance, turning to disguises, though having more robberies than he committed pinned on him. Too late, he realized his mistake of not trusting his lawyer.

Harlen crushed out his smoke in the bucket of sand beside his bed. It might be too late for him now. He could be headed for a lengthy jail stay. All he knew was if that were the case, he'd rather be given a death sentence. He'd been too long in the open to be caged up like an animal. He'd never survive it.

The trial lasted three days. The jury was only out of the room for five minutes, if that. Harlen got to feeling sick to his stomach when the foreman handed the bailiff the verdict.

Judge Peabody requested, "Will the defendant rise."

The clink of the cuff chain on Harlen's wrists seemed to be deafening in a stifling courtroom that had gone deadly silent. He could barely breathe. He could barely see through the sweat clinging to the lids of his eyes. The suit he wore was wool. His expensive shirt stuck to his chest and his legs; the tie seemed to be cutting his throat.

It seemed that every railroad official had come in for the verdict. Up here in the Idaho Territory, this was big news, though Richard had told Harlen that the news was contained to this area. No one in Colorado knew of his whereabouts, nor had any of the other boys been apprehended.

"Has the jury reached a verdict in the case of the People Versus Harlen Shepard Riley?"

"We have, Your Honor," the foreman replied.

"Bailiff, if you'll remit the verdict to me."

The folded paper exchanged hands. Harlen's fate depended on that paper, and he wasn't feeling as hopeful as he should.

The judge opened the note, scanned the contents, then put the paper on top of his Bible. "Harlen Shepard Riley, you have been found guilty of the crime . . ."

But Harlen didn't hear anything more above the frantic rap of the judge's gavel and the loud voices in the courtroom. Richard put his hand on Harlen's forearm as reassurance.

"Order! Order! I demand order!"

The buzz faded to a drone when Peabody continued. "Since I have full jurisdiction of the court, and seeing as I have already evaluated this case should the verdict be such, I see no reason to delay sentencing. I have given the matter great thought. For the crime committed, and the guilty verdict rendered, there is no penalty of death. Or else I would have imposed that sentence."

Harlen didn't know yet if he was relieved or not by that news.

Peabody slipped a sheaf of paper from his notes and began reading. "Harlen Shepard Riley was on the fourth day of October, eighteen hundred and eighty-seven indicted for the crime of armed robbery to the premises known as the Montpelier City Bank in Montpelier, Idaho, on November third, eighteen eighty-five. The said defendant was duly tried before the court and a jury, and on October twenty-eighth, eighteen eighty-seven was by verdict of the said jury found guilty of grand larceny. Also on October twenty-eighth, eighteen eighty-seven, the court, in accordance with said verdict, proceeded to and did pronounce to the effect that the said defendant, Harlen Shepard Riley, be on the eleventh day of November A.D. eighteen eighty-seven, at the hour of twelve P.M. of said day, being a twenty-year sentence in the Idaho Territorial Penitentiary." Letting the paper rest on the desk, Judge Peabody looked directly at Harlen and said, "May God have mercy on you as you pay your debt to society. This court is dismissed."

The gavel's slam was dry and final.

❊7❊

If you wish to know the mind of a man,
listen to his words.

—Chinese proverb

Leah was disappointed.

The mail from the midmorning post had arrived ten
minutes late. And when the few envelopes had fallen from
the brass slot next to the front door, there had been no letter
from Mr. Giuseppe Ciccolella of Italy. Nor had there been
the package she was expecting from the Littlefield Publish-
ing Company of Rochester, New York. She'd sent them one
dollar and a stamp, and was waiting to receive a copy of *The
Complete Guide to Italian Cooking.*

Rather than be despondent about the lack of good news,
she'd rummaged through the toolshed searching for Tug's
tackle box and fishing pole. Though Owen had been in the
last stages of his illness after Tug's birth, he'd insisted on a
trip to the hardware emporium. He bought his son base-
balls, bats, a striking bag, Indian clubs, boxing gloves, a
football, rubber balls, and boxes of other sporting accesso-
ries Leah had never opened. They were heaped in the toolshed next to the shelves of paint, gardening tools, and a
hammock Leah hadn't figured out how to assemble.

As Leah gathered the creel and poles, she couldn't remember Tug's ever having used any of it. He'd gone fishing a few times with other boys and their fathers, but he'd never asked to use his own things. And she'd never had the hindsight to offer them to him. She doubted he knew he had them. Her heart swelled when she thought of him borrowing without making a fuss.

The day was perfect for a picnic, and Leah had quickly put her office in order earlier in the morning. Afterward, she'd packed a dinner basket. The bottom was heavy with canned deviled ham, a quarter loaf of bread, and a jar of American Clubhouse cheese spread, sweet pickles, two Swiss milk chocolate bars, and six bottles of Hires root beer, with a bottle opener, butter knife, and napkins. A bound writing tablet rested on top for Rosalure to use to press wildflowers.

Leah managed to walk to Geneva's while holding on to the food basket's handle with the crook of her arm, as well as Tug's tackle box, along with two fishing poles and her Kombi camera, which was small enough for her to carry in her skirt pocket.

Reaching the impressive walkway of the Kirkland home, Leah trudged toward the veranda supported by decorative spindles. As she neared the steps, Leah couldn't help admiring the lovely craftsmanship of the home. The clapboards were cream, while the trim and railings were white. The sashes were of dark green, and all the outside doors varnished. The home was the finest in all of Eternity, but one would expect the banker's residence to be of the utmost expense and taste.

Leah juggled her burdens as she struggled to crank an electric doorbell that chimed the first twenty notes of "Oh Promise Me." Hartzell had had the rather whimsical bell installed on his and Geneva's silver wedding anniversary as a token of his undying affection, though Leah suspected the costly gift was more of a pacifying show of attention to his oft-neglected wife.

The melody played through, and soon thereafter the click of shoes could be heard on the opposite side of the door.

The entry swung open and Leah was greeted by Geneva's housemaid, Posie.

"Good morning, Mrs. Kirkland," she said with a sunny smile. The young girl was too good for Geneva, putting up with the older woman's stormy disposition and commanding of orders. But Posie seemed to handle the situation just fine. She looked no worse for the wear, her coiffure of blond hair tidy beneath the smart white cap she wore, and her complexion rosy as ever. "Do come in."

Leah managed to slip inside without catching anything on the doorway. She set her things beside the umbrella stand, then straightened. "I've come for Tug and Rosalure."

"Oh, the children have been having a wonderful time. I believe Miss Rosalure is in the gazebo sketching, and Master Tug is apt to be aiming his slingshot at the ground squirrels who run across the electrical wire hooked up to the house." Apparently seeing Leah's look of horror, Posie added, "Don't you worry. He's never hit a one yet."

The death of a squirrel wasn't what had Leah worried. Tug could knock his eye out if the slingshot backfired.

"If you could pack Rosalure and Tug's things and round them up for me, I'd appreciate it," Leah said. "I'll let Mrs. Kirkland know that I'm taking them. Where may I find her?"

"Upstairs in the boudoir." Posie rolled her eyes. "She's got a new health aid she's trying out. The gadget scares me. I told her I wasn't going to touch it when she was finished cooking herself inside those walls. She called the thing a Turkish bath. It came on yesterday's freight stage, so big it was."

Leah nodded, used to Geneva's unconventional home treatments. Laying her hand on the balustrade, she climbed upward, reached the top landing, then headed down the hallway to Geneva's room. Though it wasn't spoken, she and Mr. Kirkland didn't share a bedchamber. This was apparent by the masculine decor in the room across the hall from the opposite room which was in shades of pink—Geneva's favorite color.

A hissing sound spilled into the hallway as Leah lightly knocked on the wall next to the open door.

"Geneva?" Leah asked with fright, unprepared to view the cabinet that was at least four and a half feet tall, with only Geneva's head exposed through a tight hole in the top. She was sitting inside the box, on Lord knew what, with some sort of steaming mask on her face that was attached to a thin hose.

"What?" Geneva hollered above the loud noise of a large vaporizer. "I can't hear you! Come closer, Posie, and remove the mask!"

Leah went to the cabinet and tentatively took hold of the facial gear and set it on top of the box. Geneva's face was as red as a beet, and sweat trickled from her every pore and strand of wilted hair.

Seeing Leah, Geneva was obviously taken aback, and flushed an even deeper shade at being discovered in such a contraption. "Leah . . . how pleasant you've come to call."

Leah knew Geneva's feelings were anything but pleasant.

"Excuse me at the moment," Geneva sighed on a tired note, "but I'm trying out what the Racine Bath Cabinet Company declares is a sure way to shed extra inches and improve upon one's health."

"Is it working?" Leah asked, reining in her skepticism.

"I'm not quite sure yet. I haven't stepped out, though I'm just about ready. The alcohol stove I'm sitting on is cooking me to well done. So surely the cabinet must work. I feel pounds lighter already and I've only been in for half an hour."

Leah grimaced. A half an hour of torture. No thank you.

"What is it that you wanted?" Geneva inquired, slipping an arm through a false top and swabbing a towel over the rivulets of perspiration running down her temples.

"I've come for Tug and Rosalure. To take them on a picnic."

Geneva's drooping brow arched. "A picnic?" she quipped.

"Yes, I packed a dinner—"

"Of what? You can't cook. The poor darlings are starved for decent food. All those Chinese vegetables and herbs are bad on their digestive systems. Why, the only well-balanced meal you eat is when you come to my house for supper."

"I've managed to pack a nice dinner for this afternoon," Leah maintained, bridling a loose tongue.

"Well, I think the children would be better off here for dinner. Posie is going to fix some egg sandwiches and give them each a slice of the blueberry cobbler Rosalure and I made yesterday. She so loves to cook, but hasn't the resource to learn her way around the kitchen."

As much as she didn't want to, Leah let that remark pass. "I'm certain dinner here would be lovely, but not today."

"What about your studio?"

"I hung up my Closed sign."

"You did what?" Geneva's strained her voice over the noise. "You never close."

"I did this afternoon. I want to spend time with my children. I know you'll want them to enjoy the outing I've planned."

Geneva feigned great hurt. "You know how attached I am to little Owen. He's such an angel boy, and so like my Owen . . ." She sniffed very melodramatically. Leah had seen the routine over a hundred times.

At first, Geneva's sniveling had moved her. Geneva had lost her son and needed to hold on to a part of him, and she'd done so through Tug. Only now that attachment was turning into a fixation. She was trying to turn Tug into the son she'd buried. Well, he wasn't, and he never would be.

"I'm sorry, Geneva, but I've already made other plans."

Tug burst into the room, his overalls stained at the knees from grass. "Whose fishing poles and stuff is that downstairs?"

"Yours."

"Mine?"

"Yes, your daddy bought all that for you when you were born. I thought you may like to try it out with me and go fishing."

"Fishing?" Geneva squeaked, fumbling for the on–off

switch to the vacuum. "You can't go fishing. You don't know how."

"I was hoping Tug could show me."

"Me?" Tug's eyes widened.

"Yes, you, Rosalure, and me. The three of us on a picnic."

"But what about your work?"

"I don't have to work today."

"You don't?"

"No."

"Well, gosh, I'll go fishing with you."

"Owen, darling," Geneva cooed softly, having shut the Turkish bath off. "Don't you want to stay here with Nanna? We could go to the emporium and Nanna will buy you a new cowboy hat."

Leah's heartbeat worked into a strong staccato. How dare Geneva undermine her authority and bribe her son with a hat to replace the one she'd withheld as punishment? The offer would be too tempting to a five-year-old; Leah was sure he'd choose the new hat. Then she'd have to make him come with her. The purpose would go out of the picnic if Tug was forced into going.

"No thanks, Nanna," Tug said, two dimples appearing in his cheeks. "I want to go fishing with my mom."

The eagerness in Tug's eyes gave Leah unlimited joy. Keeping the animation on her son's face would be worth every body-shivering minute of baiting a slimy, wiggling worm on a hook.

Sitting astride July, Wyatt skirted the scattered gray sage that grew around him. The day was hot but with clouds to pass under and give him a few minutes' cooling respite from the heat.

All he'd seen for the past hour was rolling hills and posts strung with barbed wire. Those offending wires weren't shiny and new. They were rusted and weathered from many seasons of brutal elements. The tarnished coloring meant they'd been up for a while, not only caging things in but keeping things out.

Back in the old days, ranchers hadn't used too much

barbwire. People trusted their neighbors not to mess with their cattle, though Wyatt knew all too well that rustlers had been around for as long as anyone had been openly ranging herds. He supposed once he purchased his ranch, whether the property was already built up or whether he'd have to start from the beginning and furnish the buildings and pasture himself, he'd have to use the wire, too.

Just before noon, Wyatt had encountered a nice-sized spread that ran a hundred miles southwest of town. In talking with one of the hands out doing repair work on a drop gap, he found out that the cattle belonged to a man by the name of Half Pint Gilman. The brand identifying a group of Longhorns chewing their cuds in the shade of a juniper stand was a three-peaked mountain with a line running beneath the points. The emblem stood for the Rocky Mountain Cattle Company. Wyatt had been informed that Gilman's spread was the richest in this part of Colorado, with an estimated herd size of some fifty-thousand head.

Wyatt had ridden on, leaving the cowboy to his work, feeling envious and deflated. He nudged July in the direction of the Aspenglow River, having the need to cool off in one of the pools formed by the falls.

He'd spent four hours this morning up to his elbows in bits of sandstone. With the pick and shovel, he'd pawed through the rock, the calluses on his hands rising to tough flesh. He'd never had the comfort of using gloves before, so he was used to going without. Besides, the damage was already done to his abused knuckles. And his body wasn't much better off. His muscles had burned and ached from the speed with which he worked, and by the time the sun had made a near-high zenith in the sky, he was ready to quit.

His frustration had mounted twofold. No money. No hopes. No nothing. Had he not hidden those apricot cans in that spot himself, he would have sworn he was digging in the wrong place. But he had. The cross was an unmistakable marker. There was no second guessing.

The landslides must have been worse than he'd originally estimated. There could be layers upon layers of rubble, and he was only breaking the surface. But he couldn't give up, not when he knew what the money could buy him. He had dreams, and prison hadn't squelched them. If anything, they'd become more precious. He had no choice but to continue to dig. His prior outlaw ways were too much of a temptation, even knowing he was too old to start that kind of life up again. He'd known the comfort money could buy. Living without the sixty thousand wouldn't be living at all.

The smell of grasses and water came to Wyatt in the still air. Thursdays were slow for Leo, and he'd told Wyatt he didn't have to come in until two o'clock. From the angle of the sun, Wyatt had a couple of hours left to appreciate his surroundings.

Rumbling falls, with pressure enough to crush a man, reached his ears. In the distance, high on the ridge where the flow began, there was some kind of building next to the water's raging edge, absorbing all that power, though Wyatt didn't know its function. He kept on riding by, staying safely away, taking note of the multitude of wires, lines, and pipes.

Steering July to lower grounds, Wyatt knew which spot he was headed for. He'd found it yesterday: the gentle basins of clear water, sloped banks of moss, colorful wildflowers, and brambles of dewberries and elderberries. He appreciated the finer things in life, but nothing compared to nature's beauty. It was free for the taking. And he was free to enjoy every detail.

The shin-high grass had lost its spring green and was baked a brown like the edges of a pie crust. As he pulled into a lush thicket of aspens, he heard Leah Kirkland's voice. Through a part in the twirling leaves, he saw her sitting on the bank across the lazy river with her skirts hiked up and her bare legs dangling in the water. Her discarded shoes and stockings lay on a pile with Tug's and Rosalure's. Her boy sat next to her, the two of them holding fishing poles and talking about who'd have the next nibble. Rosalure was nearby, a basket in her hand as she plucked flowers. She hummed to herself as she hopped on random rocks to cross the river. Wyatt was so moved by the scene, that he couldn't tear himself away. He'd imagined himself in a picture such as this many times. It was the one real photograph that he wished he had of himself.

"Hello."

Jerking his head, Wyatt saw Rosalure standing several feet away. "Hello," he replied, damning himself for getting caught staring.

"That's a pretty horse. Can I pet him?"

Wyatt nodded.

The girl approached, a bouquet of colorful flowers in her grasp. July's nostrils widened to sniff at them as Rosalure drew up alongside his head.

"Pet him on the side of the neck," Wyatt said. "That's where he likes it best."

"What's his name?"

"July."

July's lips flapped as he tried to eat Rosalure's flowers. Laughing, she pulled them out of his reach. "These aren't for you, silly."

"Rosalure?" Leah called. "Who are you talking to?"

"Mr. Holloway's horse." Rosalure giggled when July sneezed.

"Mr. Holloway?" Leah replied lightly.

Wyatt couldn't determine by her tone if she was displeased by his invasion of her privacy. "Yes, ma'am. It's me." He nudged July out of the aspens, Rosalure trailing along.

Leah remained sitting at the water's edge, though she'd modestly lowered her hem. He realized she'd abandoned her tie and her business-like mode of clothing for an oyster-colored skirt and simple blouse. No hat protected her face from the sun, and a delicate blush of pale pink dusted her nose and cheeks. She shaded her eyes with one hand.

"Would you care to join us for a root beer, Mr. Holloway? It's awfully hot."

Surprise halted his immediate reply. She was making an

offer of alcohol in front of her children—and including them. "I don't drink, Mrs. Kirkland."

Puzzlement overtook her face, then a smile lit on her mouth. "Why, Mr. Holloway, how funny you are."

Was he? Once again, Wyatt felt out of place. Like an actor playing a part he didn't know. Heat burned his neck.

"There are extras." Leah lowered her hand, the warmth of her smile echoing in her invitation.

Tug's pole jiggled in his fist as he proudly declared to Wyatt, "I got thirty-one bites."

Wyatt's brows lifted in overstated amazement. "That's a lot of fish. How many have you caught?"

"None yet. But they've taken every worm clean off my hook."

Rosalure scampered across the river to join her mother. Plopping down next to a picnic basket, Rosalure opened the lid and took out a bottle that looked much like a cola. Using an opener, with a flick of her wrist, she popped the cap and took a drink.

"Do you want one?" Rosalure asked.

Wyatt needed no masterful persuasion. The yearning for innocent moments missed was too strong for him to say no. "Sure, Rosalure, I'll try a root beer."

Swinging his leg high over July's rump to clear the pack of accoutrements and water he'd tied on the back of his saddle, Wyatt dismounted and led his horse a few feet to a strong-looking branch. He tethered July, giving him enough length to graze. Then Wyatt turned toward Leah, suddenly aware that he presented one hell of a sight. Glancing downward, he saw that the toes of his boots were dusty, as well as his pants legs. He'd torn the sleeves out of his oldest shirt to keep cool while he was digging, only the lack of fabric hadn't given his arms any protection from the sun. His tan had deepened to a dark honey color. He was cut up with thin scrapes and covered with a fair amount of dirt and grime.

As he forded the river by stepping on the boulders that blossomed from the water, he was resigned to the fact that he wasn't much to look at. He found the thought very discouraging when it was applied to Leah's impression of him.

Leah thought there was something appealing about a man who wasn't afraid of hard work. She couldn't guess what Wyatt had been up to. His arms were powdered with fine dirt where the sleeves to his shirt were missing. The faint definition of strong veins on the insides of his arms stood out against his tan skin. He was more muscular than she could ever have guessed, the firm contours of his strength making her mouth go as dry as cotton.

Suddenly, Leah needed a root beer herself. She reeled in her line and set her pole down. Standing, she let her skirts fall to her ankles. Her petticoats stuck to her wet calves as she strode to the basket. She opened two Hires and handed one to Mr. Holloway.

"Thanks." His voice was deep and sounded parched. His expression was one of wonder as he drank long, slow gulps.

"I gather this is your first taste of root beer," Leah said after sipping hers. "How is it?"

Studying the label, he commented, "I like it. Not as much as Coca-Cola. But I like it."

"You should try a glass of root beer with a scoop of vanilla ice cream floating in it. You might change your opinion."

"Momma can I go over there?" Tug pointed downstream. "That spot's better."

"Yes," Leah replied. "Rosalure, you go with Tug to keep an eye on him. Make sure he doesn't fall in." She wasn't overly worried about Tug in the shallows. But the current in the middle of the Aspenglow was forceful enough that an advanced swimmer would be challenged. She'd taught both her children to hold their breath and float in the event of an emergency. She'd practiced with them in the bathtub every night for a month after Pinkie Sommercamp had nearly drowned last year by the falls.

The children went off to a little inlet where beavers had been active. Tug climbed up on a fallen log and dug inside the creel slung over his shoulder for another worm. Rosalure's eyes followed his hands and she scooted away.

"Keep those stale old worms to yourself," she shuddered.

Leah smiled. "I don't think it's the fish taking the bait. The worms are falling off."

Mr. Holloway stood close enough for her to catch a hint of the salty sweat and leather smell clinging to his skin. She grew pleasantly flustered. "Do you have any special technique for putting a worm on a fishing hook?"

His eyes were a very disarming shade of blue when he answered, "I stick the sharp point through it a couple of times, and cast."

Grimacing, Leah admitted, "Tug tried to show me that, but I had to look away. I'm not sure he knows exactly what he's doing. We're both new at this."

"I think it's admirable that you're trying with the boy. Most women wouldn't go fishing with their sons."

"I have to be his father as well as his mother. It's hard. There's a lot I don't know."

Biting her lip, Leah pondered asking Mr. Holloway to give her some insight into the world of little boys. She'd approached Leo once, but he thought Tug's antics were amusing and was of no help. And she would never go to Geneva, because it would be one more thing Geneva could tell her she was being silly and ignorant about.

After a long pause, Leah asked, "Would you care to sit down?"

"I reckon I would." He said the words tentatively, as if testing the idea.

Leah settled onto the blanket, Mr. Holloway beside her with a respectful distance between them. For a while, they watched Tug sling his line out, then reel it in short minutes later, declaring his bait had been snatched once again. His little arm would chug to wind up his bobbin; no doubt in the hurry, that's when the bait actually fell off. Then he'd squish a fresh worm on his hook and repeat the process. Leah suspected he got more enjoyment out of whipping the line into the river and reeling in than he actually did the art of fishing itself. Even Leah recognized that to catch a fish, one needed patience and to leave the bait in the water long enough for the trout to swim by it. Tug's method gave those fish a lot of free food, but he was having a good time, and that's all that mattered.

Leah allowed her subconscious thoughts to surface. "Tell me, Mr. Holloway, when you were a boy, did you carry a pocketknife?"

"Of course."

"Why?"

Shifting his legs so that he sat Indian style, he shrugged. "So I could whittle myself a slingshot."

"Hmm." Tug had done that. "Go on."

"And carve my initials in trees. Or anything else wood. Boardwalks. Porch railings."

Tug had done that, too.

"Why did you feel it necessary to carve your initials in the porch railing?"

"To show that I was there."

Leah grew pensive. "And did you like snakes?"

"Sure." Wyatt rested the bottle's bottom on his knee. "Your boy likes snakes?"

"He found a red-and-brown snake in the lot next to our house and put it in a jar. He wanted to keep it in his bedroom, but I forbid him. It could have gotten out. I'm sure it was poisonous."

"I doubt it. It probably was a grass snake. I used to catch those myself."

"But why?"

"Mostly to look at."

"But why?" she repeated. "They're ugly."

Wyatt's laughter was rich and warm. "Not to a boy they're not."

Sighing heavily, she stared at Tug. "I just don't know. I've tried, but I don't understand how Tug thinks."

"Because you're not a man who's been a boy. And you don't have a husband to show you the way." Mr. Holloway lifted the Hires to take another drink. Leah's gaze fell on his mouth, the way his upper lip sort of sucked into the bottle opening as he pulled the foaming drink into his mouth. A tingling began to fizzle beneath her breasts, much like the fizzle in the bottle.

Mr. Holloway set his empty bottle next to the basket. He hesitated, measuring her for a moment. "Have you given any thought to remarrying?"

His question caught her by surprise. "I would if I found someone who interested me," she replied, toying with a blade of grass.

Leah raised her eyes to find him watching her with curious intensity. His gaze probed to her very soul. And in that moment, something special flared into existence between them. Something fragile, yet tangible. The very air around her seemed electrified. She'd never felt anything like it before, and she needed a moment to reorient herself to their surroundings.

They sat in silence for a time, each of them perhaps trying to make sense out of what had just happened.

"Would you mind if I showed the boy how to bait his hook?" Mr. Holloway asked after a spell.

"I'd like that."

He went to Tug, and Leah stayed on the blanket. She watched as he took her son under his wing and guided him, offering his advice and sharing stories of when he'd been a boy and had gone fishing. About chasing water skippers and skimming stones.

The afternoon wore on with Mr. Holloway sitting on the log next to her children. Rosalure showed him her flower collection, and he asked her to name each variety. She delighted in telling him, pointing out the differences in petals and leaves.

Leah settled back on her elbows, taking in the scene as if she were considering the best angle with which to capture it on film. No tone or texture went unresolved in Wyatt's eyes. His reactions to things filled up the space from corner to corner. He appreciated simplicity. What she took for granted, he was in awe of. Rosalure's daisies, buttercups, and meek-eyed violets charmed him. He gazed at the sky as if it were more than a vast, empty space of blue. And when he lifted his ears to the coos of doves in the trees, he listened with the same passion as she did her opera.

If he were to stay in Eternity, she would regret the timing of her trip to Italy and miss the opportunity to get to know him better. She wanted to photograph him once. To develop on paper his seductive, yet deceptively uncomplicated manner. To capture his mystery and make him true to life.

She'd read in one of her magazines that in trying to persuade them to use the whole space of a picture, a photography teacher pointed out to his students that a peanut in the bottom of a barrel was merely a spot, whereas a peanut in a penny matchbox was a piece of sculpture. Wyatt was that sculpture. He emerged from an overgrown background of giant and towering trees and a wide river with rushing power, yet the strength in the scene was his.

When the sun lowered, Leah was sorry when he said he had to ride back to town.

"I want to pet your horse good-bye," Rosalure said as she hopped down from the log.

Not to be left out, Tug sloppily reeled in his line and rushed to say, "Me, too." Juggling his pole and creel packed with the three rainbow trout he and Mr. Holloway had caught, he traipsed after Rosalure via the shore route that got the bottoms of his denim overalls soggy. One of his turkey-red suspenders was missing a button again—the third she'd replaced in a month.

"Come on, Momma," Rosalure said. "You should see Mr. Holloway's horse. He's awfully pretty."

Leah wasn't too keen on fording the river. She lacked a confident balance when it came to crossing on rocks.

"Yeah, come on, Momma," Tug hollered, sloshing toward her.

Leah rose and mustered her courage. "Okay."

The children had no problem getting from one side to the other. Mr. Holloway held back, looking over his shoulder at her. "Do you need a hand?"

"Go ahead," she called. "I'm all right."

Mr. Holloway braced his foot on a boulder, then started to cross. Leah hesitated. His method called for coordination—something she lacked but was loath to show him. She positioned a bare foot on the top of a rock. Its surface was warm from the sun, and thankfully, dry and secure. Holding her arms out a little for stability, she crossed the river without mishap—until she got to the last anchoring stone and slipped. A dragonfly dove straight for her. She shooed it and lost her balance.

She hoped Mr. Holloway hadn't noticed, but from the groan and splash she'd made as her feet hit the sandy bottom, how could he not? He turned around, saw her standing ankle deep in water, then checked his smile.

Leah couldn't say why exactly, but she'd wanted him to laugh. So what if it was at her expense. Hearing him laugh made her happy.

"Yes . . . well . . ." She gave him an airy wave of her hand. "I'm not much for sports. I always lose at lawn tennis and croquet. I can't even pitch a ball a foot away."

"I'm sure you have other outdoor talents, Mrs. Kirkland."

It made her feel better to know that he was trying to point out her adequacies. "Thank you, Mr. Holloway. That was very kind of you to say." She drew up alongside him with a giddy sense of relief. "Mr. Holloway, might I suggest that since we seem to be heading in the direction of a friendship, that we drop formalities and address each other by our given names. My friends call me Leah."

He said nothing immediately, and Leah thought she'd made a terrible mistake by her assertiveness.

After a few second's thought, he said, "My name's Wyatt."

She smiled at him, delighting in standing next to a man and not having to be at eye level with him.

Tug had dumped his fishing gear by the bank, and he and Rosalure fed Wyatt's horse handfuls of grass. The black chewed and shook his head when a fly landed close to his eye.

"Wyatt, could I sit on your horse?" Tug asked.

Wyatt turned to Rosalure. "Do you want to sit on July, too?"

She eagerly smiled. "Yes."

Reaching down, Wyatt lifted first Tug then Rosalure into the saddle and let them sit astride the horse while he untied July. He moved the black out, and Rosalure slipped her arms around Tug's middle to keep him steady.

"A short trip around those junipers and back," Wyatt said.

The horse's swaying gait made the children giggle. They'd been on few horses in their lives. Anywhere anyone wanted to get to in Eternity, they could walk to. And for farther trips, Leah rode in a buggy with an experienced driver at the reins. But she could see that Tug was fascinated by horses, because he wanted to be a cowboy. And even Rosalure enjoyed the ride.

The moment was too monumental to let pass by. Leah slipped her hand into her pocket and took out her Kombi. The camera was small enough to fit in the palm of her hand, and she brought the viewfinder to her eye. Aiming at the trees where the children would come around and out, she anticipated their appearance so that she could snap their picture with Wyatt.

Wyatt came into view first, then the horse. She had Tug and Rosalure in focus when Wyatt turned away and pulled his hat brim low on his brows just as she clicked the shutter.

Lowering the camera, Leah spoke in jest. "You decided to fix your hat the moment I took the picture. Now I'll have to take it over."

"Don't bother." He kept his chin down. "I don't like being photographed."

"A lot of people don't like being photographed. I'll be kind," she assured with a smile.

"Please don't take my picture." His frank eyes met hers, sending the message that he meant what he said.

"All right," Leah replied quietly. "I won't."

Wyatt brought July full circle, ending up where he started. "Ride's over, kids." He set Tug and Rosalure on their feet.

"Nice horse." Tug gave July a final stroke on the velvet of his nose.

"Thank you, Mr. Holloway," Rosalure said.

Wyatt nodded, placed his boot in the stirrup, and swung his leg over the saddle. "I'm beholden for the root beer." Then he tipped his hat and rode off.

Disappointment left Leah with an inexplicable feeling of emptiness, and the day seemed to fade into the churn of dust kicked up by July's hooves.

❊ 8 ❊

> Money comes like earth scooped
> up with a needle; it goes like sand
> washed away by water.
>
> —Chinese proverb

When Leah invited Wyatt to her daughter's birthday party on Sunday, his first inclination had been to say no. But he remained quiet as Leah went on about how her mother-in-law would be there and how she hoped he wouldn't be put off by her. She'd said that she understood if he didn't care to be subjected to Geneva's snobbery, but she'd love to have him attend. Other people besides family would be there and he'd be able to make new acquaintances. And bringing a gift wasn't necessary. Wyatt had told her he'd have to think about it.

He hadn't been to a celebration of any kind in ages—not counting the fireworks he'd seen from his boarding-room window in Boise City last month. That had been a sight to behold, and he had been all the more reverent because it marked his own independence. The lights in the sky as they rained brilliant color against the darkness had been his inspiration for naming his horse after a month filled with meaning for him. But other than recently, Fourth of Julys and Christmases as well as other holidays had dissolved from his life. There were no exchanges of presents. No birthdays observed. Each day had been the same. Nothing days. Days of gray. Lonely hours and lonely times. He longed to hear singing. To witness an innocent moment of pure happiness, no matter how fleeting he'd be allowed to share it.

Wyatt figured Leah had swallowed her pride to ask him to the party after he'd told her not to photograph him. He trusted that she wouldn't try to again, but she probably had thought up a half-dozen convoluted excuses for why he didn't want his picture taken. Whatever her conclusions, none of them would have been correct.

The honest truth was, Wyatt couldn't chance anyone seeing a likeness of himself, no matter how far-reaching the possibility. Though his body and face had gone through changes of hard years, he could still be recognized. He didn't want the boys finding him. Not after what Manny had told him about their thinking he'd deceived them. For that, Wyatt could never forgive the other three.

The closer the party came, Wyatt caught himself thinking more and more about it. If Geneva Kirkland was going to be there, Hartzell would be there, too. Wyatt needed to talk with the banker about his land without being obvious. A party would be the perfect setting.

Sunday came, and Wyatt found himself getting spiffed up in a brand-new double-breasted blue shirt. The cotton smelled pleasantly of dye and the faint odor of store-bought, not supply room. His pants were clean. He'd washed them himself in the bathtub, scrubbing until the water had run clear on the rinse. With a damp towel, he'd buffed his boots, wishing he'd had some polish to give them a nice luster. To suffice, the day before, he'd rubbed some campfire soot on them to lessen the scratches in the black leather. He hadn't been able to afford a new hat, so his old one had been slapped against the iron footboard of the bed to swat off the dirt.

He'd taken a shower bath, then tried out one of those double-edged Gillette razors with blades that you threw away after thirty close, smooth, comfortable shaves. He got the closest shave he'd ever had. For years, all he'd been allotted under strict supervision was a straight razor that chewed up his face after months of reuse. Wyatt had combed his hair away from his forehead after a thorough shampooing, then reached for his hat. He was ready to go.

The day before, Wyatt had pored over the items in Corn's emporium, trying to decide on the right gift for Rosalure. Despite what Leah told him, he'd never show up empty-handed. He knew he'd found the perfect choice when he spied a rosewood music box that played two melodies. Rosalure had told him Tug had disposed of her musical bird. If the boy got nasty again, this would be too big to fit through drainpipes. But the price tag was two dollars and sixty-five cents. Wyatt's spirits had fallen. He barely had that to his name. Looking through the rest of the store, nothing had appealed him better than that music box. He returned to its shelf and took it down, damning the consequences of being short next week. There was nothing else he wanted to give to Rosalure.

He would have bought her the most expensive music box in the store—thirty-five dollars—if he'd been sixty thousand richer. He used to be able to make anything happen just because he wanted it to. Only now he couldn't. And not for the lack of trying. He'd devoted every morning to searching through the rocks, to no avail. Today, he decided to give his efforts a rest.

Leaving the Starlight Hotel with the paper and string–wrapped gift tucked in the crook of his arm, Wyatt ran into Leo on the boardwalk out front. His boss balanced some empty crates in his arms.

"Hey, Wyatt," Leo greeted around the cigarette in his mouth. "Where are you off to all slicked up?"

Self-consciously, Wyatt replied, "Leah Kirkland's house."

"To Rosalure's party?"

"Yes." Wyatt had seen Leo's invitation at the restaurant and had presumed the other man would be there. But Leo was dressed in work clothes that were stained with garden soil. "Aren't you going?"

"Nope."

"I wish you were."

Leo made no reply, and the two of them walked down Main Street together, Leo inhaling and puffing on his Nestor with no hands. Though Wyatt wanted to go to Leah's, he wasn't looking forward to being with a roomful of people he didn't know. His nerves needed quieting, so he followed Leo through the open gate that led behind the Happy City, taking a short diversion.

A rectangular expanse of garden thrived in ten neatly furrowed rows. In the far corner, a scarecrow with an oriental mask as its face did the job of keeping unwanted pests from eating the fruits and vegetables.

The ash from Leo's cigarette fell into the top crate he held, and he set his boxes down next to a pile of dried manure.

Wyatt rested his foot on the bottom step leading to the back door. "Why aren't you coming to the party? You and Leah are friends."

"Our friendship has perimeters." Leo pitched his cigarette in the dirt.

Wyatt didn't fully understand. "That are?"

"I am who I am. Her family doesn't care for me."

"You mean because you're Chinese?"

"I'm an American," Leo said proudly. "They think I'm Chinese."

"But that's not Leah's way to draw lines."

"Things are the way they are. We're friends at the restaurant. Nothing more." Leo moved down a row of tall corn, checking the ears where the silks were beginning to brown. He twisted some free and motioned for Wyatt to take them. "Put these in that crate, would you?"

Wyatt carefully set his package down and took the corn.

"What did you get Rosalure?" Leo asked.

"A music box."

Leo paused, his face half in shadow from the straw hat he wore. "She'll like that." He left the corn and walked the rows of low-growing, leafy vegetables. Wyatt trailed along.

"Did you know Leah's husband?" Wyatt ventured.

"I saw Owen Kirkland around town, but I didn't know

him. He never came into the restaurant, and Leah didn't go anywhere without him. She was a different woman then. Rosalure was an infant, and Leah stayed home a lot. Alone. Her husband wasn't around much. He went on business trips for the bank."

"How did he die?"

"Malaria."

"Jesus," Wyatt whispered. "How'd he get that?"

"The Spanish American War." Leo walked to the crates and layered the corn and cauliflower, then reached for a bucket of strawberries on the back porch and laid them on top. "Did you have to fight in it?"

Wyatt was vaguely familiar with the Spanish American War from an outdated newspaper he'd read. "No."

"Me neither. Bum leg." Lighting another cigarette, Leo talked through the smoke. "Owen Kirkland was fool enough to enlist. His momma wept so loud at the stage, Doc Hochstrasser had to sedate her for a week after her baby boy went off to war."

Wyatt visualized Leah left with Rosalure, uncertain whether her husband would come back safely. Only to have him return and die at home.

"Hey, tell Rosalure happy birthday for me." Leo unlocked the back door and hoisted a crate over the threshold.

"Sure, Leo."

Wyatt gathered his parcel and left with the thought that Leah Kirkland was a strong woman to have lived through what she had. He knew all too well about having to cope in hellish conditions and coming out of it a changed person. From what he'd observed of Leah's confidence, he'd say she'd changed for the better.

Reaching her house, Wyatt unhinged the gate and let himself inside the yard. He stepped up to the door and rang the bell, but no sound came out. His twist on the knob caused a noise that was more a sick grating than a ring. Voices drifted from the back of the house.

He was late. The party had already started.

Walking around the veranda to the side of the house, Wyatt saw a group of people dressed in fine clothes. Brightly colored paper lanterns dangled in trees. Streamers adorned the awning posts, making them look like pink-and-white barber poles. Ladies milled at tables filled with finger foods, and a group of gentlemen stood off to the side smoking. Children ran through the bushes, while others played a game on the lawn with balls and long-handled hammers.

A screen door to Wyatt's right opened and nearly banged him in the arm. He turned as Leah stepped out carrying a tall arrangement of flowers. "Wyatt!" she exclaimed in a startled greeting. "I'm so glad you came."

Awkwardly, he cleared his throat. "I rang the bell, but nobody answered."

"The bell is broken."

"Yeah . . . I figured."

Wyatt couldn't help staring at her. She'd done something different to her hair. It wasn't so wispy around her face, except for one tendril that curved beneath her cheek and rested on the underside of her jaw. He wondered if she'd done that on purpose. The effect was provocative.

Before he could say anything further, a robust man puffing on a fat cigar and wearing a twill suit appeared. "Who's this, Leah?" he asked with a broad smile of intrigue.

"Mr. Hartzell Kirkland, this is Mr. Wyatt Holloway," Leah replied affably.

"Holloway!" Hartzell laughed in jovial recognition, giving Wyatt no time to firm up his opinion of the banker. "You're the one Marshal Scudder said was squatting on my mountain. Good grief, man, come and join the party and tell me why on God's green earth you'd want to camp up there? Quigley," he bellowed to a portly man sitting off to the side with a pudgy face red from the heat. "Come take this present into the kitchen."

Wyatt was relieved of his package and given the once-over at the same time. Hartzell Kirkland's hand rested on Wyatt's back like a lead paperweight as he steered him toward a throng of people who gave him furtive glances. His presence created a buzz of speculation that aroused his uncertainties. Perhaps he'd made a mistake in coming.

* * *

Leah ducked into the house and quickly walked to the foyer to check her appearance—a characteristic totally unlike her. But finding Wyatt on the porch had been a wonderful surprise and she wanted to make sure she looked her best. She'd been holding on to the hope that he'd come.

She'd taken great care this morning to wear her best ladies' jumper dress of green wale serge with its two rows of buttons that reached the floor and its narrow sleeves that tapered across her arms. She had wanted to look chic and sophisticated. But the reflection that greeted Leah was not that of a stylish New York woman.

She'd laid open *Vogue* magazine on her dressing table and had tried to imitate the hairstyle of the model. Only Leah's hadn't turned out quite the same. She fussed with a loose strand of hair, trying to tuck it back in her chignon, but she had no luck and left off trying with a sigh. The heels of her Cleopatra tie oxfords clicked across the floor as she carried herself with a dignified walk back to the party.

As Leah rounded the wide gallery to where the festivities had been set up, she paused. Hartzell had taken Wyatt toward the group of businessmen standing in the shady comfort of the gazebo with its pretty decorations of pink ribbons and fresh cuttings of Geneva's royal-pink roses.

Leah couldn't make out Wyatt's expression, but his stance was stiff and unyielding. She did note that he'd dressed handsomely, and recalled he'd smelled nicely of some sort of masculine tonic that she couldn't put her finger on. The ends of his hair curled softly on his blue collar, which belonged to a flattering new shirt.

Hartzell kept his arm around Wyatt's shoulder, moving in for the kill. Leah was more or less helpless to save Wyatt from her father-in-law. Once Hartzell met a man who hadn't yet opened an account in his bank, he'd be on him until he did.

She still felt terrible for having upset Wyatt at the river. It wasn't an uncommon reaction from some people, not to want their photograph taken. She'd had other clients who had had to be dragged to her studio for a family portrait on their wife's insistence. Some men didn't think that she was capable of doing what had been known as a man's job until widowed women found themselves taking over their husbands' businesses. But that wasn't the way that it had happened for Leah. She'd inherited some of her equipment, and all of her talent, from her father. She'd been taking pictures since she was seven years old. The only reason she hadn't pursued her artistry was because she'd gotten married. And then after Owen had died, it seemed only natural that she revert back to what she knew to raise her family and bring in an income that wouldn't see her seeking charity from the Kirklands.

Oh, she really should rescue Wyatt. But she couldn't think of how at the moment. Hartzell was clever and not easily swayed. A plan quickly took shape and she headed purposefully toward the refreshment table and fixed Wyatt a plate of food. She arranged a sampling of Geneva's cooking, selecting two pieces of chicken marengo, coleslaw, macaroni pie, a jam-spread popover, and cheese straws, then strode to the loud guffaws of men—none of which belonged to Wyatt, who stood rather stoically listening to Hartzell.

As soon as she neared, the gentlemen checked themselves in her presence. She easily climbed the whitewashed steps and initiated her plan into motion. "Gentlemen, the poor man hasn't had an opportunity to eat. Mr. Holloway, why don't you come with me and I'll show you where you can sit."

"Sit?" Hartzell queried. "He can eat right here. Standing up makes the food go down easier."

Hartzell patted Wyatt on the back, took the plate from Leah, and shoved the goods at Wyatt, rendering him unable to refuse. One of the peas from the cold salad rolled over the plate's edge.

"Then why don't you forsake business for a moment while he eats," Leah suggested, meeting Wyatt's gaze and offering him a silent apology.

"It's Sunday. What else is there to do?" Hartzell claimed. "Geneva won't let me go to work, but she hasn't barred me from talking about it." His laugh was baritone and resounding, but it halted on a serious note as his bushy brows arched. "I haven't seen you at the bank to open an account, Mr. Holloway."

Wyatt didn't eat a bite of the food. "Banks and I don't get along."

Hartzell gave off another bellow. "Then you've been with the wrong bank. Part of my job is investment, Wyatt—if I may call you that. Making an orchard out of one apple seed, shall we say. My institution pays an accrued interest. You come on down tomorrow and I'll have Biggs here set up a general interest savings account."

Shifting his weight, Wyatt calmly said, "I really don't trust my money being in a bank vault."

Leah held back a gasp. You could say a great many things to Hartzell Kirkland, but you never questioned the soundness of Eternity's one and only bank, which prided itself on nightly balancing its ledgers to the penny.

"The Eternity Security Bank is as safe a bank as you'll ever find," Hartzell defended. "I've got a top notch National No. 5 fireproof, bulletproof, and bandit-proof safe. There never has been, nor will there ever be, a robbery at my bank."

Wyatt said nothing further as Geneva came up to them. "Mr. Holloway, it's nice to see you again," she said with a semblance of forced politeness because of her husband's and others' presence. Then to Hartzell, she cautioned, "Must you always talk business? And about such unpleasantries as robberies that will never happen here. Let the big cities have the outlaws. We want no part of them. They are common hoodlums and should all be locked away for life."

"I was just reassuring Wyatt here that his money would be safe from theft. I never miss an opportunity to set a man on the path of financial security. What he saves today will be his future tomorrow."

Leah found the necessary opening in the conversation and took it. "Speaking of the future, did anyone happen to see the front page of the *Eternity Tribune* yesterday? I photographed the newly completed Benevolent and Protective Order of Elks, Lodge No. 406. It's the building of tomorrow, with nearly every conceivable convenience."

"We saw it," Biggs commented. "Sheesley is not only the editor in chief of the newspaper, he's also the exalted ruler, so of course he'd want to show off the new building. He got most of the money raised for it."

"And for a worthwhile cause," Leah remarked. "The architecture is taken from the French, Queen Anne, and Romanesque. It's so lovely. And all the amenities in the lodge will be modern. I heard talk of putting in a telephone."

"Who needs a telephone?" Hartzell commented.

"I do," Geneva piped in. "I went down to the new office they're constructing, and the demonstration model should be up just in time for the Aspenglow River Stampede and Eternity Grange No. 321 Exposition. Think of it. My mother won't have to make the trip over from Bently three times a year. I can simply call her on the telephone each month."

"A phone might be just the ticket," Hartzell amended, thoughtfully puffing on his big stogie.

Wyatt stood with the plate in his hand, still untouched. He was so plainly ill at ease, Leah wished she'd never given it to him. At least Geneva was minding her manners so far. Keeping the conversation going on light topics would best insure that things stayed that way.

"Who do you think will win the World Series this year, Mr. Holloway?" Mr. Biggs asked. The accounting clerk was a great fan of the sport and never missed an opportunity to discuss baseball.

Wyatt's expression was ambiguous. "I couldn't say."

Hartzell offered his opinion. "After the Boston Red Sox trounced the Pittsburgh Pirates five games to three last year, I'm putting my money on the American League teams this year."

"You'll put our money in no such place," Geneva chided.

"Figuratively speaking, dear."

The conversation stayed on baseball and Mr. Biggs drew

in a handful of gentlemen to debate the playing capabilities of teams. Hartzell momentarily forgot about Wyatt and gave his viewpoint of namby-pamby players.

"Come with me," Leah whispered. "You can sit at a table on the porch."

Hartzell stepped away and looked amusingly at Wyatt, who was headed for the steps. "We'll talk later, Wyatt," he called, then chuckled. "I want to get the full story why you were camping on that mountain. There's something about that spot that attracts a man, but hasn't always been the sunrise like you told Bean Scudder. The last fellows to set a camp up there found a lot of gold."

Wyatt froze in his steps. "Gold?"

"A big chunk that was the foundation for this town. You could say the money those men found was what got Eternity going."

Turning, Wyatt told Leah, "I'll stand while I eat."

❧ 9 ❧

**Do not thrust your finger
through your own paper lantern.**
— Chinese proverb

Wyatt didn't have an appetite for food. He hungered for
Hartzell to elaborate about the gold, but Geneva Kirkland
hovered over him like an annoying pest.

"Is there something wrong with the food, Mr. Holloway?"

"No, ma'am."

"You haven't eaten any of it. Why not?"

Wyatt pointedly took a bite of popover and nodded his
approval. "Very good," he commented, but it was Hartzell
who drew his full attention. "You were saying these men
found some gold? When?"

"I can't think history when my mind is cooking. Let's get
out of this blasted heat, shall we, and move closer to the
house," Hartzell suggested. He strode down the gazebo's
steps as if he owned them. To Wyatt, Hartzell seemed to be
a person who got his way most of the time. He was a typical
banker: in command of the conversation, and thinking his
advice was the best and only advice. Wealth gave him a
great deal of boldness.

Rosalure rushed up to Hartzell, her springy brown curls
bouncing and her face flushed. She wore a lace-trimmed

pink dress with pleats on the skirt, and fresh roses adorned her hair. She took his hand and attempted to pull him in the direction of the lawn game with colored balls. "Poppa, come play croquet with us."

"Poppa was on his way to cool off, Rosie girl. You play without me."

"But you could be on my team and we'd win. We're playing Pinkie and her father."

Hartzell's mouth thinned. "Sim Sommercamp is a—"

"Hartzell, watch yourself," Geneva reprimanded. "Pinkie is Rosalure's friend. Besides I think you should play against Sim Sommercamp. Show him that you don't need his stale account at your bank and that you don't care that he wires his funds to that fancy Denver Bank and Trust."

Hartzell pondered the thought, then frowned. "I don't want to play him. He's a—"

Geneva lowered her voice so that Rosalure couldn't hear, but Wyatt could, and he assumed Leah could as well. "While you're playing the game, flatter him. You're very persuasive. You could sway him to transfer his money by offering him an incentive."

"You're a very shrewd woman, Geneva."

Geneva straightened, her robust bosom thrusting forward. "I take offense at that."

"None was intended, dearest." Hartzell turned fondly to Rosalure. "Okay, Rosie girl, we'll play them. Come along, Geneva, and hold my coat for me."

They walked off, leaving Wyatt and Leah alone among a flock of younger children who were running across the clipped grass while their parents conversed under the trees and sat on lawn chairs.

Wyatt stood still, though he was sorely tempted to tag after Hartzell to ask him what he'd meant by the gold. Apprehension gnawed at him. Thinking that someone had found the satchels before he could get to them tore his insides. He had to know right now, because the clench of his fingers on the plate were making his knuckles ache.

Facing Leah, his question was direct and to the point.

"Do you know anything about gold being discovered on that mountainside?"

"I didn't live here when the town was founded."

Wyatt's stomach churned. He scanned the shaded area of croquet for a glimpse of Hartzell. Finding the man with his sleeves rolled up and a mallet in his hand, laughing at something Rosalure said to him, Wyatt couldn't exactly barge in and demand to know about the gold find. It appeared as if Wyatt was going to have to wait.

With his eyes still focused on Hartzell, Wyatt asked, "How long does it take to play a game of croquet?"

"An hour or so."

Leah's reply didn't alleviate the troublesome thoughts running rampant in his mind. *An hour.* That was a long time to sweat things out. Maybe there was an explanation. Maybe it wasn't his gold coins. These hills had been full of miners in the mid-eighties. Could be that some of them struck a rich vein of gold ore. Wyatt tried to convince himself that there were a dozen possibilities, none of which was that the gold in question was his money. That made him feel somewhat better, though his stomach was still agitated.

"I didn't get you a fork for your coleslaw and macaroni," Leah dutifully said as the hostess, though Wyatt wasn't concerned. "I'm sorry you had to hold on to your plate for so long. Why don't you come this way and I'll seat you at a table on the gallery so you can eat?"

"All right," he replied, not wanting to insult her.

As he walked around the veranda, music drifted outside from the open screened windows. There was no band that Wyatt could see, but the tune was familiar to him. He'd heard it played in the plaza square of Boise City. The words sung were about the good old summertime.

"Sit here and I'll get that fork for you." Leah gestured to a round patio table. He lowered himself into the wrought-backed chair but didn't eat. His gaze once again traveled to the croquet game. Hartzell had Sim Sommercamp in a head-to-head discussion in which Sim kept nodding, his arms folded across his chest. The two children were giggling and running around a multicolored stick pounded into the grass. It wasn't a time to intrude, Wyatt concluded, and pulled his attention away.

He'd just picked up a piece of chicken when two men strode up to him and stopped several feet shy of the table to stare. One was the man who'd taken Rosalure's birthday present from him. He was a stocky fellow with a receding hairline. The other, thinner and more gaunt, had a smile that was too exaggerated. His teeth were too white and perfectly shaped for Wyatt to want to smile back at him.

A drumstick in his hand, Wyatt returned their stares. "Something I can do for you?"

"Are you Mrs. Kirkland's special guest?" the taller of the two asked.

Wyatt set the drumstick down. "I think we're all her guests."

"But she got you a plate of food. She's never gotten either one of us a plate of food, and we've been invited here before," the other replied. Sweat made a wet ring around his starched collar.

Leaning back in his chair, Wyatt stretched one booted leg outward. "If you're asking if I'm her beau, I'm not."

The two looked at each other with a great deal of relief. The toothy man extended his hand. "Leemon Winterowd, owner of Everlasting Monuments and Statuary. This is Mr. Fremont Quigley, Eternity's postmaster."

Reluctantly, Wyatt shook both gentlemen's hands. Quigley's was moist and warm. Winterowd's felt like a cold slab of headstone marble.

Quigley spoke up. "You haven't notified the post office you'd be receiving mail."

"I wasn't planning on staying too long."

Quigley and Winterowd exchanged looks, then Winterowd voiced, "That's too bad," though there wasn't too much sincerity in the tone that Wyatt could make out.

Both men remained at arm's length of the table, observing Wyatt and sizing him up as if he was a bull at an auction. "Is there anything else?"

"No," they both replied.

Leah returned with the fork and a glass of punch, stopping short when she saw the two men. Her attempt at holding back a frown wasn't successful, for Wyatt saw her displeasure. "Mr. Winterowd and Mr. Quigley. I see you've met Mr. Holloway."

"We have, Mrs. Kirkland," Quigley said with a broad grin that emphasized his double chin. "He won't be staying in town for very long."

"No, Mrs. Kirkland." Winterowd shook his head with a *tsk* and a smile that was nothing but long teeth. "Not long. Got to be moving on soon, he said."

Wyatt had said no such thing, but he didn't contradict the man. He noticed that both Winterowd and Quigley called Leah Mrs. Kirkland. They apparently weren't casual friends. A degree of satisfaction filled Wyatt at Leah's invitation to address her by her given name. He shared something with her that these men did not.

Handing him the fork, Leah surprised Wyatt by sitting in the chair across from him. "If you gentlemen would be so kind as to select another recording and keep the Edison cranked for me. Fern Sommercamp has been in charge for the past hour and all she plays is 'In the Good Old Summertime.'"

"Surely I can, Mrs. Kirkland," Winterowd countered.

"The pleasure is mine, Mrs. Kirkland," Quigley assured.

Then the two men went into the house through the double-curtained doors and the music was immediately interrupted with a scratching noise.

"There goes that record," Leah announced with a frown.

Wyatt didn't know exactly how an Edison worked. He'd seen them in Corn's store, but he hadn't ever operated one.

Leah toyed with a flower petal that had come down from one of the roses in a bouquet that was the table's centerpiece. Wyatt couldn't help staring at her, much in the same way that Winterowd and Quigley had: with deep longing. She was a handsome woman, and looked especially handsome this afternoon. He liked her dress, the way the soft fabric caressed her breasts. Her blouse sleeves molded against her arms, the cuffs straight and trimmed with cutout beaded lace.

Wyatt slid his fork back and forth in a small motion across the tabletop. "I didn't mean to slight your photography the other day."

"I'm sure you didn't."

He wasn't fully convinced she felt that way. "I'm sure you're good at what you do, and because you're a woman doesn't mean that you can't be a photographer—if that's what you were thinking I was thinking."

"The thought had crossed my mind," she confessed openly. "Only because it's happened before."

"Well, that's not my reason. I just don't like my picture taken."

Leah's eyes were forgiving, and the brows above them arched with thoughtfulness. "I'll respect your wishes. But if you change your mind, I think you'd take a fine picture."

Wyatt felt better that they'd gotten that straightened out. Picking up the fork, he tried a bite of each savory dish and realized that he was hungry. Leah said nothing as he ate, and oddly, he wasn't uncomfortable while she watched him. He was used to sitting with a full table. With Leah, he relaxed as she rolled the flower petal beneath her fingers while alternately gazing at the people in her yard and shyly at him. The fragrance of roses perfumed around him. Settling into his chair, he allowed himself some time to enjoy the food and the silent company of the woman across from him.

When he was finished and full, he commented, "You're a fine cook. It's been longer than you could believe since I've eaten this well."

Leah laughed, but he didn't understand the reason for her humor.

"What?"

Through a wide smile she embellished, "I can't cook worth a darn. Why do you think I eat so often at the Happy City? The kitchen isn't a friendly place to me. I've tried, but *non va bene.*"

When she spoke in that Italian, the inflections got to him. They sounded as if she should be saying them in a bedroom. Actually, whispering them in his ear in a bedroom.

"Geneva prepared the food," Leah admitted. "She's the one you should be complimenting."

"I'd rather be complimenting you." The words slipped out before Wyatt could take them back. Like some infatuated fool without an ounce of common sense, he'd said the first thing that had come to his mind.

He should have been relieved when she didn't become coy with him and lower her lashes. And yet when a look of discomfort crossed her face, he was disappointed. "I don't need compliments. I'm a fair judge of my attributes, and thus far I haven't done anything deserving of praise."

"That's a pretty hard statement."

"No," she countered seriously, "it's a true statement. It's just that there is one thing in my life that I haven't attained. I dream of it often, and until I fulfill that dream I don't believe in undue flattery. If I win, and if you're still here, you may compliment me to your heart's desire and I shall revel in your every word."

Whatever she was after sounded important. "What is it you want to win?"

Leah tipped her head to the side and stole a slanted look at him. "The New York Amateur Photography contest. It's sponsored by a magazine and judged by Alfred Stieglitz, a famous photographer. This year will be my third submission and my third try at first place."

"Is that why you were taking pictures of dishes?"

"Heavens, no. I wouldn't enter a photograph of something so mundane as a saucer from my china cupboard." An instant of wistfulness entered her expression as she put the tip of her forefinger to her lips, pulling his attention toward her mouth. "After giving my prior two submissions a strong critique, I realized I misunderstood the creative freedom of my profession. To win the contest, I believe that I need to replicate something with a balance to the picture by gentle but firm counterposition. The points of deepest conjunction generally lie in the center of the picture. Therein was my error with the picture of the clouds last year. They were a good subject for an artist who sought the broad, poetic view of things. But there was no life to them." She mused a moment, then continued, though he had little clue as to what she was trying to convey to him. "Clouds provide an inexhaustible supply of infinitely variable forms, richer and less predictable than everyday images, but that is just that. Clouds are everyday images. I need to think along the lines of the extraordinary. But thus far, the only soul my camera has captured that I would feel comfortable entering is Mr. Quigley's dog, Skeeter, lying down on my porch with a dead gopher in his muzzle. This may not sound winning, but the dog came to my porch on his own with the gopher, lay down, and seemingly awaited for me to snap him before he went along his merry way." Leah shrugged. "Though you probably wouldn't see it my way, Skeeter was an inspiration."

Wyatt drank the last of his punch. The only relevant thought he could offer was, "It sounds like you know what you're doing. I bet you win this time."

"False hope doesn't soothe disappointment when it comes."

And Wyatt knew that. He'd had his hope minced and cut up so many times, it was amazing he'd even held on to any at all.

Music came to them, sung in that foreign language he'd first heard when he'd entered town. He didn't understand a word of it then, nor did he now. But he finally realized that the music hadn't been performed by someone in her parlor. It was coming from the Edison.

"Do you like opera?" Leah asked, breaking Wyatt from his thoughts.

He toyed with his glass, rolling the bottom in a tight circle while his fingers lightly held the rim. "I don't know. I can't make out what they're saying."

"They're singing in French. Mr. Winterowd and Mr. Quigley found my Delibes. They know I'm partial to 'Lakmé.'"

Wyatt sat back. "I think it's those two who are partial to you."

One corner of Leah's mouth pulled into a slight smile.

"Yes, I know. Trust me when I say I don't encourage their attentions. Geneva invited them. She thinks she can pair Leemon and Fremont with the Clinkingbeard sisters."

"Did somebody say our names?" The question came in unison as two women strolled around the gallery to the table.

Wyatt gazed at the twins, taken aback at how their looks mirrored each other perfectly, from their matching feather hats right down to their patent shoes. He couldn't tell one from the other as they gaped at him expectantly.

It took Wyatt a second to remember he should rise to his feet. When he did, Leah introduced him.

"This is Netha and Wilene Clinkingbeard. Ladies, this is Mr.—"

"We know," Netha said, stretching out her gloved hand in a manner that told Wyatt she was presuming he'd kiss her fingers. Instead, he awkwardly took her hand in his and gave her wrist a slight shake. He did likewise for Wilene. Both tittered in what sounded to be harmony.

He waited for them to move on, but they didn't.

"We've seen you at the Chinese restaurant," Netha said.

"Yes. Sister and I eat there every Saturday. We were there last night." Wilene's eyes were wide and blue as a pair of delft saucers. "Did you see us?"

Wyatt hadn't noticed them. "I get pretty busy in the back."

Leah had opened her mouth and was about to say something when a towheaded boy came dashing across the nicely appointed veranda with its colorful potted plants placed in between the spindles of the porch banister. Not several feet behind him was Tug, closing in, both hands raised and holding toy guns.

"Jary Keithly, you slow down this minute," Leah admonished.

"Pow! Pow! Pow!" Tug spouted. He accidently knocked over a terra-cotta pot with the toe of his boot. Fluffy coral geraniums and clumps of soil tumbled out. "I got you, Jary!"

Leah quickly moved to stand in front of Tug so he could get no farther. "Excuse me, Mister Cowboy. What do you call that?" She dropped her hand on his head and turned him to face the overturned geraniums.

"I didn't do it."

"Of course you didn't."

The Clinkingbeard twins sniffed in an affronted manner at the young boys. Wyatt thought it was a good thing neither sister had married, for they seemed to have no tolerance for children.

"We should ask if Geneva needs our help serving the cake," Wilene said, giving Tug a disapproving purse of her lips.

"Yes, we must ask if she needs our help." Netha nodded in agreement. Then the pair went off, their skirts swaying in sync with one another.

Tug lowered his guns into his sagging holsters to approach Wyatt. "Hey, mister, I got my hat back." He took off the Roughrider Roy hat and held it out to Wyatt. "It's got a real jet bead on the strings. Made from genuine Indian rock."

"Looks like a fine one," Wyatt said, testing the brim and giving the hat his full attention before returning it to Tug. "You must have been a good boy."

"Yeah. I didn't do anything bad all week."

Leah smiled. "Nothing overly bad."

"And see these guns?" Tug exclaimed, disregarding Leah's observance. "They shoot real bullets and I could kill a man dead if I took a mind to."

"Tug, they don't shoot real bullets, and you will not go around threatening to kill anyone," Leah corrected.

"They do too," he insisted. "And I wouldn't *really* kill anyone, much less him. He let me ride his horse."

Wyatt noted the boy's Wild West woolly chaps were a size too big for him. They'd had that brand around since he'd been a little guy. Tug also wore a leather vest with a beat-up tin star on the breast and mule-ear cowboy boots. He was ready for a shootout.

"Who you aiming to go after, Marshal?" Wyatt asked,

playing around with the boy and enjoying every minute of it.

Tug's face lit up. "I'm hunting down those bad guys from the O.K. Corral."

Wyatt was impressed by the kid's imagination. "Where's this O.K. Corral, Marshal?"

Tug scowled. "You never heard of the O.K. Corral and the Earp brothers? You're named after one."

"Oh . . . sure. Them." But Wyatt didn't know. He'd picked his name after his Uncle Wyatt Harper who lived in Eastdale, not some Earp brothers.

"Tug, I want you to be my helper and gather all the children to the cake table. It's time to sing happy birthday to Rosalure. Can you do that for Momma?"

"Can I have a piece with an icing flower?"

"I'm sure that can be arranged."

Tug scampered off, hollering for kids to follow him.

Leah gazed at Wyatt with soft color on her lips and her lashes thick and sweeping. She lifted her hand to adjust the wayward strand of hair beneath her chin, but the curl didn't cooperate. The tendril fell right back down after she tried to tuck it in her bun. His response to her was strong, his heartbeat pounding in his ears.

"You look real pretty today, Leah."

A blush colored her cheeks the same shade as the roses filling the yard. "Thank you, Wyatt. You look especially nice, too."

"A little spit and polish," he said with a shrug and a smile.

She laughed. "Come this way and we'll join the others."

Wyatt followed her around the veranda. Behind the rear-entry door was a large porch and patio where ivy had been trained to grow up trellises. The area was lush and green, sprinkled with color from hanging flowers the names of which he didn't know. There was a circular table covered with a silver cloth, and in its center a white frosted cake decorated with pink roses. Rosalure stood in front of the cake with Geneva behind her as guests circled round. Tug had a close-up view on Rosalure's left, his nose twitching as he sniffed the sugary frosting. Hartzell was off to the side, still talking with Sim Sommercamp.

"Excuse me," Leah said, and took her place by Rosalure so they could light the ten candles on the cake. Soon everyone broke out into the song of "Happy Birthday."

Wyatt stayed back, leaning against a post with one of his legs crossed over the other. He'd thought he'd be able to listen without thinking of the other times he'd heard the words. But he couldn't. Unbidden, he saw Ardythe, Daniel, Robert, Todd, and Mary, his brothers and sisters. They had sung at birthdays, too, only the trimmings had never been as fancy as this. They'd been a poor ranching family, but a tight-knit family. Though Wyatt had been the man of the house when his dad had been away working, times had been hard for him. There were a lot of pressures and he'd felt every one of them by the age of fourteen. It had been the year Mary was born that Wyatt had fallen into trouble and had to leave. She'd been only three months old. For her, he'd never sung "Happy Birthday."

Softly singing it now, he tried to envision what Mary looked like. What the others looked like. If they'd married. How they were getting on. If he was an uncle. If the home place was still there. He wondered how his parents were. If they'd fared well in years kinder to them than the ones he'd lived.

But he'd have to go on wondering. It was better that everyone back home thought he was dead. And the truth was, that boy they had known so long ago really was. He'd thrown away his whole life, and there was no point in digging up a grave that would only cause heartache.

He watched Leah singing, their eyes meeting for a second before she lowered them lovingly onto Rosalure's face. How old would he be when he got to sing to his child? He had no prospects for a wife. And the one woman for whom he felt something was a banker's daughter-in-law.

"Happy birthday, dear Rosalure," the party attendants sang, "Happy birthday to you!"

Wyatt's throat had closed up, and the hot sting of tears swelled in his eyes, but he refused to succumb to any show of emotion. He was beyond that. For him, the road only went one way. Forward, away from Utah and what he'd left behind. What was gone would have to stay that way. He had to make his own family now.

❄ 10 ❄

**Blame yourself if you have no branches or
leaves; don't accuse the sun of partiality.**
                              —Chinese proverb

Leah's house was nearly empty. All of the guests had left but
immediate family and Wyatt. They'd retired into the parlor
where the cooler air was more comfortable for conversation
while sipping refreshment from the armchairs and davenport. On a side area of the cabbage-rose carpet, Rosalure
and Tug played with Punch and Judy puppets—the present
from Hartzell and Geneva.

Coming from the kitchen with a fresh pitcher of ice tea,
Leah asked, "More tea anyone?"

Hartzell nodded, then turned his attention back to Wyatt,
who sat in the overstuffed wing chair by the hearth. That
was Leah's favorite chair, and she'd made it available to
Wyatt because he looked as if he was suffering from the
effects of uneasiness. When the others had begun to leave,
he'd stayed. But not without reluctance. To Leah's observa-
tion, he was searching to speak with Hartzell, only Hartzell
was still busy with Mr. Sommercamp. The Sommercamps
were the last guests to depart, and Wyatt had attempted to
engage Hartzell's attention, but by this time, Hartzell was
ready to sit down and stretch his feet out while watching his

grandchildren play. Wyatt had followed him inside and Leah had directed him to the chair. That had been fifteen minutes ago, and the tension in the room hadn't lessened while she'd left to get the tea.

Wyatt lifted his gaze to hers and declined the beverage. "I'm fine," he said. His fingers meshed together over the crown of his hat resting in his lap, then he slipped them apart to rest his hands on the arms of the chair. She noticed the band had made an impression on his dark brown hair. She had an urge to smooth away the ripple, to feel the texture of his hair beneath her hand. He caught her looking at him and she quickly turned away.

Leah freshened Hartzell's glass, then set the pitcher on a tea cart and sat down herself. The children were exceptionally quiet in their play as they acted out the voices of the characters they wiggled on their hands. Geneva sat erect on the davenport, her skirts fanned around her ankles and her eyes leveled on Wyatt.

"That was a very extravagant gift you gave our Rosalure," Geneva ventured. "A music box like that wouldn't be affordable to most men of your position. You must be very frugal with your pay."

Wyatt made no comment other than, "I thought she'd like it."

"I do like it. Very much." Rosalure lifted her head with a smile, then she paused from the puppets a moment to wind up the music box beside her, near her other presents. "It plays one of my favorite tunes."

"The music box is wonderful," Leah added, wanting to throttle Geneva. "Thank you again for your thoughtfulness."

Wyatt's eyes slid away from Rosalure to rest on Leah. Her heart started its crazy double-fast thumping. That magic spark sprang into the air between them again.

"We didn't see you in St. John's this morning," Geneva said, her tone cool enough to douse Leah's slipping composure. "What denomination are you?"

"I was dunked in the Baptist church," he said with quiet emphasis. "But the waters didn't soak in."

Geneva's eyes rounded at the bluntness of Wyatt's admission. "I take it you don't believe in the Lord, then."

"If I didn't believe in the Lord, I wouldn't be alive."

As much as Leah's curiosity was piqued about Wyatt's background, she didn't want Geneva taking a piece out of his hide.

"Mr. Holloway, would you care for another slice of cake?" Leah intervened.

"No, thank you," Wyatt declined. "Although it was the best cake I've ever eaten. You're a fine cook, Mrs. Kirkland."

Smart move, Leah thought. Compliments were best served to Geneva when she was in a mood to get to the bottom of someone's personal nature.

Geneva was momentarily waylaid by the flattery. "That's good of you to say, Mr. Holloway." Keeping a pleased blush at bay, she plucked at one of the full gathers in her novelty gauze skirt. "I was well tutored by my mother when I was younger. I believe that is one of the reasons I landed my Hartzell. He was appreciative of the supper table I could set."

Hartzell leaned his arm over the back of the davenport, but not so that his hand rested on Geneva's shoulder. "I don't doubt that good cooking is desirable in a wife, but there are other things to consider as well."

"Which are?" Geneva asked in a pretentious tone that Leah hated. She knew where this was leading.

"Compatibility," Hartzell replied.

"But is that enough?" Geneva pondered aloud.

Geneva had always made it clear that she didn't think Leah was a suitable bride for her one and only son. He'd been educated at Harvard and had graduated with high honors. From there, he'd gone into business with his father in the financial end of the Eternity Security Bank, traveling to cities and seeking sound investments.

Leah didn't want to think that initially Owen had regarded her and her father as charity cases. But in all likelihood, he had. For he'd heard about the misfortunes of the nine-year-old girl and her father. That had been Leah, and she'd been going through the worst time in her life. If it hadn't been for Owen, she and her father would have lost everything. Even hope. Owen had been her savior of sorts.

But his family was upper-class, while Leah had come from humble stock. At first, Geneva never missed an opportunity to point this out. But now that Tug and Rosalure were older, she had to mind her tongue more often because of the children's presence. Which suited Leah fine.

"I thought the party was a success," Hartzell offered after taking a sip of his tea. "You two women outdid yourselves."

It was nice that Hartzell tried to include Leah, and she appreciated that. She'd never had any reservations about his sincerity.

"It was a lovely party," Leah added. "Most everyone could come."

"Everyone I invited came," Geneva mentioned. "Who did you invite who didn't?"

"Mr. Wang."

Geneva had nothing to say on the subject of Leo Wang, and Leah counted the small blessing.

Wyatt fingered the brim of his hat. "Leo said to say happy birthday, Rosalure."

"Oh, that was nice," she replied.

Leah turned to Wyatt. "Leo told me how much your help at the restaurant has improved business."

Hartzell set his cup down on the plant stand next to him. "Scudder put the claws into you to get that job, didn't he?"

"I needed a job."

"And he probably said he'd run you out of town if you didn't have one," Hartzell remarked wryly. "You can say a lot of things about Bean Scudder, not all of them kindly, in my opinion. Some men think that just because they've been appointed to a civic position, they can tell people what to do and run lives with the excuse that it's for their own good. Scudder is too dumb to hold down any other job, so I guess it's all our bad luck we have to put up with him." Hartzell took out a pipe and a bag of tobacco. "Surely you've got other aspirations than being a dishwasher, Wyatt. What are they?"

Leah glanced nervously at Wyatt, waiting for him to reply, yet at the same time not blaming him if he didn't. In a small way, Hartzell had insulted him. Maybe Wyatt liked being a dishwasher.

Wyatt sat straighter. Stiffer. He ran his palms down his denim-covered thighs, then cleared his throat. "Cattle. I've got my mind set on picking up a spread."

"That's a tall order. Takes a lot of money," Hartzell countered while packing the tobacco in his pipe. "And sound investments are what make the money."

"You could say I've already got an investment."

Hartzell paused with a lit match in his hand. "Where?"

"Not far from here."

"Whatever interest they're paying you, our bank will offer the better return. I can guarantee you that."

Hartzell puffed on his pipe, the smell an odor that did not offend Leah.

"I'd thought about mining," Wyatt said slowly. "Though I'm no expert, your mountain land looked like it had some potential."

Geneva, who had been quiet for the better part of three minutes, could be silent no longer. "Where is it you said you were from, Mr. Holloway?"

Wyatt was visibly disturbed by her sudden inquiry, but he supplied her with an answer—albeit a curt one. "Moab, Utah." Then to Hartzell, he continued. "Have you ever had the land tested?"

"As I said, some fellows found gold up there." Hartzell puffed thoughtfully. "That was back in eighty-eight, a year after this place started putting up tents. The country was overrun with miners back then. A group of them cut a shaft into Infinity Hill—right where that cross is, and I'll be damned if they didn't come up with a cache of big money. Wish it had been me with them, but I was just getting started and couldn't afford to put up the collateral for the mining equipment. They came out richer than anyone would have ever expected. Sunk most of it into the city. Sheesley at the newspaper was one of them. He bought a whole city block. Beaumont at the Beaumont Hotel was another. Wright at the opera house got his start because of it. And three other men made out good. But they took their shares back east. One's a broker now on the New York Stock Exchange."

Leah thought she saw Wyatt's face pale a shade. "How much did they come out with?"

"Newspaper never reported it. Sheesley didn't want anyone to know."

"Anything unusual about the find?" Wyatt smoothed his hair from his forehead. Leah followed the movement of his strong and slightly trembling hand.

"Nothing save that that was the only gold ever found in these hills. Others dug around after that, but nobody ever found anything."

"Mr. Holloway, are you ill?" Geneva asked with real concern. "You don't look well. Leah, get him a glass of water."

Before Leah could get up, Wyatt stopped her. "I don't need any water."

He slumped back into the chair, his eyes distant. His expression was overtaken with grief and a misery she could actually feel. He looked as if he'd just found out someone close to him had passed away.

"Are you sure I can't get you that water?" she pressed.

"I'm sure."

"But you look as if you've seen a ghost," Geneva observed, sitting forward on the cushion of the sofa.

At the mention of a ghost, Tug lifted his head. "Where's a ghost?"

Geneva smiled at him. "There is no ghost, darling. That was just Nanna talking figuratively."

Tug returned his attention to the puppet, making noises and head strikes at the one Rosalure was operating. She stuck her tongue out at him, but he merely giggled at her.

During the exchange, Wyatt seemed to have collected himself. He rubbed his brow with his fingertips, his forehead furrowed in deep thought as he gazed at Hartzell. "How did they explain the apricot cans?"

"What apricot cans?" Hartzell tapped his pipe on the ashtray at his disposal.

Wyatt sat straighter, his brows pulled into a tight frown. "You mean they didn't find gold coins?"

"Never saw gold that came out of the ground already minted into coins. Why would you think that?"

Shifting in the chair, Wyatt shrugged. "I heard rumors that miners in these parts stored their money in old tin cans before a bank hit a town. I just wondered if that's what was found."

"No, what they found was ore. Pockets of it. Took them weeks to pick it all out. Then the vein just died. Too much sandstone up there and not enough mineral rock. Not only that, too many landslides. That section where they found the gold must have slid twenty feet down toward town after all these years."

To Leah's total surprise, Wyatt laughed. Rich and deep. A relieved sound, and a little too loosely to be considered in good taste. Geneva sputtered at the outburst and Rosalure wanted to know what was so funny.

"Nothing." He shook his head and planted his boots firmly on the floor beneath him as he tried to rein in his laughter. "I'm sorry."

"Well I should say so," Geneva remarked. "In our family, we don't display such tasteless outbursts."

"Perhaps we should," Hartzell added, tapping out his pipe. "You're a little too stiff, Geneva."

Geneva glared at him, then settled her observant eyes back on Wyatt. "As I said, our family conducts itself with restrain."

"Maybe his family doesn't."

"What kind of family do you have, Mr. Holloway?" Geneva inquired, using the change in subject to her advantage.

Wyatt's smile dimmed, though his spirits didn't darken too much when he admitted, "My family is gone."

Geneva's brow lifted. "Are they departed?"

"Yes."

"Such a shame. I know how devastating that is. My

Owen, Leah's husband, left us. I grieve for him still. No one can replace him in the children's lives. They would be better off with no father than a replacement. I can give little Owen what he needs, and Rosalure is my sweet girl. Leah doesn't need another husband; she has Hartzell and me to take care of her."

Hartzell stood. "Geneva, I think you're beginning to overstep your bounds. It's time for us to go."

She went to her feet with a protest. "But I'm not ready to go home."

Leah rose, and Wyatt did likewise. He held on to his hat, exchanging glances with her. She didn't want him to leave yet. Not when they'd finally have an opportunity to sit and quietly talk. "Mr. Holloway, stay a moment and I'll get some cake for you to take home."

Geneva bustled, "Hartzell, I can't leave. I have to help Leah clean up. There are lots of dishes to do. I'll get that cake for Mr. Holloway so he can be on his way." She attempted a beeline for the kitchen, but Leah stood in her way.

"That's not necessary, Geneva. I can manage the cake. And as for the dishes, I'm too tired to clean up tonight. I'll get up first thing tomorrow and take care of them."

Geneva was appalled. "You can honestly say you have no qualms about going to bed with dirty dishes in the kitchen?"

"No, I don't. The dishes can wait until I'm in the mood to tackle them."

"But I say never put off until tomorrow what you can do today."

Geneva's attempt at assistance was transparent. Leah's mother-in-law was against the idea of Wyatt staying in the house with her. Not only that, but Geneva was a hypocrite. She never did dishes. Posie, her housekeeper, did all the cleaning. Whenever Geneva did make the attempt, she complained that the dishwater gave her a rash. And as soon as her skin reddened, she would quit helping, to apply numerous lotions and vegetable glycerin. By then, her hands were too slick and she couldn't hold a dish to dry it. So she ended up sitting on a kitchen stool directing Leah's culinary conduct with advice that was more often than not critical.

"Hartzell, I really can't leave until I get the kitchen in order. I won't sleep until every dish is put away."

"I'll help Leah with them." Wyatt's forthright offer surprised Leah, but none more than Geneva. Her mouth dropped open.

"You'll help her? You're a man."

"If a woman can be a photographer, a man can wash the dishes in her home. It is what I do for a living."

"Yes, but . . ."

For the first time Leah could remember, Geneva was speechless.

"There, not to worry," Leah said, walking her in-laws toward the foyer.

"But you two will be alone in the house," Geneva blurted.

Hartzell lay his hand at the small of Geneva's back. "What do you call the children? Do you think our Leah would engage in hanky-panky in front of them?"

"I should hope not!"

"Then don't worry."

Hartzell took his hat from the hall table. Rosalure went to her grandfather and hugged him. "Thank you for the puppets, Poppa."

He kissed the top of her head. "You're welcome, Rosie girl. Happy birthday."

Then Rosalure embraced her grandmother. "I loved my cake, Nanna. Thank you for decorating it for me."

"Any time, darling." Geneva tied the wide sash of her hat beneath her chin, all the while staring hard at Wyatt. "No, this isn't proper. Forget about the dishes, Leah. I'll send Posie over in the morning. Mr. Holloway, you needn't stay."

"I haven't given him his extra cake yet," Leah replied, rather enjoying having the upper hand over Geneva for a change.

Hartzell kissed Leah on the cheek and gave her shoulders a squeeze. "If you need anything, you call on me."

Leah nodded.

Geneva gave her a perfunctory hug. "I shouldn't have made mention of it."

"But you did."

"Owen," Geneva called. "Come give Nanna a kiss good-bye."

Tug's chin lifted and he hopped to his feet. His shirt had a red stain of punch down the buttoned front, and the corners of his mouth were sporting a mustache of the same color. He dutifully kissed his grandmother.

Geneva didn't budge when Hartzell grasped the door-knob. She imposed an iron will and drew a deep breath. "You run along without me, Hartzell."

"Geneva, I'll do no such thing. I need a good night's rest without you fiddling with the shower pipes after I'm in bed. Tomorrow is a workday for me and Sommercamp is coming by first thing in the morning to talk about a transfer."

"But—"

"No buts. Let's go."

Hartzell opened the door and took Geneva with him down the steps. She turned once, glancing at Leah. Then Wyatt. Reluctantly, she faced forward and went down the walk with her husband as Leah closed the door.

Turning, Leah returned to the parlor. The children had abandoned the puppets and were engrossed in the Ouija board Pinkie Sommercamp had given Rosalure. Wyatt stood by the hearth with one hand lazily tucked inside his pocket. His hat had been casually tossed onto the chair. Ordinarily she was in complete command of herself when in the company of gentlemen, but Wyatt was handsome enough to make her go weak at the knees. She had the strongest urge to hug him.

Rather than give in to her whim, she said, "You were kind to save me, Wyatt, but you don't have to wash the dishes."

"Good, because I didn't really want to. I just wanted to get her out of the house for you."

Leah's teasing laughter bubbled from her throat. "Do you dare come into the kitchen with me for that cake? Or will all those dirty dishes make you want to run?"

"They might," he said in a low voice. "But if you're in there, I'll stick around and not look at anything but you."

She grew giddy, like a young girl attending her first dance. She didn't dare let him see how he was affecting her. Things were happening at a rapid pace all of a sudden. She didn't know how best to handle her feelings. They were foreign and new. Leah Kirkland never flirted with men; she was too serious for that. But she found herself engaged in the fun of light banter with Wyatt and enjoying every minute of it.

Picking up the empty glasses, she walked into the kitchen, Wyatt behind her.

Even to her, the room was unpleasant with the stacks of plates, mounds of silverware in the sink, and dishes, cups, and dessert service taking up all the available counter space.

Wyatt came alongside her at the sink. His sleeve barely brushed hers. But enough so that she shivered with warmth as he said, "Maybe we ought to do these."

"Heavens, no." Leah turned her eyes to his. "Geneva said she'd send Posie over in the morning. I intend to make her keep her word. She offered."

"She only offered because she didn't want me here with you."

"It's not you personally. She doesn't want me to be with anyone other than her son. And that's quite impossible."

Wyatt reflected softly, "Sounds to me like she thinks you should have buried your heart with her son."

Lowering her eyes, Leah gazed at the span of his chest, the soft billow of his shirt where the tails tucked into his trousers, the iridescent gleam of his buttons as they caught the light from the kitchen's electrical fixture.

His large hand took her chin and gently lifted it. A familiar shiver raced through her. "You're a good woman, Leah. Don't let her hold you prisoner. Go on living."

Leah's heart thundered and she could barely think. *Go on living.* Such a natural statement, and one she'd adhered to. But that was before Wyatt brought complexity into the meaning. She hadn't realized how little living she'd done until she met him. He'd showed her without words that creativity couldn't revolve around the four walls of her studio. Seeing the beauty that he had found in the colors and sounds of the outdoors had given her a new perspective and dimension in a world that she'd viewed through her camera, yet hadn't seen until she'd seen it through his eyes.

Needing a minute to gather her thoughts, Leah went to the sideboard where the leftover cake had been set out. An unsettling combination of emotions rocked her. She felt as if she was on the brink of falling in love, but she couldn't let herself surrender. The timing was horrible. She was leaving Eternity. Wyatt was leaving Eternity. Each was headed down his own separate path of life.

"Where do you intend to ranch?" she asked with her back to him, forcing herself not to think about what could never be. She grasped a knife and reached for a clean plate.

"Montana. Wyoming. Wherever I can find the best land for the best price."

Despite her resolve, her hand on the knife stilled. "Would you ever consider Eternity?"

Wyatt's answer was delayed, then he replied in a voice that seemed to come from a long way, "I don't think I could."

Leah let out her breath, unaware that she'd been holding it.

"What about you?" He strode to the table. She liked the man-sound of heavy steps in her kitchen. They made her think of strength and the large man wearing the boots. "What happens if you win that contest?"

"Well, I'd win five thousand dollars for starters."

"Jesus. Five thousand."

"Yes. Mr. Stieglitz is very generous."

"You mentioned him before."

"He's a genius."

Wyatt leaned his hip against the sideboard's edge. "I've never met a genius before."

She sensed a hint of a smile in his tone, and she boldly met his eyes to defend her mentor. "Mr. Stieglitz really is a genius photographer. And if I win, I'll be welcome in his New York gallery where I can study from the master himself. He can teach me what it takes to be famous."

She didn't mention that her Italy trip might interfere—provided she was accepted into the Veneto Academy. She'd return to the states immediately if she won. Nothing could keep her from the Little Galleries on Fifth Avenue if Mr. Stieglitz invited her there. Absolutely nothing.

"What about Tug and Rosalure?"

"They'd come with me."

"To a big city?"

"Certainly. The city is full of culture and the arts."

Wyatt folded his arms across his chest. "There wouldn't be any place for Tug to go fishing."

"I'd hire a carriage to take us into the country on the weekends."

"But it wouldn't be the same as having a river at your back door any time you wanted to see it rushing over rocks."

"No . . ." Leah cut a big wedge of cake and covered the plate with an unused linen napkin. "But there would be other things for the children to do. Museums. The Metropolitan Opera house. Libraries."

"Rosalure couldn't collect flowers."

They'd reached a point in the conversation where Leah didn't want to continue. She'd thought of what Rosalure and Tug would be losing, but she'd also thought of what they'd be gaining. Broader experiences, wider knowledge, and opportunities that didn't come along in a small town like Eternity.

She handed the plate to Wyatt. "This should take care of your sweet tooth."

"Thanks." His clear, observant eyes prolonged the moment. She sensed he could read through her. Guess that she had her reservations about whisking her children to New York, much less Italy. But she'd reasoned the trip would be good for them. It wasn't as if they were never coming back to Eternity.

"I wonder what the children are up to?" Leah mused, ducking out from Wyatt's gaze. "It's quiet in the parlor."

She went toward the swinging door, pushing through with Wyatt behind her.

Only Rosalure sat on the carpet in the corner. The Ouija board had been abandoned for tiddledywinks. The colorful buttons were strewn across the carpet. Tug was nowhere in sight.

Rosalure came to Leah with a beribboned basket filled with bath salts and other toiletry articles. "Look, Momma. I got crab apple blossoms toilet soap for my bath. And even real perfume." Hooking the handle through her arms, she picked up an atomizer and puffed some of the fragrance on Leah's hand. "It's genuine Eau de Cologne No. 4711, used by the royal and imperial families of Europe. The bottle says so."

Leah fought the urge to sneeze. The perfume was pleasant but too sweet for her tastes. And she doubted royalty used a fragrance given a number of authenticity, but she didn't discourage Rosalure's faith in the product. "It's an exquisite smell."

Rosalure doused herself with the Eau de Cologne No. 4711, then went back to her pile of presents to sort through the goodies she'd gotten. This time Leah did sneeze. "A little lighter hand next time, Rosalure. A lady never dips herself with perfume."

"But I wanted to smell sweet as a kiss. The bottle says that, too. That if you put on a lot, that's what you'll smell like."

"Yes, well . . ." Leah cleared her throat and gave Wyatt a hasty glance. He stood next to the hearth perusing her wedding portrait on the mantel. "I think at even the mature age of ten years old, you don't need to smell sweet as a kiss. There isn't anyone you should be kissing."

Rosalure's cheeks turned pink, and she whispered beneath her breath to her mother, "I think I would let Donny kiss me."

Leah kept her own voice soft. "You'll do no such thing."

Then she strode to Wyatt. He thoughtfully kept his gaze on the photograph. "This is your husband?"

"Yes."

"He was quite older than you."

"Twelve years." Though the difference had seemed much broader than that. Owen wasn't much for spontaneity. He wore his tie rather tightly. Leah wondered how old Wyatt was. She guessed he was in his mid to late thirties. The same age as Owen would have been. But with Wyatt, age seemed to be a matter of feeling. He didn't show his years through his speech and manner. He acted as if life were just beginning for him, rather than being half gone.

The upstairs lavatory flushed and Tug came thundering down the steps and rounded the pocket door opening to the parlor, not missing an opportunity to disturb the tasseled fringe hanging from the grille.

"Tug, you didn't do anything just now, did you?" Leah asked, over the sound of rushing water through the pipe in the wall.

"Yeah. I went to pee."

"Oh, honestly. We didn't need to hear that."

"But you asked me."

Wyatt cracked a smile and ruffled Tug's hair. "You did ask the boy."

"Yes, well, my mistake." Then to the children, "It's time to clean up and get ready for bed."

"But I'm hungry," Tug complained.

"You've been eating something or other all day." Leah lay her hand on his shoulder and directed him toward the stairs. "I'll be up in a minute to fill the bathtub."

Rosalure held as many of her gifts in her arms as she could manage. "Momma, when he's done with the bath, can I fill it with my crab apple blossom soaps?"

"Yes."

With a smile, Rosalure mounted the steps behind her brother. That left Leah and Wyatt alone in the room. The surroundings became very quiet. Only the ticking of the clocks could be heard. And perhaps Leah's beating heart. For some reason, she was very aware that they had been left on their own. It wasn't as if she hadn't been in her parlor on numerous occasions with gentlemen. But those gentlemen had come seeking her services, or in the case of Mr. Winterowd and Mr. Quigley, they'd come to discuss their observances of her attributes, conversations she found very embarrassing. But she knew how to handle those men. She was smarter than them and she could usually figure out what they were thinking before they said it. That gave her the upper hand. With Wyatt, she hadn't a clue as to what could be on his mind. His face was unreadable. Holding the plate, he stood there, putting his weight on his right leg, his hip semicocked and causing her attention to fall in the general direction of his abdomen.

"Would you care to sit down?" she offered.

"I should go."

"You don't have to."

"But I should." He reached for his hat and put it on. Then he walked toward her and her breathing hitched. Coming very close, he walked by. That masculine scent she'd detected on him earlier was still there. Still appealing to her senses. She, on the other hand, smelled too strongly of Corn's emporium perfume.

Leah escorted him to the door. Once there, Wyatt turned to face her.

"Thanks for the invite," he said, leaning into the jamb.

"You're welcome. Though I don't know how much you could have enjoyed the party. Geneva can be . . . well, herself. And Hartzell likes to talk only of the bank."

"It was a family gathering, and they sometimes go that way."

Leah felt a pang in his words. "How long has it been since you lost your family?"

"Too long to be feeling like I miss them."

Without thought, Leah rested a comforting hand on Wyatt's forearm. "How very sad for you, Wyatt."

He gazed into her eyes and she had the strangest desire for him to kiss her. She hadn't been kissed or held in a man's embrace in three years. She'd thought that she didn't require that closeness. But suddenly, she had an overwhelming need to be in Wyatt's arms. It was the most peculiar sensation. Her body came to life in places that had long since been reserved and shut down.

She had only herself to blame that Owen had been the one man to kiss her. She'd had the opportunity with Frederick Warrick, but hadn't allowed him to get close enough to her. Though why, she wasn't sure. She'd liked him, but she hadn't felt what she was feeling now with Wyatt—those deep emotions that swirled inside her and went beyond a physical attraction. She couldn't let the moment pass her by and not find out what it was.

So when Wyatt moved a few short steps closer to her, she took one closer to him. His face was inches from hers and she tilted her chin upward. Waiting . . .

"Sweet as a kiss." Wyatt spoke in a low tone that rippled across her skin. "I wonder if it is."

Rather than kiss her on the mouth, he took her hand in his and kissed her wrist. Right at the point where her pulse zipped at a frantic pace. His mouth was warm and moist against her, and when he lowered her hand, he closed his eyes tightly for a second and then stared at her.

"I have to go."

"Good evening, then," she managed to say in a voice heavy with longing.

He looked as if he wanted to do more than just kiss her wrist. His fingers touched her cheek and he caressed her. "Fame fades away, Leah. It's a vain prize that isn't worth it."

Then he turned and departed, leaving her to ponder the wisdom of his words.

❧ 11 ❧

**Beauty does not ensnare men;
they ensnare themselves.**
> —Chinese proverb

Wyatt should never have reached for Leah's hand. It had
been a stupid thing to do. But it had been either that or kiss
her fully on the lips. The far less damaging was the wrist.
For he was afraid that if he'd embraced her and taken her
mouth, he would have wanted to take more.

In retrospect, the perfume had been what made him act
without thinking. Despite Leah's not caring for the eau de
cologne, Wyatt had. There was something to be said about a
good-smelling woman. She belonged in the arms of a man
who appreciated the floral scent and the soft curves behind
the fragrance.

Even knowing that he was going to complicate things
between them, he couldn't help taking her wrist. Bringing
that eau de cologne to his nose and smelling how sweet it
really was, where the oils were warmed by the beat of her
pulse. His subconscious mind went in one direction while
his common sense went in the other—the wrong way. It had
been a culmination of the day, he'd reasoned on the walk
home. He'd been thinking of his family and missing them;
he'd been thinking of a woman and missing one. It was only

natural that he reach out to her. Oddly enough, she was the closest friend he had.

He'd been watching her among the guests, trying to decide what it was about her that appealed to him. He kept telling himself that she was an ordinary woman. But Leah wasn't. She had ambition. Even while delivering something as common as a birthday party. She wanted to succeed. It was written all over her face and in the way she talked to Geneva. He admired Leah's determination, for he felt the same intense steadfastness to make a success of himself. To turn his life around and finally do something meaningful.

But where Leah seemed headed for fame by garnering attention if she won that contest she had her heart set on, Wyatt just wanted some peace and quiet. No fanfare. No hoopla. Just a ranch, some cattle, a half-dozen or so hands . . . and a wife.

Montana and Wyoming were beginning to feel too far away. He'd ridden most of Eternity's boundaries and saw a great potential in this land. The grasses were good and the water clear and abundant, and the drive over the foothills wouldn't be too taxing on the stock when the seasons changed. Colorado did have something to offer a man with his purpose.

But Colorado also held bad memories he wanted to get away from. Namely, Telluride and Silverton. The places he'd used to haunt. But Eternity wasn't any of them. Eternity was its own city. What good would a ranch in Montana or Wyoming be if he didn't have a woman by his side? A woman like Leah. It was what a husband and wife put into the house that made it the right place to live, no matter if that house was a sod hut on the plains or a cabin in the mountains.

What Wyatt couldn't reconcile was that Leah wanted different things out of life than he did. There was no point in figuring out a way to be with her if she wasn't going to be with him. Her plans included a broad scale of people she didn't know, knowing her. He'd had that before. Notoriety came with a penalty. There was no place else to go once you got to the top, but down.

At first light, Wyatt had gone to his diggings wanting to forget about something that couldn't be. He had the whole day to work. Leo and Tu had ridden over to Denver to buy hard-to-find oriental spices. Despite the backbreaking labor he'd been doing most of the day, Wyatt hadn't had any luck. After what Hartzell had told him about the land shifting, Wyatt had lain in bed most of the night thinking that those men who'd cut a shaft hadn't found his satchels because they weren't beneath that cross anymore. They had slipped some twenty feet down and weren't in the same spot. That's why Wyatt hadn't been able to find them yet.

He'd surveyed another angle at which to dig. He'd been at it until well after dinner, barely stopping to drink a cup of the Arbuckle's he'd brewed and eat a tin of lunch meat. He'd been hoping that he'd be rich by evening and his troubles over. But so far, not a sign of the apricot cans enveloping his future. Nothing. And Wyatt had dug fairly deeply. He could stand in a hole that came up to his navel.

Discouraged and angered, the summer sun beating down on him not helping the situation, Wyatt decided it was time he widened the hole. With a great amount of muscle, he took up his pick, held the iron tool above his head, and swung hard into the layers of sandstone in front of him, all the while thinking how good it was going to feel to tell Leo he had to quit his job. All the while thinking that it had been a hell of a Monday and he hadn't a damn thing to shout about after hours of sweat and aching joints.

A cracking sound rendered the air on the pick's impact. Wyatt had heard that noise too many times to be mistaken about what it meant.

He'd split the handle right down the middle.

Leaning forward and bracing his left hand on the bank, Wyatt let the pick slip out of his fingers.

"Son of a bitch," he yelled, then slumped down the side of the hole and glared at the sun baking his skin to a deep tan. He could use a beer right now. A cold one with beads of moisture rolling down the sides. Just like Scudder had had. Only Wyatt couldn't drink. No liquor, anyway. So the next best thing to a beer was a Coca-Cola.

Wiping the sweat and dirt from his brow with a piece of his old shirtsleeve, Wyatt put his hat back on and climbed out of the hole. Dusting himself off, he made fast work of covering the shallow pocket with branches and brush. He didn't want to spread the sandstone out now. He was too hot. And he was too tired. He doubted that Scudder would come out on a hot day like today. Chances were, the marshal was at the Monte Carlo with a beer bottle cooling off his forehead.

But someone else might stumble on the spot and wonder who was digging around and for what. It was that thought alone that gave him the strength to level out the ground to a certain degree and recover it with the branches. By the time he was finished, he was so thirsty, he could think of nothing but that cold cola.

Wyatt began walking down the mountain, calculating that the new handle was going to cost him twenty cents, and the cola a nickel. At least there was some luck on his side today. He had exactly two bits on him.

"What kind of doorbell did you have in mind, Mrs. Kirkland?" Mr. Corn inquired. He stood behind the building supplies counter where the wall drawers were stocked with locks, keys, chain bolts, shutter knobs, steel sash pulleys, cupboard turns, cabinet hardware, screws, washers, and hinges.

"I'm not exactly sure," she replied. "Nothing too fancy."

"You mean none that play a melody?"

"Precisely." Leah gazed at the many boxes he'd gotten down from the top shelf while using his roller ladder. He'd displayed over a half-dozen for her on the hardwood counter. Not knowing anything about electric doorbells, she couldn't decide. "Perhaps if you told me about each one."

Mr. Corn lined the boxes up in meticulous order, pointing to the first one. "Stratford design with nickel-plated gong." The second. "Emerald escutcheon with chimes and antique copper sand." The third, and so on. "Chicago design with electrocopper-plated cast gong. Mayfair with electroplated finish and metal gong. Royal with easy spring action. Fulton chime strike with latch bolts. And Regal with genuine bronze metal with either a flat or astragal face."

His descriptions were of no help and she grew more confused than ever. "Which is the easiest to install?"

"They're all about the same." Mr. Corn waited for her to make up her mind, his stance anxious. He had another customer who needed fly screen cloth measured, and that gentleman was obviously impatient for services, by the way he kept drumming his fingertips on the cutting board.

Leah hated making rash purchases, especially when the product in question was mechanical. She wasn't all that handy with a pliers and hammer, but she'd managed to fix the leaky kitchen faucet, tighten the wheel on Tug's wagon, and replace a few of the split-rail fence boards. Electricity, however, was a different matter entirely. Its potency scared her. When she hooked the new bell up, she'd have to make sure she unscrewed the fuses before she handled any of the wires. But at least the house had been wired for an electric doorbell when it had been built, even though Owen hadn't wanted a modern ringer. He'd preferred the old-fashioned crank type.

Mr. Corn cleared his throat and Leah frowned. "I'll need another minute. Go ahead and help your other customer."

He did just that, leaving Leah with the boxes of doorbells. She picked up the Mayfair. It did have a pretty turn plate. Without wanting to appear ignorant, she didn't open the box to read the instructions thoroughly. If they were all the same, what was the point? She didn't know how any of them went together. But she guessed that it would be a simple matter of coupling the wires. Any nitwit could do that.

The shop bell above the front door rang and distracted Leah from making an immediate selection. Chicago, Fulton, Regal. They all looked sufficient. Eeny meeny miny mo. But she wanted a nice-looking bell, so she couldn't use a

children's rhyme to choose something that made a statement when callers came to her door. Her pick would have to
come down to personal preference.

Hard-falling footsteps of boots went toward the hardwood ice chest Mr. Corn kept at the front of the store by the
cash register and furnace, and where the cracker barrel took
center stage on wintry days with nothing better to do than
sit and complain about the foul weather. Inside the cooler,
Mr. Corn had ice-cold soda pop for sale: Hires root beer,
Coca-Cola, and grape Fizzle.

She resolved to pick one doorbell, make her purchase,
and be on her way. Geneva was watching the children until
supper, and that gave Leah only two hours to get the new
bell installed without being pestered and interrupted to
referee squabbles.

The lid to the icebox opened and closed, and the *phist* of a
bottle cap being removed sounded awfully refreshing. She
might just treat herself to a root beer to drink on the walk
home.

All this thought about cold soda pop made her look
toward the icebox. When she did, she recognized the
familiar figure beside it and her heartbeat came to life.
Wyatt Holloway had come into the hardware store.

Leah hadn't expected to see him until tomorrow. The
Happy City was closed today, because Leo had to go into
Denver. If she'd known she'd run into Wyatt, she would
have changed her dress. She had on her working outfit, and
though the fabric was supposed to be waterproof, the sizing
had been washed out, allowing for accidents. She'd splashed
some solution on the gathers, and although the spots were
minuscule on her cravenette skirt, she knew they were there.

And if she really wanted to feel disheveled, she remembered her hair. That same old stray lock that never stayed
put. Leah reached up to try and tuck the strand beneath the
brim of her untrimmed straw sailor hat. It stayed for a
second, then came right back down.

At least he hadn't seen her. Yet. Did she want him to? *Yes.*
No! Why not? Just because he'd kissed her wrist didn't
mean they couldn't speak to each other anymore. Just

because she'd put more into the kiss than he probably had didn't mean she had to lose her head. She was a sensible woman. She knew better than to act like one of the Clinkingbeard sisters.

Feigning an engrossed interest in the doorbells, Leah glanced at Wyatt from the corner of her eyes. He was leaning up against the cash register counter, sipping his cola and gazing out the window. Deep brown hair curled at his collar. His face was dirt-smudged, and the sleeves on his shirt had been rolled up. He looked as if he'd been digging holes to plant gigantic trees, or mowing a lawn.

Unbidden, she imagined him mowing her lawn. Pushing that stupid Sears, Roebuck, and Co. two-bladed thing she had that made her huff and struggle the one time she'd tried to use it. Since then, Hartzell had paid for his handyman to come over and tend to the grass, bushes, and trees. She'd never fantasized about Hyrum Pfeiffer when he cut her grass. He was . . . well, he sure wasn't of the same physical composition as Wyatt Holloway.

Mr. Corn took his customer to the register and wrote up a bill. The man paid and exited, leaving Mr. Corn to return to Leah.

"So which one will it be?"

She had no answer. Wyatt pulled her attention, yet she didn't want to be obvious and stare at him, so she kept her gaze intently on the doorbells. What would she say to him when she walked by on her way out? Or would he speak first? Should she let him be the first to talk? Or would that be too standoffish? She should square her shoulders and say how do you do, as if the kiss hadn't affected her at all.

Leah was only marginally aware of Mr. Corn's agitation. His voice intruded like the scratch of fingernails on a chalkboard. "Mrs. Kirkland, I have another customer. Do you want me to pick the bell for you?"

"No, that isn't necessary. I've made up my mind." On a whim, she chose the one that sounded the most romantic. "I'll take the Emerald escutcheon with chimes and antique copper sand."

"Very good. Let me wrap that up for you."

Leah nodded and was left alone while Mr. Corn went to tear off a piece of brown paper and cut a length of twine. Without the doorbells to concentrate on, Leah had no central place to thoughtfully put her gaze. She glanced at her shoes to see if the laces were tied, then at her hands with a frown at the stain of ink on her fingers, then at the . . . icebox. She just couldn't help herself.

But Wyatt wasn't there anymore. She hadn't heard him leave, and frantically stood on tiptoes to see through the window. She didn't spy a portion of his broad shoulders or the shape of his hat on the bench outside. Where could he have—

"Looking for someone?"

Leah started and turned around at the deeply voiced query. Wyatt stood directly behind her, giving her pulse a terrible jump.

"Why, good heavens, no . . . I was just . . . That is . . ." She couldn't think of an ample lie when he was staring at her as if she was . . . pretty. His boldly handsome face smiled down at her, as if he were telling her he knew he'd caught her in the act of looking for him. Reflected light from the sunshine outside shimmered in his blue eyes, making them contrasting pleasingly with his sun-browned face.

Any witty thing she had to say went up in a *poof* when his mouth melted into a buttery smile just for her. "Lovely weather, isn't it?" she remarked.

"It's hot."

"Yes, very." She would have put a shoe length more between them if the small of her back hadn't already been pressing into the counter. He stood so close. His massive shoulders seemed to loom over her. She was acutely conscious of his tall, well-proportioned body and the rich outline of his chest straining the chambray fabric of his damp shirt. "You've been working outside?" The question was more of a squeak than an observing comment.

"Yes."

"It is very hot," she countered, agreeing with him. "I may buy myself a root beer."

"Here you are, Mrs. Kirkland." Mr. Corn came up to them and placed her package on the counter. "Would you like me to put this on your bill?"

"Yes." But she still required one more item. "About the old doorbell. When I remove it, there'll be a hole in the door that I'll need to cover. What can you suggest?"

Mr. Corn turned and opened a drawer. Setting two covers before her, he said, "Astoria push plate with matching screws. You have your choice of antique copper or lemon brass finish. Penny more for the latter."

This time Leah didn't delay. "Antique copper, please," she replied without hesitation. "And if you could be so kind as to add a root beer on my account as well."

"Consider it done." He turned his attention on Wyatt and said, "I'll be with you in a minute."

Wyatt leaned his hip into the counter's edge and held the cola loosely in his soiled fingers. "I'm in no hurry. All I need is an ax handle. I know where they are."

"You break that one I sold you already? Thought you weren't going to mi—"

"I just need a new handle, Corn, not an interrogation."

Mr. Corn grumbled, "I told you they were cheaper by the dozen, but you wanted just one."

"And one's all I'm buying today," Wyatt replied as he pushed from the counter and went to the barrels containing saws, picks, axes, hammers, and the accompanying hardware such as handles. Leah watched as he tested several in his grasp, swinging a little and adjusting his grip. It looked as if he chose a solid ash, but as he returned she quickly averted her gaze.

Carlyle A. Corn put Leah's purchases together with string, making a loop for her to carry them. "You're all set, Mrs. Kirkland. I hope that doorbell works out for you."

"I'm sure it will," she replied, not really wanting to leave yet but having no other option without it appearing obvious that she was dawdling to talk with Wyatt. She headed for the cooler, lifted the lid, and took out a Hires.

"I'll get that top for you," Mr. Corn offered. He took the

opener, which was tied to a string on the wall beside the icebox, and popped the cap off. "There you are, Mrs. Kirkland."

"Thank you, Mr. Corn."

Leah pretended as if she needed to take a few sips before starting on her way. Wyatt slipped his hand into his pants pocket and came out with two coins, which he put on the counter.

"Paid in full." Wyatt grabbed his cola. "I hope I won't be seeing you soon."

Leah took that opportunity to exit first, but slowly so that Wyatt would have a chance to catch up to her if he wanted. She went to open the door, but his hand came up quickly on the knob and opened the door for her.

She gave him a light smile. "Thank you."

They went outside together, and both headed in the same direction. Her house and the Starlight Hotel were on the same street, but four blocks apart. The heat came in waves and showed no signs of letting up until twilight. She really didn't feel like installing the bell right now, but was resigned to doing it. As Wyatt stayed by her side, silently drinking his Coca-Cola and holding onto his new ax handle, she wondered what he needed the ax for.

"Are you working on a project for anyone?" she queried, trying to sound offhanded.

"A project?"

"You know. Handy work. That's why you need the ax."

Wyatt gazed at the handle in his grasp. "I'm trimming back some overgrowth at the drop gaps for one of the ranchers."

"Oh." Leah wondered if it was Half Pint Gilman. He owned the biggest ranch outside of Eternity. It surprised her that Mr. Gilman would have Wyatt doing such a job. He had plenty of ranch hands for that sort of work.

Walking down the western side of Main, they past Everlasting Monuments and Statuary. Normally, Leah made it a point to walk on the eastern side so she wouldn't have to encounter Mr. Winterowd *or* Mr. Quigley. The post office was right next door. It was too late to change course.

No sooner had they passed the door to 96 Main Street, with its advantageously large front windows, than Mr. Leemon Winterowd stepped out.

"Mrs. Kirkland," he heralded. "What a surprise."

Indeed. "Mr. Winterowd."

Then to Wyatt, Leemon gave a speculative stare. "Mr. Holloway."

"Winterowd."

Leah had wanted to keep right on walking, but Leemon remarked, "It'll be a nice evening for a buggy ride, Mrs. Kirkland. I could come by and pick you and the children up for a little roundabout."

"I'm afraid I'll have to decline. You see—"

"Mrs. Kirkland!" came Mr. Quigley's greeting. He'd left the post office, probably having heard their voices, and strode upon the group with great enthusiasm at finding her. "What a pleasure. Mr. Holloway," he said in an obligatory tone. "Mrs. Kirkland, did you get the mail I delivered to you this morning?"

"Of course. It came through the slot on time." Right along with the poem he'd written to her and folded in three. She wouldn't dare make a comment about it now, and hoped to heaven he had the good manners not to mention it in public. The heartfelt sentiments had disconcerted her, while the bad rhyming had made her wince. He meant well, but she'd been quite honest with him when she'd told him—and Mr. Winterowd—over two years ago that she simply wasn't interested in their courtship.

"It's going to be a grand evening," Quigley said, his full face obviously beaming with the prospects of a cricket serenade on her porch swing. She'd allowed him to stay for such a night once and she'd always regretted it. But he'd brought her a fancy box of chocolates and had been so sincere, she didn't have the heart to turn him away at the door.

"I was saying it's going to be a grand evening," Mr. Winterowd interjected, giving Fremont Quigley a frown. "I was asking Mrs. Kirkland to go on a buggy ride with me and she was going to say yes."

"Actually," Leah jumped in, "I told you I had to decline for the reason that I've got to install a new doorbell. So you see, I'll be otherwise occupied this evening."

Mr. Winterowd, who was known to be quite handy with his hands since he carved picturesque scenes in marble headstones for a living, perked right up. "Why bother yourself over that, Mrs. Kirkland, when there is a capable man standing right here?"

Fremont bounced in. "Yes, I'm quite capable. I can install that for you, Mrs. Kirkland. It would take no time at all."

Leah shifted her gaze from one to the other. A dilemma was brewing and she could see no polite way out. Either way, she'd hurt their feelings, but the offer sure was tempting.

"I could close up shop early, Mrs. Kirkland," Leemon said. "Come right over now so as not to disturb your supper hour." He gave Mr. Quigley a triumphant smirk. "Quigley has to keep the post office open until five."

This got Mr. Quigley's goat and he puffed his face up with a snort. "If you were any kind of businessman, you wouldn't close up early just to install a doorbell. Somebody could need your services from now until five, Winterowd."

"I don't have any appointments, and even if someone did kick off right this second, it takes Old Man Uzzel at least two hours to perform an embalming. And by then, it would be five and I couldn't sculpt a stone on the spot. Besides, even if I was to engrave a monument on the spur of the moment, Reverend Bunderson doesn't do burials after he eats his dessert cobbler. So I don't see as I've got a problem, Quigley. You, on the other hand, are an officer of the United States government. You can't close on a whim. I'm in business for myself. I can do what I want."

Leah's gaze landed on Wyatt, who'd been quiet during the entire transaction. Rather than see the amusement she was certain would be written on his expression, she saw a slight scowl and a brittle smile. His eyes were level under drawn brows when he butted in, "I'm installing Leah's bell for her."

"Leah?" both men said in unison. "You mean Mrs. Kirkland." They looked at one another.

"I've never addressed her as Leah," Fremont complained to Leemon.

Leemon nodded. "Neither have I." Then to Leah, "Have you given him liberties to call you Leah?"

By this time, Leah was getting dizzy. She said to both gentlemen, "I appreciate your concern, but my name is Leah and I don't see any reason why Wyatt"—she pronounced the name in an even tone—"can't call me that. My mother-in-law does, and so does my father-in-law. In fact, several people in Eternity address me by my first name."

"But you never let us," Mr. Quigley grumbled. "And you fixed him a supper plate."

Then as if the news soaked in, Mr. Winterowd crossed his arms over his chest. "Mr. Holloway is going to install your doorbell? Is that the truth?"

Leah had to pause a minute. Wyatt had made the offer. "Yes. As a matter of fact, Wyatt has been very kind to offer to install my doorbell for me. So if you gentlemen will excuse us."

Wyatt tipped his hat at both men, whose mouths were agape as she and Wyatt continued on. Leah couldn't breathe, much less make sense out of the rapidly changing circumstances. But she had to say, "You don't really have to install my doorbell. I appreciate you making the offer just to let them down."

A glance at his profile and she saw that the set of his chin suggested a stubborn streak. "I made you an honest offer. I intend to keep it."

They were in front of the Starlight Hotel now and Wyatt stopped. Leah paused with him, her senses awakening.

"Let me clean up first, and I'll stop by in about fifteen minutes."

"All right."

They both turned and continued on, she with the sudden compulsion to change into a good dress and fix her hair properly before he arrived. But that would be too noticeable. She didn't want to be obvious. About what? That she found the prospect of him coming over something to look forward to. That her life had been mundane before she'd met him.

Wyatt didn't know the first thing about electric doorbells. But he'd offered to install hers because he'd had to stand back with his teeth gritted, unable to buy Leah that root beer she'd wanted because his cash was all tapped out. Before, he'd always been able to buy the lady in his life whatever she had her fancy set on. Frustration over his lack of money was eating away at him. In his youth, money had burned a hole in his pockets and he'd spent it carelessly. What he wouldn't give to have some of it back right now.

At least he didn't need a fat wallet to put in the bell. Because he'd be damned if he let Winterowd and Quigley come by her place. An unexpected surge of jealousy had hit him when those two goons stepped over each other to be with Leah. Neither one was enough man for her.

After cleaning up, Wyatt hesitated about which shirt to wear. He had two clean ones: his old cotton or the one he'd recently bought. Since he'd already had it on yesterday at the birthday party, he opted for the old one. As he slipped his arms through the worn and comfortable sleeves, he hoped like hell that she knew what she was doing and could direct him. If not, he'd have to rely on the instructions. He wasn't a really good reader, so unless the guidelines were printed in very simple terms or there were lots of diagrams, he was going to be a complete goner and look like an idiot.

It didn't take him long to get ready. He left his room and ran into Almorene in the hallway on his way out. She had crisply ironed sheets folded over her plump arm, and a delicate lace cap over her silver hair.

"I was going to make up a fresh bed for you, Mr. Holloway."

"That'd be fine."

She went past him to his door, the circle of brass keys attached to her waist through a loop jingling to a halt when she stopped and faced him with a faded smile. "You're a pleasant guest, Mr. Holloway. Not loud or disorderly, and you keep the room tidy. So I think I ought to tell you, Marshal Scudder stopped by after breakfast to ask me about you. Specifically, if you've broken any laws and if you're paying your bill on time."

Wyatt's lips thinned with agitation. "What did you say to him?"

"Precisely what I just said to you. That you're not loud and disorderly, and you keep the room tidy. And that you pay your bill."

"Thanks for letting me know."

"You're quite welcome."

Wyatt pushed on, thinking that Scudder was like a bloodhound with his nose to the ground, sniffing after any trace of scent that could see Wyatt thrown in jail. Bean Scudder should be ferreting out real criminals instead of riding his heels, waiting for Wyatt to do something that was grounds for lockup. It was cock and bull that a lawman of his dim-witted caliber could throw such weight around, thinking that he exemplified the full extent of Eternity law.

This grated hard on Wyatt as he strode to Leah's. When he came to Seventh Avenue, his eyes narrowed on the marshal's office across the street. Scudder was on the porch, slouched in a straight-legged chair. He balanced his weight on the two rear legs, flirting with a backward fall. His feet were stretched out in front of him, the heels of his western boots propped on the beer cooler. From the sporadic jerking nod of his head, with his eyes closed, he was on the verge of snoozing.

Wyatt had the strongest urge to shoot the back legs off that chair and show Bean that he was nobody's business but his own. But because it was felonious to raise a firearm against a U.S. marshal, and seeing as Wyatt wasn't armed, the likelihood of fulfilling that tale of dime novel fiction just wasn't to be. However, that didn't stop Wyatt from thinking about how much fun it would be to see the expression on Scudder's ruddy face when he fell on his ass and went groping for his revolver to retaliate.

A block later, Wyatt stopped at Leah's gate and put his

hand on the latch. He let himself in, and as he approached the veranda he noted the front door was wide open. Leah sat cross-legged on the threshold with a screwdriver in her hand and a heavy furrow of concentration on her forehead. Her hair was in a different style than she'd had earlier when she'd worn her hat. Rather than being twisted at the nape of her neck in a braid, she'd twisted it into a loose knot at the crown of her head. She'd also replaced her dress for a skirt and blouse. Though the clothing was nothing fancy, the flared navy skirt pooled around her legs, and the form-fitting mushroom-colored blouse got his attention. She had a figure he could appreciate, right along with Winterowd and Quigley.

Upon his ascent of the wooden steps, she lifted her chin and smiled. "I've already removed the old doorbell. I'll give it to Tug. He likes to take things apart with his Buck's tool set. I suppose you did likewise when you were a little boy."

Wyatt bent down to a crouch, absently picking up a discarded screw. "When I was eight, I took the hinges off the outhouse door and threw the bolts down the hole."

"You were a naughty boy." There was a trace of laughter in Leah's voice.

"It sounds funny now, but it wasn't back then. I got a whipping, because we didn't have the extra money to replace the bolts. For the next couple of months, we had to use the privy with the door off until my dad could afford new ones."

"What line of work was your father in?"

"He did a little of everything. He cut ties for the railroad and studded out silver mines. Mostly he hauled freight. He wasn't home much when I was young."

"I couldn't imagine not having my father with me when I was growing up." Leah took the Astoria plate out, held it flush over the hole left by the old ringer, and made markings around it with a pencil. "He was everything to me. My mother, too." Her voice drifted on a sad chord. "But they're both gone. Like your parents."

Wyatt didn't really want to get to talking about families. The subject depressed him and he fought against all the wondering, all the imagining of what everyone was doing with their lives.

Picking up the drill brace, Wyatt at least knew how to bore a hole to set screws. "Let me get that for you," he offered when she took the plate away after making her scribes. But to get a level hole started, he'd have to sit where Leah was. Leaning forward, he motioned to where her knee was close to the doorjamb. "You have to slide over."

"Oh, certainly." Leah began to move out of the way, but the door opening was just barely wide enough for two people to occupy. When he bent to his knees, he accidentally pinned her skirt and trapped her before she got too far. Rather than apologize for it, he didn't say a word, keeping her there next to him. She made no comment either, and he took that as a sign she wasn't all that sorry to be sitting so close.

As Wyatt lifted the drill and began boring out the necessary screw holes, he caught himself trying to detect a hint of that sweet-as-a-kiss eau de cologne. She wasn't wearing any that he could distinguish above the faintness of wood and new copper. He told himself that he wasn't disappointed, but he was.

Holding the bit by the handle, he rotated the tool until he completed all five holes. Leah handed him the plate and held it against the door, then she passed over one of the screws. Their fingers touched and he fleetingly stared at her hand with rapid thoughts. She had a fine, capable hand. Soft as the skin of any peach and warm as the sunny side of a meadow; yet there was an unmistakable strength in that hand. Her fingernails were cut on the short side, though not so short as to lessen the sensuality of her slender, tapered fingers. He imagined those fingers gliding across his naked chest like the tickling whisper of down . . . those fingers reaching into his hair and pulling his head toward her mouth for a kiss . . .

Wyatt's shoulders tensed. He couldn't allow himself to be sidetracked by such vivid thoughts, and took the screw from her outstretched hand. "Screwdriver," he said in a brisk tone.

She lay one in his open palm and he made a fast job of sinking the first screw.

"Do you ever think about inventions?" Leah asked, throwing him a little offtrack.

"No," he replied honestly. "I think that there's already too many inventions for people."

"Oh, but I disagree. There's so many wonderful things being developed. Why, Mr. Corn says he's getting flyers everyday about products that will make our lives easier. The other day, he got one on an electric carpet sweeper."

"I don't need an electric carpet sweeper."

"But I do."

"I guess a woman would," he conceded.

Leah sighed. "Don't you think about telephones? About talking to people who are in a whole different place from you? I wonder if they will ever design a washer that can wring out the clothes automatically. Or if there'll ever be such a machine that you can put flour and water into and have a loaf of bread come out?"

Wyatt finished with another screw. "There'll never be a machine that can bake bread. It's impossible. How would you flour a board? How would you knead it? Or put it in a pan to bake it?"

"I don't know. You just would, because the inventors would make sure it could be possible."

"Something like that isn't possible."

"I would have thought so myself a few years ago, but Mr. Corn sells a New Queen sewing machine with sixteen different attachments including a ruffler and even a quilter. He also has a new and improved gramophone where the records sound just as clear as if the music and singer were right in your parlor. His newest delivery was a genuine Bohn Syphon icebox, that has hurry-up air circulation so you don't have to replace the block of ice as often. Now that's progress," she stated, plopping another screw into his hand. "I'd march right down there and buy it if it wasn't so darned expensive. Mr. Corn wants twenty-two dollars and fifty cents for it."

"I don't see how newfangled objects can be so useful if no one can afford the price tag."

Leah shook her head. "People in Eternity said they couldn't afford electricity before the electric light plant was built and the power wheel installed. But almost everyone in town is wired to it now and can't see themselves going without the convenience."

"It's no inconvenience to strike a match and light a lamp."

"But with a lamp you have the hazard of fire. With electricity, you don't."

Wyatt could find no argument. He didn't know the laws of physics when it came to electric light plants and the wheels that generated that monstrous power. A switch turning on a glass bulb perplexed him.

"We're in a time of great inventions." Leah toyed with the crank on the old doorbell and got no sound from it. "And I for one think it's very exciting. No one thought man could fly, but the Wright brothers did in it the *Kitty Hawk* just nine months ago."

Wyatt hadn't heard about any Wright brothers and a Kitty Hawk. Men flying like birds was infeasible. "You mean they flew up in the air with hawk wings on?"

"Not with wings on them, silly." Leah's enchanting smile was irresistible. He fought against covering her mouth with his. "Though that's been tried without much success. But in a flying machine that they built and called the *Kitty Hawk*. It had a body and two wings, just like a paper bird. Didn't you read about it? The flight in North Carolina was monumental. The story ran in every newspaper last year; even the *Eternity Tribune* had an article about the historic event."

"I missed it."

"Well, I was quite impressed. I'd like to ride in a flying machine one day." She put her finger thoughtfully to her lip. "But I'd like to ride in an automobile even more."

"I hate automobiles," Wyatt mumbled.

"But why? They're so keen and modern. Automobiles are going to be the wave of the future. Everyone will have one."

"I hope to God not. They smell like rotten eggs and their backfire scares horses." Wyatt put the last screw in place. "If you want to get somewhere, either ride a horse or hitch a buggy to a pair of them. Horses don't need gasoline to run. All they need is grass and water, and there's plenty of that. *For free,*" he added with punctuation.

"Well, I have to disagree with you." Leah removed the new doorbell from the box. "Automobiles are going to be big."

"I'll bet you they don't last another year. By then, people will figure out they're nothing but costly trouble."

"When I buy one, I'll let you have a ride in it, and you can eat your words when you see how wonderful and comfortable it is. You better hold on to your hat, because I'll put my foot down on the pedal and speed down Main Street at fifteen miles an hour."

"You want speed, darlin', I'll sit you in front of me on my horse, July, and run him fast enough to knock every last hairpin out of your pretty hair."

Leah's bright laughter pulled at his heartstrings. It had been longer than he could remember since he'd been affected by the sound of a woman's voice. "You can be so funny, Wyatt. Why, I think you were a man who was supposed to be born for the Dark Ages, resistant as you are to progress." Her smile was as intimate as any kiss. "Where have you been living? In a cave?"

Wyatt's good feelings faded. Leah didn't know how close she was to the truth, but he'd never let on. "I've been out of touch for a while," was all he would confess to. "But I'm going to be doing some expensive living soon, so just you wait. I may even buy you that icebox you want."

With that admission, Wyatt realized he was thinking about sticking around to prove his wealthy status to her. It was a stupid mistake on his part. One that he should have been more careful about. But it seemed as if his mind had a will of its own by implying he was staying near Eternity.

"With your investment money?"

"Yes."

She dropped the subject of money, but he could tell she

wanted to ask him something by the change on her face from animation to soft curiosity.

"Why is it that you aren't married, Wyatt?"

Her question weighed upon him, his thoughts jagged and painful. "I blundered my youth. I wouldn't have made a very good husband then." Then to veer the topic of conversation down a path that was less defeating to him, he queried, "Do you have everything to put the bell in?"

Reluctantly, Leah glanced at the parts she'd spread out around her. She looked as if she knew what she was doing. Which was good, because he didn't have a clue.

"Yes. I unscrewed both fuses so we don't have any current running into the house. Everything is dead."

That sounded like a wise maneuver. "I'll just—" He picked up the bell component and turned it over. Two wires, one black and one white, stuck out from the back. "—just put these where they go."

He moved his knees and Leah scooted backward away from the left side of the door. He instantly missed her closeness, yet at the same time he didn't want her watching him too astutely. He was liable to do something stupid. Make a mistake and ruin something. About four feet up on the wall was a cutout in the wallpaper where a plate had once been. Two wires dangled, and he figured the ones hanging off the bell connected to them. Simple enough.

"I'll go outside and hold the bell in place for you." Leah attempted to rise, but her foot caught on the handle of the screwdriver, and before she was fully standing, she had to put her hand on his shoulder to keep from falling. She landed on her knees and would have fallen to her backside if he hadn't caught her. "Oh," she gasped, her face inches from his. "I'm sorry . . ."

Her eyes were an entrancing shade of golden brown, the lashes framing them thick and sweeping. The ivory of her skin was flawless, the structure of her cheekbones high and alluring. If he were to move his head ever so slightly, he would be at an angle in which to thoroughly ravage her lips with his own. The temptation was so strong, he couldn't make it go away.

He brought his chin up and put his hand on her jaw, his lips gently meeting hers in a quiet but potent kiss. The forced calm he'd been holding onto shattered through him as he drank in the sweetness of her mouth against his. He kissed her harder, moving his lips over hers. He didn't touch her anyplace but her mouth, and though he craved her arms around him, he didn't push her to do so. This had to be enough, because he couldn't risk frightening her away. His lonely soul melted into the kiss and he wanted it to last forever.

The flame had been struck, and Wyatt felt himself burning up and craving more. Time had all but dimmed his recollections of kissing. He'd never kissed a woman he cared more about than the moment of pleasure she could give him. He'd never felt such passion that his blood pounded through his chest, his head . . . his heart. His mouth on Leah's erased his preconceived thoughts that there was no harmony between a man and woman without sex. He was wrong. With Leah, just kissing her was satisfying.

He would have taken the kiss further, made it more intimate, but Leah wasn't one of the girls down on River Street. And they were sitting in her doorway. She was respected and not apt to fall on the floor with him, despite his wanting to.

Leaving her mouth, his own afire with the heat consuming him, Wyatt held her at arm's length. Very shaken, he released his hands from her shoulders. Several seconds passed while he found his voice, and when he did it was raw with passion. "That shouldn't have happened."

Leah pushed a lock of hair from her cheek. She licked her damp lips. They were soft, and still so very inviting. "I'm not sorry," she whispered.

He almost took her into his arms and kissed her again, but he had to wonder what good could come of a romance between two people going in opposite directions.

Not quite sure what to make of her honesty, Wyatt tucked down the brim of his hat so she couldn't see his eyes when he admitted, "I haven't seen or touched anything soft in a long time. I'm no person of great virtue, Leah. You tempt me. You have from the first minute I laid eyes on you. I had to know if a woman's mouth was as sweet as I remembered, or if I dreamed the whole thing up."

"Wyatt . . . I don't know what to say."

"There's nothing to say." He raised his head. "You've got a crowded big city on your mind. I've got wide-open spaces on mine. I don't see the two of them ever meeting at a crossroad. We should leave things as they are. Without complications."

Leah's lashes swept across her cheekbones as she cast her eyes downward. "I'd still like to consider us friends."

"Nothing's changed."

Her gaze lifted and they stared at one another. A clock inside tolled the hour. Leah spoke in a velvet murmur, "Rosalure and Tug will be home in thirty minutes. They'll be underfoot."

"Then we better get on with what we were doing."

Only Wyatt's thoughts weren't on black-and-white wires, reading instructions or doorbells. The harder he tried to ignore the truth, the more it persisted. He wanted to stay in Eternity, and he wanted Leah to stay with him. But he wouldn't hold her back. The only problem was, how long could he wait for her?

Wyatt had cleaned up the tools and was putting them away in the toolbox when the children came to the gate. Rosalure held a basket with a cloth covering the top, and Tug had a toy whistle between his lips.

Rosalure waved as Leah returned to the doorway from the back of the house after reconnecting the fuses.

The gate slammed closed behind the boy and girl, and Tug began to march with soldier's arms. He blew the whistle with a repetitive cadence as he stomped over the flagstones.

The shrill of that whistle made the blood in Wyatt pound to a roaring beat. He willed himself to block out the sound. He told himself he was immune to it and that the noise didn't mean a thing to him anymore.

Rosalure came up the steps while Tug did an about-face and marched toward the gate again. "Hello, Momma. I brought home some orange fritters." Her gaze fell rather speculatively. "Hello, Mr. Holloway. You're here again?"

"Your mother needed help putting in the new doorbell."

"How does it work?" Rosalure asked.

"I don't know," Leah said. "We haven't tried it. Do you want to be the first?"

Rosalure nodded her enthusiasm, grasped the keylike turn and gave it a single motion to the right. From above the front door where Wyatt mounted the chime box came a repeated trio of three notes.

Whhhrrrrrrrr! As Tug neared, the piercing sound of the whistle made Wyatt tense so tightly, he felt as if his bones would snap. Instead of dwelling on the noise, he looked at Leah. She'd lifted the cloth off Rosalure's basket and was investigating the contents.

"They look yummy, Rosalure."

"Tug even helped make some."

Tug ceased his marching and yelled toward the porch. "I made the lumpy ones."

Leah smiled. "I'm sure they taste very good."

"They do. Nanna let me eat five."

"There goes his appetite," Leah sighed. Then she gazed hesitantly at Wyatt. They hadn't spoken much for the past half hour. "Would you care to stay for supper? It won't be much. Just hot dogs."

Wyatt had no set plans. The idea of staying with Leah, of watching her, listening to her, hearing the sounds of a family was too much to walk away from to eat alone. And if Leo could eat hot dogs, Wyatt figured he choke a few down, too. "Sure," he replied. "I'd like to stay for supper."

"I'm glad." Her smile was genuine and kind. As if she truly wanted to hold onto the fragile relationship they were forming. "It won't take me long to fry the dogs. Rosalure, could you set an extra place?"

"I guess, Momma." Rosalure gazed at Wyatt, then went into the house.

"Tug," Leah called. "You come on in and wash your hands."

Tug marched toward the door. *Whhhrrrrrrrr! Whhhrrrrrrrr!*

Whhhrrrrrrr-Whhhrrrrrrr-Whhhrrrrrrrr! Over and over, he blew that whistle.

Wyatt felt as if his head was going to split open. He would have put his hands to his ears if he could have stopped the sound from pulling him back. But it was too late. . . .

The dark memories surfaced, much like water working its way up a well shaft. The past burst to the surface, and Wyatt was helpless to keep it from gurgling to life.

⚜ 12 ⚜

The past is as clear as a mirror,
the future as dark as lacquer.
—Chinese proverb

November 11, 1887
Idaho Territorial Penitentiary

From the guard tower, the warden's deputy blew his whistle,
announcing the arrival of the new prisoners. As flakes of
snow sifted from the gray sky, the cagelike cart holding eight
prisoners rolled through the open double gates of the Idaho
Territorial Penitentiary. Harlen Riley got his first glimpse of
the cold-looking two-story brick building that was to be his
holding place for the next twenty years—if he allowed
himself to think on those terms. Which he didn't. Richard
was going to get him out. Soon. He'd already petitioned
Governor Edward A. Stevenson for a pardon. Harlen knew
he could count on his attorney to plea successfully for his
release. Robison had never let him down.

The icy clink of ankle manacles and the short lengths of
chain that dangled from the cuffs of prisoners made the
autumn air seem colder. Harlen wished for a thicker coat,
but his Mackinaw and a worsted shirt were all he'd been
allowed. His clothing, except for what he was wearing, and
his expensive possessions had been taken from him at
Montpelier.

The wheels of the cart hit a rut, and the convicts sitting

on the three benches bumped into one another. It had been that way the whole ride. Knocking and hitting shoulders and knees on a trip that had lasted nearly four days without much of a letup except to change horses at various posts. They were given only the distance of the stage stop entrance to walk to. Then they had to sit and eat an unpalatable meal in minutes before walking back to the cart. Harlen was dying to stand up and exercise his stiff legs.

After rolling to a rattling stop, one of the guards came over to the cart and took the key from the driver, who unlocked the cage.

"Out with you! Now!" he barked, with his hand on the butt of his gun to stress that he meant business.

Harlen rose and put his foot on the narrow strip of wood that served as a step-down. Needles shot through his feet, and his knees almost buckled. He wasn't able to move much with the constricting confines of iron on his legs.

The whistle blew a marching tune, as if the prisoners were required to step to the beat and march in line. Most of them wobbled, Harlen included. He could barely walk much less march.

As soon as the men were lined up to the deputy's specifications, a man dressed in a shin-length coat with a scarf around his thick neck came out of a building off to the side and behind the guard tower. He was solid-looking, built like the stone edifices surrounding him. The soft crust of frozen snow crunched beneath the heels of his polished boots as he approached them.

The deputy ceased his whistling when the man halted and gave the prisoners a narrow going-over. After a thorough inspection that started from one end of the line to the other, the man nodded to the deputy guard.

"You may proceed," he decreed, as he rubbed his gloved hands together.

Withdrawing a small paper-filled ledger from his coat pocket, the deputy let the whistle drop from his mouth to hang around his neck by a leather thong. "It is my duty, on orders from Warden Ezra Baird, to inform you of the prison rules. They will be strictly enforced. Anyone caught breaking a rule either will be penalized by privileges being taken away or, if the punishment so allows it, will be held in the solitary known as Siberia for a duration of time appropriate to the severity of the disobedience. The rules are as follows in accordance with the government of prisoners . . ."

He rattled off a long list. Harlen comprehended a few, noting key words and phrases, cursing them in his mind.

Perform labor . . . no profane language . . . no loud talking . . . no loafing in the shop area . . . no gambling or card playing . . . allowed to write only two letters . . . conversation at the dining table prohibited . . . no files, saws, or chisels . . .

"At the blowing of the first whistle in the morning," the deputy bellowed sternly, "each prisoner must arise, make up his bed neatly, sweep up his cell, empty his night bucket, and prepare for the morning meal. At the second whistle each will take his cup and march, in single file, to the table and remain standing till the whistle sounds the signal to be seated. At the close of the meal the signal will be given to rise and pass, in single file, to the cells; at the next whistle everyone will pass out into the yard to be assigned to their respective works for the day. At the blowing of the whistle at noon every prisoner will enter his cell and will await the signal for dinner, which will be the same as for breakfast. The signals for supper are the same as above; after his meal each prisoner will return to his cell and close the door to be locked. After the final lockup, the whistle will sound and everyone must arise, place his right hand on the door of his cell, and wait until he is counted by the turnkey or the guard. At the blowing of the whistle at nine o'clock P.M., all lights must be extinguished in the cells and the prisoners retire and preserve absolute silence till the blowing of the whistle in the morning. When for any reason the whistle shall blow out at any time, every prisoner will march to his cell without delay.

"These rules will be strictly enforced and any infraction hereof will incur in severe punishment and forfeiture of one or all of the privileges allowed good conduct.

"The aforementioned is signed by the warden of this

territory, the governor, the secretary of state, and the attorney general, and has been presented to the Board of Prison Commissioners for Idaho. So long as you all obey the rules, you will serve your time in relative comfort."

Harlen didn't want any part of the rules and regulations. They were outlandish and would be impossible to abide by. No one could tell him when he had to get up and when he had to go to bed. Christ, he hoped Robison was working hard on his case this very minute.

The deputy's whistle shrilled, and the warden went back into the building from which he'd come. Harlen speculated that the man had a nice toasty fire and a bottle of brandy to keep him warm. What Harlen wouldn't have done for a drink and a smoke at this moment. He'd been sober since his capture, and he'd been having a hell of time going straight. His hands shook and his fingers trembled. He was sick to his stomach and his pants were loose around his waist.

No sooner had the warden left than the deputy motioned for them to follow him. Harlen went, because he had no choice. As he walked across the yard, pain shot through his legs from not having used them in so many days. Trying to keep an even stride, he gazed at the forlorn structures of the compound. Men in uniforms pitched hay into piles at a stable, while others huddled in front of another building over a laundry tub. The flames beneath the black iron kettle looked so inviting, Harlen had a mind to walk over and warm his hands. But there was a guard at his side with a mean-looking Colt Harlen had no desire to test.

Along with the others, he was led into the two-story cell block where the air inside was so cold, his breath misted in front of his face.

"You'll change into your uniforms and report to the doors of your cells in five minutes for work detail," the deputy said as the guards ushered them into vacant cells. There weren't more convicts than cells, so the men didn't have to double up. At least Harlen could be grateful for that one thing. He wasn't any good rooming with strangers.

After his chains had been removed, he was shoved into a

six-foot-by-six-foot barred cubicle with a solitary cot, two wool blankets, a uniform and patched coat, and a utility bucket. The iron door closed with a harsh clank that rang more lamentably than a blacksmith's anvil as he shaped a grave arch.

Harlen stood in the center of the sandstone floor, the cold seeping through the soles of his boots. He'd wronged a great many people in his young life, and he supposed he owed them and should be paying the penalty for doing such. But this seemed beyond reasonable restitution. This was hell in the worst way.

Lowering himself onto the cot, Harlen put his head in his hands and stared at the tips of his wet boots. Christ Almighty, he had to get out. He couldn't make it. Twenty years in here was certain death. He'd wish he *was* laid out on an undertaker's table. The words from that little girl in Telluride would come true.

Little Darling . . . If she could see him now, she'd have her satisfaction.

"Three minutes!" That damn whistle blew several sharp notes, causing Harlen to grimace hard.

He lifted the shirt on the bed and gazed at the number that had been sewn onto the breast pocket. He was no longer a man with a reputation to be reckoned with. All that was in the past. He was one of society's outcasts now.

With a shiver of understanding, Harlen Shepard Riley lost his notorious name to a number. He became known as Territorial Convict Number 628 and put in Cell House Number One, where forty-two double-brick cells were occupied by some of the worst delinquents he would ever have the misfortune to encounter.

❧ 13 ❧

**The light of a hundred stars
does not equal the light of the moon.**
— Chinese proverb

The *Complete Guide to Italian Cooking* arrived in the morning's post and Leah had immersed herself in the tome, reading up on the various preparations of Italian dishes. For this evening's supper, she'd chosen to tackle the main staple: Italian gravy with pasta.

It had been a fluke, really, that Wyatt was coming over to try her first attempt at something extravagant. Leah had gone to the Happy City after dinner to get some fresh garlic and tomatoes from Leo's garden for the preparation of the dish. She'd found Leo weeding and Wyatt watering with a garden hose. Normally, the two should have been inside readying the restaurant for opening.

Leah had approached them with a friendly greeting as she entered the short gate that kept stray dogs out of the garden. "I didn't expect to see you two outside."

Leo had lifted his head, and Wyatt turned in her direction.

"Good to see you, Leah," Leo replied.

Leah found herself studying Wyatt's lean face and features. He'd wrapped a faded red bandanna around his forehead to keep the hair from his eyes, and he'd rolled the sleeves to his pale blue shirt above his elbows. Shifting his weight, he kept aiming water on a row of peas as he said, "Hello, Leah," in a voice that was resonant and made gooseflesh rise across the nape of her neck.

She'd done everything she could to erase Wyatt's kiss from her memory, but it was useless. She could no more forget than she could stop breathing. His words had had a profound affect on her. She'd wondered what kind of life he'd had where softness had no part. Where had he been?

She wouldn't press him for details. She'd detected that he was a private man about his past. She respected that, but at the same time she longed to know all there was about him in the time they had together.

"Hello, Wyatt," she replied as she drew up to Leo. "Are you opening late today for some reason?"

Leo straightened and rested his fist over the top of the hoe's handle. "Not opening at all. Tu Yan is sick. He can't cook."

"It's nothing serious, is it?"

"Just a cold," Leo said around the cigarette gripped by his lips. "He should be better tomorrow and we'll open." Grinning, he gave her a short wink. "I guess this puts you in the kitchen tonight."

"Well, actually, I was planning on cooking anyway."

"You're kidding?"

"I'm not. My Italian cookbook came this morning."

"Ah."

Wyatt went to turn the valve and shut the water off. Then he came over and ran his damp hand down the side of his pants. She never got over how good he looked when he was working outdoors.

"Since the Happy City will be closed tonight, and since I've got a new recipe I was planning on trying, you're both welcome to share supper with us."

"Not me, Leah," Leo replied, pitching his cigarette. "I've got things to do."

She had invited Leo over once before for Christmas

cheer, but he'd politely declined for unstated reasons. She feared he wasn't comfortable in her house because of his ethnicity, even though he was as American as she. Leah would have never allowed Geneva to make any untoward remark, but Leah also knew there were others who wouldn't have been kind. It was accepted that she was friends with Leo because she patronized his establishment. But outside of the Happy City, a personal association that could be misconstrued wouldn't have been approved of. Still, that didn't stop Leah from trying to include him.

"But Wyatt, you go," Leo said, "and tell me what you think of Italian cooking."

Wyatt slipped the flats of his hands into his denim pockets. "I reckon I could."

Leah had to slow her breathing. Not because he'd said he was coming; she hoped she didn't mess up or burn anything. The hot dogs had gone over marginally well, because the margin for failure was minimal. But Wyatt had kept kidding about them, asking what kind of dog they used to make them. He'd had Tug in stitches, but Leah couldn't help thinking that Wyatt really didn't know that hot dogs weren't made from dogs.

"That's wonderful," Leah replied. "I'll have supper ready at six."

"All right."

Then Leah had gotten the garlic and tomatoes from Leo and had ensconced herself in the kitchen for the next three hours. She'd scorched the garlic twice and had to throw it out. The third time, she knocked the coals down low enough so that she had more control over the heat. The garlic softened to clear yet didn't turn brown, just like the instructions said. After that, she'd added onions and the rest of the ingredients. And there were a lot of them. She made sure each one was measured out exactly. But when she got to the basil, she accidently poured too much in and had to try and fish out the excess. When the last mashed tomato had been added, Leah put the lid on the pot and let the gravy simmer.

That done, she went upstairs to freshen up and change while Rosalure and Tug were outside in the gazebo playing house. When Leah had done a decent job of arranging her hair with a lavender ribbon, and buttoned on her eleven-gored jumper dress with its puff-sleeved blouse and smart lace bow tie at the throat, she went downstairs as the clocks were chiming the half hour. She hoped nothing would go wrong from now until six. *Thirty long minutes.* Most especially, she hoped Geneva and Hartzell had made up from their tiff so Geneva wouldn't show up on her doorstep again.

Earlier, her mother-in-law had come over in a tizzy because Hartzell had threatened—once again—to cut off her allowance. The pricey bill had come for her Quaker Thermal Turkish cabinet, along with an order statement from the Niagara Manufacturing Co. for a double-spigot Niagara bath spray. Not to mention the bills from L. P. Hollander & Co. on Fifth Avenue for the winter fur coat she'd sent away for, *and* the bottle of Ed Pinaud's Famous quinine hair tonic had arrived—C.O.D. All of which had Hartzell in a royal fit, or so Geneva claimed.

Leah listened to the tirade for as long as she could stand, then sent Geneva on her way with forced reassurance that everything would be all right. But her mother-in-law went down the walk blowing her nose into an embroidered handkerchief, and Leah had the feeling that the end was not yet soon to come. Geneva would be harping about the unfairness of her tightwad husband and would get her way in the long run. As usual.

After putting on the water for the noodles, Leah selected her favorite Puccini Grand Opera recording for the phonograph, *La Bohème.* Just as Signora Resky's clarion voice carried through the parlor, making Leah smile, the new doorbell rang.

Taking a deep breath, Leah walked to the foyer, paused at the oak-framed mirror, smoothed her hair and any unseen wrinkles in the gored skirt, then opened the door.

Wyatt stood at the threshold, hat in hand, hair damp and

combed away from his forehead, holding a bouquet of pastel sweet peas that were slightly droopy from the heat. Leah was touched by his thoughtfulness.

"Please, come in." She stepped aside so that he could enter.

"Something smells good," Wyatt commented as he hung his hat on a coat tree hook.

Yes, Leah thought, and breathed in shaving soap. It was nice to have the masculine smell of Mennen back in the house. She gazed at him with a warm feeling. Wyatt's fresh, clean hair was thick and ever so slightly the color of polished silver at the temples. She liked that. It gave him distinction and strength in his face.

"These are for you, from Leo and me." Wyatt stretched out his hand to present the sweet peas. Leo grew the flowers on a trellis in his garden and he knew she enjoyed their subtle fragrance.

"How kind."

Though they had been in each other's company enough times not to get tongue-tied, the stress of formality weighed on Leah. She felt very self-conscious and nervous, as if this were her first encounter with Wyatt alone.

"Well . . . come this way," Leah managed to say. "Supper is about ready. All I have to do is drain the noodles. Why don't you sit down while I get a vase for these?"

Leah walked into the parlor, Wyatt following. Turning to face him, she asked, "Would you care for something to drink? I have brandy. My late husband occasionally indulged and there is a bottle left."

"No thanks."

"Oh, well, would you like a Coca-Cola, then?" She'd gone to the mercantile and stocked up on twelve bottles.

"I'm fine for now."

"All right." She could smell the pasta and water . . . and the scorch of a pan. Alarm flashed through her. "Ah, excuse me. I have to check something."

Leah went through the connecting pocket doors that led into the dining room with as much grace as she could muster, given the sure emergency of removing the pot from the burner. She headed straightaway for the kitchen, plunked the flowers on the sideboard, and reached without care to remove the pan.

"Ouch!" She pulled her hand back and sucked on her fingers while grabbing a pot holder. Whisking the pan off the stove, she realized that it hadn't been the noodles burning. There was sufficient water. It must have been the drops of moisture bubbling over the sides and landing on the stove top. But for some reason, her noodles were stuck together in a glob. Perhaps she should have kept on stirring them.

"Is there a problem?" Wyatt's intrusion gave her a start. Dropping the pan in the sink, she whirled around. He stood less than a foot away from her.

"N–No," she stammered. "There's no problem. Everything's fine." *I hope.*

The wheeze of the dry-hinged screen door in the mudroom slammed closed in Tug's wake. Entering the kitchen, he wrinkled his freckled nose and announced, "Something stinks in here."

That was the last thing Leah needed to hear. "Oh, do be quiet, Tug, or I'll box your ears."

Tug shrugged, then seeing Wyatt, braced his hands on his six-guns. "Hey, Wyatt, are you part of the posse?"

Wyatt folded his arms across his chest. "I reckon I could be. Who you going after today?"

"More bad guys."

"Sounds like they'll be tough."

"I reckon."

Rosalure came inside and set the porcelain doll she'd gotten for her birthday on the counter. "Tug, you were supposed to be watching the baby. You just left her in the grass on her face." She frowned. "Some father you are."

"I'm no dad. I'm a cowboy."

Rosalure stared at Wyatt with reservation. Earlier, when Leah had told the children Wyatt was coming for supper, Rosalure had asked if she was planning on marrying Wyatt. The question had caught Leah completely off guard and she'd told Rosalure that she and Wyatt weren't courting. They were merely friends who enjoyed each other's company.

"Why doesn't everyone sit down?" Leah suggested. "Rosalure, show Wyatt to his seat."

"Does he have to sit where my dad sat again?" Rosalure asked. The question wasn't voiced with malice, but Leah sensed a trace of resentment in her daughter's tone. Rosalure had been five when Owen died, and she remembered her father. She knew that the head of the table had been his. When Wyatt had stayed for hot dogs the last time, Leah had been uncertain whether to seat Wyatt in that particular chair. But logic outweighed sentimentality. There were four chairs at the table at all times—one east, west, south, and north, with two extras in the corner of the room. It would have been foolish to get an extra chair and set it next to Tug or Rosalure just so Wyatt could avoid sitting where Owen had.

It wasn't until now that Leah realized there was another solution. One that wouldn't disrespect Rosalure's feelings about her father's importance at the table when he'd been the head of the household.

"No, Rosalure," Leah replied. "I'll sit where Dad used to sit, and Wyatt can sit in my chair."

Rosalure smiled. "Okay."

While everyone went into the dining room, Leah carefully poured the Italian gravy into her best ironstone bowl with its lily and lotus pattern. She dumped the noodles into another. They landed in a chunk. Thoughtfully biting her lower lip, she wished she knew a way to fix them. Perhaps if she broke the noodles up with a fork. She tried that method and it worked somewhat, though there were still lumps.

With a sigh, she picked up the gravy and brought it to the table. Setting the bowl in the center, she was rather proud of herself. The dish looked appetizing and smelled very edible.

"Looks good," Wyatt said, and Leah's heart soared. Now if only it would taste just as good.

She made several trips to the kitchen, bringing the

noodles, bread, a water pitcher, and the flowers. When everyone had been served, Leah motioned, "Well, everyone, *buon appetito.*"

Tug gazed at his minuscule portion. "I thought you said this was gravy. How come it's not brown?"

"Italians call tomato sauce gravy."

Leah put a small amount of the sauce and noodles on her fork, as did Wyatt, Rosalure, and Tug. It seemed as if they all sampled her efforts at the same time. So it was at that corresponding moment that Leah was sure they all knew something was terribly wrong. The flavor was so pungent with garlic it was practically dangerous. She immediately set her fork down and took a long drink of ice water. Rosalure did likewise, but Wyatt was more discreet. At least he nodded with a tight smile while chewing, then put his utensil on the edge of his plate and drank his water without a breath in between gulps.

It was then that Tug said, "I like it, Momma. Almost better than American cheese." Then he scooped a huge bite onto his fork, shoving the wad into his mouth and staining his cheeks tomato red in the process.

"Well, I don't know what could have happened," Leah said for the fifth time as she cleared the table.

Wyatt sat back, watching the efficient way she moved and not caring all that much that the gravy had been so riddled with garlic even he couldn't force his serving down.

"I suppose I got mixed up on cloves of garlic and heads of garlic. I thought they were the same. So when the recipe called for six . . . I just assumed you put all six whole clumps in. I guess that's where I went wrong."

"It's all right," Wyatt reassured her as she took his empty plate. Leah had brought out an emergency substitute of Armour's beef sandwiches with the offer of Bromo Seltzer for anyone who needed it. Only Tug polished off his Italian meal without a single complaint, which Leah couldn't stop commenting on. She'd even risen from her chair and tested his brow for temperature.

"Well, now that I've finished humiliating myself," Leah said as she wiped the last crumbs from the table. "We can retire into the parlor."

Rosalure and Tug had already left the dining room and were in the parlor. Leah had asked Rosalure to rewind the Edison. The symphony notes drifted in a soft melody as he and Leah entered the room together. He didn't know what the foreign opera lady was singing, but he sort of liked the way she sounded when the man sang with her. She had a high-pitched voice, and though he couldn't decipher a word, from the lilting tone alone he figured they were singing about being in love.

"Please, sit down." Leah offered him a chair by the hearth once again, and he obliged. Then she took a seat opposite him and folded her hands in her lap, though she didn't appear to be relaxed. "Would you like a cup of coffee?"

"No, thanks."

Wyatt began to have reservations about coming. He'd been so starved for moments like this that he'd made a rash judgment in accepting Leah's invitation. Throughout supper, he realized that by sharing her table, her home, her children, he was torturing himself. All this around him was something he couldn't have.

Rosalure brought out a tablet and pencil, sat on the davenport, and began to sketch, while Tug sat down at Wyatt's feet and stared at him. Wyatt was fond of Tug and enjoyed fooling around with him about cowboys and make-shift bad guys. In a way, Tug reminded Wyatt of his youngest brother Todd. Todd had always gone around with an exaggerated swagger and a chest puffed out with bluster as he hunted for rustlers on their land.

Crossing his legs at the ankles, Wyatt asked Leah, "Do you know what she's singing about?"

Leah straightened, licking her lips. "Well, yes, I do. That's Musetta's aria. She's walking down the street thinking how—" A hint of color marked her cheeks. "—how beautiful and desired she is. How graceful and charming she is as people turn to admire her. She loves their glances, and Marcello and Alcindoro comment on her as she passes by."

The tempo changed and Wyatt wondered, "What's she saying now?"

"That passion has betrayed her. And deep in her heart she'd never tell. She'd rather die."

Wyatt grew more interested. "Tell what?"

Leah's lashes lowered along with her voice when she gave him an explanation. "About the passionate affair."

"What's a passionate affair?" Tug asked, scooting over to Leah.

"Never you mind." Leah cut him off with a stern warning.

But Wyatt wanted to know more about the passionate affair. He was beginning to see the allure of this opera stuff if it was about lovers and liaisons.

Easing back in his chair, Wyatt brought his foot onto his knee. "How do you know that's what it's about when it's not being sung in English?"

Leah smoothed a shock of hair from Tug's brow. "Though most would think it's a foolish waste of time, I've been studying the Italian language so I can speak it."

"I noticed that you talk that way sometimes."

Her eyes were a golden brown, her seductive brows arched. "Does it bother you?"

"No. In fact, I like it."

The radiant smile on Leah's lips was enough to lure Wyatt into asking her to engage in their own passionate affair and damn the consequences.

"If you don't mind," Leah said, rising from her chair, "I'd like your opinion on something." She went to the black-lacquered upright piano and took a folio from its fringe-scarfed top. "I've narrowed down my entries for the contest to these two. Which photograph do you like the best?"

She handed Wyatt the folder and opened it for him. Putting the pictures side by side, she stood back and crossed her arms beneath her breasts. Wyatt lowered his gaze, feeling hers on him with expectancy. On the left was a photo of a ladies' dress pinned to a clothesline. Long shadows were created by the grooves of the skirt gathers. These lines were a contrast to the lighter-colored fabric that stood out on the scoop-necked bodice where ribbons dangled. Beneath the dress, pale rose petals littered the grass. He liked the representation of femininity.

The photo on the right of the folio was of a delicately constructed corner curio cabinet filled with glass figurines of miniature clocks. Sunlight streamed in through an unseen window, creating the illusion that there were two of each clock—one real and one shadow.

Both were fine photographs, and he was impressed with Leah's ability to capture something so simple and make the image jump off the paper to catch his attention.

Lifting his eyes to meet hers, he asked, "I suppose the judges are men."

"Yes."

"Then I'd enter the dress."

"Really?"

"The clocks are very good. I would have never thought to take a picture of something like that. But the dress will capture a man's attention better." Wyatt closed the folio and handed it back to her. "It captured mine. You're a good photographer, Leah."

Their knuckles brushed as she took the pictures. The touch left a jolt in his heart and he looked at her in a way that he had no business doing. She tried to disguise her blush by turning away, but he saw the heightened color on her cheeks.

The music ended and Tug jumped up. "Can I crank the Edison this time?"

"Yes," Leah replied in a composed voice after she replaced the folder and resumed her seat. "You may."

Wyatt thought it best to rein in his wayward thoughts. So he watched as the boy lifted a heavy-looking arm off the black disk. Then he opened the grillwork cabinet where a large horn was located. There was a handle—the type Wyatt had seen in front of automobiles. Tug grasped it and gave the handle many turns, as if winding a clock. The plate above began to rotate and spin, and Tug set the arm down on one of the grooves. Music sprang forth once again.

"Haven't you ever seen a phonograph before?" Leah inquired as the opera wrapped around them.

"Frankly, no."

She gave him a perplexing gaze. "How is it that you haven't seen phonographs or eaten hot dogs?"

There had been many clues he'd given her to kindle her interest about where he'd come from. They hadn't been intentional. They had merely been the truth of things. To a certain degree. The absolute truth was too harsh. But he began to wonder how she would feel knowing where he'd been. Would she look at him as if he were dirt? Or would it matter to her?

Wyatt would never know. Because telling anyone the truth was not in his cards. That part of his life was behind him, so there was no point in discussing it. Common knowledge of his background would only cause people to shun him. He just wanted to get on with living and make up for all those years. Get on with his freedom and make a fresh start with the money. His future was tied up in those satchels. He had to find them. And then, when he was well-off, maybe Leah might . . .

Maybe she might change her mind about New York and settle in with him.

Wyatt had imagined himself wed to a younger woman and starting his own house full of children. But at thirty-eight, any woman of a companionable marriage age would have to be a spinster or widow. Recalling the Clinkingbeard sisters, Wyatt amended his thought that his intended probably wouldn't be much to look at if she was a spinster. In the west, men outnumbered women, and those who weren't yet married past the age of twenty would have to be about as handsome as a sack of horseshoes. She'd sure be no parlor ornament, not like Leah.

But Leah didn't come alone. She came with a package, part of which was a dead husband's memory, another man's offspring, and a loaded Kodak camera.

Wyatt should have shied away, but Leah was so like him in spirit that he couldn't back off. And neither could he outright lie to her when she gazed at him so openly.

His answer was long in coming, but at least he didn't stretch the truth too far. "I've been a cowboy, so I haven't been to too many built-up towns. I've mostly seen the back country of Wyoming, Montana, and Utah." He purposefully omitted Colorado. "I haven't seen much." It wasn't a total fabrication, though he hadn't been an honest-to-goodness cowboy for over twenty years. Ranging and branding herds had been a sideline during his teens until he'd gotten into more lucrative ways to earn a buck. But throughout some freezing winters when traveling was rough going, he and the boys would fall back on what they knew to get them by. Cattle was about as good a way to make a few dollars as any when the nearest bank was between here and a blizzard.

Tug came to life and scrambled back to Wyatt. "You're truly a cowboy? I never thought you were for real 'cause you wash dishes."

"I'm just working here until I can get my place going."

This news unleashed a torrent of questions from Tug. "Can you rope cows? Can you ride broncs? Can you brand steers? Can you ride bulls?"

"I can." *Or I could.* There'd been a time he could ride anything with hair on it, be it bronc or bull. He'd been damn good at it, too. Won himself a few stakes in some traveling rodeos. But that was back when he wasn't as heavy with muscles as he was now. His arms and legs had grown stronger and hardened in places that prevented him from being the willowy lad he once was.

"Could you show me how to rope?" Tug was looking at him through hopeful eyes and practically panting with excitement like a lapdog. "I got a genuine Bob Lassiter lariat with a rawhide honda. It's got a good grip."

"I reckon it would with a rawhide honda."

"Yep." Tug vigorously shook his head. "It works real good. . . . I mean, I think it does. I've never been able to lasso anything, but I'm sure it works real good. It would work better if you showed me how to make it lasso my swing horse. I've been trying, but I can't get it quite right. Could you *please* show me how to throw it?"

Wyatt shifted in the chair, thinking that he was getting in deeper than was wise with the boy. But seeing that heartening grin on Tug's face had Wyatt nodding. "Go fetch it then, and we'll have a go of it."

"Gee! Thanks."

Tug was on his feet and bounding up the stairs.

"That's very nice of you, Wyatt," Leah said. "He's asked me to show him, but I don't know how to throw a rope. Neither does Hartzell."

"There's not much to it." Wyatt figured he could still snag a cow. That was one thing a cowboy never forgot once he learned.

Tug came back and halted in a breathless skid. Proudly, he presented Wyatt with his lariat. "See. I got it last Christmas."

"You've had the rope for nearly a year and haven't caught anything yet?"

"Nope."

"Where's that horse?"

"In the front yard."

Wyatt glanced at Leah and Rosalure. "You ladies coming?"

Rosalure set her sketch pad down. "Sure."

Leah was already on her feet. "I wouldn't miss it."

"Come on then. Cowboy Tug is going to get his first bronc."

Leah rested her arms on the porch railing next to Rosalure, watching as Tug swung out the rope over and over in an effort to snag the loop around the neck of his rocking horse. Each time, the circle fell short or didn't hold its shape. His little face was determined when Wyatt corrected his throw and had him try again.

After the thirtieth-odd time, whether it was the faint breeze, pure luck, or skill that suddenly kicked in, Tug got the rope around the horse's neck. He let out a whoop so loud, he could have knocked the apples out of the tree.

"I did it! I did it!"

Rosalure left the veranda to check out the rope, as did Leah. Tug ran to her and took her hand to show her his accomplishment.

"See, Momma. I did it."

"I see that."

"I've always wanted to be a cowboy, but Poppa keeps saying I'm going to work at the bank when I get bigger, like my dad did. I don't want to. I'm going to be just like Wyatt when I grow up."

Leah spared a glance at Wyatt. Wistfulness had stolen into his expression.

"I'm going to do it again," Tug declared.

She ruffled his hair, still gazing at Wyatt. The sunset was behind him, casting the brim of his hat and his broad shoulders in hues of gold. His handsome face had captured a place in her heart, and the obvious hit her. She desired him as a wife desired her husband. She was thinking about asking Wyatt Holloway to share her four-poster bed. It was a very liberal thought. Even too modern for her own beliefs, but she couldn't stop wanting him.

Leah had to get that notion out of her head immediately. What kind of mother was she to think such a thing in the company of her young children?

Dismayed, Leah answered her own burning question. Maybe she was a mother who was missing intimacy. That closeness and bond with another person that came from touches and caresses of warm skin and naked embraces. Though she and Owen hadn't been fervent in the bedroom, tenderness and cuddling afterward had made Leah feel loved.

She missed feeling that now.

She missed loving a man.

Before she got too sentimental, Leah turned away and went for the porch. Unbidden, she felt the sting of tears well in her eyes. It was ridiculous to be feeling lonely. She had her children. She had her career. She had a lot to keep her busy.

But there was no one to kiss good night, no one's strong arms in which to sleep . . . or to wake up in the morning with her cheek on a chest, her hair fanned around them.

Wyatt's voice intruded on her musings, near to her ear. "What's the matter?"

With her knuckles, she brushed a stray tear from her eye and refused to let another slip. "W—Why, nothing."

He followed her up the steps and stood at the railing with her. Very close. Too close for her to stay clearheaded. "Something upset you."

She shook her head and took in a fortifying breath. "I was just thinking, that's all."

"Thinking about something that made you cry."

"I was sad for Tug," she hedged. "I was thinking it would have been nice if his father could have shown him that trick. Not that I don't appreciate what you did. I just worry about Tug's not having a man's influence."

Wyatt nodded and grew thoughtful as they both watched the sun lower behind the feathery tops of pines on the mountain. "Has it been real hard on you, losing your husband?"

"His illness was lengthy and watching him slip away was difficult. When he finally let go, I was filled with grief, yet guilty with relief he didn't have to suffer anymore."

"What happened?"

"He contracted malaria in the Spanish American War, though it wasn't until he returned home that the symptoms began to show nearly a year later. He'd had intermittent bouts, but we never thought they were anything but the flu. After awhile, when he was getting sick once a month, the doctor thought it was a case of pneumonia, because Owen would respond to the treatment for chills; but two weeks later, his fever would come back. There were days of delirium, then he finally went into a coma and died a week later. Tug was only a baby when Owen died. He doesn't remember." Leah gazed pensively across the yard. "But Rosalure does. It devastated her to see her father so sick."

Leaning forward, Wyatt put his elbows on the rail. "I'm sorry."

"Me, too. Mostly for the children."

"You should be for yourself, too. It isn't easy for a woman to be alone."

Leah didn't want to appear weak and incapable of taking care of herself and her children. "It's no harder than a man's being alone."

A slice of quiet passed between them in which Marshal Bean Scudder came up to the gate and fiddled with the latch to let himself in.

Leah straightened and stepped a respectable distance away from Wyatt. "Marshal," she welcomed, though she didn't find his visit particularly welcome at this moment.

Wyatt remained tight-lipped.

When Scudder was inside, he lumbered toward them on the chunky heels of his oiled-hide boots. "Boy," he said to Wyatt. Leah didn't regard Bean's slight as friendly by any means. "Last place I'd expect to see you on a Wednesday night. The Chinaman fire you?"

"Leo's closed tonight."

"Is he now."

"The cook is sick."

Scudder huffed to a stop, snagged his hat off, and wiped his forehead with the cuff of his sleeve. "So you get a free night to spend here." Then to Leah, his caterpillar brows rose. "Surprised to see you and Holloway out on the veranda. Any special reason?"

Leah didn't like her privacy infringed upon. It was bad enough Geneva wanted to know about her personal life and her comings and goings. She wasn't going to report any such thing to the marshal.

"No special reason," she replied. Before Scudder could question her further, she plunged in with a question of her own. "What brings you out here this late in the day?"

Scudder smashed his hat back on his head, then absently twirled and smoothed the waxed end of his full mustache. The bush of facial hair was in its prime; the marshal had been grooming the wiry hairs as if they were a ewe he was getting ready to present at the fair. Bean Scudder entered the Whopper Mustache contest at the Aspenglow River Stampede and Eternity Grange No. 321 Exposition every year. And every year he won hands down.

Scudder hooked his fat thumbs into his suspenders and rocked back on his heels with his neck out like a turtle. "That old saddle tramp Earl Stretch drifted into town again tonight. I just arrested him for attempting to pick a pocket over at the Clipper Saloon. I'll need you to come by the jail first thing tomorrow and update his mug shot. He's got whiskers now."

"I can be there."

"Good." Scudder's marble-sized eyes narrowed in on Wyatt. "Mrs. Kirkland is a fine woman, boy. Wouldn't want you causing any trouble over here for her."

If Leah didn't need to keep her job with the law office taking those mug shots, she would have shooed Bean Scudder off her stoop.

"I don't cause trouble," Wyatt remarked, adjusting the angle of his hat so that the brim rode up, as if he meant business. He thrust out one hip in the process and stood with a hand in his pocket.

"Not in my town, you don't." Then Scudder lay his fingers to the brim of his hat. "See you in the morning, Mrs. Kirkland."

Leah said nothing as he walked down the path and continued on to the boardwalk.

Wyatt readjusted his hat against the setting sun. "I should be getting on myself. Thanks for everything, Leah."

"Must you?" Leah didn't want him to leave. She wished he could come back inside and they could talk for a while.

"Yeah, I've got an early morning to put in." Wyatt's hand slid over the railing and he went down the steps. Leah stayed behind, afraid that if she went with him she'd slip her hand in his and steer him back toward the house.

"Hey, Tug, you keep on practicing."

"I will, Wyatt."

Wyatt went to Rosalure, who sat in the swing. He gave her a big push that made her laugh.

Knowing that Wyatt liked it when she used Italian, Leah called, *"Buona sera, il signor Holloway."*

His mouth curved into a smile, then he turned and walked to the gate.

As Tug kept up his roping, and Rosalure sat in the swing on the live oak singing softly, Leah stayed on the porch and watched Wyatt walk down Main Street until he disappeared from view. When he was gone, the homey picture in her yard lost its life. Suddenly, nothing had dimension any-more . . . everything seemed gray and flat.

✦ 14 ✦

There is no high road
to happiness or misfortune.
—Chinese proverb

Leah came down the stairs from her studio to answer the
persistent ring of the bell. When she opened the door, she
was met by a uniformed Mr. Quigley. The strap of his
mailbag cut across his shoulder, and the government-issued
cap on his head had a letter sticking out from the band.

"Good morning, Mrs. Kirkland," he said solicitously.

"Good morning, Mr. Quigley."

His hand grasped several letters addressed to her, and
Leah held back a frown. "You could have dropped those in
the mail slot. No need to hand deliver them."

"Oh, on the contrary." He removed his hat by the bill,
slipped the letter out from the band, then tucked the hat
under his arm. "Seeing as this came all the way from Italy, I
couldn't treat it like ordinary U.S. mail."

Leah's breath quickened as she caught a glimpse of an
envelope with many inked cancelations and a bold, slanted
script. Putting her hand to her throat, she reached for and
grasped the letter. She could hear her heart beating as she
scanned the postmark.

Lombardy, Italiana.

"Oh, my," she whispered, feeling as if it were Christmas and she were about to get the best present of her life. She began to close the door, paying no heed to the prying gaze of Mr. Quigley.

A size nine wide-width storm shoe belonging to one Mr. Fremont Quigley wedged in the path of the door before she could fully close the panel. "Who do you know all the way in Italy?" he queried with the assertion of a man who wouldn't be satisfied until he got an answer.

Leah would never in a million years tell the postmaster why she'd written to Italy. She'd known this day would come when he'd be nosy enough to ask, so she'd been ready with an answer for over a month. "I have a pen pal."

"Pen pal?"

"Yes. It's all the rage. Writing to Europe, that is." Trying discreetly to nudge his foot away from the bottom of the door with the tip of her shoe, she succeeded in easing his Goodyear tread back a few inches, because he hadn't been paying attention. She spoke in the narrowing crack of the door as she closed it. "Well, thank you so much for the mail. Good day, Mr. Quigley."

Leah shut the door with an *oomph* and pressed her back to the heavy wood. Looking down at the paper in her hand, she was almost afraid to open the seal. She had waited so long for this. With quivering fingers, she broke open the flap and began to read the words penned in Italian.

La Signora Kirkland—
Mi dispiace di informi è stato rubato il mille denar con Il Signor Giuseppe Ciccolella . . .

Leah had to be mistranslating. She thought that the letter had said . . . No, it couldn't have. She walked to the stairs and sat on the last tread to reread the message calmly.

Mrs. Kirkland—
I am sorry to inform you, your one thousand dollars has been stolen from you by Mr. Giuseppe Ciccolella. I regret to say, Mr. Ciccolella has been arrested for

embezzling funds from the Veneto Academy for Image Artists. Every effort is being made to recoup students' funds, but at this time, the academy will not be operating.

> *Yours—*
> *Ezio Buzzati*
> *Investigative Commissioner of Fraud*
> *Lombardy Constable District No. 41*

The parchment fell like limp cabbage into Leah's lap, and she stared at the colors of stained glass in the door. It couldn't be true. Her money was gone . . . so were her expectations of studying where Alfred Stieglitz had. What was she to do now?

The children had gone swimming with the Sommercamps at the lake for the day, so Leah had stuffed the letter into the slash of her skirt pocket and walked the length of Main Street to think. She did that on occasion—take walks to clear her head, usually when she was stumped on a project and was lacking inspiration and in dire need of some. The fresh air did her good, and observing people and their habits on the streets while going about their business most times got her out of her slump. But today, Leah didn't think a walk on Main Street could possibly fix what was now broken beyond repair.

After passing Carlyle A. Corn's Hardware Emporium, Leah knew she needed to talk to someone. She'd always gone to Leo with her troubles. But at this moment, she felt compelled to talk to Wyatt. His name constantly lingered around the edges of her mind. She sensed he'd be able to offer her advice on how to rid herself of the jagged disappointment she was feeling. But that would mean she'd have to tell him about the Veneto Academy. It would be embarrassing to admit she'd been swindled.

Leah passed the Eternity Security Bank just as Geneva briskly walked out the door with her starched muslin petticoats in a flitter. "Leah!" she exclaimed. "My goodness! A friendly face."

Something was definitely amiss with her mother-in-law.

"It's dreadful!" Geneva squawked, the silk fruits anchored in her hat bobbing. "He's really done it this time."

Leah was scarcely in the mood for Geneva's problems when she had her own, but she felt obligated to ask, "Who has done what?"

"That husband of mine has threatened to divorce me if I spend one more cent on what he calls 'the worthless products of flimflam men.' He's being impossible, I tell you."

Leah kept on walking with Geneva trailing along.

"I told him to be reasonable," the older woman declared. "But no. Even to *accuse* me of misappropriating household funds is unthinkable. I spend no more than he does on his Republic cigars and Cascaret brandy. Am I to be denied the same luxuries as my husband? Am I a second-class citizen in my own home? Don't *I* count for anything? I mean, honestly, if I don't get my Dr. John Wilson Gibbs electric massage roller, I'll be covered with wrinkles and have facial blemishes. Really, why shouldn't I have the massage roller when it guarantees to take off a pound a day? Does he want me fat? I should say not. If I don't get one of those massagers, it will be the ruin of me. My life will be over," she lamented. "My—"

"How about *my* life?" Leah snipped off her tirade as if it were a dead flower that needed pruning. She couldn't listen to another word without going crazy. "My life is in a sorry state of affairs, too. You're not the only one with problems."

Leah had rarely if ever spoken out of turn to Geneva and her harsh words halted the woman in her tracks. "Well, I dare say, someone is having her monthly time."

Leah walked on, hoping Geneva would go away. But she didn't and Leah ignored her as she came to the Anvil and Forge. The double-wide doors were thrown up, and a blacksmith's hammer rang out from the dusky interior.

Leah thought about going inside to ask Mr. Tinhorn if he knew where she could find Wyatt at this time of the day, but Wyatt rode toward the livery on July, saving her from asking.

The sunlight shined across the horse's black mane and coat, pouring its warmth over Wyatt and leaving his eyes in shadow beneath the brim of his hat. With the dark stubble across his jaw, he appeared unscrupulous enough to be an outlaw. But she knew better than that. All the same, she was drawn to the rugged and vital strength of his powerful body as he sat in the saddle.

She was glad he'd shown up, but not that Geneva hadn't gone on her way. A sincere conversation with Wyatt couldn't be personal with her mother-in-law around to listen in.

"Leah, we're not finished with—"

"I believe we are, Geneva." Leah smiled at Wyatt.

Wyatt gave the reins pressure, pulling back and bringing July to a halt at the curb. "Nice morning for a ride," he said to both women. "It's going to be a scorcher again."

"Yes, it is," Leah remarked, shading her eyes against the sun as she lifted her chin to gaze at him.

Leah was about to aggressively suggest that Geneva run along and buy herself the September issue of the *Ladies Home Journal,* then treat herself to a pink lemonade at the Coffeepot Cafe, when there came an explosive chugging. Though the noise was distant enough for Leah to have overlooked the *pop-popping,* that sound was definitely out of place for Eternity and was cause for notice.

Both she and Geneva gazed down the road and saw dust rising at the far edge of Main.

Cap-pow!

That gunpowder-like eruption came again, along with a *chug, chug, chug.* A sputtering and a wheeze sounded just the same as a ninety-year-old man with a case of far-gone tuberculous. Then the *toot-toot* of a bulb horn burped out a warning to a group of pedestrians in the middle of the street crossing over to the Beaumont Hotel. They ran as if they were a flock of chickens being scattered by a fox.

Wyatt's horse nickered and snorted, making Leah jump and take several quick steps toward the livery.

"Easy, boy." Wyatt ran his hand over the horse's neck in an effort to sooth the skittish July.

As the blur of metal approached, Leah could make out the automobile. She didn't know enough about them to decipher the make or model, but it was a fancy one. Plum in color where it wasn't coated with chalky dust, with a fine leather interior and a detachable tonneau. The top was folded back in an accordion manner, and the rear part with seats was loaded with a parcel of black trunks and cases. A steady hand had painted the white script on the auto's door:

T. N. T. Vibratrel

The smoke coming from the motor puffed out in a cloud of gray, and was likely to choke out the snoozing horses tethered on the posts in front of City Hall. They all started shifting their weight, eyes rolling upward.

July's pointed ears were thrust back, his teeth and lips chomping and working over the bit in his mouth.

"Whoa, July. Whoa." Wyatt gave the command in a low and soft voice, but with a chord of full control.

Coming into town lopsided on three rims and one tire that looked ready to burst, that heavy touring car rolled to a stop right in front of Geneva and Leah. The driver cut the engine, and a report of backfire began. July's feet did a nervous dance, and Wyatt's muscles were bulging in his arms when he took command of those reins to calm the black horse down.

One of the horses that'd been tethered by the reins rather than a lead rope at City Hall jerked his head and snapped the leather in two as he broke free and took off in a run up Seventh Avenue.

The car died on a vapor of stinking smoke and with Wyatt's curse of eternal damnation. An automobile in Eternity was such a rare sight that not even Geneva bothered to scold Wyatt for swearing, because she—like the other citizens exiting buildings and gathering around for a look-see—was in awe over the machine that was radiating enough heat a person could fry an egg on its hood.

Doffing his smudged goggles and roadster hat, the man behind the dash spoke in a voice as slick as the pomade in his rust-colored hair, "Afternoon, folks. The *T. N. T.* stands for Tiberius N. Tee." He slapped the lettering on the door with a loud whack. "Vibratrel! That's what it's all about! The best dang treatment you'll ever find for curing cases of nervous headache, neuralgia, muscular rheumatism, insomnia, et cetera. Stimulates the entire nervous system." Without taking a breath, he pointed his finger at Wyatt and spouted, "Son, I believe that horse of yours is in dire need of this product. He's spooked so bad, I'd swan he's a shaking in his iron shoes." With that, Tiberius gave a little chuckle. Several of those in attendance laughed with him.

Wyatt frowned with cold fury, his eyes hooded. "That rotten smelling contraption you're in is what's making this horse's hair stand up."

"This rotten smelling contraption?" Tiberius parroted with mock horror. "Why, son, let me tell you a thing or two about this here automobile. It's a top-of-the-line nineteen-ought-three Oldsmobile with power transmitted to the rear axle by a roller chain of four thousand pounds of working strength, running *dee*-rect," he pronounced with a twang, "from the motor shaft. It's operated by a single lever from the seat and responds instantly to the will of the operator. Not like that horse of yours, son, whose just about ready to bolt outta his hide."

"At least he's got four solid feet, not like those chewed-up rounds of rubber you've got there." Wyatt eased forward in the saddle, sitting taller. "Let's see how far you get on them now that they've gone flatter than a shadow." Then he wheeled the prancing July around and gave him the spurs.

Though Leah didn't share the same animosity for automobiles as Wyatt, she had found Tiberius N. Tee to be rude and brash.

"Never mind about him, folks," Tiberius went on. "I can tell he won't be sampling the benefits of the Vibratrel, and be sorely lacking in health for it." The huckster stood up and motioned the crowd in with his right hand, where he wore a gold Masonic ring on his pinky finger. "Gather around, folks. Gather around."

Leah gazed down the street, hoping to find Wyatt. But he

had ridden out of sight. Geneva brushed past her to move in closer to Tiberius, and Leah held back, letting the onlookers walk ahead. She went to the bench in front of the livery and sat down, wishing Wyatt would return soon, that she could have the opportunity to speak with him.

"Let me testify to this statement," Tiberius hawked, "that the Vibratrel vibrates five thousand times a minute, folks, and is under perfect control with a switch that regulates the vibrating mechanism. The machine is so simple to use, it can be handled by a child. Now if that hasn't got your attention, ladies and gentlemen, you are surely not the customers for me."

Geneva piped up like a church organ. "What did you say your name was?"

"Tiberius N. Tee, but I believe it's going to be Tibby to you, good madam. All my customers call me Tibby." He grinned like a fat cat. "Now then, folks, the Vibratrel is nickel plated and comes complete in an attractive case, and it's a bargain for the price."

"Just what is the price?" someone asked.

"Anyone who cares about the fortification of their body can't afford *not* to have a Vibratrel," Tibby countered in a crafty tone.

A few of the spectators scoffed at the way he was hedging and wandered off, and Tibby acted fast. "I agree, folks. It's hot out here." He flipped the car door open and hopped out. "No sense in doing business on the street. I'll be checking into a room at the nearest hotel and giving a demonstration in the lobby at eight this evening." To the disbanding crowd, he announced, "And by the by, not only do I endorse the Vibratrel, I have a complete line of wigs, hairpieces, toupees, and mustaches that are of the finest quality and can't be bought in a catalog anywhere."

Geneva lingered, her teeth catching her lower lip.

Tibby tipped his hat to her. "Pretty lady, would you be so kind as to point me to the nearest hardware store. It would seem I have three flat tires and am running that eight-horse power engine of mine on mere gasoline fumes. Time for a fill-up."

"Oh, my . . . well . . ." Geneva blushed brighter than a new penny. "Why, I could show you where the hardware store is, if you want."

"I would be delighted to share your company on the walk." He offered her the crook of his arm and Geneva took it without blinking an eye. "And may I say, good madam, that the Vibratrel could work wonders for you. Though I'm sure you are in excellent health as we speak. Not a day over forty, to be certain."

Geneva tittered. "Oh, you're too kind."

"Never, my dear. I know classic good health. But one can never take fitness for granted. I believe that the Vibratrel could make a new woman out of you."

Their voices droned to murmurs, and Leah could hear no more. Not that she wanted to. Geneva wasn't acting her age, nor herself, and Leah hoped Hartzell gave her what-for when he found out his wife had bought a T. N. T. Vibratrel when he'd specifically told her not to purchase another newfangled doodad to restore her youth and beauty.

"If there's some justice in this town, Bean Scudder's going to kick that man's hide out of Eternity before sundown."

Turning toward the sound of Wyatt's voice, Leah mutely nodded, following his hard gaze leveled on the Oldsmobile.

"I came through the back of the livery," Wyatt explained, taking off his hat and wiping his forehead with the back of his arm. "That drummer rubbed me the wrong way."

Leah rose from the bench and agreed, "But I bet he's going to sell a few of those Vibratrels before he leaves town."

Slapping the dust from his hat, Wyatt replaced the Stetson on his head and thrust his hands into his back pockets. "I've got a half hour before I have to be at the Happy City. Can I buy you a cola?"

"I'd like that, Wyatt."

Wyatt put his hand on the small of her back and guided her toward the cafe.

Casswell Tinhorn's voice beckoned before they got too far along. "Hey, Wyatt!"

Turning, Wyatt lifted his chin a notch. "Yeah?"

"Found y'all a bronc you can practice on." The creases at the corners of Tinhorn's eyes were lined with soot, and his flushed face shined with sweat. "A friend of mine pastures a gelding down yonder by the Aspenglow on a forty-acre place. Ax Miller—that's his name, said you could help yourself to B. B. tomorrow. Ax and his wife'll be at church in the morning, so if you go out early, B. B. is the fleabitten roan. I didn't have any luck with the bull though, but I've got one more possibility."

"Obliged, Tinhorn."

"Y'all are crazy, you know." Casswell wiped the grime from his neck with a handkerchief that hadn't been white in some time. "You're too old to be getting y'self throwed off a pony."

Wyatt shrugged dismissively. "I've still got all my teeth."

"Not for long," the blacksmith snorted. "Y'all are going to get 'em kicked out if you get your mouth in the line of fire."

"Don't plan to."

Tinhorn waved them off and went back inside. Wyatt went on with Leah and she gave him a speculative glance.

"Are you really going to try and break a wild horse?"

"Yes."

"What for?"

"I need the practice."

Leah was given no opportunity to inquire further, as they'd reached the Coffeepot Cafe and Wyatt held the door open for her. A bell jingled overhead announcing their arrival. The small restaurant was tiny but cozy with round tables covered by hand-embroidered cotton cloths. No matter what time of the year, a patron could always find a seasonal centerpiece on his table. Whether it was fresh-cut garden flowers, pine boughs and cranberries, or corn husks and miniature pumpkins, Shelva DuChenne ran a nice little eatery. She did mostly all the cooking herself, and was best known for her brown Betty. Her daughter Grace ran the dining room and appeared from the back with an apron around her slim waist and an order pad in her hand.

The noon dinner rush had a ways to go before it commenced, so Leah and Wyatt pretty much had the cafe to themselves. The only other customers were the eldest members of the B.P.O.E. No. 406, Wither Fosdick and Huff McMasters, two of Eternity's best checker players. They'd set up a board near the dotted swiss–curtained window where the sun blazed across their table. Each was dozing through a game half finished.

"Hi there," Grace DuChenne greeted in a friendly tone as Wyatt removed his hat. "Good to see you, Mrs. Kirkland. Been a long time since you come into the cafe. Sit wherever you want. The place isn't near full-up yet."

Wyatt chose a table in the corner nearest to the back wall. He held a chair out for her and Leah sat as Grace flapped menus down before them.

"We'd like two Coca-Colas, darlin'," Wyatt said, handing the menus back.

An unexpected pang of jealousy knocked Leah in the ribs. Though the owner's daughter was pretty with her corn silk–colored hair in a fashionable twist, and meadow-green eyes that were trimmed with thick blond lashes, she had barely turned seventeen this summer. She was awfully young for Wyatt . . . but too comely not to turn his head.

Suddenly, Leah felt every bit her twenty-six years. She found herself reaching to the back of her neck to fuss with the baby-fine wisps of hair that always seemed to fall from her bun. When Wyatt's gaze followed the younger woman as she went off to get their drinks, Leah quickly pinched some color into her cheeks and wet her lips to make them shine.

"Do you come here often?" Leah asked in what she hoped was a tone as casual as Sunday.

Redirecting his gaze on Leah, Wyatt adjusted the lineup of the salt and pepper shakers. "Not all that much. I sometimes buy breakfast. The food is always hot and the service is pleasant."

"Hmm." Leah didn't feel any better.

Grace returned with two colas she'd already popped the caps to, and with glasses tipped upside-down over their narrow mouths. She set each bottle and aligned the glasses next to them, then pulled a bill from her apron pocket and set it between Wyatt and Leah. "If there's anything else you'll be wanting, just give a holler. I'll be in back."

Leah watched the girl retreat, wondering why Grace had put the ticket in the middle, as if the refreshment might just be Leah's treat. But Leah supposed she could see how the young girl had gotten that impression. All Grace had ever seen was that Leah Kirkland paid her own way, so why would she accept a Coca-Cola from Wyatt Holloway?

Wanting to groan, Leah silently poured the drink into the glass and took a small sip. She refused to think about how she must appear to be the self-sufficient dowager to those surrounding her. Instead of dwelling on that, she reached into her pocket, took the letter out, and smoothed the wrinkles from the edges as she flattened the paper on the table.

"You never asked why I wanted to learn Italian," she began.

Wyatt drank his cola from the bottle rather than using the glass. "I figured so you could make out what those opera records were talking about."

"Partially, but that's not the entire reason." She fingered the corner of the envelope, then lifted it to show Wyatt. "It's from Italy. A few months ago, I mailed my enrollment fee to the Veneto Academy for Image Artists in Lombardy so I could study photography where Alfred Stieglitz had. I sent the school a thousand dollars."

Wyatt whistled softly and let the pitch fall slowly silent. "A thousand dollars is a lot of money to spend on some academy."

"I would have paid two thousand if it could have gotten me into the school. But that doesn't matter now. My tuition was stolen. Embezzled by the school's director. The Veneto has been shut down, and I'm out the money with no place to go."

Wyatt grew thoughtful, "I thought you wanted to win that contest and go to New York?"

"Oh, I do. But Italy is where all the master artists began."

"So forget it and stay here." Wyatt's eyes held hers, then he quietly added, "Or if you want to be so much like this Stieglitz guy, go to New York and meet him."

The air in Leah's lungs compressed. "I only wish! But heavens, no. I couldn't just knock on his door and say hello. He's just the most famous photographer that there is—for a man. There are women with great talent—E. Alice Austen, Anne Brigman, and Gertrude Käsebier—but none have captured his success. He's like Leonardo da Vinci was to art. He's . . . well, he's simply the best in the business. He's won every conceivable award. No, I couldn't just show up at the Little Galleries without being invited."

"Then win the contest."

"Would I that I could." Leah ran her fingertips over the letter's surface, grazing the slanted words that had been written in a city so far away. "But in order to win, the artist's work has to be so outstanding and compelling that the images leap off the paper. I don't have that kind of talent."

"I thought what you showed me the other night looked good."

"Amateurish," she countered. "I realize that now. I don't have a chance of winning that contest with those photographs. I don't know why I even considered them."

Bringing himself forward, Wyatt leaned toward her and touched her fingers. The light contact sent a warming shiver through her. "That's not true. I think you have a lot of talent."

"I appreciate the confidence, Wyatt. Truly I do. But you don't understand what it's like to be a woman photographer. Men have so long held the most advantageous place behind cameras, and in various professions, simply because they are expected to make a business and not a pastime of what they undertake. Because of my gender, what I do is looked upon as a hobby." She absorbed the warmth from his fingers, pausing to gaze at the connection of their hands. His comfort gave her the courage to admit, "I thought that if I could go to the Veneto, I could be famous and prove everyone wrong. But now it's not to be, and I don't know where to turn or what to do."

He captured her eyes with his, a window of compassion and commiseration lighting the blue depths. "Sometimes life can kick you in the butt."

Wyatt gave Leah's fingers a slight squeeze before letting go. He hadn't planned on holding her hand, but it had seemed natural that he'd reach out to her. She didn't seem shocked by his cynical words, or even that he'd referred to a part of the anatomy.

"Your plans for a ranch aren't going well?"

"Yeah. The money I need hasn't turned up like I thought it would."

"If you need Hartzell to draw up a draft at the bank, or to contact the branch where your money is to come from, I'm sure he'd be happy to assist you."

"It's not that easy." Wyatt gazed at the calluses on his right hand, running his thumbnail over the ridge of hard skin on his palm. He'd never dreamed he'd still be in Eternity weeks after he'd arrived. All those years he'd plotted and gone through the motions of digging up those satchels, his visualization had never had him picking at sandstone for days on end with nothing but aching joints to show for his time. Hell, it was just like he was still on Table Rock, with a pick and a ten-hour day without a thought to call his own. His spirits were so low, and his paycheck from Leo just barely getting him by, that Wyatt had to face the fact that it could be weeks, maybe even months, before he ever found a hint of apricot can . . . if even that. But he couldn't accept that he'd be flat busted and broke after he'd put so much into looking for that sixty thousand dollars.

"You already have a banker handling your account?" Leah's inquiry broke through his reflections.

"The money isn't going to come from any bank." Wyatt had had ample time to come up with a story. One that would accommodate anyone who asked—namely, Scudder.

"I'm waiting on a fellow to arrive in Eternity with some payoff funds I invested in long ago. Only he hasn't shown up yet, and I've got to do something while I'm waiting."

Leah's brows rose. "Do what?"

Wyatt dug into his denim pocket and took out the quarter-folded flyer that had been pasted up over every available electric pole and fence plank. Smoothing the crease out, he showed Leah. Her gaze lowered to the lettering and she quietly scanned the advertisement. Wyatt knew it by heart.

The Aspenglow River Stampede and Eternity Grange No. 321 Exposition had printed the circular calling would-be buckaroos to take a ride on the wild side. One-hundred-dollar cash awards for best bronc bareback skills, bull riding, calf roping, and steer wrestling. Wyatt intended on winning all four. That'd be four hundred big ones in his threadworn pocket. Money he couldn't afford not to go after.

Leah's eyes met his, their color a fiery brown. "You're going to get yourself killed."

"Naw. I've got rawhide gloves and spurs. That's all I need. That and some practice." Wyatt fingered the stubble on his jaw, thinking he would have shaved this morning had he known he'd be sitting across from Leah at a table.

"I assume you know what you're doing when it comes to cattle. But that doesn't mean you have to tangle with a bull for a hundred dollars." She caught a bead of moisture on her bottle before it rolled to the tablecloth and wet the surface. His eyes followed the tip of her finger moving slowly across the glass. He found the gesture to be innocently erotic, making his insides tighten and giving him a run for his concentration on what she was saying. "Last winter over at Half Pint Gilman's place, a ranch hand was gored to death. I didn't know him personally, but I knew of him. Everyone said he was a nice young boy, and his dying like that gives me a case of the shivers."

Snapping his gaze from her hand, Wyatt ventured, "I can't argue with you that it's dangerous. It's been some time since I gave a bull the chance to put me in a funeral parlor, and I have no desire to get my guts ripped out by sharp horns. I think once a man knows how to go about dropping a steer, the method'll stick with him all his life. But first things first. Tomorrow, I'm going to give B. B. a try and see if I can stick my seat to him for a wild ride."

"But what if he throws you?"

"There's no what if, darlin'," he said, unable to quell her concern. "He will buck me off, and that's a fact. What counts is how long I can stay on him before I take flight."

He could see by the determination on her oval face that she was fixing for a debate about the logistics of having the wind knocked out of his chest, so he quickly maneuvered the subject to ram home his point. "Leah, sometimes you've got to take life by the horns and run with it no matter that what you're doing isn't what you'd call comfortable. Maybe you ought to take a picture that's totally unlike you. Something that will make those judges stand up and peel their eyes wide open. Make yourself stick out a little more."

She hung on his words, her mouth a perfect cupid's bow. He thought of when he'd kissed her, wishing that they were alone now so he could kiss her again. "Like do what?"

Her words didn't quite penetrate; he was visualizing her mouth against his. "I don't know," he replied in a voice too gritty to go unnoticed. Fingering the bill, he picked up the edge and palmed the paper. "You're the expert in that area. You'll have to come up with something."

Wyatt stuck his hand into his pocket to retrieve some coins, finding the pressure of fabric against his crotch somewhat tighter than when he'd first sat down. At least he was able to buy her the Coca-Cola. He'd gotten paid and took satisfaction in flipping a dime and a penny on the table. It was a hell of a note when spending eleven cents made him feel like he was something. Wyatt finished his cold cola, letting it chill down his body.

"I've got to be heading over to the restaurant," he said, setting the empty bottle on the table.

"Hmm." Her reply was noncommittal, as if she was thinking over what he'd said and trying to produce an image that would be beneficial to winning that contest.

Wyatt stood, went around the table, and helped Leah with her chair. She smiled at him over her shoulder, and he captured in his mind for later recollection the way her lips curved ever so slightly and were of the softest shade of pink he'd ever seen.

"I appreciate the advice," she said while they walked toward the door. "Though I'm not quite sure what type of photograph I should take. There are so many avenues . . . I just don't know what would be doing too much."

"Do whatever inspires you."

"Yes, I suppose." Her answer was heavy with thought. Then as they crossed Main Street, she abruptly put her hand on his forearm. The contact left him hot where her fingers were on the thin cotton of his shirt. Her exclamation bordered on being distraught. "You only have a week to practice before the rodeo."

"I know that."

"But that's not enough time."

"It'll do."

"I guess it will have to," she murmured, a furrow on her brow. "Just be careful, will you?"

"Sure."

"All this cowboy talk. It makes me think about Tug and his wanting to be one. He'll be tickled to know you're entering in the contests."

"You'll be there to watch?"

"Of course. The whole town comes."

"Then I reckon Scudder will be there."

"He wouldn't miss it. Why, every year he enters the Whopper Mustache contest. He's won five years in a row." Leah let her hand slide from his arm, and her expression grew thoughtful. "Tug has his heart set on being a cowboy. I've never said this to you, but I think it's a dangerous occupation."

"It's only dangerous when you don't know what you're doing. When Tug's older, you can talk him out of it if you still have a mind to. But for now, why don't you let him keep on pretending? I think it's good for a boy to have a fancy that he lives and breathes." Wyatt paused, wondering if he'd overstepped. He'd never given her an opinion about Tug before. Maybe he shouldn't have now. He wasn't the boy's father.

Any qualms that he'd had were laid to rest when Leah laughed softly. "Well, of course you'd encourage him to be a cowboy."

They were at the Happy City's doors where the plump statues stood guard on either side. Leah fidgeted with the letter in her pocket before saying, "Thanks ever so much for the cola. And the advice."

"No problem."

She gave him another tentative smile. Nervous. Blushing. "Well . . ."

"Well."

"Well . . . I don't mean to be following you, but I'd like to talk to Leo and tell him what happened. He knew about Italy."

Wyatt opened the door for her. "Leo's probably in the office."

As they walked past the Chinese watercolors on the walls, and the grinning cat, Wyatt was thinking that it wasn't going to be so bad washing dishes early in the day when he could catch glimpses of Leah sitting at her usual table talking to Leo.

It dawned on him then that there really wasn't anything shameful about doing menial labor. Especially versus robbing banks. He still didn't want to accept that his lot in life was to be elbow-deep in suds. But being able to buy Leah that cola to make up for the root beer put him in a good frame of mind. If she only knew how rich he was going to be. He could buy her new cameras, get her the best equipment. He wanted to make her happy.

Real love was a rare thing for him. Aside from the way he felt about his family, he'd never experienced love before. He'd desired many women and had had many, but he had never craved for what was beyond: a soul and a spirit. It was difficult to know when his thoughts of Leah turned to such, and even more difficult to know what to do with them, seeing as how he had no experience in sorting out such feelings.

Right now, he had nothing to offer her. So there was no point in thinking along such premature lines. Until he could make himself financially sound enough to support her and her children, he had to remind himself not to let his imagination run away.

And there was no sense in wishing he could change his past and be honest with her about being an ex-con, because he couldn't ever come clean about who and what he'd been. She might turn away from him, and he wasn't willing to jeopardize losing her to a man who no longer existed.

❧ 15 ❧

A great fortune depends on luck.
— Chinese proverb

Wyatt undoubtedly could have used more than a week to get the kinks out of his wrangling technique. He was no match for B. B., whose initials stood for Ball Buster. An apt name for the green roan, as Wyatt's backside and crotch had taken abuse each time he managed to land a ride on the bucking and kicking horse.

By Tuesday, Wyatt was so saddle sore he spent a full hour soaking in a steaming tub bath, trying to ease the aches out of him before going to bed.

Leaving the bathroom wearing a fresh change of clothes and a damp towel slung over his shoulder, Wyatt hobbled down the hall on stockinged feet to his room. He fell short when he saw Hartzell Kirkland jiggling a key into the lock of the door across from his. An alligator traveling bag sat on the carpet beside him.

Hartzell lifted his head and swore, "The damn lock is gummed up. See if you can get the key in there for me, would you, Wyatt?"

Wyatt eased forward, wondering what Hartzell was doing

at Almorene East's place when he had a stylish house up on Colorado Street.

Taking the key from Hartzell's trembling fingers, Wyatt wiggled the end into the lock and clicked the door open.

Hartzell bent to pick up his bag, reached around the edge of the wall to switch on the light, and stepped inside while Wyatt stayed back in the open doorway. He needn't go in. The room was much like his. Plain, but clean. He could tell by the slump of Hartzell's shoulders that disappointment hit him as soon as he saw the patched quilt and yellowed curtains.

Leaning into the frame, Wyatt wasn't sure if he should ask the set of circumstances that had brought the well-to-do Hartzell Kirkland, esteemed owner of the Eternity Security Bank, to such a humble establishment.

Hartzell turned and uneremoniously released the handle of his traveling bag. *Thump.* The bottom smacked an oval rag rug at the side of the bed. "I've left Geneva," he announced just as unceremoniously, causing Wyatt to lift a brow. "It looks like you and I will be neighbors."

Then Hartzell choked back a sob and sat on the sagging edge of the mattress with his face in his hand. "I gave that woman the best years of my life . . . and how does she repay me? She spends money as if I printed every last dollar of it." Raising his chin, he gazed at Wyatt. "But I'm through with her. From now on, it'll be just us men. And I, for one, intend on living the good old bachelor life again. Just like you, Wyatt."

Wyatt straightened, the weight of Hartzell's words sinking in. "My life's nothing to pine after."

Ignoring Wyatt's counsel, Hartzell took out a handkerchief and loudly blew his nose. "Take it from me, don't get married. We're going to have one rip-roaring time, you and I. We'll go down to the Bon Ton Saloon for brandy and take in a girlie show at the Temple of Music, then go fishing every Sunday because that's what men do, and eat bacon, fried eggs and potatoes over at the Coffeepot Cafe seven days a week. It's going to be living on the high hog, Wyatt."

Drawing in a breath, Wyatt folded his arms across his

chest. His mind filled with questions, but he broached the one that was foremost. "It seems to me that you've been happy with your wife up until now. I'm sure whatever happened between you and Mrs. Kirkland will work itself out. So, seeing as your accommodations are likely temporary, what made you choose the Starlight when you could have gone to the Beaumont Hotel?"

Hartzell propped his elbows on his knees. "Well, there are two reasons for that. One, that Tiberious N. Tee is staying down at the Beaumont, and he's to blame for all this trouble. And two, you're here, Wyatt."

No answer could have surprised Wyatt more. "Me?"

"You're the only young single man I know. And I wanted to get in on all the bachelor fun you have."

"I don't know about my being so young, and I have to tell you, the bachelor life isn't all that it's cracked up to be."

Hartzell's face fell, and the color in his eyes faded.

The back door to the Happy City was open, allowing the cooling September breeze to filter in and bring a fresh fall atmosphere to the kitchen. Wyatt had always liked autumn and places where the four seasons were prominent. The palettes of golden color on the leaves of aspens and oaks brought a good feeling to him.

With his hands sunk into warm dishwater, Wyatt eased the stiffness from his knuckles by rubbing them. Tomorrow was the rodeo, and he wasn't as ready as he would have liked.

His mind kept on wandering to how he would do. He hoped like hell that his competitors were unskilled, and that he'd out ride them all with his best scores ever. But Wyatt doubted it would be so. He massaged a bruise on the top of his right hand. Jesus, thirty-eight years old, and he was feeling it.

He was getting on in age to be putting in an eight-hour workday, exercising his horse, quarrying for money that wasn't showing up, and getting himself thrown off a bronc. It was a lot to take for any man. Jesus . . . all this for four hundred dollars. But four hundred was a fortune to him right now.

Every fiber of every muscle and every bit of marrow in his bones was screaming out at him for mercy. It wasn't as if he wasn't strong. He was just as strong as he'd been when he was a kid. But now he had more body to keep on the horse's back, and more weight to use to try and heft a steer to the ground.

Tinhorn had come through with the bull, and that had gone about as smoothly as with B. B. flinging him over the corral post. All Wyatt could hope for was the best. That and drawing a bronc and bull that weren't snorting for blood.

It might not have been so bad if he'd been able to leave the Happy City and fall into bed for some much-needed sleep. But he swore Hartzell listened with a glass to the wall to hear when he was unlocking his door. The other man would spring out from his room wanting to play a hand of gin rummy, since Wyatt wouldn't go to the Bon Ton with him.

If Wyatt had known a way out without sending the other man into a worse depression, he would have declined. But the expectant look on Hartzell's face while he held on to a pack of Bicycle cards was just too much for even Wyatt to close the door on.

Hartzell and Geneva were no closer to reconciling than they had been the first night Hartzell had checked into the Starlight. Wyatt had talked to Leah about it the next day, but she was at a loss over what to do. Geneva was being stubborn, refusing to talk about patching things up. In fact, she'd been stepping out with Tiberius N. Tee while he waited in Eternity for the Standard Oil shipment to arrive with a supply of gasoline.

A gust of early evening wind shot through the kitchen, ruffling the proverbs Tu Yan kept tacked to the wall. A few tore free and floated around the room. Tu looked up from the cookie batter he was stirring and spouted a few harsh words of Chinese as he left the mixture to grab the flying papers.

"Howdy, partner." The tiny voice came from the bamboo

curtain doorway, and Wyatt glanced at Tug. He was armed to the teeth with his toy guns and western gear. He'd been routinely stopping by the Happy City ever since Wyatt had shown him how to lasso his hobbyhorse. And in the evening when he came for supper with Leah and Rosalure, he'd waltz into the kitchen to check on what Wyatt was doing and talk about cowboys.

"Howdy, partner," Wyatt returned.

Punching through the curtains, Tug approached. The sound of metal scraping across the floorboards sang through the kitchen. Wyatt lowered his gaze to the two tin cans Tug had smashed over the heels of his boots.

"What's that you have on your boots?"

"Spurs."

Smiling, Wyatt wiped the suds from his hands with the towel tied around his waist. "They look like authentic Mexican spurs."

"Yup. They're the real thing."

"They're as big as soup plates."

Tug clamored to a halt directly in front of Wyatt. "I know that." Standing on tiptoes, he poked a hole with his pudgy finger in the mound of bubbles filling the sink before he swirled the white clouds around as if he was stirring sourdough. "I've decided I'm going to be a dishwashing cowboy when I grow up. Just like you, Wyatt."

A frown drew Wyatt's brows down. "I've got nothing against dishwashers, but I think a boy with your potential ought to be planning on a college education. Your grandfather told me he's got expectations of you taking over the bank for him when you get old enough."

"Nope." Tug withdrew his hand. "Money stinks like dirty socks."

But it was sure a nice stink to have wadded in your pocket, Wyatt thought. He could have used some smelly green stuff right about now, but it wasn't to be. So for tomorrow's big event he was going to have to settle on wearing his old boots with the loose rowel spurs, and a hat that was just about done for, with denims so thin in the seat he might just disgrace himself before the day was over.

Wyatt began to dry the dishes stacked in the drainer. "I just think you should consider your options before you go making up your mind."

The boy's face screwed up like a jar lid clamped on too tight. "What's an option?"

Leaning against the counter, Wyatt paused. He wasn't very good with words and even had a harder time putting them to paper. He knew what *option* meant, but wasn't quite confident he could get the exact definition across. "Well, an option is like a choice. Let's say you go to Corn's Hardware and he's got a black licorice rope and a red licorice rope; you have the choice to decide which one you want. It's your option whether or not you buy the red or the black."

"I don't like the black."

"Then your choice would be red."

"My choice is to be a dishwasher cowboy like you," Tug replied with a straighter face than any poker player.

The boy was dead serious, and it distressed Wyatt that his presence could make such an impression on him. Wyatt didn't want anyone, much less Leah's son, pining to take after him. He was not a good example. The road he'd traveled to get to the man he was had been hell. He wouldn't want that for Tug.

Wyatt put a stack of plates up onto the cupboard shelf. "Well, I wouldn't want you to choose until you're at least—" He cast a glance over his shoulder at the boy's upturned face. "How old are you now?"

Tug held up five fingers. "And a half."

"Until you're at least ten." That'd give him twice his age to ponder the prudence of having his hands stuck in dirty water for a living. Choosing the cowboy life was hard enough. There were kitchen duties a man could opt for if he wanted to be on the range. "Maybe you ought to take up cooking if you like being in a kitchen."

"I don't like it."

"Then don't wash dishes."

"But I could like it because you do."

"I don't like it."

"Then why do you do it?"

"I like the stinky smell of money."

That went a hair past Tug's head, and his velvet-brown eyes wrinkled at the corners.

"There you are," came Leah's voice from the curtain. "It's time to sit down. Supper is being served."

Tug scuffed toward his mother.

Pointing to the cans, Leah directed, "And take those off. You're going to ruin Mr. Wang's floor."

"They're my spurs."

"Real cowboys don't wear their spurs indoors."

Tug quickly glanced at Wyatt's boots, but he didn't have the opportunity to stand out of reach from the boy's gaze. Wyatt was indeed wearing his Texas stars with jingle bobs. He hadn't taken them off after riding B. B. before coming on shift. It was a bad habit of his, keeping his spurs on after a workout with a horse. He rather liked the sound they made across Leo's kitchen floor. The jangle kept him focused on what was important to him in life. Securing a ranch and becoming a full-fledged cattle owner.

"Wyatt's got his on," Tug debated hotly.

"Mine are the indoor models," Wyatt said before Leah could respond. "They're guaranteed not to scratch floors."

Tug turned to Leah. "I want some genuine spurs, Momma."

"We'll talk about it at the table."

She put her hand on the crown of Tug's cowboy hat and steered him toward the beads. Whispering over her shoulder to Wyatt, she said, "No luck with Geneva. Mr. Vibratrel Home Wrecker is still in town and he's taking her to the exposition tomorrow."

"Hartzell is going, too."

"Oh, dear. If they run into each other . . ."

"It won't be pretty."

"We'll have to think about what to do," she said as she left to return to her table.

Wyatt nodded. He was no marriage fixer, but he and Leah had been talking about getting Hartzell and his wife to settle their differences and make up. Geneva was driving Leah to distraction on her end, and Hartzell was making it near impossible for Wyatt to get any sleep.

Later, when the supper rush had slowed, Wyatt was able to go into the dining room with Leo as he brought a plate of cookies to Leah's table.

"These aren't Tu's best," Leo said as he set the dessert in front of Leah. "I don't know what happened to them. They have lumps."

Rosalure and Tug immediately grabbed them while Wyatt awkwardly held back. He still wasn't comfortable having Leah see him in an apron and with chapped hands, even though she'd never said anything derogatory about his job.

Leo patted Wyatt on the back and grinned. "So you think Wyatt's going to be a lucky buckaroo and win all the big purses tomorrow? He's entered all four events."

Tug dropped his cookie to his plate. "You're going to be a lucky buckaroo? The real thing? The one who rides on bulls and doesn't get himself bucked off?"

Wyatt had to admit, "I was planning on it."

The boy's face lit up like a candle. "Gee!"

Rosalure stopped eating her cookie and picked it apart. "There's something in here." A tiny piece of paper was revealed in the crumbles. "It has squiggly writing on it."

Leo took the paper from her. Wyatt recognized it as being one of Tu's proverbs that had been floating around the kitchen.

"What does it say?" Rosalure asked.

Leo squinted at the tiny chicken scratches. "A well-known friend is a treasure."

Rosalure mused, "Pinkie Sommercamp is my best friend."

Tug pounded his cookie with his fist to get to the paper. "Mine. What does mine say?"

Leo read, "Full-fledged birds fly away."

"What's that mean?"

Leah sighed and answered for Leo, "It means that you'll grow up and be your own man."

"Oh. That's nothing." Then to Wyatt, he grinned broadly.

"I'm going to be right in the front row so I can watch you win."

Wyatt held back the sinking feeling that was giving him a pain in his belly. He sure as hell didn't want to fall short on showing the boy he was a capable rider, but he had no guarantee that he wasn't going to fly off that horse's back as soon as he was out of the gate. He didn't want to let Tug down, and he didn't want to look like an ass in front of Leah.

"What's your cookie say, Momma?" Rosalure asked.

Leah picked up her cookie and broke it in half, handing Leo the scrap of paper.

Leo took the proverb, reading the symbols, glancing at Leah, then returning his gaze to the paper. He hesitated before translating, "Words of unspoken love are not known."

Leah cleared her throat and abruptly stood. "Well that certainly doesn't mean anything." But as she was speaking, she stole a glance at Wyatt. He gave her a guarded stare back, thinking that the blush on her cheeks was far too high. Was she thinking loving thoughts about him?

Wyatt wasn't sure of anything at the moment, only that he had to win those contests tomorrow or Tug would never look up to him again. And he was getting used to having that boy thinking of him as larger than life.

September had begun to ignite the mountains the colors of glowing hearths: yellows, reds, and oranges. Warm, earthy tones were replacing the velvet greens of summer, leaving withering brown leaves to cartwheel through yards, streets, and alleyways. August's kaleidoscopic of flowers faded to goldenrod and purple asters that inspired gentler moods and reflections on naked woods to come. A bounty of apples ripened to the core and were picked for ciders and pies. Orchard fruits had been plucked and put up to be brought to tables and savored during the long winter months ahead.

Leah and the children had done their picking over the

course of the week, and Hyrum Pfeiffer had stocked brimming baskets of juicy apples alongside her back porch to await canning. But Leah had never done the peeling, slicing, boiling, and sugar preparations all herself. She'd always had Geneva to help supervise; however, with Geneva's having taken leave of her senses, the fruits were left alone to fill the air in the gallery with their delicious sweet smells for Tug and Rosalure to snatch and eat at their will.

Saturday morning dawned clear, and with high cottony clouds slugging in from the east to provide a picture-perfect day for the annual Aspenglow River Stampede and Eternity Grange No. 321 Exposition. The event marked the last get-together before the frosts came, and the next social activity would be forced indoors into barns with cornstalks underfoot and jack-o'-lanterns lit on the hayloft rails.

Everyone in Eternity came out for the crowning festivity of autumn. Chapter Twenty Order of the Eastern Stars set up wares in the cowhouse of the old Cloudtree Dairy Farm at the rural end of Ninth Avenue. Stanchions had been removed and became nooks with tables where there were culinary sweets aplenty to sample, sewing and stitchery handiwork to admire, and contests for largest and smallest garden vegetables to vote on. Leo would no doubt spend the entire day in the vegetable pavilion, talking about gardens with the local green-thumbs and Mr. McWhorter—who had taken first prize with his essay on gardening and her photograph as accompaniment.

Half Pint Gilman and his crew came in every year to judge the hopefuls, and was known to hire several on if they were good enough for the arduous job. Mr. Gilman had put up the money to build the arena and grandstands, with donations coming from the citizens for concession booths and a first aid hut supported by Doc Hochstrasser and Reverend Bunderson.

The fairgrounds were located across from Cloudtree Farm at the base of the Infinity Hills, the outcropping of sandstone from Eternity Ridge. In the flattened area below, meadow grass had grown taller than buggy wheel hubs, and a week before the exposition, men had brought out scythes and mowers to clip the blades down before bringing in Mr. Gilman's cattle to clean up the job.

By Friday evening, everything was in place that should be, and what wasn't, usually was done at the last minute with a lot of laughter and good cheer.

Leah bustled down the stairs to meet Rosalure and Tug, who waited on the porch, calling for her for the umpteenth time.

"Yes, yes," she breathed quickly. "I heard you."

"We're going to be the last ones there," Tug said with a sour pout. He had taken a bath earlier that morning and donned his freshly aired chaps and laundered vest. His cowboy hat hung behind his back from a cord around his neck. Leah had combed his hair to the side from a meticulous part, and the blondish brown tufts were slicked back behind his ears.

Rosalure had made plans to meet Pinkie Sommercamp at the hoop toss game, and the two girls had decided to dress alike in rose dimity with matching hair ribbons.

Leah paused to grab her gloves from the foyer table and gaze at her reflection for an instant to make sure her hat was pinned on straight. All looked as good as could be expected. She'd tried to dress fashionably but without appearing as if she were trying to catch Wyatt's attention. She'd arranged her long hair into a neat bun with springy curls, which she'd painstakingly taken the iron to, framing her face. Her Eton jacket was smart, yet serviceable in case the weather took a turn toward a chill, while her polka-dotted silk skirt and challis waist were a nice complement to the sleeveless coat. Her aubergine-colored straw hat was the current style, with its trimming of cream chiffon, leaf-green ribbon, deep purple roses, and ostrich plumes.

"Momma, I told Pinkie I'd be there by eleven." Rosalure gazed at her chatelaine watch. "It's five minutes until. We'll have to run if I'm going to make it on time."

"Then let's get going." Leah shut the door behind her, not

bothering to lock it. She seldom did. She figured if anyone wanted something badly enough to break in and steal it, they were welcome to whatever she had. Except her cameras. But no one in Eternity was going to steal them, as no one else would have any use for the complex devices.

Hand in hand with Rosalure and Tug, Leah led them to the fairgrounds. Though she and Wyatt hadn't made plans to meet up, she was hoping they would. She wanted to spend the day with him. Perhaps enter a few contests together and have fun before the rodeo. She still wasn't keen on the idea of his risking his life on one of those untamed horses or bulls. The thought of his being thrown off into the fence scared her. She didn't want anything to happen to him. She was . . .

She was what?

She was falling in love with him.

How and why had her feelings taken such a turn? She hadn't set out to fall in love with Wyatt; it was just happening. Maybe the feelings began the first day she saw him talking to Marshal Scudder and he'd said she had a smudge on her cheek. She'd about died when he'd told her, but had put on a straight face not to let him know she was flustered. Ever since, the heartbeats and tingles across her skin had been gaining momentum, until her blush was so easy to rouse in his company, it took everything she had to fight it off and remain calm and composed. Not to give her true feelings away.

Beyond the physical attraction, there were many things that drew her to Wyatt. The way he looked at things. His sweetness with Tug. His patience with Rosalure. The way he'd encouraged her after her disappointing news from the academy. His suggestions about her photography. She hadn't thought she needed a man, but she was astonished at the sense of fulfillment she felt when she was with Wyatt.

Leah never thought she'd be feeling this way. She had never been bubbling inside with lightheadedness when Owen was near. With him, they'd fallen into a comfortable love that was neither passionate or stirring. But like a well-worn slipper, they had fit and complemented one another. She'd known him for so long before they'd married, their marriage was a natural course to take. Leah didn't regret marrying Owen, but now she realized that by denying herself the same passion for a man that she felt for her photography, she had shorted herself.

Would she . . . could she dare . . . an affair? There was a lot to consider. The smallness of the town, her children . . . her broken heart when he left. The unabashed thought continued to trouble her as they entered the exposition grounds.

Tiberius N. Tee's glossy Oldsmobile, equipped with three new tires, sat parked amid the horses and buggies beneath the shade of an oak. Apparently Standard Oil had come to town and he'd been able to fill his tank so the automobile was operable again.

"I'll meet you at one by the home-and-garden pavilion," Rosalure said with a beaming smile.

"Have fun, and stay with the Sommercamps."

"I will."

Rosalure went off, Leah watching. Her daughter was growing up, venturing into early womanhood with her dainty carriage and easy sprint. A few boys from school passed her by, saying hello and gawking after her as she left them behind. *Oh, Rosalure . . .* Leah mused. *You'll be getting married before I know it.*

"I want to see the horses and bulls," Tug declared.

Leah gave his shoulder a reassuring squeeze. "There will be plenty of time to see the animals later."

Leah really should check in with Geneva at the booth, but for what purpose? Leah had none. She was still angry with Geneva for being so chummy with the salesman, and to actually have made plans to attend the exposition with him. Had she no shame? No commitment to her marriage? Leah had never cared much for what the gossips said about her being in business for herself, but Geneva was a central figure in the community and a prime target for loose tongues. Just to step out with another man while married wasn't appropriate. It was scandalous. And Geneva had always loathed and despised scandal—unless it was about someone outside her immediate family.

"When are we going to the barn and corral? I want to find Wyatt."

So did Leah. But she didn't want to be obvious.

Scanning the crowd for a glimpse of Wyatt's familiar hat, she replied on an optimistic note, "Maybe we'll run into him."

And ten minutes later, they did. Wearing his calf-length duster, scruffy boots, and spurs, Wyatt stood at the Independent Telephone Company's display, examining a telephone that had been hooked up to a live wire. A temporary pole behind the decorated stand had a cable that dipped down to the table and the false wall where the phone was mounted. No doubt that fat black wire was generating power from the main office and was connected to the switchboard Leah had gazed at through the store's window when the building had been completed just last week.

A line of people gathered behind Wyatt, waiting for their turn to see how the phone worked.

"Look, Momma, Wyatt's talking on the telephone. Can we try it out, too?"

Leah nodded and took his hand.

Wyatt hung up the receiver, as per the instructions from the man demonstrating the telephone. Then a *brrringg!* sounded from the black instrument and the people moved in closer for a better look.

"Pick up the handle, sir." The vendor pointed to the ringing telephone. "See who it is."

Leah smiled as Wyatt reached out to lift the receiver and bring it to his ear. His eyes grew wide with wonder, then he held the receiver out and declared, "There's a lady talking in there. Says her name is Tilly."

"Sure is. She's operator number one down at Central. She can connect you with whomever you want to speak. Anywhere in the country that the party on the other end has a telephone."

"I don't know anybody with a telephone."

"You will. Telephones are springing up everywhere, folks. Just think of the possibilities. We've got two models to choose from down at the store. Installation is nothing more than a wire run to the house and a hookup. Then you can enjoy hours on the line with those you love."

Wyatt cradled the receiver back on the phone mount, then let the person behind him crank the handle to ring the operator.

"Was there really a lady in that talking machine, Wyatt?" Tug burst out, catching Wyatt's attention and causing him to turn in their direction.

"Hey, Tug." Seeing Leah, he gave her a smile that melted her to her toes. "There was somebody on the other end. Somehow. Don't know how they make her voice come through that wire."

Tug yanked on Leah's jacket hem. "I want to hear!"

Leah directed him into the line, and they waited while Wyatt stayed off to the side, his hands in the front pockets of his duster. "You sure look pretty today, Leah."

He stood so close, she could feel the heat from his body. Her answer was a rapid thud of her heart. "Thank you."

He toed a rock on the ground, gazing down, then lifting his eyes and giving her a casual shrug. "I wasn't going to look at that telephone, but I had nothing else to do."

She didn't feel the need for him to play down his curiosity about the phone. She herself was curious about how it operated. Though she doubted she'd ever install one, listening in as the operator spoke to her would be an experience. "You don't have to defend yourself," she said. "I've been wondering about it, too."

"I never thought I would," he confessed.

"I believe you're a tad smitten with progress."

Minimizing her observance, he sounded nonchalant when he replied, "Maybe a little."

Leah smiled, and the line moved forward. When Tug's turn came, he gripped the receiver to his ear and grinned so widely, Leah had never seen the like on his face. "She's jabbering away at me, Momma! Said she can see the flag on the top of the dairy from where she's sitting." Tug swiveled around to gaze at the American flag waving softly from the stout pole on the top of Cloudtree's.

"Here, Momma, you try."

Leah extended her hand for a listen, amazed with the female voice on the other end as she identified herself. "Tilly Vandermeyer, operator number one. Eternity, Colorado. Who may I connect you with?"

"My . . ." she sighed, then gave use of the telephone to the ladies next in line and stepped away.

"Can you take me to see the bulls and horses?" Tug pleaded, not to his mother this time but to Wyatt.

Wyatt inched his hat back some, giving Leah a questioning gaze. "It's up to your mother."

"Only for a minute. We don't want to get in the way."

"Yippee!"

The attendees had thickened to the point where casual strolling was almost impossible. Tug loped next to Wyatt's right, not looking where he was going half the time, so Wyatt grabbed him and lifted him onto his shoulders for a ride. A large group of people had stopped by the fiddler's platform and were holding up the flow to listen to the music.

Leah accidently bumped arms with Wyatt and shot away from him before she could catch his reaction. Veering in a different direction, she held on to the smell of his shaving soap and the dusty scent of his hat. The second time she made contact with him, it was the fault of the man striding quickly to her left, jostling her toward Wyatt and causing her to brace her hand on his shoulder. Without a word, Wyatt took her elbow and kept her close to him.

A companionable stride flowed between them as they stayed together. She gave him a tentative look, soaking in the hard edge of his profile, where determination marked his brows and the corners of his mouth. She sensed his demeanor had nothing to do with concentrating on steering them through the crowd, but rather the courage it was going to take him to ride in the rodeo.

Though she didn't see the logic in self-made suicide, she did sort of thrill at the prospect of seeing him holding on until he won. Her skin prickled pleasurably at the thought of his standing in the arena afterward to thunderous applause, and his seeking only her in the crowd to wave his hat high as if to dedicate his win to her. It would be a communication that needed no words. And the moment would be theirs alone.

Leah's near-step on a discarded candy apple made Wyatt lurch her to the right.

"Head in the clouds?" he asked with a glint of humor.

Flushing, Leah stammered, "Ah . . . yes. I guess. I was thinking about that telephone."

"Could we get one, Momma?" Tug chirped.

"We don't have anyone to ring."

"We could call Nanna. She said she's getting a telephone."

That was all Leah needed—to enable Geneva to phone her at will. It was bad enough her mother-in-law dropped by without any notice at all.

"No, Tug. We are definitely not getting a telephone."

They approached a copse of young aspens that clustered down the center of two long barns with low-pitched roofs. The buildings were new as of last year, but already the boards were weathered and bleached by the blinding sun. Wide double doors made up the entrance, and the odors of dung and sweaty animals wafted through the air.

Since the swarm of people had thinned considerably down to mostly wranglers and their sweethearts, with a few of Eternity's citizens interested in the horses, bulls, and calves, Wyatt let go of Leah's elbow. She instantly missed the warmth of his fingers seeping through the light fabric of her shirtwaist.

Wyatt set Tug on his feet, and he dashed inside the dim interior before she could stop him.

"Tug! Wait!"

Wyatt picked up the pace, but assured her, "Only the roping horses are in stalls. They won't hurt him. It's the broncos and bulls corralled out back that can get him into trouble. But he won't get that far before we catch him."

That didn't appease Leah's worry. Tug was foolhardy enough to climb through one of the rails to try and meet face-to-face with a workhorse if he thought the animal would let him pet it. Horses of any kind were unpredictable.

Gathering the fabric of her skirt, Leah hurried after Wyatt into the barn that was poorly lit in the middle, even with the doors thrown open. She skimmed past the horses whose heads stuck out from their stalls, looking for her son. She couldn't see him anywhere.

Wyatt ran through the back doors and called out to Tug in one of the severest voices Leah had ever heard him use.

"Hold it right there, Tug!"

Leah's heart did a double-trip when she saw Tug frozen to the side of the corral, his hands and feet stuck fast to the railing as if he had been planning on climbing inside.

"Owen Edwin! You get down from there right this minute!" Leah ran forward while Wyatt snagged Tug around the waist and pried him off. A billow of dust rising from inside the corral captured Leah's attention, and her heart slammed in fear as a fleshy bull snorted and kicked at the dry ground with his front hooves. "Owen Edwin," Leah reprimanded with less steam than she ought to, but she was fairly petrified, "I should tan your hide."

Wyatt let Tug go, and the boy tried to keep some of his dignity. "I wasn't doing anything."

"You sure were," Leah admonished. "That animal could have killed you."

"I was just lookin'."

Wyatt said, "Just lookin' and climbing over the rail are two different things."

Tug hung his head but didn't seem all that sorry.

Catching her breath, Leah stood back and took a really hard look at that bull. A hump protruded from between his shoulders, and his flesh seemed a half size too big for his ungainly body. The gray-dappled skin hung in places, especially beneath his neck and belly. Foot-long horns that could disembowel a man sprung out at his cropped ears with uptilted points.

"Wyatt," Leah said, wishing now more than ever he wasn't actually going to sit on the beast. "You can't ride on that bull."

"I've already entered." Wyatt put up a foot on the bottom corral rung and gazed at the bull. "I hope I draw him. He's small."

"Small?" Leah squeaked.

"Small for a bull. His name is Cricket."

Cricket conjured up a leaping bug, nothing like the ungainly bull before her. But crickets were known for their spring-air action, and the thought didn't make her feel the least bit better.

"What's some of the other ones?" Tug asked, pointing to the pens.

Wyatt directed his finger on a few. "That one there is Boot Hill. Squirrely. White Lightning. And Popcorn." Wyatt's eyes narrowed in on the latter. "From what I've seen, Popcorn is a son-of-a—" He cut himself short and rephrased, "He's a mean customer."

"Bet you could ride 'em, Wyatt," Tug said with all the adoration in the world. "I'll be watching you."

"Yeah . . ." Wyatt's voice trailed. "I reckon the whole town will. Will you, Leah? Or have you changed your mind?"

"I'll be there."

"But you don't like rodeos."

"No."

"You wouldn't go for a rancher, then?"

"A man's occupation wouldn't sway me from having feelings for him, if that's what you mean," she replied.

"Yeah, that's what I was meaning."

❧ 16 ❧

In haste, there is error.
—Chinese proverb

At one, Leah collected Rosalure by a gardened pavilion and Wyatt said hello to Leo, who proudly held up his first-prize ribbon for the largest ear of corn. Afterward, Wyatt spent the last of his pay buying Leah and her children a dinner of cold fried chicken, corn oysters, and apple snow. He himself couldn't eat a bite. His stomach was too tangled in knots over the impending rodeo. The four of them sat on a bench beneath the shady boughs of an elm.

Wyatt's gaze continually landed on Leah and he thought about what she'd said. She'd consider being a rancher's wife. She was willing to give a man who drove cattle for a living a chance. That's all he wanted, a chance. Her not going to Italy meant she'd be sticking around Eternity . . . unless she won that photography contest and packed up for New York. But until then, if that happened, he had the chance to win her over.

In his rowdy days, he wouldn't have thought to settle down with a missus and set up house. But that notion had been foremost on his mind since getting out. And he'd decided Leah was the woman for him. If she'd have him. He had to prove himself to her by winning those contests to keep him above water. He was sinking so fast in the wallet that he was getting desperate. Everything he wanted to do for himself and for Leah relied on money. He was so sick and tired of being nearly busted, he could puke.

The shimmer of silver winked at the corner of Wyatt's eye and he veered his attention to the source: a tin badge pinned on a navy lapel. U.S. Marshal Benard Scudder swaggered through the crowd wearing a sugarloaf hat as high as four hands, with his revolver swaying against his beefy thigh. A fat Cuban cigar was clamped between his lips, and his whopping mustache kissed the round of that stogie while he puffed contentedly as if he hadn't a care in the world. But Wyatt knew better.

Scudder wasn't on the up-and-up.

Last night when Wyatt had been walking home from work, he'd passed the marshal's office. The window shade hadn't been drawn, and Wyatt saw Bean sitting in the electric light at his desk swilling down a bottle of beer. If Bean hadn't been irritating him, Wyatt would have kept on walking, but since the marshal seemed out to get him for some trumped-up offense, Wyatt had sneaked closer to investigate the marshal for a change and turn the tables on the lawman.

Standing in the shadows, Wyatt had watched Bean tip back on his chair in a good drunk that nearly had him upending himself. He sang under his breath, some obscene barroom ditty Wyatt had heard a thousand times. Then he fumbled for a cigar box and had withdrawn one. Skunked as he was, after he had the stogie in his mouth, he had a hard time striking the match. When he finally got the end to sizzle to a flame, his shaking hand brought the burning stick to his cigar. Only Bean hadn't been steady enough to light the weed in his mouth. His mustache had gotten in the way. All that wax he'd twirled into it caught fire and went to a quick burn. Scudder bolted out of the chair, and had Wyatt thought he was in jeopardy of going up like tinder he would have bolted inside to lend a hand.

As it was, Scudder had dunked his head into the ice chest

and came out with a wide-eyed look of shock. A mirror hung on the wall, and he'd stumbled toward it. Wyatt had held back a chortle when he got a glimpse of what Scudder had done.

The marshal had singed the best parts of that mustache, and rather than having a damn good Brillcream twist of facial hair, it was more reminiscent of cat whiskers. And an ugly cat at that.

Wyatt had walked on, thinking that Scudder was lucky to be alive, for an inept fool.

Seeing Bean Scudder today sporting a mustache finer than the one he'd had yesterday had Wyatt wondering how in the hell he'd come about such a growth overnight.

Wyatt would have gone out of his way to avoid Scudder if he could. But sitting with Leah, he couldn't just get up and walk away, so he stayed. Scudder spotted him and came over with an expression on his face as if he was full of more information than a mail-order catalog. Wyatt's stomach turned even more.

"Mrs. Kirkland," the marshal dutifully greeted. "Kids."

Rosalure and Tug weren't impressed with Scudder and kept on eating their meal.

"Is there anything wrong, Marshal?" Leah asked in a monotone. "Do you require my professional services?"

"No." Scudder's eyes stayed on Wyatt, boring in on him while he kept up a slaphappy smile. "Actually, I needed to speak to Mr. Holloway a minute."

Leah made a quick protest. "Do you really have to now? We're about finished with dinner and had plans to enter some of the field races."

Wyatt flashed Leah a brief exchange of thoughts. He didn't know about any plans to enter races, but appreciated her attempt to get Scudder off his back.

"This won't take but a minute, Mrs. Kirkland." Then he motioned Wyatt toward the back of a popcorn vendor's cart.

Reluctantly, Wyatt rose, feeling his dander rise. Once he drew up to the red wheels of the handcart, Wyatt stuck his hands in his back pockets and took on his most intimidating stance. "What do you want?"

Scudder had the gall to finger that mustache of his, petting and smoothing the two sides from the inside out before saying, "I got a firsthand crack at that new telephone this morning. I used it to make an official inquiry up north." Scudder eased his hand over the butt of his service revolver, but Wyatt wasn't in the least bit threatened by the gesture. "There ain't nobody in Billings, Montana, ever heard of a Wyatt Holloway. Not anyone in the sheriff's office nor down to the city census bureau. You're yanking on my chain, boy, and I don't like it."

Though making ignorance a paying job, Wyatt figured Scudder would eventually get around to checking out the Billings story. The marshal had nothing else to do. But Wyatt had also figured he'd be long gone from Eternity before such a question would be asked. Since Wyatt was still in town, and since he was staying, the question became relevant. Scudder was due an answer for his duplicity—if only the man wasn't such a pain in the ass. Seeing that he was, and that Wyatt now felt he had one over on the marshal, Wyatt decided to be downright obnoxious.

Pulling himself up to his full height and bracing a hand on the top of the popcorn cart, Wyatt looked down at Scudder as if he was an ant. "A drunkard for a lawman can be abided mostly because he's so useless it's no skin off anyone's nose. But a liar with a tin star on his chest is just about as low as a fellow can get."

Scudder sputtered with such injustice, droplets of spit landed on the underswell of his mustache. "What in the Sam hell are you implying?"

"I'm not implying anything, Scudder. I'm just stating a fact."

"I don't like your tone, boy."

"And I don't like you calling me boy. Just about as much as I don't like your new mustache."

Scudder's face went pale as chalk. "W–What was that?"

"Looks real enough, though. I doubt the judges will notice. I reckon you figure on winning this year again, too."

For the first time since Wyatt had had the misfortune to be in Bean Scudder's company, the marshal was at a loss for words. If Deputy Ferris Moon hadn't come along, there was no telling what Scudder would have said in his defense, because he had none.

"Eh, Marshal Scudder," Ferris said, his thin neck lumped with a bobbing Adam's apple. "We got a problem. Luke Creed and his cronies got a crate of firecrackers out of the auxiliary storage and are setting them off in the middle of Main Street. A rocket shot through the tree in your yard and busted up the bottles. Another broke one of the windows at the bank."

Scudder stiffened and pulled out from Wyatt's spell. "Hang it all! Those damn hoodlums. I had just about every available branch covered! How many did they get?"

"I didn't stop to count. I was more worried about the bank window being shattered. I can't find Mr. Kirkland to tell him."

Wyatt broke away and went to Leah. What was between him and Scudder wasn't as important as Hartzell's setting things right down at the bank before someone got the urge to vandalize the place. "Do you know where your father-in-law is?" he asked her.

"Is something wrong?"

"He needs to get to the bank and see to a broken window. You don't have any idea where he could be?"

"I imagined you would. He's been with you this past week more than anyone else except at the bank."

Wyatt thoughtfully gazed in a slow half-circle at the crowd in an attempt to spy Hartzell Kirkland. By pure luck, he saw him standing in conversation with a group of businessmen at the crepe paper–festooned gazebo.

Turning to Leah, Wyatt said, "I found him. I'll go tell him what happened. He may need some help getting that window boarded up, so go on ahead to the field races without me."

Tug poked with a greasy finger at his uneaten chicken. "Will you be back in time to enter the sack races with me, Wyatt?"

"I don't know. If I'm not, your mother can enter with you."

"She won't race in any gunnysack," Tug declared.

Wyatt gave Leah a cursory glance. "Sure she will. She said as much to the marshal."

"Ah, I was referring to something less physical," Leah said. Eyes as brown as walnuts took on a hue of panic. "Such as horseshoes."

"I'll play you horseshoes if you sack race with Tug."

Before Leah could offer further debate, Wyatt was off.

The big east window to the Eternity Security Bank lay in shards on the floor in front of the teller's cage. Glass had flown behind the radiators and spewed across the deposit stands. A streak of black powder left a trail as the skyrocket had scudded to a stop at the rear wall and mercifully burned itself out before razing the building.

"Will you look at that?" Hartzell blazed peevishly. "The trouble with kids today is they have no respect. Luke Creed's daddy is going to be paying for this, I can tell you that."

Wyatt stayed in the doorway, his chest heavy. If he crossed the threshold to the inside, he'd be swept back in time. And he didn't want to make that journey. When he'd volunteered to help nail up the board until a new plate of glass could be installed, he hadn't volunteered to stick around. But Hartzell had wanted to unlock the bank and make sure nothing had been tampered with. He'd asked Wyatt to stay, and in the light of everything that had happened to Hartzell, Wyatt couldn't deny him. The problem was, Wyatt didn't want to be in any banking institution. Ever again.

A bank held nothing but sour memories for him: his days of reckless drinking, disobedience to society, and the need to cause trouble.

"Come give me a hand with this glass, would you?" Hartzell had grabbed a broom and was sweeping the worst of it into a pile.

Wyatt moved forward, torn by conflicting emotions. The

dark-paneled walls seemed to close in on him. Lemon oil and ink permeated from the wooden tables and hardwood floor. The odor of ledgers and old papers oozed from the shelves behind the cage. And all around was the smell of money. Dirty. Pungent. Rich. He could hardly breath. His head ached to think of all that cash locked up in the vault.

Forcing himself to forget where he was, Wyatt bent down and picked up the dustpan. He and Hartzell cleaned up most of the glass, dumping the sharp pieces into several trash bins.

"Those ruffians can blow my window to smithereens, but nobody can crack open my National safe," Hartzell said as he unlocked the teller's cage door and entered. Wyatt held back. He couldn't get close to the metal cage, not without seeing Pierpont Farnham sitting behind it at a desk and looking mad as all hell when he realized he was being robbed.

"Come on over here, Wyatt." Hartzell moved around the clerk's counter. "I want to show you something."

"You don't need to show me anything."

"You said you didn't trust your money in a bank. Let me show you just how protected your money would be in the No. 5. Just take a look at this here."

"I'd rather not."

"Oh for chrissake, Wyatt. Humor me and come see my National safe."

Wyatt heaved a sigh and walked through the teller's cage. He drew up alongside Hartzell, who stood at a gigantic black safe with gold trim and lettering.

Hartzell patted the side with pride. "Nobody can pick out the combination of this safe. The tumbler is silent." To prove his point, Hartzell spun the dial. "Nothing. Not even with a stethoscope could you pick up the numbers. Can't blast through the casing either. Solid steel. Won't even rip a hole in it. Come on, take a spin at it."

"I'd rather not," Wyatt repeated.

"I just want you to see that the safe is secure. One spin. Give it a whirl."

To appease Hartzell, Wyatt grasped the dial and turned it.

"See there!" Hartzell beamed proudly. "Not a peep."

Sweat popped out on Wyatt's forehead, his underarms. What Hartzell didn't understand was that Wyatt didn't need dynamite or the ability to crack a safe to get to the money. None of that mattered. The bank's layout was so common, he could walk through the building in his sleep. All he'd need to pull off the job was a disguise, his Colt aimed and cocked as if he meant business, and he could be in and out within minutes. People did whatever you wanted when they were scared. And Wyatt had scared a great many people in his life.

He could rob again. He knew that now. The old instincts and reactions hadn't left him. That's not to say that he wanted to pull off a holdup. It just meant that some things were never forgotten. How he could move through a bank, take command of the occupants, and leave with bags of money was something that once learned was still in his head. He fought off thinking about the money in the vault. He needed some so badly, he could taste the metallic gold coins as surely as if he were biting on one to test it for authenticity.

Money.

A man was nothing without it.

Wyatt's fingers began to tingle, and he had to get a lung full of fresh air or he'd bust. "I've got to get going, Hartzell." Backing away, he gave the elder man no opening for argument. "I promised Leah I'd meet up with her and the kids. I'm running late."

Hartzell made no motion to stop Wyatt, but he did ask, "You like Leah?"

The question threw Wyatt off a little. "I like her."

"And the children?"

"Yes."

A distant memory faded the light in Hartzell's eyes. "My son was a good man, but he was very ambitious. He wasn't at home much for Rosalure. And Tug was only a baby when Owen died. A boy needs a father around to look up to so he'll know how to be a man. I fell short of that with my own son." Hartzell flecked a speck of dust off his lapel. "Leah's

been alone for three years now. She's never seriously
entertained a caller since the day we buried Owen. There
was that *National Geographic* writer, but he was here and
gone within a couple of weeks, and she sure didn't pine after
him when he left. I don't count the postmaster and the
headstone carver as callers. Quigley and Winterowd are
about as bright as dogs barking at knotholes. But she's
friendly to them, because she's that kind of woman." He
lowered his head a fraction.

"Are you getting at something, Hartzell?"

"You're the first man she's encouraged since she became a
widow. I wanted you to know that if you have any intentions toward Leah, I wouldn't be against the two of you. If
that's where you're headed." Hartzell's expression grew
somber. "And if you ever need a loan, I think I've gotten to
know enough of your character this past week to vouch that
you'd repay your account."

Wyatt didn't know what to make of Hartzell's offer. "I
don't have anything worth a damn to put up as collateral."

"You have your integrity."

The statement fell hard on Wyatt. Just minutes before,
he'd been thinking about how effortless it would be to steal
Hartzell's money from the vault, and now that man was
telling him he had integrity. The two thoughts didn't go
together.

"Thanks for the faith," Wyatt managed to reply.

Then he strode from the bank without a backward glance.

Leah wasn't any good at gunnysack races. She and Tug
lost, but they did come in fifth and not last.

Standing off to the sidelines to catch her breath, Leah
watched Tug and Rosalure participate in the wheelbarrow
races. Their laughter and attempt at walking on their hands
made Leah recall the times she hadn't participated in Anti-
I-Over, "How Many Miles to Miley Right," pop-the-whip,
or shinny-in-the-hole. Her fun came in solitary play, and
what she could recall at the moment was when she'd found
a discarded wagon in the alleyway behind the Gunnison
mercantile and hitched a turkey to it.

Grown-up now, with children of her own to raise, it seemed as if she'd never been a child herself. Her childhood had been one of moving from one mining town to another so her father could take portraits of the miners and their working conditions for the various unions. Her early years had been spent in Wyoming, but as soon as she was of school age, they settled in Silver Cliff—only until she was seven. After that, it was Querida, Bonanza, Cripple Creek, and White Pine. Leah didn't have any bosom friends, and those whom she did start to feel close to, she distanced herself from because she knew soon they'd have to be moving on again.

School would be starting up next week for Rosalure and Tug and she didn't want them to have to go through the same taunts as she had been. Arithmetic had bewildered her, and her passage through the five readers was a grim march. Instead of concentrating on school, she'd begged her father to teach her how to use his camera. Just as she was teaching Rosalure and would teach Tug when he grew old enough.

It was on those mining streets, where at least one man was killed each week in either accidents or gunfights, that she gained her independence. It was also where she followed her mother, desperately craving attention and nurturing from the woman who had given birth to her.

Loath to the idea but having no choice in the matter, Momma took in laundry while they were at the Cornucopia Mining District. Leah went along to deliver the fresh clothes and linens to the women and establishments her mother took in work for. One of them was a bordello, and Leah had the strangest feeling Momma wanted to be one of the fancy women who sat around in satin all day waiting for gentlemen callers. But Momma never left, and she never smiled either. Leah always thought it was somehow her fault her mother was so unhappy. But that didn't stop her from wanting Momma's love and affection.

When she was old enough to understand the double-edged words her mother would sometimes speak to her, she realized that Momma hadn't been able to pursue her acting

career because she'd gotten pregnant with Leah. She'd had
to stay home and take care of a daughter. When Leah had
been five and her father made a living out of photographing
sod house folks on the Wyoming prairies, she'd overheard
her mother telling her father that the first opportunity she
got, she was hitching a ride to Denver. Only she never made
good on her threat. She found out she was going to have
another child. But resentment had made her reckless, and
she'd miscarried.

The loss of the child had left her bedridden and close to
death. Momma begged Leah's father not to let her die.
Father nursed her back to health, and Momma had promised she would stay with him if he made her better.

Momma kept her promise, but she wasn't happy in the
mining towns. Leah tried all her young life to make her
mother smile and look at her with love. But it was never
to be.

"Momma!"

Rosalure's excited shout brought Leah from her memories, and she looked up to see Rosalure and Tug running to
her waving a blue ribbon.

"We won!" Rosalure cried. "I can't believe it, but Tug
actually can run on his hands."

Remnants of pink sugar strands from cotton candy
smudged Tug's cheeks. "'Course I can!"

Leah embraced them both, but Tug wiggled free.
"Where's Wyatt? He said he'd be back."

"I am back."

The three turned together. Leah's heart skipped a beat, as
it did whenever Wyatt was near.

"Am I too late for horseshoes?" His smile was white and
dazzling.

"Nope," Tug said.

Rosalure held up the ribbon to show Wyatt. "Tug and I
won the wheelbarrow races."

"Well, good for you."

Leah composed herself and tried to keep her demeanor
calm. "The horseshoes are over there."

"Let's go."

An area of graded sand with a slight pit had been groomed by the ushers of the First Presbyterian Church. Rather than traditional stakes, the pegs were crosses. If a person made a ringer on the horizontal of the cross, he automatically had to make a donation—of whatever he could afford—to the church.

A free court became available, and Leah challenged Wyatt to a game. Once in position, she took aim while Wyatt stood next to her before walking to his end of the court.

"I don't think you can throw that fifty feet," he remarked with a half-smile.

"This is the one sport I'm good at. Don't try and distract me."

"I wasn't."

She gave him a knowing smile in return. "Yes you were."

"A little."

"A lot."

"Yup."

"Hmm."

Leah took on the correct form, trained her eye on her target, and released the horseshoe. It fell short of the mark by a mere inch. She straightened. "I was close."

"You were."

"Let's see you do it."

Wyatt walked to his end of the court, took aim, and threw. His horseshoe hit the cross with a *ping* before thudding into the sand several inches from the base of the stake.

"Not bad for a novice."

"I'm out of practice," Wyatt commented as he walked toward her.

A giggle worked its way up her throat. "I'm sure."

"Momma knows how to play horseshoes, Wyatt." Tug sat next to Rosalure, eating his third cotton candy, while his sister had gone off to purchase a pecan bar.

"It looks that way, doesn't it."

"Yup." Tug repeated Wyatt's cowboy reply.

Leah got her bearings, looked down the court to the cross,

and threw with a steady hand. *Zing!* She made a ringer. Her triumph made up for coming in fifth on the gunnysack races.

Unable to contain her joy, she jumped up and grasped Wyatt by the arm. "See! I told you I knew how to play this game!"

Wyatt leaned in close to her, his mouth inches away. "I guess you do, darlin'."

Explosive currents raced through Leah. A familiar shiver of awareness melted her bones and she was barely able to stand. "The game isn't over yet," she managed to say in a murmur.

"Nope. But I think you'll be the winner of this one."

"The church is the winner," Leah said, trying to keep her mind off Wyatt's firm lips. "For every ringer you make, you have to contribute a donation."

His eyes were a blue so deep that it was all Leah could see when he replied, "That a fact?"

"Hmm." She was walking down to the end, but she wasn't really thinking about where she was walking. "The First Presbyterian has been sponsoring this event as a fund-raiser ever since they had to pay for a new cross on the hill."

Wyatt slowed down midstride. "That one up there?" He pointed to Infinity Hill.

"Yes. That's the one."

"What do you mean about a new cross? The old one wear out?"

"Actually, the old one got struck by lightning."

"When?"

Leah was puzzled by Wyatt's sudden concern about the cross. "I couldn't exactly say. Before I moved to Eternity. At least fifteen or sixteen years ago."

"But they put up the new one just where the old one was."

"No."

His eyes had chilled with reserve. "Where was the old one?"

Leah pointed to the clearcut on the mountainside where the timbers had been shorn down to stumps amid grass and pockets of sandstone. "I believe the original was there.

Some twenty feet west of where the cross now stands. Wyatt, what's wrong?"

His face had grown the color of ash and his hands balled into fists. He swore beneath his breath.

She touched his sleeve, truly concerned about his upset. "Wyatt?"

"It's nothing. Never mind." He stalked to the end of the court and picked up a shoe. "Forget about it." But his hand was gripping the iron so tight, his knuckles had whitened; and when he threw the shoe, he missed by a foot.

❧ 17 ❧

**To see a man do a good deed is to
forget all his faults.**
—Chinese proverb

Wyatt's lack of concentration threw him off for the rodeo.
He didn't make the points needed to advance in the final
round of either calf roping or steer wrestling. When it came
to the bronc riding, he'd drawn a sorrel mare known as
Grasshopper and was bucked in the first four seconds. A
greener by the name of Tuff Callister won the hundred-
dollar purse. To come this far with his determined practice
and fall flat on his ass was humiliating. But his mind
kept being pulled to what Leah had told him not an hour
earlier.

That cross had been moved.

The cross that he'd buried his money under seventeen
years ago was not the cross that he'd been digging under.
Landslides or not, he'd been picking in the wrong spot all
this time.

"Next event," the announcer called. "Bull riding."

Wyatt snapped himself from his thoughts and remembered that Tug was in the audience, right smack on the front
bench, watching as he lost three events in a row. This was

his last chance to dazzle the boy, and misplaced cross or no, Wyatt was going to give it all he had, or die trying.

"Come on, Wyatt!" Tug's high shout carried through the anxious noise of the outdoor crowd, but Wyatt didn't turn to acknowledge the boy. He had to focus on the pens of Brahma bulls and hope like hell he wouldn't pull one that was known for his one-way spinning. That would mean he'd have to initiate his spurs to get him to turn in the opposite direction for a better ride.

The officials gathered the bull riders together, and they drew lots. Wyatt ended up with Squirrely for his first attempt. Squirrely had no pitfalls that Wyatt had heard of, but that didn't mean the bull was a dream to ride. Several riders went before Wyatt, and then it was his turn to ease his legs around Squirrely's flanks and adjust the rope as two men kept the bull from bucking in the narrow pen.

Sitting atop a ton of muscles, bone, and guts, Wyatt's adrenaline surged sharply through his veins. Squirrely's hide was loose on his body, making it hard to hang on. The cowbell beneath the bull's belly jangled as he shifted and snorted, rearing to go.

Wyatt withdrew inside himself, putting his concentration on the core of what he must do: hang on for eight seconds.

Lifting his chin, he mentally checked his position. He'd pounded the rope into his gloved fist as tight as he could make it, his hat was slung as low as the brim could be without blinding him, the heels to his boots were down with spurs poised to the inside, his chaps—borrowed from Casswell Tinhorn—protected his legs, and his spine was erect yet fluid. Keeping his gaze on the official standing on a high platform with a stopwatch, Wyatt saw nothing else and tuned out every sound except for the one that would give him the go-ahead.

The official held his arm up, staring at Wyatt, then abruptly lowered his hand and hollered "Time!" in the same instant.

The gate was pulled open by a rope attached on the other side, and Wyatt ejected out of the shoot.

Squirrely bucked and kicked, thrashed and bawled. Wyatt

held on with his right hand, while his left arm was shaken out of its socket. Twisting and pounding and skyrocketing muscles tried to hurl him off, but Wyatt kept his head down and squeezed with his legs in those fractional seconds until he was sure he'd be bowlegged for life.

The bell beneath Squirrely's belly clanged out. Wyatt stayed on tight as the bull turned around to the right, changing directions as many times as a woman changes her mind. He kept his shoulders tall and squared Squirrely up for a ride that was taking endless seconds to complete.

When the official yelled "Dismount!" into the megaphone, Wyatt released the rope and leaped from the bull's back. He had to make a run for it, as Squirrely turned around and was set to charge. The cowhands who were trained at handling the bulls once a ride was over took command and herded Squirrely back into the pen area.

Wyatt bent and picked up his hat, not realizing until he saw it lying upside-down in the churned-up dirt that he'd lost it.

"Wyatt! Wyatt!" Tug leaned over the railing, nearly toppling from the bench seats. "You hung on!"

Replacing his hat, Wyatt nodded briefly to Tug, not meeting Leah's gaze or responding to Rosalure. Wyatt was only as good as his last ride, and he had two more if he wanted to win the purse.

His ability to stay on, and his scores, advanced him to the second round. Tuff Callister also proceeded to the next phase of the contest. He rode to a near-perfect score on Cricket. When Wyatt was up next, he drew Boot Hill and had a time keeping the bull from whipping him down. He felt himself starting to fall and lifted himself up square, not wanting just to hang on, but to impress the judges with his control of the animal.

When the dismount was called, Wyatt made the same smooth release as he had before, earning him a respectable score and a round of applause. His pulse hammered double-time, and he spared a glance at Leah, who had risen to her feet with the others. She clapped with enthusiasm and he felt good. Her fears about the sport had apparently dimin ished. He hoped that meant she'd give Tug a chance when he got old enough.

Going into the final round, Wyatt and Tuff Callister were tied for the lead. Wyatt's last bull was Popcorn. Halfway into his eight-second run, he figured out why. The Brahma hopped and skipped like hot popping corn on a griddle. He jumped back and under, swung his head to the left, then abruptly to the right. Wyatt began to fall, the thrust of the bull more than he could handle. But before he ran back off his rope, the call for dismount was given and Wyatt got off that bull with a quick snap of his wrist for a release.

Popcorn recoiled, hung his head low, and aimed those vicious horns of his at Wyatt. Wyatt ran for it, not wanting to be disemboweled or have his teeth crammed down his gullet and tromped on besides, with Leah and her children witnessing. With a quick strut and high leap, he flung himself over the pen rail as Popcorn smacked into the planks.

The bull was subdued by the cowhands and taunted into the pen. Wyatt took a deep breath and leaned his forehead against the rail post. His heartbeat was battering, his legs like jelly, and his guts so stirred up, he felt liable to throw up. Christ Almighty, he was just plain too old for this kind of craziness. And all his innards jarring could be for nothing if Tuff Callister scored higher than he.

Wyatt gazed at the scoreboard and saw that he'd scored his highest mark yet. A degree of relief flooded through him, but the knot of tension remained. He didn't want Callister gored, but he'd sure like to see that kid sail off his bull before the eight seconds were up.

The crowd had risen to its feet once more, and Wyatt could only wait and wonder with them. Tuff was let out of the pen and took a wild ride on White Lightning, Tuff's head lashing against his chest as the bull bucked and kicked.

Tuff Callister appeared to be having the ride of his life, until his bull went down wrong on his left foot and stumbled. Tuff went headfirst over White Lightning's neck and caught a hoof in the ribs as he scrambled to stand. The cowhands got the situation quickly under control, getting Tuff out of the arena and the bull into the pen.

The crowd gave the young kid an ovation for his bravery, and Tuff came out and stiffly waved his hat, holding onto his side. Disappointment painted a painful picture on his face as he came over to Wyatt.

"Looks like you have it, Holloway. Congratulations."

"You're a hard man to beat," Wyatt replied. "I had a stroke of luck."

"No luck about it. You knew what you were doing."

The announcer proclaimed Wyatt the winner, and Wyatt went to stand on the podium to collect his purse from Half Pint Gilman.

A man as brawny as a hundred-year-old tree, and just as tall, loomed over Wyatt to hand him an envelope of cash. The skin on the rancher's face was leathery and burned brown from the sun. Eyes the color of mint stared through the weathered cracks at the corners. The name Half Pint was clearly a misnomer, as the man was bigger and taller than anyone Wyatt had ever encountered.

"Nice work, Holloway." Half Pint shook his hand. "You finally set your concentration on what you were doing. Keep that up and I could use you at my place."

Wyatt appreciated the offer, but replied, "I plan on getting my own going. Nothing as big as yours, but enough to keep me from starving."

"There's enough grazing land around here to do it." Half Pint inched the brim of his high hat further up his forehead. "You need some quality cattle to start up; ride on out and pay me a visit."

"I'll do that."

Wyatt tipped his hat to both Gilman and the crowd, then stepped down and ambled on sore legs to Leah. She was a pretty sight amid a sea of onlookers who were mostly drab-dressed cowpokes. Her colorfully decorated hat stood out against the blue background of sky and the grays and tans of Stetsons.

Tug scrambled to the top of the railing that kept the

stands separate from the arena, straddled the barrier, and shoved off over the side to land in Wyatt's arms.

The boy's familiarity startled Wyatt more than the sudden impact. Tug's hands clasped around Wyatt's neck, and his short legs tightened around Wyatt's middle. In a quick flashback of his childhood, he saw his brother Daniel doing the same thing to him when he'd been ten years old to Daniel's three. To Wyatt's fast calculation, Daniel would be a man of thirty now. Too big to tag after his older brother and pester him about riding. Wyatt would have given anything to get those days back.

"I never seen a better bull rider, Wyatt!" Tug declared in a tone so heavy with hero worship, Wyatt became embarrassed. "I—I want to ride 'em just like you!"

The sweetness of cotton candy came from Tug's breath and drifted to Wyatt's nose. He felt the stickiness of sugar on Tug's cheek as it bumped against Wyatt in a jarring movement while the boy turned his head toward his mother to say proudly, "Wyatt's the best buckaroo I ever saw."

Leah put her hands on the railing and leaned forward slightly. "I think Wyatt was very good, too."

Wyatt had hoped to win all the events to impress Leah, but having her look at him the way she was now, he guessed that one was enough.

Rosalure presented him with a cola. "Momma said you may be thirsty, so I got you this."

"Thanks, Rosalure."

"Tug, let Wyatt go so he can have some room to breathe." Leah held her arms open. "Climb back up here. You shouldn't be down there. What if a bull got loose, or something?"

"No bull's going to get loose, Momma. And even if one did, I could ride 'em like Wyatt."

"Don't be smart," Leah countered. "You couldn't pet one of those bulls, much less ride one. It takes years of experience."

Tug reluctantly shimmied from Wyatt's grasp and slipped through the railing to stand by Leah. Wyatt took the Coca-

Cola from Rosalure and practically drank the entire bottle without taking a breath. He had been thirsty, and the drink was just what he needed.

Wiping his mouth with the back of his hand, Wyatt viewed Leah—who looked around the arena with a frown at all the stomping bulls and broncs in their pens, Rosalure—who cuffed Tug on the shoulder when he stepped on her toe, and Tug—who clambered onto the railing again to straddle it as if he was riding a bull, with one hand swinging in the air and letting out a "Yi-high!"

The scene made Wyatt reflect. Watching his siblings Ardythe, Daniel, Robert, Todd, and Margaret grow up was not to be. With Leah, if she'd let him, he could have a second try at family life. See how Rosalure would develop into a young woman. See how Tug would change into a man. Experiences that men like him didn't usually get, because nobody wanted to love ex-cons.

That's why he couldn't let Scudder drag up information about his past. As far as Wyatt was concerned, he'd paid his debt to society.

"Mighty fine showmanship." The drawled compliment came from Tiberius N. Tee, who came up to the group with Geneva Kirkland as his companion.

"Owen, darling, Nanna doesn't think it's a good idea to be straddling that railing. You could fall off." Geneva gave Leah a worried appeal. "Leah, you should tell him to get off."

Leah looked as vexed as a hive of disturbed bees. "He isn't hurting anything."

Wyatt noticed Leah refused to acknowledge Tiberius.

Moving in, Tee tried to cluck Tug's chin, but Tug growled at him. Tiberius merely chuckled and leaned his elbows on the railing so he could look down at Wyatt. "I mean it. Mighty fine showmanship. But you know, you did look a little tired on that last bull. The Vibratrel could make a new man out of you. Get your heart going. Put some fire of ambition into your blood."

"I don't need any gadget to put fire into my blood. It burns pretty good on its own." Wyatt folded his arms in a gesture of defense.

Tug struggled to get down and ended up on the arena floor again next to Wyatt. He ran around a small circle, pretending he was riding a bronc.

"I didn't see you at the booth, Leah," Geneva said, her chin high.

"No. I was busy."

"With Mr. Holloway?"

Wyatt was the recipient of an arched, penciled brow.

"As a matter of fact, yes."

Leah kept her tone down, but Wyatt could see she was on the verge of yelling at her mother-in-law. Wyatt couldn't blame her. A married woman shouldn't be going around with a man who wasn't her husband. And Hartzell was a likeable enough fellow. Wyatt sided with him over his wife's indulgences. A man could only put up with so much.

Tiberius wouldn't give up on the sales pitch, and went into a long litany of the benefits about the Vibratrel, while Leah and Geneva got into a whispered argument about propriety and Rosalure eavesdropped with wide eyes.

After a spell, Leah abruptly snapped her head up and exclaimed, "Where's Tug?"

Wyatt, who'd been listening with half an ear to Tee, spun around in search of the boy who'd been doing circles around him seemingly not more than a second ago.

"I don't know. He was just here."

"He's not now." Panic issued forth from Leah's cry. "Tug! Tug! Where are you?"

No reply came.

The arena had been a bustle of activity earlier, as hands took the steers and horses back to the corrals. But things had seemed to be quieting down, with only a few of the cowboys lingering over smokes.

"Tug!" Leah shouted to no avail. Turning helplessly to Wyatt, she uttered, "You don't suppose . . . He wouldn't have gone back to . . ." Her voice cracked, but Wyatt knew what she was talking about and had already taken off in a run.

"Tug, don't move."

Wyatt's voice was calm, unlike Leah's heartbeat, which was so frantic her chest hurt. They had found Tug in Cricket's corral, trying to sneak up on the bull while holding a lasso he'd picked up somewhere. Her son froze upon Wyatt's words, and turned with round eyes at being caught.

"But—" Tug began, but Wyatt cut him short.

"Be quiet. And don't move."

Some twenty feet away, Cricket grazed on a portion of hay that had been thrown in his pen. Had the food not been there to distract him, surely the animal would have been bothered by Tug's intrusion. As it was, Leah was so angered that no one had been in attendance in the corral area to keep on eye on the bulls, she could scream.

"Oh dear Lord in heaven," Geneva breathed softly, squeezing Leah's hand so tightly, Leah's bones throbbed. "Mr. Holloway has to get our Owen out."

"He will," Leah reassured. If anyone could rescue Tug it was Wyatt.

Inside the pen, Cricket's chomping went deathly silent. His ears pricked and he raised his head. Slobber ran from his nose where a ring caught a glint of the sun.

"Tug, oh, please stay still," Leah whispered, closing her eyes, unable to view the scene for a moment. But when she heard the gasps and soft, excited voices of the crowd that had gathered to witness what was going on, she had to open her eyes.

Wyatt had crouched and was in a fast walk directly toward the bull. He held a red bandanna in his hand and was waving it like a flag to distract the bull from looking at Tug.

"Run, Tug!" Wyatt hollered. "Get the hell over that fence!"

Tug kicked up his heels and ran faster than Leah had ever seen. She broke free of Geneva and went to the fence, where she held her arms open and ready to help Tug up and over the railing. When he was there, she grasped his sweaty hands in hers and pulled, taking him into her arms and holding him close.

"Tug, Tug, Tug." She couldn't get enough of his boyish smell as she buried her face in his hair. "You scared me."

His hot tears wet her cheek and melted any scolding she would have given him. He'd paid for his mistake in cold fear.

"Owen Edwin! Darling!" Geneva was in tears herself, cooing over Tug while Leah held him tight. "What were you thinking?"

"I wanted to be like Wyatt."

Her son may have been saved, but Wyatt was still in the corral. Leah's chin lifted. Cricket had found the red bandanna more interesting than his hay and had turned with a snort in Wyatt's direction. The bull began lumbering toward him on legs swifter than Leah could imagine. Wyatt made a dash for the nearest railing and pitched himself over it before the bull could spear him with his pointed horns.

The crowd gave Wyatt rousing applause for his heroism as he slapped the dust from his pants legs and walked to Leah. She let Geneva take Tug from her. A rush of feelings came to her as she gazed at Wyatt. The pull on her heartstrings grew and made her feel warm inside.

She had fallen in love with Wyatt.

In little ways that were now a whole, he'd become a part of her life. That he'd risked danger to himself to save Tug only made her love Wyatt more.

"I don't know how to thank you," she said when Wyatt came to her side. "What you did . . ." Her throat closed and she couldn't continue.

Wyatt touched her hand and her pulse leaped. "It wasn't anything."

"It was a lot."

Even Geneva, who'd made no bones about her reservations for Wyatt, said, "Mr. Holloway, if it weren't for you, our Owen Edwin might not have—"

"Somebody else would have done the same thing."

"I doubt that," Tiberius piped in. "You showed exemplary courage."

"Of all the stupid things to do." Rosalure gave Tug a mock punch in the shoulder. "What would I do without a brother to pester?"

Trying to put on a brave front, Tug wiped his tears with his knuckles. "I dunno."

"Well." Geneva took in a shaky breath and released Tug to his feet. "You gave Nanna quite a scare, young man. But in the process, you've made me see that I've been—" Her gaze shifted to Wyatt." —hasty in my assumptions of your character, Mr. Holloway. May I thank you for your unselfish aid?"

"You don't have to."

"But I want to, and I think that the whole town should know." Standing on her tiptoes, she waved her hand at the editor of the *Eternity Tribune*. "Yoo-hoo! Mr. Sheesley!"

Delmar Sheesley's outdated, pin-checked suit stuck out like a sore thumb as he passed through the crowd to meet with Geneva. "What is it, Mrs. Kirkland?"

"I believe an honorarium is due to our Mr. Holloway for his heroism." Geneva beamed in the spotlight as others gathered near to hear her words. "His photograph—with my grandson of course—for the front page of the newspaper. I'll write the article myself and recount every harrowing second of little Owen's death-defying rescue."

Others nodded in agreement. What Wyatt had done was out of the ordinary. His actions were front-page material. But Leah was the only one who knew Wyatt's aversion to having his picture taken, much less reprinted in a newspaper. She would have made the attempt to help him bow out graciously, had she not agreed with Geneva. Wyatt should have his story told.

"I'll pass." Wyatt slipped his hands into the pocket of his duster. "What I did was nothing."

"On the contrary," Mr. Sheesley sighted. "I watched from back there the way you took charge of the situation and brought that boy to safety. I was planning on running a story about the winners of the lawn-and-garden entrants, but what you did is far more important." Delmar addressed Leah. "Mrs. Kirkland, I'll have my assistant run you home in my buggy so you can get your camera. I think the shot ought to be right here. Right in front of the corral. And maybe we could encourage the bull over so he could be in the background."

"I want my picture in the paper!" Tug jumped up and down, his chaps flapping. "No kid has ever had his face on the front page. I'm big news! I'm big news! Just me and Wyatt. Come on Wyatt! You and me."

Leah thought it a wonderful idea, but she could see that Wyatt wasn't going for any of it. She wished she could make him understand that he was special to her and she wanted the whole town to know just how much. Contrary to what he said, nobody who had stood by and watched Tug sneak up on Cricket would have jumped into that corral to save him. But Wyatt had. What was the harm in letting everyone know about his bravery?

"Please, Wyatt," Leah said softly. "I think what you did was marvelous, and I'd love to take your photograph."

"I don't like having my picture taken."

"But it's I who'll be taking it. You can trust me."

Before Wyatt could reply, Hartzell broke through the crowd with a frantic expression, shouting, "What's this about Tug? I heard he was hurt."

"I almost roped him, Poppa." A blush of excitement colored Tug's cheeks.

"Roped who?"

"Cricket, the bull."

"A bull?"

"You missed it all," Tiberius butted in, his words directed at Hartzell. "Your grandson was quite a trooper. Too bad you weren't around."

"It was too bad," Geneva said beneath her breath, her chin low. "Hartzell . . . I . . ."

"Don't get wishy-washy on me, Geneva," Tiberius said, hitching his suspenders higher. "It's you and me for the rest of the day."

"I don't believe so." Geneva appeared to be embarrassed.

Leah could only speculate that it had taken a near tragedy in the family to bring Geneva to her senses. "I need to speak with my husband."

"You don't want to be with him," Tee spouted in his theatrical croon. "You said yourself he spends all his time at the bank standing around and scratching his seat."

Geneva drew herself up tall and pursed her lips. "I never mentioned anything about his posterior. And even if I did, don't you say one bad word about my husband. That's my job." She brought out an embroidered handkerchief and dabbed at the corners of her eyes. "Or at least, that used to be my job."

"Geneva, dearest . . ." Hartzell stepped forward, taking his wife's hand and padding her fingers. "Don't cry."

"I can't help it. I've made a fool of myself." Lowering her voice, she added, "And in front of everyone. What must you think of me?"

"I think that I still love you."

"You do?"

"Of course I do."

"Oh, Hartzell." Geneva threw herself into his arms and rested her cheek on his chest. "Do you forgive me?"

"I do."

"Oh, Hartzell," she said again on a sigh. "Will you come home?"

He smoothed his hand across her shoulder. "If you give up that damn Vibratrel, I will."

Geneva stiffened. "My Vibratrel?"

"Yes. For a cash refund."

Leah waited for Geneva to refuse adamantly, and when she consented with a nod, Hartzell let out a breath. He put Geneva at arm's length and turned to face off with Tiberius N. Tee. But when all eyes moved to the salesman, he was gone.

"Right there," Mr. Sheesley directed. "In the center of the railing. I believe that's the spot." The editor gazed at Leah. "But you are the expert, Mrs. Kirkland. If you feel they should stand elsewhere, speak up."

"Where they are will be fine."

Wyatt stood stiff as a slab of sandstone. He'd been moved and nudged for the past ten minutes while holding Tug in his arms. If there had been any way out of the photograph, he would have bolted. But he'd been trapped. Trapped by a town that hung around like flies on a strip, waiting for the camera's shutter to open and snap him and Tug. Trapped by a stuffy newspaper editor who claimed the article would sell extra papers. Trapped by Geneva Kirkland, who insisted Tug's photograph in the *Eternity Tribune* would be the proudest day of her life. Trapped by Tug, who jabbered away at those asking him to tell them what had happened, and how excited he was to have his picture taken with his hero, Wyatt.

And trapped by Leah herself, whose gratitude had permitted her to return to her house and retrieve her camera, knowing how he felt about them. Knowing that he was not pleased to stand before a lens, and smile.

"A little to the left, Wyatt," Leah instructed from beneath the dark cloth of the camera. Her head popped out momentarily as she frowned when he moved left. "I meant right. In the camera, you're upside-down and I sometimes get my rights and my lefts mixed up." Rosalure stood at her mother's side, watching with interest as Leah made adjustments.

Tug felt heavy in Wyatt's arms, even though he wasn't all that heavy. The minutes he'd been standing seemed to turn into hours. Sweat dampened his forehead at the band of his hat. Wyatt held his teeth tightly together and when Leah finally said, "Smile!" in a cheerful voice, he could no more muster a smile than a corpse.

"Hold still!" Leah took a new plate from Rosalure. Wyatt remained where he stood, the crowd and heat pressing in on him.

"That's good. I want to take another, just in case. Now, smile!"

But Wyatt remained smileless.

Rosalure's laughter came to his ears. "Mr. Holloway, you look like you're laid out on a table waiting for embalming."

Her analogy hit him as if she'd slapped him across the cheek.

"W—What, Rosalure?"

"You look like you're laid out at Mr. Uzzel's waiting for him to . . ."

But her words drifted with a gut-wrenching pull that took Wyatt back to the past.

He sat in Darling's Photography studio with Colvin, Nate, Thomas Jefferson, and Manny. They wore their finest suits and, hidden beneath, the guns that had given them their reputations. That day in Telluride had been the start of a journey to hell.

What Rosalure had just spoken had left him shaken and frozen in limbo in a place he didn't want to be. Those very words had been said to him before when he was having his portrait taken. But back then, Little Darling had been the one in the studio to speak them, and she'd been about ten years of age. Rosalure couldn't have been there to know, because today that girl from Telluride would be in her mid-twenties. Just like . . .

. . . just like Leah.

⚹ 18 ⚹

There is a day to be born and a day to die.
                                        —Chinese proverb

February 13, 1888
Idaho Territorial Penitentiary

For several months, while lying on the stiff cot of his cell in the pitch dark, Harlen Shepard Riley relived the words of Little Darlin'.

"You all look like you've just been laid out on the undertaker's table and are waiting to be embalmed."

Harlen had stolen from fat-pursed banks, cattlemen, and railroad owners without conscience, for he knew that those men could afford to be robbed. A crime was a crime, and by committing one an outlaw flirted with the inevitability of paying his debt to society in prison. Harlen had never counted on being caught, but if he had to do time for a single criminal act, it would have been for that day in Telluride.

A burden of guilt had fallen heavily on him for what had happened on those streets. He'd gone over and over the incident in his head until he'd committed to memory a picture of the events. Yet, with all his intense thoughts and reflections, he still couldn't sort out which one of them had been holding the gun that had shot and killed Evaline

Darling as she crossed the street. The uncertainty of not knowing and the depressing horror of penitentiary life drove him a little crazy.

Like a wild animal caught and caged, he resisted the rules and paid dearly for his disobedience. Beatings and lockups in Siberia were his punishments. In those darkest hours sitting on the cold, damp floor nursing his bruises, he would close his eyes and try and conjure the warmth of the sun . . . the kiss of a breeze.

Freedom.

He never realized how valuable freedom was until it had been taken away from him. He'd thought himself strong enough to own up to his failings, but days spent in solitary confinement in an area that had a heavy plate and door with ventilating holes no more than three-quarters of an inch mentally tortured him. The guards had a saying about Siberia. You put a normal man into the box, and an animal would come out. When Harlen came out, he wasn't an animal, but he was a shell of his former self and bowed his head in submission. His attitude toward his time had changed.

He would spend his days subservient to the penal codes and be a model prisoner, but his nights would still belong to him. Those were the nights he laid awake thinking about Evaline Darling and her little girl. About the boys. His parents. His brothers and sisters. And his attorney, Richard Robison.

Harlen wasn't allowed to write more than two letters a week, which really didn't mean a thing to him, because he couldn't write a letter to where a person could read it. By brief and strictly monitored visits, Richard had informed Harlen that his request for an appeal had been denied. There had been no errors in the first trial to constitute a second one.

Richard had assured Harlen he was doing everything possible to get him out. But by February, Harlen's hopes were dying. On a Friday afternoon that swirled snow in drifts and blankets against the building of the laundry where

Harlen had been assigned, Harlen was informed that his attorney had come to report to the commissary for visitation.

Harlen did so, and the look on Richard's face instantly gave him away. All hope had been exhausted. Robison's petition to the governor for restoration to citizenship to one Harlen Shepard Riley had been denied, and the best Harlen could hope for was another hearing in five years.

Alone in the dark that night, time ceased to have meaning. A second, minute, and hour all became one. With a thin blanket to keep him warm, Harlen went over the letter he'd been writing to Little Darlin' and her father. In it, he voiced his sympathy and his sorrow for the death of Evaline. He told them he understood real regret for the first time in his life, and would do anything to make up for what had happened, if he could.

As the beads of water that had collected on the stone walls from the moisture of warm breath in a cold room dripped in a steady rhythm to the icy slabs of floor, Harlen composed the letter until he got the words perfect. Any letter that went out, the warden would open and read, and even then, Harlen wondered whether the letter would be mailed at all. But that really didn't matter, because Harlen didn't have the skills actually to write the words on paper, so his thoughts were never shared with the girl who'd looked at him through the window with open hate in her eyes.

Little Darlin' never knew how sorry he was.

Manny Vasquez was brought to the pen the next day to serve a sentence of fifteen years for his part in the Montpelier robbery. Harlen didn't have much of an opportunity to speak with him, but he found out that Manny had been arrested down in Alma, New Mexico. He'd never found Nate, Colvin, and Thomas Jefferson, but people were saying the boys had ridden into Mexico without him.

In the ensuing days, Manny was given a job in the sign shop. Harlen learned more in their brief passings. Manny said rumors were circulating on the outside that Harlen had gone up to Canada and was living high on the hog with the sixty thousand dollars. The boys had supposedly bought this rumor and were calling Harlen a traitor to the Loco Boys.

Harlen was sickened by the news that his riding partners had thought he turned against them, betraying them and spending their money. He swore that when he got out, he'd set them all straight with his fists.

August 21, 1889
Idaho Territorial Penitentiary

When Harlen turned twenty-three, he became a member of the Quarry Gang. The men had been assigned work detail in the hills to cut sandstone for the building of the new cell house. The guards held long rifles and kept bloodhounds at their hips in case any of the inmates took it into their mind that they would escape.

Harlen had resigned himself to the pen until 1892, but Manny could see no life in confinement. He resisted. The outcome was a face that always wore a cut across the cheek, or an eye that was bruised. Manny was solidly built and strong as an ox, and therefore too useful to be put in Siberia anymore once the warden was told he had the funds to build a new wing.

Manny was assigned to the Quarry Gang with Harlen.

As the heat stung Harlen's skin, sucking out his sweat while he picked away at the stone, he gazed at Manny. Manny was his only friend on the inside, but he wasn't the same as he'd been before. His movements were edgy and confined, not limited to the shackles on his ankles, and he took every opportunity to bait the guards' dogs and have them snapping at him.

The bloodhounds looked docile enough, but Harlen had seen them choking against their collars before being let off their leashes to run down some fool inmate who thought he could scramble down the side of Table Rock to freedom. An escape wasn't to be had with those dogs and the guards' shotguns in sight.

But Manny Vasquez would try anyway.

June 25, 1890
Idaho State Penitentiary

Cell House Number Two was near completion the year Idaho became a state and the penitentiary's name was changed. Manny had slowly been losing his mind in his cell and would swear many times to Harlen that he would break out. Harlen had thought along those lines himself, but still held out hope Richard Robison could pull something off. Harlen was tired of running, and were he to gain his freedom by escape, he'd have to run.

Richard's visit earlier that day had been full of news about the boys.

Sitting in a suit across from Harlen, Richard said quietly, "Words been circulating anew about you. Now it's told that you made off with a hundred thousand dollars from that Silverton robbery. There are some rumors that the boys are in Mexico and are swearing to see you dead for cheating them."

"It's still not known where I am?"

"Court documents are sealed, Harlen. The judge thinks that if the boys want revenge against you, they'll come out of hiding and the law can apprehend them."

Harlen put his hand on the flat of the table. "You hear anything about that photographer in Telluride?"

"I'd have to investigate."

"No . . . don't." Harlen was afraid to know. He'd just been wondering if the family had gotten on all right without the mother. But maybe it was better not to bring all that up again.

Richard flicked the edge of his notepad. "I ran across some news about your mother, Harlen."

Harlen's eyes lifted, and he saw his mother's face in his mind's eye. "She's all right?"

"She's been sick. The family had to take her to Hanksville for medical treatment for her blood."

"Is she okay now?" Harlen's pulse beat inside him like the kick of a guard.

"She's better. The girls are watching over her."

Despite himself, Harlen asked, "And my dad? He's okay?"

"He's working close to the place to be near your mother."

Harlen nodded.

"Harlen, I think you ought to tell them where you are."

"No." Harlen adamantly shook his head. "I'm not going to bring them any further shame. It's best they think I'm in Canada, or six feet under. Any place but in here. It'd kill them to know."

Richard gathered his notepad and slipped it into a portfolio. "If you ever change your mind—"

"I won't."

Nodding, Richard stood. "I have an appointment with the governor next week to speak to him about you. I can't promise anything. Your pardon hearing won't be for another two years, but if he's abreast of your case now, that could help us."

Harlen slouched in his chair. "But you're not hopeful."

"The Idaho courts haven't been granting any leniency in the last few years, because the public is demanding that criminals be kept for their full incarceration time. The pressure is making it hard for me to argue with the government. They feel it necessary to act on the full extent of the law."

Disappointment barely registered in Harlen. He had too much to think about. His mother. His father.

Harlen rose and shook Richard's hand. "I appreciate your coming by, Richard."

Going back to work detail, Harlen bottled his feelings for his family inside. It was unsafe to take them out during the day. At night, when time slipped by slowly, Harlen could afford to let his mind wander. For now, he had to keep a clear head. There was Manny to look after.

Fearing Manny would try and put together a futile plan, Harlen had talked to him while they worked on the line side by side. Without backup men to cover him, or a waiting horse, Manny had no chance of escape. But Manny didn't see things that way, and Harlen feared he would lose the only friend he had.

The sweltering sun buzzed with flies, beating down on the rock and the prisoners who'd been stripped to the waist to work. The guards sat in the lethargic shade, the bloodhounds panting nearby.

"When I get out, do you want me to send word to your family?" Manny whispered.

He'd asked Harlen that question many times, and Harlen had always replied they would both get out together.

Sweat ran down Manny's sun-browned face. "Come with me, Harlen. It'll be you and me. We can start up where we left off."

"It's pointless, Manny. You can't get out until they're ready to let you out."

"No talking on the line!" W. T. Fulton, one of the day guards, yelled out to them from his cool spot in the shade where he sipped a drink of water.

Manny swore beneath his breath. "I could kill him. It would be so easy. I've never wanted to kill, Harlen, but I do now." He wiped his brow with the back of his hand as he leaned over to dig the tip of his pick into the rock. "You know, this place made me a criminal. I never really was an outlaw until they put me in here. Now I think of killing. I think about it all the time. I could kill Fulton. And the warden. And half of the men in this stinking place."

Harlen gave Manny a sidelong glance, but kept up with the motions of his pick. Manny had turned into someone Harlen didn't recognize. Siberia had done it; Manny hadn't been the same. "You quit thinking thoughts like that, Manny. We'll get out together. You and me."

Manny straightened his spine, his eyes moist as he stared

at Harlen. "I can't take it anymore, Harlen." His parched voice cracked like a clump of dirt. "I just can't. I've got to get out now. Freedom . . . I have to feel it or I'm going to die."

"Manny, don't."

But Manny had already started to walk. Slowly at first, and then with an uneven gait from the chains on his ankles. At first, the guards thought Manny was going for the water bucket, but when Manny walked past it, the men in the shade rose, calling the dogs to their feet as well.

"Number 452! Hold your steps!" Fulton yelled, his rifle raised and pinned on Manny's back.

Manny kept on walking down the hill to where an apple orchard was spread across the valley above Boise. On balmy days, the smell of those blossoms drifted up to the inmates and nearly made Harlen sick with the longing to put his nose in the buds and drink in the fragrance of something sweet instead of greasy.

"Number 452! Hold your steps or I'll shoot."

"Manny!" Harlen couldn't contain himself, and he shouted to Manny. "Get on back."

Without a word or backward glance, Manny started to run down the embankment. Fulton gave the order for the dogs to go after him. The hounds caught Manny by the legs, but Manny wasn't put off by them. He took one by the neck and strangled it. This set Fulton off in a frenzy, and without another warning, he pulled the trigger and shot Manny in the back. A crimson stain spread across the prisoner's soiled shirt as he crumpled to his death in the dust and weeds.

Harlen squeezed his eyes closed and the pick slipped from his hand. His chin fell to his chest. Manny was his last link to his old life, and though the life had been lawless, it was a life that Harlen knew. He'd had a bond with Manny, even Colvin, Nate, and Thomas Jefferson before the trouble had come. And now Manny was dead. His family was gone.

Standing under the oppressive sheet of the sun's rays, Harlen didn't want to find the boys anymore. He hoped to

God he never saw Colvin, Nate, or Thomas Jefferson again. He wanted nothing further to do with the past. He didn't want to see or hear them ever again.

For all intents and purposes, Harlen Shepard Riley died that afternoon with Manny Vasquez. There just wasn't any grave marker to prove it.

❧ 19 ❧

Light a fire in seven places,
and there will be smoke in eight.
—Chinese proverb

The headline of the Sunday edition of the *Eternity Tribune* read:

CHILD RESCUED!

Wyatt and Tug's photograph was directly beneath the bold headline. Leah gazed at the paper, wishing Wyatt would have had a more enthusiastic expression on his face. But that she'd been able to give him credit for his heroic deed was enough. Now all of Eternity would know what a good man he was.

"Momma!" Rosalure's voice carried up the stairs into Leah's studio, where she sat in her dressing robe. "Oh, Momma!"

Leah rose from the plush chair in her studio and went to the landing. "Rosalure, how many times must I tell you not to yell like that in the house? If you want me, come up and get me."

Rosalure stood by the door and let the panel turn inward while saying, "Wyatt's here."

Putting a hand to where the fabric of her dressing robe met across her breasts, Leah stammered, "W—Wyatt. What a nice surprise."

Seeing him on a Sunday morning truly was a surprise. He didn't attend church and kept to himself on the Lord's day. So finding him at her doorstep put her at a loss. Not that she was disappointed. She was glad to see him. She only wished he'd come sooner.

Last night, in all the excitement of Tug's encounter with Cricket, Wyatt hadn't walked her home. Leah's house had been filled with family and friends, all wanting to know about what had happened to Tug. Geneva had taken notes on a tablet and went frantically to work on the article at the secretary in the parlor while Tug basked in the moment on his grandfather's knee and Rosalure called Tug's escapade just another dumb thing to do.

Wyatt hadn't returned with them, even though Leah had invited him. As soon as she'd taken his photograph, he'd withdrawn and moved away from the crowd. She'd thought it was because he hadn't wanted his picture taken and she'd done so anyway. So she'd chased after him to apologize and tell him that he truly was a hero and should be recognized for it.

But Wyatt had had a far-off look on his face. A distance in his eyes that made her think he wasn't with her, but rather recalling some other moment. She'd asked him what was wrong, but he refused to talk to her. Instead, he'd walked away, only to be swallowed in the throng of exposition goers.

"Hey, Wyatt!" Tug tromped through the foyer in his cowboy boots and met Wyatt, pulling Leah from her thoughts of yesterday.

"How you doing today, Tug?"

"Okay."

"Good."

Though it wasn't appropriate for a man to enter a lady's home when she wasn't properly dressed, Leah sensed by the serious look on Wyatt's face that he wanted to discuss something important with her.

"Let Wyatt in, Rosalure."

"Sure, Momma."

Wyatt entered and removed his hat. The locks of his dark hair were neatly combed, and his clothing was clean and pressed. He might have come for a social call were it not for the somber line of his mouth.

"You two run along and finish getting ready for church. If you don't dally and argue, I'll let you go to Nanna's right after services for cookies and milk," Leah said, thinking it best for her and Wyatt to be alone. Both Tug and Rosalure bounded up the stairs past her, and she heard the doors to their rooms slam closed.

Leah lay her hand lightly on the banister as she continued her assent. "Wyatt, is something wrong?"

He looked down a moment, then up at her. "No." His voice cracked and he cleared his throat. "I just wanted to tell you that I saw the paper and the picture looked nice."

Leah could tell there was more, but wasn't sure how to bring it out of Wyatt. "I know you weren't thrilled about the idea, but I was hoping you'd be pleased with the results."

"If you've got a minute, could you show me your studio? I'd like to see where you developed the picture. I'm just a little curious now how everything goes together."

Wyatt had never had an interest in her business apartment before. Not that he was disinterested, but seeing that he didn't want his portrait done, Leah had had no reason to show him upstairs before. She was proud of her working area, but hadn't wanted to appear boastful and encourage him to step inside her studio. Now that he was asking, even though her time was tight she couldn't refuse.

"I'd be happy to show you, Wyatt. But I've got to be at the church in a half hour."

"I won't keep you."

Leah turned and went up the stairs, feeling Wyatt's eyes boring into her back as she did so. It was as if he were trying to look at her from the inside out and see who she really was.

* * *

For Wyatt, finding the money on the mountain had become inconsequential for the moment. He hadn't given the moving of the cross and its new whereabouts more than a passing thought after Rosalure had made the comment about being laid out on an undertaker's table. As soon as he started figuring facts and dates, he began putting together a far-fetched scenario.

Leah Kirkland could be Little Darlin'.

He didn't want it to be true. But too many pieces to a complex puzzle were falling into place. She was a photographer. She was of the age Little Darlin' would be today. Her son's middle name was Edwin, as in Edwin Darling in Telluride. Leah had no living family; that meant no mother. Too many clues. Too many fingers pointing in her direction.

Wyatt hadn't slept all night. All the places, all the people he could have picked to be and befriend, he couldn't have turned full circle and met up with Little Darlin' again. He just couldn't have. What kind of cruel fate would that be for a man who'd suffered years of incarceration . . . years of not knowing whether he'd killed a child's mother. Years of trying to put the past behind him, only to have it confront him headlong in the face.

He had to find out who Leah was. And he had to know without asking. If Leah had been that girl in Telluride, and if she ever found out who he was, she'd hate him.

He wouldn't blame her. But he'd become too close to her to let her go. Too many feelings were riding the line here. He was afraid to lose her without ever having had her heart. Leah had taken his life and given it meaning. Because of her, he wanted to stay in Eternity and start afresh. But he could never stay if she was Little Darlin'. He couldn't face her each day knowing that he'd had a part in her mother's death and outright deceiving her as to who he really was.

Wyatt wanted to go to her studio for the simple reason that if she was Little Darlin', there could be a picture of her when she was younger. The photograph parlor that he'd been in had scads of pictures. Some of customers, some of family. All sorts of *cartes de visite,* cabinet photos, and cards. If only she'd kept some of her old photographs downstairs, he would have known sooner. But the only ones she displayed in her parlor were of her children and her wedding portrait.

Needing to see a likeness of her parents had made him come to seek the truth. Though it had been a long time, he felt he could identify Evaline Darling. She'd been a striking woman. The kind of woman a man didn't easily forget.

The hallway carpet buffered his steps as Wyatt followed. The odor of chemicals grew and he had the same feeling he had the first time he'd entered her home: an overwhelming need to hold his breath and run. Leah went through an open doorway into a room bright with sunshine from skylights, and he followed. The smells were stronger and his nostrils smarted as he was brought back in time to Darling's on that fateful day in 1887.

Wyatt couldn't be distracted by a place in time. He put a wedge of distance between himself and back then, focusing instead on the present and taking in his surroundings.

The walls were blue and ivory, colors that softened the interior and gave a velvety look to the studio. Rugs of exotic patterns laid on the floor, while pots filled with ferns and flowers dappled the free space in the corners and on the window ledges. An easel with a backdrop setting of a lush garden stood next to a window where negatives were anchored by clothespins and hung on string that sagged across the sash.

Plain as day, the transparent imprint of him and Tug dangled over the window.

"Well, this is it," Leah said as she clasped her hands in front of her. "It's nothing fancy, but it suffices quite nicely. This room used to be a bedroom, but I converted it into my work space. The water closet is my darkroom."

Nodding, Wyatt's gaze didn't meet Leah's. He took a slow stroll through the room, taking in all the photographs that were on display. At each framed picture, he paused and gave the portraits a thorough examination. None struck a chord with him. But he continued to each table until he reached one with a lace cloth draped over the surface. Amid the ornate frames of silver and etched wood, he found what he feared most.

Wyatt's palms grew damp and his nerve endings stabbed tiny needles into his pulse. Stretching his hand out, he lifted an oval off the tabletop and brought the portrait closer. The image was that of a girl in a pinafore, her hair plaited close to her head. The half-smile was unmistakably Leah's . . . unmistakably Little Darlin's.

"I was about nine in that photograph." Leah had come to stand behind him. He felt her presence, her warmth, soaking into him and making him want to take her in his arms and forget he'd ever seen the picture. Forget about everything.

Wyatt gently set the frame back on the table, trying to keep his fingers from shaking. "Where was it taken?"

"Telluride. At my father's gallery."

Closing his eyes, Wyatt cursed Harlen Shepard Riley's existence. "Your father was a photographer?"

"Yes." Leah reached for another picture. "This is a picture of him and my mother."

Wyatt could barely look at the images of the couple dressed in their best before a curtain of velvet. Edwin had a look of pride about him, while Evaline held herself with a regal pose and not a hint of a smile. She was just as beautiful as Wyatt had remembered.

With his stomach clenched tightly, Wyatt said, "You don't speak about them much."

Replacing the photograph, Leah dusted the edge with her fingertips. "My mother died when I was young, and my father passed away the year I turned seventeen and married my husband. I took my father's death very hard, but my mother's . . . I don't like to think about that." Leah's voice clogged with emotion.

Though Wyatt hated to, he had to know how Leah felt about that day. How she'd coped, how she'd gone on . . . what had happened to her. Had she known about him? What had become of him? Had she tried to find out?

His throat dry as parchment, Wyatt asked, "How did she die?"

Leah's gaze met his. "She was murdered in Telluride. I saw her get shot."

Wyatt could barely hear over the pounding of his heartbeat as it battered his ribs. "What happened?"

"A notorious gang of outlaws came into the studio to have their portrait taken, though we didn't know their occupation at the time. I don't recall much about them, other than there was one . . ." Her voice drifted as her brows furrowed. Wyatt inhaled so deeply his chest hurt. "I remember him most, because he gave me candy. He seemed like a gentleman. They all were dressed so nicely. But they were cold-blooded killers. Every one of them."

Wyatt didn't think he could listen to any more. He felt as if the ceiling were dropping down on him, closing over him and crushing his bones to dust.

Leah fingered a ribbon on her gown and wet her lips. "When they left with their portrait, I thought that was the end of it, but then the gunfire started. I looked out the window and saw my mother crossing the street. She wore a light-colored dress. I can't recall the exact shade."

Peach. The color came to Wyatt as if he were right there with Evaline Darling all over again. Why hadn't he seen that Leah looked so much like her? Her eyes, her hair, the shape of her face.

"Then the horses and riders came barreling down the street, and the next thing I saw was Mother falling . . . into the gutter, her pale dress covered with mud and blood. I'll never forget the way she lay there. So still . . ." A tear slipped from Leah's eyes, rolling down her cheek and splashing on the collar of her robe.

Wyatt wanted desperately to comfort Leah. To touch her. But his hands were stained. He couldn't betray her in such a way as to console her about himself.

"And then he rode by and our eyes met," Leah went on. "I don't know if he was the one or not, but I had to blame someone for what had happened. And since he'd looked at me, I've always known Harlen Shepard Riley had to be the one who killed her."

She spoke the name with such disdain, Wyatt wanted to erase it from her lips, putting passion on her mouth instead of hatred. But what had been done could not be undone.

"Did they ever capture him?" he asked in a voice so heavy with pain, he could barely speak.

She shook her head. "No. No one ever saw him again. We heard he'd fled to Canada with money he'd stolen from a bank in Silverton. That was all. He never had to suffer for what he did to my mother. He never had to pay the way my father did. Living alone with his heart broken."

If Leah could know, could understand that Wyatt's heart had broken that day, too, perhaps . . .

Wyatt lowered his head, letting go of hopes that made him feel pitiful. There was no way to make her understand that he'd been young and reckless. There was no way to tell her that he'd spent seventeen years in hell paying for what he'd done. None of that could bring Evaline back.

"I'm sorry about what happened," Wyatt offered in a tone so chock-full of emotion, he thought he might break down and spill his guts. But words of sympathy would be too little, too late.

Leah lay her hand on his shoulder. "It's not your fault."

Shame ate at him so deeply, he felt the marrow of his bones being chewed.

"I didn't mean to cry," Leah said. "It's just that . . . I loved my mother, but I never told her that I did. I tried to show her, but she couldn't see. I think that's why it's so important that I be successful in my photography. She wanted to be an actress and wasn't able to, because she was a wife and mother. I want her to be proud of me."

"I'm proud of you." Wyatt's words were whispered softer than a feather. His breathing was labored and he had to get out of the room before he suffocated from the strong components of developing liquids that permeated from the walls, the floor, the very air he was sucking into his lungs.

"Are you all right?" She lifted her hand to his cheek. Her fingers burned him and he wanted to crush her next to his chest and breathe in the perfume of her hair. He wanted to close off everything inside him but her. But wanting to and being able to were tearing him in two. He had to leave. To get away.

Slipping away from her touch, he said, "I've kept you too long. I've got to go."

"Wyatt?" Leah followed him to the door. "Are you sure you're all right? You don't look well."

He didn't feel well. His stomach was lurching and punching his guts to bits. "I've got to be going." But seconds before he turned, he put her face to memory, drinking in every detail until he could draw her portrait in his head.

Then Wyatt left, taking the stairs two at a time before they could swallow him whole.

Once he was out the door, he gulped in the cleansing air and nearly ran for the Starlight Hotel. He needed a plan.

But he needed money worse.

He thought seriously about robbing the Eternity Security Bank. He had to get out of town. Away from Leah before he broke down and told her the truth about everything. Before he told her that he loved her. But nothing good would come of her knowing who he'd been. Revealing who he was would just dredge up her hurt and add to her scars.

There were some loose ends he had to tie up before he left. One was getting hold of that negative of him and Tug and destroying it. He couldn't stop his photograph from circulating in the local newspaper, but he didn't want any more copies produced. If any of the boys ever saw that picture, they'd come hunt him down with a vengeance.

Wyatt thought of all that cash on the mountain and hated to leave it. But unearthing the money would take time. Time he didn't have. He couldn't afford to stay another day.

When Leah was at church, he'd have to break into her house and take the negative . . . then he'd figure out what to do about the bank. Just the thought of wielding a gun against Hartzell and telling him to put up the cash made Wyatt grow stone cold.

What kind of man was he, that he could turn around and rob a friend? That he could even think about it, much less go through with it.

Hadn't he changed at all? Or was he fooling himself? Was Wyatt Holloway nothing more than a shadow of Harlen Shepard Riley?

The house was quiet when Leah returned home from church alone. Removing her hat and gloves, Leah climbed the stairs with the intentions of changing her moiré dusty-rose dress for a simpler ivory linen. As she neared the top landing, she froze, thinking that she heard a noise from her studio. She listened closely but could discern nothing further. Taking extra care with her steps, she proceeded. She knew which areas on the floor to avoid, which planks that groaned beneath her weight. Nearing her studio, she held back in the doorway and peeked around the jamb.

Wyatt stood at the window where she kept her negatives. He had one in his hand and folded it before she could stop him.

"What are you doing?" Her unflinching question rang through the room. She wasn't nearly as upset about finding him in her home as she was about his destroying one of her prints.

He swiveled quickly, confronting her. "Leah."

Entering the studio, she went straight to him and took the film from his grasp. She saw the print was of Wyatt and Tug. She'd been proud of that picture. Even more so than others, because this one had Wyatt in it. She'd planned on making a copy for herself to keep on display. Now it was ruined. Lifting her gaze to his, she asked, "Why?"

"I don't want my picture in a newspaper again. I don't want my picture showing up anywhere. If you don't have the negative, you can't make another copy."

"But I wouldn't have. Not without asking you."

"You couldn't ask me if I wasn't around."

Leah's earlier apprehensions about Wyatt's strange behavior rose, but even more concern about his implication. "Are you leaving Eternity?"

His steely blue eyes held hers. "Would you miss me if I did?"

"Of course I would miss you." Fear knotted inside her.

He'd always said he'd leave. But she thought . . . hoped . . . he changed his mind. "We all would miss you. Tug and Rosalure. Leo. Everyone." Less troubled over his sneaking into her home, she took his hand in hers. "Something happened yesterday, didn't it? It's not just the photograph that has you acting so unlike yourself. Tell me, Wyatt. Please." She gave his fingers light pressure. "You can tell me anything."

He drew away from her, removed his hat, and ran his hands through his hair, tousling the locks. "There are some things I can't tell you."

"No, there aren't. There can't be. We're friends . . . more than friends," she added quietly. "At least you are to me. I trust you, Wyatt. Whatever it is, it can't be all that bad. I could help you."

"You can't help me." Replacing his Stetson, he went to the window once more and gazed through the pane at the cross high on the mountain. His words were as far off as the icon. "You don't know me. I've done things in the past."

"I know who you are now. That's all that matters." Leah stood behind him, putting her hand on his shoulder and thinking how right he felt next to her. She'd known for some time that he was special. That she'd grown in her desires since she'd met him. Wyatt was strong and caring. His presence was good for Tug and he treated Rosalure as if she was a grown-up young lady. Hartzell was fond of him, and even Geneva had turned around in her opinions.

Wyatt was everything she could want in a man, and more. That she'd held out for something better, not in the sense of a companion, but by wanting more for her life through her photography, she'd been deluding herself. Her art wasn't important without love. Men like Wyatt didn't come through town everyday. She didn't want to let him go.

Leah struggled with her emotions, wondering if she dared reveal to him what was in her heart. The fear that he wouldn't feel the same way, or wouldn't want her in return, had kept her silent. But now that he was implying he was moving on, she couldn't let him go. Not without telling him.

Sliding her fingers down his shoulder, she reveled in the

hard feel of his muscles beneath the soft fabric of his shirt. "I can't make you tell me what's troubling you, but I don't want you to go away. I . . . I love you, Wyatt."

He didn't turn toward her and take her into his embrace declaring similar feelings as she'd hoped, but neither did he flinch and move aside so she couldn't touch him. "You can't love me." His voice was heavy. "I don't want you to."

Without moving, Leah asked softly, "Could you ever love me?"

This time she felt his bicep bunch beneath her palm, his body grow tense, and his chin lower a fraction. "Don't ask me that."

"Then you don't."

"What I feel for you can't be."

Leah sighed with frustration. "You're acting like Tug, you know that. You're saying one thing but wanting me to think another." She withdrew her hand. "Do you love me or not, Wyatt? It's a simple enough question. One that with an honest answer, we can deal with anything."

He abruptly spun around and gripped her by her shoulders, startling her while giving her a soft shake. "You want the truth? Yes, dammit, I love you."

Leah reeled from his tight grasp, the intensity burning in his eyes as he pinned her beneath him.

"I wish I didn't," he said. "I wish I'd never come back to Eternity."

His words were late registering with her, and when they did, she questioned, "You've been here before? I never saw you."

"You wouldn't have. I passed through town seventeen years ago on my way to . . ." He exhaled deeply. "Well, you could call it the road to restitution. I wasn't able to come back until now."

"But what does any of that have to do with today? I don't understand."

"There is only one thing that you need to understand, Leah. And that's if I could go back in time, if I could make a difference, I would." His shadowed face slowly lowered to hers until their foreheads touched. She could feel his breath on her cheeks, the suffering in his voice when he spoke, "I would give anything to make you forget you ever knew me."

The sting of tears in her throat thickened her reply, "I don't want to forget you, Wyatt. I have wishes, too. I wish that we could be together. Hold each other. You're lonely some times, I can tell. So am I. We can reach out to one another. We don't have to be alone . . . we could—"

Before she could finish her thought, Wyatt held her chin in his fingers and brought her mouth to his. The kiss was hard and searing. Fraught with a passion and thirst she'd never experienced before. Her arms lifted to encircle Wyatt's neck, to bring him closer to her. His solid chest melded against her, flattening her breasts into the fabric of his chambray shirt. She could think of nothing besides his mouth on hers. His lips, the way they coaxed her to abandon herself to him.

Leah had wanted this. To be with Wyatt. To have him in her arms. She felt no shame. No regret. She was no longer a virgin with idealistic thoughts. She was a woman, and she knew the beauty of lovemaking. The closeness. The want of fulfillment and joy.

Breaking from Wyatt's mouth, Leah breathed, "I want you to stay with me. No one's here but us. . . . No one will return to the house. Stay with me . . . for a while."

He dropped a light kiss on her cheek, his nose brushing the side of hers.

"Trust me . . ." she whispered.

Wyatt held her tightly to him, his face in the curve of her shoulder. "I trust you, Leah. It's I who you shouldn't trust."

She took his hand in hers. "I'm afraid it's too late for that. I've already fallen in love with you." Easing him away from the window, she led him out of the studio and down the hall to her bedroom.

❧ 20 ❧

If what we see before our eyes is doubtful,
how can we believe all that is spoken?
            —Chinese proverb

Nothing masculine decorated Leah's bedroom. She'd packed away Owen's things, giving most of his personal belongings to Geneva and his clothing to charity. She'd gone on after Owen's death, but she couldn't help giving her husband a passing thought as she brought another man into the room they'd once shared.

There wasn't a feeling of guilt or being illicit. Only a recollection of a time gone by and a time to move on.

Without a word, Leah brought Wyatt to the French bedstead of bird's-eye maple with plush ticking rising high from the frame and the abundance of embroidered and lace-trimmed pillows. She followed his gaze as he took in the floral-patterned paper, the tall wardrobe, the dimity curtains that parted at the headboard of the bed, her marble-topped toilet table where articles for her hair and skin lay strewn in a haphazard manner. Sunlight caught her colorful perfume bottles and put a shine to her decoupage box overflowing with ribbons and silk flowers. Throughout, there were books, china plates, baskets, and vases. Memen-

tos and an array of old and new hanging photographs of Tug
and Rosalure.

The room truly did belong to her now, with Owen's
presence only a memory.

She let Wyatt's hand go, smiling subtly as he went to her
toilet table. His hands passed over the bottles of fragrance,
lifting several, then coming to the last crystal vial. Bringing
the bottle to his nose, he inhaled, then faced her. "This is
what I can smell in my sleep. It's you."

Leah came forward. "Actually, it's Carnation de Parme."

Tipping the bottle, Wyatt then righted it and popped the
stopper. "Give me your wrist."

She lifted her hand and he took the back of it in his palm.
With the end of the stopper grazing against her pale flesh,
the floral essence of carnations heated against the thrum of
her pulse. The room smelled pleasantly of fragrance and
sunshine.

Wyatt set the bottle down, lifted his hands to her neck,
and unfastened the right row of buttons to her sailor-style
dress. She trembled, standing still and yearning as he
continued beyond her breasts to her waist, where the
closures stopped. Then he addressed the left side with the
same attention, moving slowly, keeping his eyes not on
what he was doing, but on her. She felt the burning imprint
of his gaze, the longing to have his hands on her bare flesh.

She wore a lightweight shirtwaist that was held together
by a series of tiny bows down the front. After pulling each
one, Wyatt took her arms out of both the dress and the waist
until she stood with the fabric bunched at her waist and in
her chemise and corset cover.

He picked up the perfume again and brought the stopper
to the hollow of her throat, lightly caressing her with the
cool crystal. Shivering, Leah let her head fall backward, her
eyes closing. Then Wyatt's mouth was on hers again. He
kissed her until she could barely stand, his lips firm and
persuading. Parting the seam of her mouth with his tongue,
they shared a kiss in a way that Leah had never before
experienced. His tongue met hers, dancing, touching, seek-

ing. Rather than being embarrassed or shy, Leah kissed him in the same way, trying, tasting, experimenting.

When she thought her knees would give way, he swept her into his sinewy arms and brought her to the bed. The ticking molded against her backside, cradling her and Wyatt. He held his arms straight but kept his mouth on hers, ever teasing. Torturing a response from her. She gladly gave, her hands gliding around his middle and skirting down to his waistband. Tugging the worn fabric free of his pants, she tentatively skimmed her fingertips across the smoothness of his back.

His skin was warm and tight. Hard with muscles. The bones of his spine were strong and straight, unyielding. Wyatt's body was built for endurance and held a coiled power. She'd seen that when he'd ridden the bull. Now, she marveled in the flex of his muscles as he moved over her, taking her face in his palm and giving her a gentle kiss.

"I'm still going to leave, Leah," Wyatt said hoarsely. "I have to."

"But you're here now. And that's all that matters to me."

In his eyes, she saw a mixture of emotions. A depth of unhealed pain, yet a thirst for her so potent, she was almost afraid. She wondered if he hadn't been with a woman for a while. Because he touched her eyebrows, her lashes, the bridge of her nose and the curve of her cheek, the lobe of her ear and the shape of her lips . . . as if he hadn't felt the softness of a woman in quite some time. By tracing the map of her face, he made her feel special. Important to him.

His gift gave her the nerve to bring her fingers to the buttons on his shirt and begin to separate the fabric. Wyatt kept his weight on his arms, his head down and hidden from her view by the brim of his hat. When she had his shirt unbuttoned, she brought her hand to his Stetson, slowly slipped it from his head and throwing the hat to the floor.

Wyatt's hair fell over his brow, long and unruly. She took her hand and buried her fingers in the silky locks above his ear, relishing the cool feel and texture.

He dipped his mouth to hers for a brief kiss, then raised

himself onto his knees and stripped out of his shirt. Leah lay there, gazing up at him. The planes of his chest, the markings of the tiny lines of scars across his ribs and the hard swell of muscle. She hurt for him, putting the tip of her finger at a long-healed cut that was just below his left nipple.

"What happened to you?"

Wetting his lips, he refused to gaze at himself when he replied, "I've led a hard life. I paid for it."

"But somebody beat you. Hurt you." She traced the outline of his flat nipple, trailing a path to another scar, one in a deeper color of flesh.

He grabbed her wrist, stopping her from continuing. "Don't. I don't want you to feel them. Or see them." With his free hand, his fingertips fell across her eyes. "Close your eyes. I don't want you to look at me. They're ugly."

She found nothing ugly or horrible in his body. She found only wounds that needed love to heal. But rather than upset him, she kept her eyes lightly closed when he removed his hand.

The bed dipped and strained as Wyatt moved. She could hear his boots falling hard to the floor, the metal clink of his belt buckle, and the rough slide of denim down his lean legs. When he came back to her, she dared not touch him.

When his lips came down on hers, she kept her hands at her sides, her fingers clutching the covers. The heat from his naked body gave off his own perfume. His own masculine scent of horse leather and the wind, Mennen shaving soap, and a smell that was Wyatt's alone. There was no distinction or name to it. It was just him. She'd know it in the dark . . . on a sheet. Anything he touched.

Breaking free of her lips, Wyatt lifted himself to tug down her skirt. Despite her promise, Leah opened her eyes to watch him release her from the heavy dress fabric. Once she wore only her underclothing, he leaned back on his haunches and worked the laces of her shoes. She could see nothing of him below his navel, as the bedclothes had gathered at his hip. He slipped each kid shoe off in turn, then lay his hand on her anklebone, feeling, petting, then skimming upward beyond her knee and to her thigh where the garters held her stocking in place. At the band of elastic, he slipped his fingers inside to reach her skin.

Wyatt emitted a low growl from his throat, a cry of ecstasy at the simple pleasure of touching her thigh. She couldn't take her eyes from him, gaining as much just observing him. With a drawn-out movement, he rolled the stocking down her leg, then turned his attention to her other leg. This time, after removing the stocking, he fit both his hands across her legs and lightly kneaded her flesh in his palms, massaging and exploring, coming closer to her.

Leah couldn't stop from writhing when he reached the part of her legs where her frilly open drawers covered her. Rather than seek, he stopped, instead slipping the ribbon at her waist out from its bow. The seductive pull made her ribs feel as if they would snap in her corset. She couldn't breathe, and while Wyatt eased the delicate lawn of her drawers across her legs, she unfastened her corset cover, then nimbly plucked free the numerous hooks of her corset front. Tossing both garments over the side of the bed, she now lay as naked as Wyatt.

He'd risen to her, catching her eyes on him as he climbed up the bed. This time, he said nothing about her looking at him. Her gaze roamed over the surface of his muscular chest, his waist and navel where a whorl of dark hair descended. His hips were narrow, his thighs sprinkled with dark hair. She had purposefully avoided the male part of him. No sooner had she allowed herself to view the rigid tautness than he shifted and stretched out beside her, turning her toward him.

Reaching out, he dusted her breast with the calluses of his fingers, circling the fullness, yet abstaining from the nipple that had puckered. For an eternity, he worshiped her breast, rolling her onto her back so he could have access to the other. He never touched the nipples, only the soft roundness.

Leah could endure no more of his exquisite torture. With a moan, she brought his head to her breast. The stroke of his tongue, the hotness of his mouth inflamed her further. She tried to reach out to him, to the length of him, and give him the same pleasure, but he'd pinned himself tightly against her. She felt him against her inner thigh. Burning and solid.

The overwhelming passion that engulfed her was like none other that she'd ever known. Owen had been her first and only lover. Their relationship had been filled with love, but she hadn't been passionate about him.

Wyatt's hands and mouth on her body made her feel things she never dreamed. When he took her nipple between his teeth, she could stand the sweet agony no longer.

"Make love to me," she whispered raggedly, her fingers sunk into Wyatt's hair.

He came to her then, breaking away from her breasts and lifting himself above her. His breathing was like that of a man who'd been running. Running all his life with no place to go. She wanted to scream that he'd come home. That he could stay here.

Dampness put a sheen on his forehead, his control so ironclad she saw the veins at the sides of his temples standing out.

"You can't know"—he said in a half-choke—"how good this feels."

"I know," she replied in a quiet tone, "because it feels the same way to me."

On a shaking breath, Wyatt's entrance was slow and given with a heavy sigh that came from the depths of his chest. He began to worship her with everything he had inside him, moving at a pace where seconds turned to hours. She felt every inch of him, coming inside and then pulling away. So slow. She didn't know how he could stand it. She couldn't. She wanted him so badly her eyes misted with love.

Lifting her knees, she gave him deeper entrance. Her hands found the small of his back and held him close, riding the rhythm he'd set. Then his tempo grew, not by leaps but with that same control he'd kept in check since they'd come into the bedroom.

Leah felt herself spiraling, higher, reaching for the plateau she knew would come. Only this time, it was a different pull. An intensity of which she hadn't been prepared for. She felt herself shattering, coming apart. Still, Wyatt held back. She wanted him to be with her, to feel the same as she did.

And then it was as if the iron wall of his will collapsed as well, and he let himself get lost within her. She matched his strokes, coming together with him. The force of the friction pulled her over the edge and she couldn't wait for him. She was pulled into the searing need that had been building. Her breath came in long, surrendering moans.

As the waves continued to soar through her, heat rippled from Wyatt's muscles beneath her fingers. His body tremored and he growled from erotic pleasure at the raw act of passion. The electricity of his release seemed to arc through her and she clung to him as his arms buckled and he fell on top of her.

His weight was a welcoming crush to her tingling breasts. A thin veil of perspiration covered them, their hearts beating against one another. Leah held him close, kissing his shoulder and tasting him.

For a long moment, neither spoke. Leah had never known such peace. Such complete fulfillment as she felt with Wyatt. She would be content to lie here forever in his arms, listening to the sounds of his breathing. To watch him sleeping beside her, and be able to study his face at her leisure. She wanted to feel his body next to hers throughout the night, waking to his kiss and being able to hold him. . . .

But the warmth of their lovemaking was ebbing away, and reality was settling back in. When Leah thought of Wyatt's wanting to leave, she could remain silent no longer. "Stay. Don't run away."

Wyatt's voice reverberated next to her ear where he lovingly nipped at her lobe then pressed his mouth to the column of her damp neck. "I have to think."

"Then think here. Sort things out before you decide."

He nodded against her breast, his hair tickling her.

Leah dared to hope that he would stay. That they could begin a life together. But she wouldn't push him. It had to be his choice.

Wyatt's thumb stroked her collarbone, light and tenderly. "Are you still mad about the negative?"

She wouldn't lie. "Yes."

"I could say I'm sorry I did it, but I can't."

"You should know that extra copies of the *Tribune*'s Sunday edition are sent to Denver with other small newspapers. City people like to read them."

Wyatt lifted himself to his elbow and stared into her eyes. "What are you saying?"

"I'm saying that it's too late, Wyatt. People outside of Eternity are going to see that newspaper picture of you."

Wyatt couldn't leave Eternity. Not without getting that sixty thousand dollars and giving it to Leah.

Monday morning, he dressed at dawn and went to the mountain to begin work on a new excavation site. As he labored in the coolness of the early hour, he thought about what the money would mean for her. A future for her children. College tuition. Further education for Leah herself. She could go to New York and buy her way into that fancy school Stieglitz ran. Anything she wanted, she could have. She'd be financially sound while he . . .

While he eased the burden of guilt from his conscience.

He couldn't make up for that day in Telluride, but he could see to it that Leah never had to worry about supporting her family on her own. Though Hartzell would never let her become destitute, he wasn't going to live forever. Leaving the money with Leah would be the insurance she needed to keep her independence.

Starting a ranch didn't seem as important to Wyatt as it once had. Sure, he still wanted to own a piece of land, but he couldn't take the money for himself now. Not after he'd found out who Leah was. There'd have to be other ways to get what he wanted.

Raising the sharp point of the pick high into the air and crashing down in a powerful arc onto the sandstone, Wyatt's thoughts drifted to yesterday afternoon.

He hadn't planned on staying with Leah. Making love to her was time treasured. It had been so long for him . . . so long, that he had feared he wouldn't be able to give her pleasure and would take only his own. He'd held back with all he had, but once he lost himself inside her, he'd felt such a gratification and completeness, the moment erased from his mind any woman he'd ever been with.

But he shouldn't have taken Leah to her bed. Sharing and loving posed complexities in an already complex situation. And admitting he loved her had been the worst thing he could have said. The words meant hope and promises. He couldn't give her either. Not without telling her the truth.

Not when Colvin, Thomas Jefferson, or Nate could find him.

Wyatt wondered how much time he had before the newspapers hit Denver. And how much time after that that someone could hunt him down and demand their share of the money, still thinking he'd double-crossed them.

The chances were remote that the boys were even in the area. It had been seventeen years. To return to Colorado would have meant being in hiding all these years until the statute of limitations ran out. Or to assume other identities by changing names and faces. But the Loco Boys had been good at that game. That's why Wyatt knew the window of opportunity existed in which one if not all of them would find him.

He couldn't afford to have Leah learn who he was. The only choice he had was to dig up the money, anonymously leave it with her, and ride out of town before anyone could confront him. He didn't need one of his former gang members causing trouble, dredging up Telluride and the past. It would only hurt Leah to know the truth. There was no point in reopening old wounds.

In the meantime, he had to put some distance between them. He couldn't touch her again. If he did, he'd be beyond logic and reason.

Leah had never truly known fulfillment through lovemaking until she'd made love with Wyatt. He'd given her a very special gift. Not only with the gratification of his body, but with the way he'd touched and loved her. Despite his saying he would still leave, she had no regrets. And perhaps, just perhaps, he'd change his mind.

Knowing Wyatt intimately had opened her eyes to total creativity. Leah knew what portrait she would enter in the New York Amateur Photography contest. Wyatt had given her the confidence to tear down her barriers and let the sensual woman in her be free. She could be the next Anne Brigman or E. Alice Austen, going beyond that famous woman's self-portraits of cigar smoking while standing in her underdrawers. Leah's vision of the perfect entry would have the great Stieglitz noticing her. All of New York would notice her. But by the same token, all of Eternity would see her, too, when the magazine came out. Geneva would never forgive her. And could she ever face Hartzell again, or Mr. Winterowd and Mr. Quigley?

Leah couldn't think about that. What she was doing was art. There was no shame in the mastery of the human form.

Walking up the incline of Infinity Hill toting her camera and tripod, she imagined how the shot would appear. The object would be bold and unabashedly pure. In communion with nature and at one with the land. Biting her lip, Leah's second thoughts surfaced once more. Oh, could she really go through with it?

Of course she could. She was a woman in love, and women in love had no boundaries.

Wyatt drank water from a canteen, his gaze on the box elder, sage, and juniper that littered the hillside toward Eternity. He always kept a cautious eye on the path that led to his digging spot, wondering if Scudder would come back looking for him.

He and Scudder had started something at the exposition, and Wyatt had been half expecting the marshal to come to his room and demand to know what he'd meant about his remark at the Aspenglow Stampede.

Lowering the canteen, Wyatt was just about to turn and go back to work when a swatch of color captured his attention. He quickly hid behind the scaly leaves of a juniper, peering at the path and waiting to see who was approaching.

A figure never came into view.

Wyatt was certain he'd seen something, so he slowly dropped the canteen and started forward. With his thumb, he flipped up the anchor strap of his holster and put his hand on the butt of his Remington-Rider. Walking without making a sound, he used a copse of scrub oak for cover as he came to a clearing due south of his cache.

Parting the yellowing leaves enough so he could look through the branches, Wyatt saw his intruder.

Leah set up her camera with a bag of equipment at her feet. In front of her lay a fallen tree, apparently from a lightning strike. Its stump was jagged and splintered. She aimed her camera in the direction of the great piñon pine that had toppled, the slant of the hill causing her to adjust the legs of her tripod continuously.

Wyatt didn't want her to know he was there, yet he couldn't walk away. He stayed hidden, watching her work. When at last she had ducked out from beneath the black camera cloth for the dozenth time, she smiled. Then she raised her fingers to the buttons on her long jacket and began to remove the coat. He had assumed she wanted to photograph the tree, and in her effort to align her camera just right, she'd grown hot. But the air had a fall crispness to it. The type of tart nip that a cold apple from the first harvest held when bitten.

Once she had shed the coat, she carefully folded the garment and set it on the ground. After that, she removed the pin from her hat, then the ones anchoring her hair.

Wyatt stood there, stunned with awe as he witnessed the falling mass of her hair. He watched like a voyeur, envious he hadn't been the one to bring her hair down yesterday, that the tresses had remained pinned and he hadn't had the foresight to see her with her crowning glory cascading to her hips.

The wind picked up the wavy skeins, caressing and kicking at them. He couldn't remember ever seeing hair as long as Leah's. Varying colors of brown caught the sun, emblazoning her with a burnished cloak made from her hair.

So taken aback by what he had seen, it took him a

moment to register that she sat on a large rock and was now unlacing her shoes. After the shoes were off, then came her stockings and drawers.

Wyatt was at the point of calling out to her to ask her what in the hell she thought she was doing. But he couldn't speak. He remained still and infatuated with the dance of disrobing she performed.

She undid the tiny buttons of her shirtwaist, shivering when she pulled her arms free. Then came the skirt. The navy fabric fell in a circle at her feet. At last, she stood only in her corset and chemise, the shortness of the latter barely covering her.

Wyatt felt himself stir and become hard and overcome with desire for her. Leah stopped, carefully looking over her shoulders, perhaps sensing someone watching. Her gaze fell right on him, but she didn't see him standing behind the scrub. Then she continued until she stood utterly nude.

Digging inside her bag, she produced a long strip of filmy, near-transparent cloth and wadded it in her hand. Then she went to her camera and made an adjustment, taking up the long tube with the bulb on the end. Visibly letting out a shaky breath, she squeezed the bulb then walked over the pebbled earth on tender feet until she reached the fallen tree.

The breeze brought out puckers in her nipples as she faced the camera. Her hair blew in strands of chestnut as she brought the fabric to her breasts and let the diaphanous curtain fall over her nudity. What was left to the image was more sensual, more stunning, than her standing bare.

At that moment, clouds seemed to come from nowhere to fill the sky, a backdrop to her self-portrait. She flung her head back, her hair waving like a glorious banner behind her. Her left arm stretched high, reaching heavenward. Her shape became treelike. Strong, earthy, full of electricity. She became a part of nature, responding to it, reaching toward the breaking clouds as the click of the camera shattered the stillness of the clearing.

It was then Wyatt couldn't keep himself hidden any

longer. He came storming from the scrub, startling a scream out of her when he barked, "What in the hell do you think you're doing?"

Covering herself with her hands, Leah stammered, "W–Wyatt . . . w–what are you doing here?"

Wyatt made no reply. He picked up her jacket and brought it to her. "Put this on."

Leah mutely slipped her hands inside the sleeves and wrapped the jacket tightly around her as the breeze dashed her hair in front of her eyes. Swiping the tresses back, she stared at him wide-eyed. "Did you follow me?"

"What if it hadn't been me to see you? What if Scudder or somebody else saw what you were doing? What if your kids stumbled across you like this? What would they think?"

"Rosalure and Tug began their fall term at the Eternity Normal School this morning."

"That doesn't exclude Scudder."

"No one comes up here."

"Then what am I doing here?" he shot back before he thought the better of it.

"Precisely."

Leah shivered and Wyatt was tempted to draw her into his arms to warm her. But he held back, shoving his hands into his pockets instead and slouching in a defiant manner.

"Just what *are* you doing here?" Leah went on. "You look like you've been digging in the rocks again. I never pressed before, giving you your privacy, but if what you're doing up here is part of the trouble you're having, I want to know."

With her unbound hair, and bare slender legs peeking out from the hem of her short jacket, Leah's appearance distracted him. He could easily forget that he wasn't the right man for her. That he couldn't have her because he had wronged her so very long ago. And that his misdoing had cheated her from a life with her mother. He couldn't let her close to him. Not ever again. If it meant pushing her away with a shock of the harsh truth, then she would have to hear it.

"Put your clothes back on." Wyatt ground his teeth,

plucking up undergarments from the ground and shoving them at her. He couldn't talk to her when she was naked. "Then I'll tell you."

Turning his back while she dressed, Wyatt folded his arms across his chest. He gazed skyward. The clouds were edged with gray linings, their roving shapes growing turbulent and stormy. The weather seemed appropriate for the jolt he was about to give Leah. A temperate gust blew through the clearing, and he fit his hat lower over his forehead.

"You can turn around."

Wyatt did so and found Leah sitting on the rock, putting her shoes on. She hadn't done anything with her hair. A full wave fell over her shoulder next to her cheek. She absently dashed it behind her back, but the length returned to tease her throat. Sitting straight after lacing her shoes, she caught the hair in her fist and attempted to put it in order with a quick braid. In fascination, he followed her nimble fingers as they tidied her hair but left wispy curls to frame her face. Once finished, she let the coil fall into her lap where she folded her hands, and gazed expectantly at him. "Well?"

Rubbing his jaw in contemplation, Wyatt mulled over the best way to say what he had to without her being able to justify anything he'd done. There shouldn't have been any justification, but Leah had a way of seeing the good in bad things. "Some years ago, I buried something up here by that cross, but I haven't been able to get to it until now." He carefully watched her face for her reaction when he admitted, "I couldn't, because I've been in the penitentiary."

If Leah flinched, Wyatt didn't see her move. She kept her composure as cool as a spring pond. "What did you do?"

"I was convicted of grand larceny, but I've committed other crimes that the prosecutors didn't have enough evidence to bring me to trial with."

Her eyes never left his. "Other crimes?"

"Petty theft, armed robbery, and rustling." He drudged up the earlier charges, not embellishing that he'd been acquitted of some. "Illicit racehorse gambling, mavericking, horse stealing. I was not liked by the Union Pacific for relieving them of their gold bullion. But mostly I held up banks for a living. One day I got caught and was sent to prison. I'm an ex-con, Leah."

She didn't say anything for a long while, her eyes studying him. He had wanted her to be offended, to look upon him as if he were beneath her, but if she was thinking such thoughts, she wasn't showing them.

At length, she asked, "Are you sorry?"

Her question threw him off-kilter. He'd been sorry about a great many things in his life. Getting caught was one of them. But had he been left to continue his destructive ways, he might not have lived past his twenty-fifth birthday. He wouldn't be the man he was today if he hadn't had the influence of the Idaho State Penitentiary to discipline him. But had he to do things over, he wouldn't have chosen the prison system to mold him into what he was. Most every day in the institution had been torment and misery. He could not look back with any fondness. Only bitterness and unhappiness. And long, lonely hours.

"No," he finally replied. "I'm not sorry for what I did. I am sorry I was caught, though."

"How long were you in there?"

He noticed she didn't speak the word *prison*. That perhaps meant she was seeing him differently. Not as any good for her. For her children.

"A long time."

"How long? A year? Two?"

Wyatt shook his head with a crooked smile that had no warmth in it. "Seventeen, Leah. Seventeen years of my life. I went in when I was twenty-one."

Her fingers rose to her pale lips and she spoke behind them. "But how old are you now?"

"Thirty-eight."

"That means . . ."

"That means that up until three months ago, I was living as Convict 628 in Cell House Number Two."

Leah tried to digest what Wyatt was telling her. She had had no clue, no notion, that he'd been where he'd said. He

was kind and good-hearted. Warm and friendly. He wasn'
the type of man she took mug shots of for Marshal Scudder

Wyatt had never brandished a gun down Main Street o
was drunk and disorderly. In fact, she'd never seen him take
a drink at all. He didn't even smoke—a habit of so many
cowboys—and as far as she knew, he didn't gamble. He wa
generous with his time and helpful when she needed him.

Leo had told her Wyatt never missed a day of work
wasn't late or slovenly on the job. She had seen for hersel
that he had had the opportunity to steal money from Leo's
cash box. The receipts and currency were kept in the
kitchen on a shelf, but Leo had never mentioned anything
was missing. If Wyatt was a bad man with criminal
thoughts, wouldn't he have been tempted, and even acted?

Not if he'd changed. And he had. The Wyatt she knew
was no outlaw. The man she'd brought to her bed had been
loving and tender . . . mindful of her feelings and needs.

"You should have told me sooner." Leah smoothed her
hair from her eyes. "I wouldn't have thought badly of you."

"You sure as hell would have."

"But having the chance to know you, I—"

"You don't really know me," he shot back, angry lines at
the corners of his mouth. "And you wouldn't have taken the
time if I'd told you I was an ex-con right from the start.
Admit it."

Swallowing, Leah looked down at her hands, then back at
Wyatt. "You may be right."

"Of course I'm right."

"But none of that matters now. I think I do know who
you are, Wyatt. And despite what you said, I believe you are
sorry. I can see in your eyes that you feel bad."

"What I feel badly about," he said in a jagged voice, "has
nothing to do with robbing banks and living the life I did. It
has everything to do with . . ."

She thought he'd ended with "you," but the wind plucked
the word from his lips and she wasn't sure. "What do you
mean? Is there more?"

Leah didn't want to hold Wyatt's past over him. People
made mistakes. He'd paid for his. What did he want her to

do? Hate him? Push him away? Did he think so little of her that she would judge him in such a prejudiced way?

"Let it go, Leah."

She stood, going to him. "No, I won't. What else is there? Did something happen in prison?" She recalled the scars on his chest and wondered how they'd come about. If he'd been beaten and tortured. If he'd had to defend himself in the penitentiary. She'd read about the brutality inflicted by guards. One day, had he had enough and struck back?

Without backing down, she confronted him. "Did you ever kill someone? Is that why they kept you in there so long?"

Wyatt looked ready to break. His eyes were hooded and dark, his nostrils flared. The vein at his throat steadily pulsed while he tensed the muscles of his neck.

"Would it make a difference to you if I said yes?"

"You can't convince me you're a cold-blooded killer, so quit trying to scare me."

"You should be scared."

"Well, I'm not." She lifted her hand to his cheek, but he backed away from her.

"Go home and forget you know me."

She couldn't accept the dull ache beneath her breast. "I can't. I love you."

"Then stop loving me." Wyatt started walking. His stride was long and swift. Leah had to run to catch up to him, unable to leave things between them as they were.

"Wyatt! Wait!"

He spun around, putting his hands on her shoulders to keep her at arm's length. "I'm telling you right now: Go home. I haven't changed, Leah. I never will, so don't come after me. I'm sorry about yesterday. It shouldn't have happened."

When he pushed her away, she fought the tears that blinded her. As he continued toward the bluff where the cross's dark shadow fell, she called out to him with a sob, "What did you bury up here that's so important?"

Barely turning toward her, he replied without inflection, "A part of what I used to be."

⚜ 21 ⚜

Though stone were changed to gold,
the heart of a man would not be satisfied.
—Chinese proverb

Wyatt was still washing dishes at the Happy City Restaurant that Saturday. There had been no sign of the money after five days of backbreaking digging. He was beginning to wonder if he was going a little crazy to be spending so much time chasing after something that had eluded him for so long.

And without Leah, he felt more alone than he had in prison.

Her face was etched in his mind, whether smiling, serious, or thoughtful. He missed hearing her laughter, watching her gestures. The way her hair was always mussed from the camera cloth. He longed to hear her voice, sweet and clear. To listen to her talking about progress and inventions. He longed to be with her, touch her, hold her. Kiss her. He suffered the dull ache of desire at the thought of her.

But none of that was to be.

She hadn't come into the Happy City since that day on the mountain. Tug had stopped by every day after school, wanting to know why Wyatt didn't come to his house anymore. Wanting Wyatt to lasso with him and take July out for a ride. He'd given the boy an excuse, saying he didn't have the free time at the moment to get away from other obligations. Tug hadn't taken the answer too well, pressing Wyatt at least to go frog hunting with him. Wyatt hadn't had the heart to tell him no. He'd said he'd think about it and see if he could get some time off from the restaurant. But he couldn't promise.

That had been two days ago and Tug hadn't returned to the restaurant's back door wearing his chaps and the real spurs that Geneva had bought him after the close call with Cricket. Every time Wyatt heard a noise at the doorway, he half expected to see Tug standing there with adoration in his eyes. But when the space was empty, Wyatt's disappointment left a hard pain in his chest.

He'd come to love that boy, just like he did his mother.

The slow week had drawn out like the edge of a blade, slicing into Wyatt and making him restless. Hartzell had moved out of the Starlight and back home with Geneva. Before he left the hotel, he'd knocked on Wyatt's door to extend to him a teller's position at the bank.

Wyatt had almost laughed at the irony of his working in a bank, but he didn't. Hartzell had been dead serious. He'd told Wyatt that after what he'd done to save Tug, he was as good as a member of the family and deserving every opportunity. Wyatt had thanked him for the offer but turned him down. Hartzell adamantly declared that if Wyatt ever changed his mind, the job would be his.

Friday, Rosalure had popped her head into the kitchen from the bamboo reed curtain. Fancied up in school clothes, with her hair plaited in two braids close to her head, she'd stepped up to the sink while holding her books.

"Hello, Wyatt."

"How's school, Rosalure?"

"All right."

He knew what she'd say before she said it, wishing that she hadn't had to.

"Tug misses you, Wyatt. He doesn't understand why you don't like him anymore. Are you mad at him about Cricket?"

Letting out a slow breath, Wyatt leaned into the counter his hands submerged in the water. "No. I'm not mad a him."

"Is it me? I know I wasn't always nice as I could be—"

"You haven't done anything either."

"What's wrong then? Momma cries at night. I can hea her in her bed. She hasn't done that since my father die Did you two have an argument?"

Wyatt couldn't answer.

"I know that all grown-ups have arguments. Look a Nanna and Poppa. But they worked things out. You and m momma could, too." Rosalure looked at her scuffed shoes then hesitantly back at Wyatt with shyness in her eyes. " like you, Wyatt. I know you probably thought I didn't to much. It's just that I didn't want another father for a lon time. But now, it'd be okay with me if you wanted to marr my momma."

Wyatt put his hands on the sink's edge, nodding, afraid t trust his voice.

"I've got to get home now. I just wanted you to know ho I felt is all."

After she'd gone, Wyatt realized his fondness for Rosalur ran deeper than he'd acknowledged. With her maturity an candor, he loved her and wished he could have been th kind of father she needed.

Leo came into the kitchen with an armful of dirty dishe and a broad grin on his face. "Six more orders for th proverb cookies. I hope we have enough to last the rest o the day." Then he spoke to Yan.

Tu rattled off a response in Mandarin, and Leo's smile increased.

Wyatt took the dishes from Leo and dunked them into the soapy water. "You're having some good luck with those cookies, huh, Leo?"

"Better now that I've translated the proverbs into English. It was a stroke of luck they fell in the batter and Yan baked them into the cookies." Leo lit up a cigarette and waved out the match. "Customers are fascinated with ancient sayings. It's sort of like reading about omens. You know, like fortunes and destiny."

"I think I do." Among everything else on his mind, Wyatt had his destiny with Bean Scudder to worry about. Ever since the exposition, the marshal had been dogging him. Wyatt had seen his shadow in the back alley late one night after closing, but he was gone before Wyatt could walk up to him. A night later, Wyatt had caught Scudder standing across the street from the Starlight staring at his window.

Wyatt wanted to know why Scudder was still hot after him when he'd made it clear he wasn't going to be chased. Seeing as how Wyatt wasn't leaving town as soon as he'd wanted, it was time to pay Scudder a visit and set him straight once and for all that a telephone call to Billings, Montana, didn't mean jack.

"Leo, would you mind if I took ten minutes?" Wyatt asked.

"Sure, Wyatt."

"Thanks."

Wyatt removed his apron and slung it over the towel rack by the oven. Stepping out the back door, he headed down the alley and took a shortcut to Scudder's office.

Once there, he didn't bother to knock. Any U.S. marshal's office was public domain and he saw no reason to ask permission to enter.

Throwing the door open, Wyatt stepped inside with all the bravado of a dime novel hero. Swearing, Scudder bolted from his chair, knocked over a tin of kerosene oil onto his desk, and inadvertently threw the stream of his electric fan off-kilter so the blades blew into the wall and ruffled a bulletin board of wanteds. Soon, papers were flying off the tacks.

"Hey, Scudder, what are you up to?" Wyatt sauntered toward the desk where the vapors of kerosene were the strongest.

"Hang it all, Holloway! You just gypped me out of ten years of my life." His hand rose suspiciously to his mustache where the part by his left nostril drooped a little.

Patting the hair back in place, he rebuked, "What do yo
mean, barging in on me like this?"

"What do you mean by following me?"

Scudder snorted. He went for a towel on the top of his i
chest and used it to blot the oil that had already begun
sink into some papers. "I ain't following you."

"Damn sure are."

The russet hair on Scudder's lip rippled when h
breathed. And he was breathing heavily. The towel wasn
helping to clean up the mess, which was now dribbling t
the floor and spattering on some of the wanted sheet
Scudder's eyes darted around the room in frustration, the
they latched onto Wyatt's and narrowed speculatively as
he were trying to decide whether to say what was botherin
him more than the overturned kerosene. "How'd you kno
about the mustache?"

"I saw you through the window the night you burne
yours up when you were drunk. You couldn't have grown
new one so soon."

Scudder dropped his behind into the chair and groane
"You aren't going to tell anyone . . . are you, Holloway?"

Walking through the room and assessing the jail, Wyat
let Scudder stew a minute. He paused at one of the cells, pu
his hand on the iron, and tested its strength. The bars coul
hold a man. Hold him a long time. Wyatt shuddered an
turned to face Scudder. "It's not my way to put my nos
where it doesn't belong. What you do is your business
Scudder. Just like what I do is mine. I haven't broken an
laws, so I don't want you trailing after me, waiting an
anticipating that I will. That telephone isn't going to do yo
any good either."

"You aren't from Billings, are you?"

"Been through the town, but never lived there."

Scudder fidgeted with his mustache. "Who are you
Holloway?"

"Don't bother a man unless you're convinced he's guilty
of something."

"You are guilty of something, only I just haven't figured
out what."

"I'm not guilty of anything, you got that?"

"Least not in my town you aren't."

"Damn right. And that's all that you need to know."

"I reckon." Scudder kept remolding his mustache.

"It's not looking so good," Wyatt observed, letting Scudder's comment slip by. There was no point in stressing his innocence with a man who couldn't drive a nail into a snowbank. "You trying to take that mustache off? Is that what you were doing with the kerosene oil?"

"It won't come off." Scudder gave the end a yank and succeeded only in pulling out his lip into a mock sneer. Releasing the waxed end, he grumbled, "Damn and double damn that Tiberius Tee."

"What did he give you to affix that with?"

"Diamond Magic invisible cement."

Wyatt shook his head with just barely a flicker of sympathy for the marshal. "Let me make two suggestions. First, you get yourself some harness oil and mix it with a little turpentine. That ought to get that mustache off. Second, lay off the beer. It's going to kill you eventually."

Scudder yanked the wire cage of his fan from the direction of the wall and aimed the cool spinning air at his perspiring face. "How would you know, Holloway? You've never set foot in one of the saloons."

Wyatt found it odd he'd come to chew out Scudder and now he was swapping life experiences with him. "It's been a long time, but I'm no stranger to a bar. Liquor owns you when you let it. I'm not buying an early grave anymore."

A knock on the open door had Wyatt moving away from the cell.

"Here's the negative of Bodie Ledgerwood you wanted to send over to Ridgeway, Marshal."

Leah's voice gripped Wyatt, her name echoing in the black stillness of his mind. She remained at the door, a change coming over her face when she finally saw him as he walked forward. Her brown eyes grew large and liquid, but her inscrutable expression gave him no clue as to her thoughts.

* * *

Leah had been unprepared to encounter Wyatt at the marshal's office. The building was the last place she thought she'd find him.

She'd been staying clear of him ever since that day on the mountain. She had her pride. But always, his name and the memory of his face lingered at the edges of her mind. With a shiver of vivid recollection, she relived the biting words he'd spoken to her. The way he'd pushed her from him, telling her to go home.

She'd cried that night until her eyes burned from sleeplessness. Her whole body had been engulfed in tides of confusion. She'd felt drained, hollow, and lifeless by Wyatt's rejection.

She hadn't been able to concentrate on her work despite a busy schedule taking photographs of the 1904 classes enrolled at the Eternity Normal School. Her thoughts would inevitably filter back to the question of what had happened between her and Wyatt. Why he couldn't love her enough to know that his prison record didn't matter to her.

When she was near him, her heart swelled with a feeling she had thought unattainable. For the first time in her life, a true, passionate love had found its way to her, but no sooner had she recognized and admitted it, she'd lost Wyatt. The blow was devastating, trapping her within the memory of her emotions. Without him even as her friend, she'd felt an extraordinary void.

Marshal Scudder pushed himself from his chair and reached for the large envelope in her hand. "I appreciate your expediency, Mrs. Kirkland."

Though she fought against showing Wyatt what remained in her heart, her exhausted eyes smiled at him. Then quickly looked away. "I'll be leaving you to your business then."

"I'm not his business," Wyatt replied dryly, then he came toward Leah. "And I was just on my way out."

Leah didn't have anything further to discuss with the marshal, so she went out the door as well. Going down the walkway with Wyatt at her side and saying nothing, the misery of the week came at her full force. She wanted to tell him how much she missed him, but she held her tongue.

Once on the boardwalk, Wyatt paused, and she couldn't help stopping also. Gazing at him, she waited for him to speak. He shrugged into a stance that was familiar to her: hands stuffed in his denim pockets, hat drawn low. He stood close enough for her to reach out and touch him. Put her hand on his chest . . . lean into his arms . . .

"How've you been, Leah?"

"All right." She stood rigidly, afraid to even breathe.

"Things going okay for you?"

"I suppose."

Numb silence. Then he lifted his head. "I better get back to the restaurant."

The need to keep him near had her blurting, "I entered the photography contest with my photograph. I entitled it 'Soul of the Fallen Pine.'"

"I hope you win. Then you can go to New York."

"Yes . . . New York." But the lure of the big city had dimmed.

Their eyes met for an instant, then Wyatt pulled his away.

"Have you found what you were looking for?" she asked.

He seemed puzzled. "What?"

"On the mountain. What you'd left."

His brows lowered. "Not yet."

"It must be very important."

"Yeah." But he didn't seem very enthusiastic. Kicking at a pebble, he dug his hands deeper into the slashes of his pants. "Leo's expecting me back."

"Sure . . . you better go."

He caught and held her gaze, and she almost thought he caressed her with his eyes. "Take care of yourself, Leah." His hesitation was marked in his steps as he walked away. She wanted to call after him, but she didn't. Not this time.

Wyatt sat cross-legged at the bottom of the hole he'd been working on for over a week. Debris fell from the sides, crumbling down every so often to coat his shirt and pants with dirt. He only had an hour left before he had to ride out on July and get cleaned up for the restaurant. Using a hand shovel, he mindlessly pulled rock and sand from the deepest part of the cavity.

He couldn't take the strain anymore. He had to accept that the money was destined to be buried on this mountain until somebody got lucky enough to dig in the right spot for the wrong reason and unearth one hell of a surprise.

All but resigned to leaving Eternity without leaving Leah the money, Wyatt cursed himself for not being able to take care of her and the children. He knew Leah would never spend a dime of stolen money, so he'd figured he'd start by mailing her a thousand dollars with a note that said her money from Italy had been refunded. After that, he figured he could set himself up as an anonymous patron and buy her photographs for large sums of money.

But without the satchels, he could do nothing.

Wyatt had been mentally preparing himself to ride out of town. To put Eternity behind him. He wouldn't only be leaving Leah, he'd be leaving some people he considered friends. Hartzell, for one. Leo. He didn't like leaving Leo in the lurch, and hoped he could get a fast replacement for him at the restaurant.

Taking up a fistful of dirt, Wyatt threw it over his knee. He sat for a long moment, then he stood and brushed the dust from his clothing. He swore at his stupidity for wasting all those days in his prison cell thinking about the damn money. Thinking about how he was going to dig it up when he got out. How he was going to spend it. What he was going to do. It was all for nothing. He'd never find it. He'd been kidding himself thinking he could.

With a swift kick, Wyatt caved in a section of the loose sandstone wall and gave vent to a foul curse in the process. He reached to pick up his tools, hurling the pick over his shoulder and bending further for the shovel. In doing so, a streak of rust in the pinkish stone caught his eye. Crouching down, he rubbed at the spot until the reddish brown image grew. Until he could tell that the texture was not that of rock, but of metal . . .

His heartbeat pushed at his ribs.

Using his fingertips, he clawed at the earth, revealing more of a rusted surface that appeared to be in the shape of a cylinder. He dared to envision the extra gallon Yellow Crawford apricot cans he'd stuffed the leather satchels into on a cloudless night so long ago. He rubbed some more, and more. . . .

Then . . . seventeen years and ten days later, he didn't have to imagine anymore. He was touching them.

❧22❧

The wise adapt themselves to circumstances
as water molds itself to the pitcher.

—Chinese proverb

November 11, 1892
Idaho State Penitentiary

Harlen had had the dream again. That he'd been digging for
the money. Unearthing it had been so easy. He'd gone
straight to the spot by the cross, lifted a couple of scoops of
dirt with a shovel, and there they were. Those Yellow
Crawford apricot cans and the satchels. Just where he'd left
them.

It was so simple.

His life was going to be just as simple when he got out.
He'd have no worries. He'd be set. And after his application
for a pardon went through today, he'd be out free and clear
to get himself a decent soak in a tub, then buy a drink and a
woman.

Everything would be as it always had.

November 8, 1897
Idaho State Penitentiary

In 1893, the old wooden wall surrounding the prison had
come tumbling down, replaced by a new sandstone struc-

ture that convict labor had built. The town had come out in force to watch the unveiling. Harlen had wished he hadn't had to be there to see it.

After his petition had been denied, he'd spent the next five years as a stone cutter in the quarry. His body developed into that of a man's. As solid as the rock he picked at, day in and day out.

Richard Robison had an appointment in the morning with the new governor of Idaho, named Steunenberg, and the incoming warden, Charles VanDorn. Harlen had seen five prior wardens come and go. He figured not even the prison system could hold a man inside if it wasn't his sentence. The walls were full of miscreants and offenders, most of whom would never reform. Each day the dining hall message board had new notices to the prisoners tacked to it.

Suicide wasn't uncommon, though Harlen had never considered that way out. Even when his pardon had been denied in 1892, he'd taken his anger out on his cell and destroyed prison property. Putting a twisted bedsheet around his neck would have been the easy way out. Harlen wanted his freedom too badly to cheat himself out of walking through the penitentiary doors when his time was up.

Life took on a routine for Harlen. Getting up at the same hour, going to bed at the same hour, eating the same food three times a day for 365 days of the year. He stayed to himself after Manny died. To those who would try and befriend him, he made it clear that he wanted to be left alone. Fighting became a way of survival.

Dreaming about getting the money became his only thread of sanity and hope of a better existence.

That and his pardon hearing on the eighth of November. He'd composed the letter himself, struggling to get everything spelled right and having Richard correct it for him. Over the years, he'd learned to write better, having nothing else to do at night but look through the handful of books the prison offered its inmates and study how sentences were put together.

Sitting on the edge of his cot as the rain battered the rooftop, Harlen lit a match he'd hoarded and scratched a flame to life. He held the letter to the waning light to read his words once more.

Application for Pardon

Boise, Idaho
November 1, 1897

To the Hon. Board of Prison Commissioners

Gentlemen:

I, Harlen Shepard Riley, who am serving a twenty-year sentence in the Idaho State Penitentiary for Grand Larceny, arrested under Sec. 6452 of the Revised Statutes of Idaho, plead guilty to the crime of "armed robbery." I do hereby apply to your Hon. Board, for a full and free Pardon. I have worked truly and faithfully for the State, especially in the Quarry, and have observed the prison rules to the best of my ability. If granted a pardon, I promise to be a good and law-abiding citizen, and apply myself to the laws of society; in your petitioner, will ever pray.

Signed,

Harlen Shepard Riley
Convict No. 628

November 11, 1901
Idaho State Penitentiary

The new century had come upon the penitentiary without fanfare. There had been speculation among the prisoners that they would finally see plumbing and electricity. Both came. The plumbing was not without numerous notices to the prisoners about its use and what not to put down the pipes. And the electricity was nothing that any of them could operate. Lights had been installed down the middle of the cell house but none in the cells, so prisoners were kept in the dark when a main switch was thrown and those big glass bulbs shut down until the following night, when they remained on only for one hour.

In September of 1900, Harlen received a letter from Richard Robison. Harlen was able to read enough by trial and error to make out that Richard had been called out of the West to return back East to Boston to see to an estate of his wife's. In his place, he was putting a Boise attorney by the name of Stanton Mercer on Harlen's case to plea for his release the following year.

Harlen's faith had been tested for nearly a decade and a half. Though he wouldn't admit to it, he'd fallen back on some of the Bible verses his dad had read to him when he'd been a boy. Harlen didn't own a Good Book, nor did he read the several the prison made available.

On a gray November 11, 1901, fourteen years after Harlen's incarceration, he was denied one again. He fell into a grave depression that might have killed him had it not been for the intense work in the quarry and a guard by the name of Jack Holloway. Holloway had been from Utah and taken a liking to Harlen. He gave him magazines and newspapers to catch him up on the outside. It had been years since Harlen had had a cigarette, and Holloway supplied him with a few hand-rolleds every now and then.

The Petitioner's Act of 1901 came into effect that year, making it possible for Harlen to reapply for citizenship in three years instead of five.

Those next three years were nearly void of emotion for Harlen. If denied once again, that would mean he'd have to spend his full twenty years in the pen. A thought that was too dispiriting for him to accept.

April 29, 1904
Idaho State Penitentiary

C. S. Perrine, the warden who had come to the Idaho pen in February the year before, was willing to look at Harlen's application seven months early. Stanton Mercer took it over to the office, where the hearing was short, and within the hour Harlen was called to the commissary.

Harlen stood stock-still, having gone through disappointment so often. He knew the routine, the stance to take to bear the news.

Stanton lowered his lawyer's case onto the tabletop and pulled out a document that he handed to Harlen.

Harlen's hand shook as he scanned the paper.

Restoration to Citizenship
No. *11028*
THE STATE OF IDAHO
vs.
Harlen Shepard Riley

Convicted in the District Court of *Bear Lake* County, *November* Term, A.D. 18*87*.
Offense: *Grand larceny*
Term of Sentence: *20* Years.

Executive Office,
Boise, Idaho *April 29* 19*04*

For the reason that the above-named convict has served out in satisfactory conduct his sentence in the Penitentiary, for good behavior, he is granted a full pardon and restored to full citizenship and the right of suffrage.

By the order of the Governor,

J. Morrison

Harlen lifted his gaze to Stanton, unable to speak.

"There'll be some more paperwork to file. It's not like you can walk out today."

Nodding, Harlen was feeling emotions that were undescribable. There was also a numbness. A foggy sense of disbelief that he would be able to walk across the "deadline" and through the Trinity arch that he'd helped to build, without one of the guards taking a shot at him.

Harlen couldn't sleep that night. He laid in his cot imagining all that fresh air he was going to be able to smell. Would the sky be bluer on the outside? The trees greener?

A clerical error in the paperwork caused a three-month delay in Harlen's release. On June 24, all that was required was another signature by Governor Morrison and final documentation by the warden's secretary.

And then, at 8:00 A.M., on the first day of July, 1904, Harlen Shepard Riley walked out of the Idaho State Penitentiary with the clothes on his back and seven dollars and twenty-eight cents. As soon as his resoled boot hit the free ground, he left Harlen's battered shadow behind and became Wyatt Holloway, a man with a quest.

❊ 23 ❊

Money unjustly gotten is but snow on which hot water is poured.

> —Chinese proverb

Leah's week was ending as miserably as it had begun. Her encounter with Wyatt over the weekend had kept slipping through her thoughts. Despite working on the photographs for the school, she felt listless during the day. At night, sleep came only in drifts of fleeting moments. She couldn't eat much, and caught herself staring out her office's second-story window to the mountainside where Wyatt rode each morning before going to the restaurant.

This morning, as she'd been pinning negatives to print on the cording across the window, she held back when she saw Wyatt returning to town earlier than normal. He sat astride his black horse, July, who'd been loaded down with several bundles wrapped in canvas. On all other occasions, he'd ridden down Main Street without a pack tethered to the back of his saddle.

It would seem that Wyatt had finally found what he'd been looking for.

Turning away from the curtains, Leah went on to finish her work, trying diligently to put Wyatt from her mind, with marginal success. By the time the children came home from school, she'd completed only one print. In her attempt to immerse herself in her surroundings, she'd gotten sidetracked when she'd looked for special velox with a matt surface, and had ended up cleaning out her paper cabinet. That had led to the table, and from there the filing cabinets where she stored the original orders she'd taken for the past several years.

"Momma!" Rosalure burst into the room, out of breath. She must have run the entire way from the school to home. "You'll never guess."

Sitting on the floor surrounded by old files, Leah looked up. "What?"

"Donny chased me around the schoolyard and he told Pinkie that he thought I was pretty."

"You are pretty."

Tug came sauntering in the studio, unceremoniously dropping a picture book onto the settee. "Hello, Momma."

"Did you have a good day at school?"

"It was all right." Tug slumped onto the floor by Leah. "What are you doing?"

"Cleaning."

Rosalure kneeled down next to the stacks of files, absently undoing the braiding at the back of one envelope and opening the flap. "You never clean anything." Sliding a portrait out, she gazed at it.

"Well, it was time to, I suppose."

Tug crossed his legs and investigated, too. He selected a yellowed envelope that was brittle at the edges. "What's in here, Momma?"

"Oh, that's some of Poppa Darling's work. Careful of the envelope, Tug. Don't open that."

Putting it aside, Tug reached for another that was in just as poor condition. This time, he didn't ask Leah, he went right ahead and opened the envelope. A photograph fell out, along with newspaper clippings that had turned a buttery color from age.

Tug discarded the articles and studied the photograph, his pale brows furrowed. "These guys are dressed funny."

"Men used to wear clothes like that."

"Did Poppa Darling?"

"Yes."

Rosalure lifted a portfolio from the collection, separating the sides and gazing at the picture inside. "Our Nanna Evaline sure was pretty, Momma."

"Yes, she was. She wanted to be an actress."

"How come she didn't?" Tug asked.

"Because she married Poppa Darling and she had me to take care of."

Tug's gaze lowered to the photograph he held. By a glance, Leah knew which one he was looking at. Her father had taken that portrait on the day her mother had been killed. She hadn't brought the envelope out in a long time, preferring to keep the past buried. But the plate had been an important one back then, the photograph used to try and apprehend the members of the Loco Boys. Only none of them ever were caught. None of them had ever paid for having had a part in her mother's death.

Cold tingles rose goose bumps on Leah's arms, and she shivered. "Tug, put that away. Momma doesn't want it out."

"Let me see it, Tug." Rosalure leaned closer to gaze at the portrait. Pointing to one of the two men standing behind the chairs of three sitting subjects, she giggled, "That one is dressed funny." Then her laughter suddenly quieted as she grabbed the photograph's edge. "Give me it for a minute, Tug." Bringing the photograph closer, her eyes narrowed as she lifted her chin. "Momma, how come Poppa Darling took a picture of Wyatt?"

Stacking the files that were ready to be put away, Leah said, "Poppa Darling didn't take a picture of Wyatt."

"Yes he did. It's Wyatt. Right there." She held the photograph out to Leah. "See, Momma. The man with the slightly glaring watch fob."

Leah took the portrait and gazed at the man Rosalure had directed her to. Harlen Shepard Riley.

Examining Harlen's facial features very critically, Leah noted there were startling similarities. The shape of the eyes and mouth. But Harlen's nose was wrong. Wyatt's was slightly crooked. And the build of the men were different. Wyatt was big. Harlen was slender.

Still, her breath solidified in her throat. Funny how she'd remembered Harlen through a child's eyes. Dark and swarthy beneath his hat, yet in some ways kind, because he'd given her the candy. She'd been confused and distraught after he'd ridden out of Telluride. But in her memories, Harlen was a cold and ugly man. Looking at his portrait, she could see a set to his mouth that was so like Wyatt's, it made icy fear twist around her heart.

Wyatt couldn't be Harlen Riley. Wyatt wasn't a killer. And yet, Wyatt had confessed to being in prison. For seventeen years. Leah did some quick calculations and realized that Wyatt had been incarcerated shortly after her mother's death.

No, it couldn't be true.

If Harlen had been arrested, surely she and her father would have been notified that one of the gang members had been apprehended. There was no reason to keep his capture a secret.

"It is Wyatt," Rosalure said adamantly. "I know it is."

Leah momentarily met Rosalure's gaze, then lowered hers once more to the young man in the portrait. His eyes pulled her. Even without knowing the color, they came across dark and fathomless. Just like Wyatt's. The jaw, the position of his ears, the shape of his mouth . . . these were Wyatt's traits.

Wyatt had acted strangely that Sunday when he'd wanted to see her studio. When he'd looked at her mother's portrait. He hadn't been himself since. He'd pushed her away, as if he knew of a strong reason to stay out of her life.

Being involved with her mother's murder would have been a strong reason.

Leah put the photograph back into the folder and stood. "Rosalure, please watch your brother for me. I'll be back soon." Her voice was absolutely emotionless, and it chilled her.

"Where you going, Momma?" Tug asked.

"I'll be back soon."

Rosalure went after her into the hallway, but stopped short of the landing. "Are you going to see Wyatt and show him the picture?"

Leah made no reply of confirmation. "Don't let Tug open too many of the envelopes. Some are old and will fall apart."

Gripping the doorknob, Leah let herself out without bothering with a hat or gloves. Her stride was automatic and wooden as she walked to the Starlight Hotel. Once in the lobby, she went past Almorene East's curious gaze, only to be stopped by her voice.

"Is there something I can do for you, Mrs. Kirkland?"

"Is Mr. Holloway in his room?"

"Yes, but—"

"I'm going up to see him."

"But—"

"Which room is his?"

"The third to the last on the right, but—

"I won't be long."

Almorene sputtered a moment, then fell quiet. "Leave the door open."

Leah took the stairs, measuring out the doors and knocking on Wyatt's. She heard his footfall as he came to the door and swung it open.

He didn't show surprise at finding her there. His face was drawn, the lines at his mouth set. "Leah."

She didn't wait to be invited in. She merely walked past him and strode to the middle of the plain room. Taking a deep breath, she forced her beating heart to slow. If her fears were premature, there was no sense in getting worked up. Not until she knew for sure.

"I need to ask you something," she began, "and I would hope that you would be honest with me." Withdrawing the photograph from the envelope, she held it out for Wyatt to see. "Is that you in this portrait?"

Wyatt didn't take the photograph after briefly scanning the five men with hardly a glance. Then his eyes rose to hers and he turned away, a gesture that all but admitted it was him. An innocent man would have studied the portrait. An innocent man would have been curious about who the men were. But Wyatt didn't have to look long at something he was familiar with. For he'd already seen it. He'd lived it.

Leah fell into a chair at the table and laid the photograph in front of her. She could barely contain her anger, her hurt. Gazing at Wyatt through eyes that had filled with tears, she had to ask, "Are you Harlen Shepard Riley?"

Wyatt faced her. "I used to be."

Putting her hand to her mouth, Leah lowered her head. Her eyes closed against the tears burning the backs of her lids. He'd come to her as a deceiver, and she'd welcomed him with open arms. "You lied to me."

"A sin of omission."

Her gaze rose and glared accusingly at him. "I spoke your name in my house. I told you things about Telluride. I showed you my parents' portrait. You knew who I was."

"Yes."

"You knew before you made love to me."

"Yes."

She wanted to strike out and hit him. Make him suffer for what he'd put her family through. Make him know how she'd missed her mother, and how she'd had to nurse her father's sorrow while setting her own grief aside and growing up overnight. Did he have any idea what he'd done to her? How he continued to hurt? She'd fallen in love with him—one of the very men responsible for her mother's death.

"Why did you come to Eternity?" she lashed out. "What do you want from me?"

Wyatt moved toward her but stayed clear of the table. "I didn't know who you were until I saw Evaline's portrait. I don't want to hurt you, Leah."

She didn't want to hear the pain in his voice. Her own was so acute, she felt as if she were breaking. "It's too late for that."

"I never meant to come back into your life."

"But you have," she whispered, unable to trust the steadiness of her voice.

Wyatt pressed the edge of his brow, massaging, then wen to the bed and slumped onto the mattress. His bod slackened, none of its strength coming to light. She knew h was strong and virile, but the man before her looked tire and defeated. In as much pain as she. It couldn't be.

A dead quiet stretched over the room.

At length, Leah asked, "Did you lie about why you wer sent to the penitentiary? Was the charge really murde instead of grand larceny?"

"No." He rested his elbows on his knees. At his fee barely peeking out from beneath the edge of the bedcover were dirty leather satchels that appeared to be quite ol and battered. She hadn't noticed them until now. "The brought me to trial for a crime they knew they could get conviction on. I couldn't be charged with murder in Tellu ride without tangible evidence. No one will ever be indicte in your mother's death."

She didn't want to listen, for she'd been told the ver same thing by the Telluride sheriff and the Merchants an General detectives who'd been involved. Even now, it wa difficult to accept that her mother's murder would g unvindicated.

Wyatt went on. "I wish someone could be charged; then wouldn't have to wonder anymore if it had been me. But to many people were shooting that day to single out a guilt man."

Leah hadn't read the newspaper accounts in over sixtee years, having tucked the clippings and sparse follow-u articles away. She couldn't remember the exact stories th law officials told, other than the fact that none of th suspects were apprehended. Her mourning had been s filled with anguish, she'd walked in a fog for months on end trying to keep her father from forgetting he was among th living. He still had a daughter and a business. It was the that Owen had come to Telluride to help them put th studio back in order financially. And after that, Leah ha tried to go on without looking back.

"If I had known you'd be in Eternity," Wyatt said whil

raking his hand through his hair, "I wouldn't have let myself get near you."

She sought and held onto his blue eyes, watching for his reaction. "Then whatever part of yourself you left behind is so important, you'd risk my finding out who you were, no matter how remote the chances would have been."

"Yes."

"What is it that's buried, or was until this morning, on that mountain?"

His answer was simple and undiluted. "You don't need to know."

"But I think I can guess. Your share of the money you stole from the Silverton bank that never turned up."

Wyatt's gaze lowered to the satchels.

"I'm right, aren't I?"

"It's everyone's share," he said at length. "Sixty thousand dollars."

Despite herself, Leah gasped. "You have sixty thousand dollars sitting at your feet?"

"I haven't counted it yet, but that's what it's supposed to be."

"There is no man you made investments with. It was the Silverton money all along. You're planning on using it to buy your ranch."

"I was."

"This money was robbed from good people." Leah scooted away from the table with trembling hands. Once on her feet, she went toward the door. She didn't know Wyatt. She couldn't have.

Wyatt stood and walked to her, but kept a wedge of space between them. "There wasn't a day that went by in the pen that I didn't think about Evaline . . . or you. I wrote a letter telling you how sorry I was, but—"

"I never got a letter."

"I never mailed one."

Leah put her face in her hands and took in deep breaths. She could feel Wyatt's eyes on her back, but in the heat of his gaze she couldn't sense any request for her forgiveness. Not that she could ever forgive him.

"I wish you'd never come. I hated Harlen, but Wyatt . . . I . . ." Her muffled voice moistened her palms and sh[e] lifted her head but didn't turn to face him. She wouldn't l[et] him see her crying. "You've pretended to be someone yo[u] aren't, but you're still Harlen Shepard Riley. You alway[s] will be. The money proves it."

Then she walked through the doorway and down the ha[ll] without looking back. She'd been doing that most all he[r] life. She just couldn't anymore.

Wyatt parted the muslin curtains and stared out th[e] window onto Main watching Leah as she walked with he[r] head down. Her shoulders quivered, a sign she was crying[.] Letting the curtain fall, he moved away, unable to view he[r] grief without going after her and making her believe he ha[d] never wanted to hurt her. He would have given anything no[t] to have been baptized Harlen Riley. Or at least the Harle[n] Leah had known.

Crossing to the bed, Wyatt's gaze fell to the satchels. I[n] frustration and torment, he kicked them deeper beneath th[e] frame out of his sight. He cursed what they suddenl[y] represented: his failure at being Wyatt on the outside.

In the beginning, the money had meant security and [a] future for Wyatt Holloway. A fresh start. Now all th[e] satchels represented was Harlen's inability to follow th[e] straight and narrow path. They were worth no more tha[n] the very sandstone he'd uncovered them from. He realize[d] that by giving Leah the money, it would be like stealing it a[ll] over again. She'd see through his thin plan to give it to her[.] And as for himself, he could never keep a cent of it now.

A rap sounded on the door and Wyatt went to it[,] wondering if Leah had returned. Hoping that maybe . . . but not daring to . . .

When he answered the knock, Wyatt gazed into the du[ll] hazel eyes of an old friend. His voice failed him, and [a] bundle of memories came crashing in so hard, his shoulder[s] ached from the weight. If he hadn't known the man behin[d] the eyes, Wyatt wouldn't have recognized him. The once